For Alison

Matt Brolly

Following his law degree where he developed an interest in criminal law, Matt Brolly completed his Masters in Creative Writing at Glasgow University.

In addition to Zero, he is the author of the DCI Lambert crime novels, Dead Eyed, Dead Lucky, and Dead Embers.

Matt lives in London with his wife and their two young children. You can find out more about Matt at his website MattBrolly.co.uk or by following him on twitter: @MatthewBrolly

Also by Matt Brolly

THE DCI LAMBERT SERIES:

DEAD EYED
DEAD LUCKY
DEAD EMBERS

Zero

Matt Brolly

OBLONG
BOOKS

First published in the United Kingdom in 2016 by Canelo

This first print edition published in 2017 by Oblong Books

A CIP catalogue record for this book is available from the British Library.

ISBN 978-0-9957747-0-4

Chapter One

It was not a comfortable space for a man of his size. Old Blue had been in the boot of the car for five hours. He was squeezed into the foetal position, his considerable stomach pushed tight against his bended legs. Sweat dripped from his brow and cooled on his silver beard. The little oxygen which remained in the cramped interior of the car was contaminated by the fetid odour of his breath. He concentrated on his breathing, drawing the stale air in through his nose and exhaling it through pursed lips. His watch told him it was eight forty-five pm.

Old Blue closed his eyes and waited for the judge.

Twelve storeys above the basement car park where Old Blue waited, Judge Lloyd was preparing to leave for the day. He had a strict policy of finishing work at nine every evening. Anything urgent was taken home with him. Lloyd was in his late sixties but looked ten years younger. He signed off his last report and placed his paperwork into his briefcase. His personal assistant, Sarah Natal, was still working in the outer office. 'Time to wrap up now,' he told her as he walked past. He wished her goodnight with a tired flicker of a smile. The digital clock on her desk read nine p.m. precisely.

The court building was still alive with work, and Lloyd passed a number of familiar faces as he made his way down to the car park. The lift was empty so he was able to reach the car without exchanging words with anyone. His car was in its usual reserved space close to the stairwell. As always, Judge Lloyd opened the driver side door first, placing his briefcase on the passenger seat next to him.

The evening traffic was thinning and the judge made good time back to his house. He followed his favoured route, across the river at Bridge Eight and up to the winding side streets which led to his house in Sector Twelve. The pods were visible at various points through the journey. An outstanding feat of modern engineering, the glass capsules crawled through the night sky snaking across the entire city. They moved along their tracks, dangling like giant lanterns. It was claimed you were never more than one hundred metres away from a sightline of the structure. Lloyd chose not to notice. It was not that familiarity had lessened the wonder; Lloyd never looked at the translucent domes in case he saw someone within he recognised.

At home, the electronic gates sensed the arrival of his car and opened accordingly. Lloyd pressed the button for the garage doors and drove into the space. After closing the garage doors, he entered the house through a side door in the garage, which he locked behind him.

It was nine forty-five by the time the judge left the car. Wedged into the boot, Old Blue had suffered each bump and pothole of the journey. It was eleven-thirty before he moved. He managed to pop open the latch with little effort. His arm muscles flared with pain as he hoisted himself from the car, his legs buckling as he hit the stone floor of the garage. He stretched his calves and thighs, encouraging the blood to circulate. It was a slow, painful walk to the side entrance. He opened the door with the kind of ease that only comes with months of practice.

The lights were off downstairs but Old Blue knew the space well. To reach the staircase, he had to pass through two interior doors, both made of solid oak, both unlocked. He moved as quietly as was possible for a man of his weight and lack of agility. With his right hand, he reached into the inside of his jacket and pulled out a gun. Orange nightlights, the type a child would use, lined the stairwell. Old Blue eased himself upwards towards the landing, ignoring the occasional squeaks of loose floorboards. Judge Lloyd's bedroom was the third on the right. Without hesitation, Old Blue opened the door. A four-poster bed made from thick black wood filled the room. The judge was sitting up in bed reading. He looked up from his book and studied Old Blue, seemingly unconcerned. Seconds later, he nodded. 'Mr. Jacobson,' he said.

Old Blue looked at the man and shook his head.

Chapter Two

Inspector Kate Swanson knew the junior officer standing by the courtroom doors watching her. Flaherty was flushed with excitement, so desperate to get Swanson's attention that for one horrendous second she thought he might shout over to her. Swanson turned her attention back towards Judge Livermore. The accused, William Crampton, sat to Swanson's right, on a separate table with his lawyer. Little more than a child, he had been arrested six months ago for petty theft after stealing a bottle of vodka from an off-licence, a dare from his fellow gang members. Dressed in a maroon jumpsuit, his narrow eyes stared straight ahead. Swanson listened to the familiar sound of the verdict followed by the equally familiar sentence. There was only ever one sentence.

Any breach of the criminal law, however minor, was subject to an effective death sentence. After spending time in the holding zone, convicts were placed in the glass pods which journeyed throughout the city. The journey took thirty days, but after eight days the water supply was removed. No one had ever survived the pods. Luis Ciucci had been the first prisoner to be podded, not long after Swanson was born. Ciucci had murdered his wife's lover in a crime of passion. His podding had been symbolic. People had sympathy for Ciucci, and the council knew it. It would have been easier to pod someone everyone loathed, a multiple murderer, a rapist or child molester, but this way they signaled to society that whatever your crime, whatever the mitigating circumstances, you were going to the pods.

The boy barely reacted. Swanson had seen the weary look of resignation countless times before. No doubt the hope had been ground out of him during his probationary incarceration. Even after all these years in the force, all the prosecutions she'd been involved with, the verdict was still difficult to hear.

'Court dismissed,' said the judge.

Flaherty was by her side in seconds. In his grey-blue uniform, he looked like a schoolboy playing dressing-up games. He smelt of nicotine and sweet aftershave. He pulled at the grey clip-on tie dangling from his throat. 'Ma'am,' he said.

'What is it?' asked Swanson.

'It's Judge Lloyd, Ma'am. He's missing.' Flaherty's voice was an octave higher than normal.

'Would you care to elaborate, Flaherty?' suggested Swanson.

'He didn't turn up for court today and there's no sign of him at his house. His car is still parked in his garage.' Flaherty was smiling.

'And?'

'Chessington wants you over there. As soon as you finish here.'

Swanson glared at him.

'Ma'am,' he said.

Swanson packed her files away. Five foot eleven with long blonde hair tied back into a ponytail, she was wearing her standard formal issue: a black pleated skirt, white blouse, and black jacket. On her left lapel shone three silver crowns. Her voice was deep and guttural, the legacy of a childhood throat infection which had permanently damaged her vocal cords.

The public defender, Dave Legg, walked over and shook her hand, holding on longer than was necessary. 'Another victory, Inspector Swanson,' he said. 'It must make you proud, putting away such hardened criminals.'

Swanson understood the man's sarcasm, his despair at losing another client, but couldn't show any weakness. 'Defeat makes you so bitter, Dave.'

'It is not the defeat, Inspector. It is the consequences of defeat which trouble me.' He held her gaze, trying in vain to look nonchalant, then walked away. He had left a gold plated pen on his desk which Swanson placed into her pocket.

Outside, she barged through a group of journalists each barking questions at her. She made eye contact with one of their number, Jane Sutton who she occasionally shared information with. She nodded to the woman before entering her car.

As Swanson drove through the city to Judge Lloyd's house, she tried not to think about the sentence just handed down to the young petty thief. The policy of Zero

Tolerance, ZT, was fixed legislation. Its powers could not be withdrawn, only extended. At present, any breach of criminal law, subject to a fair trial before judge and jury, was subject to the death penalty. Swanson had been working in the police force for the last eight years and had never known a society without the pods.

She reminded herself that she didn't make the policy. Her job was to uphold the law, however draconian that law appeared to be. In her judgement, the petty thief, Crampton, didn't deserve to die. She empathised with the young man, and even with his obnoxious lawyer. Maybe one day there would come a time when the law was not so severe, but until then, she had a job to do.

Chief Inspector Chessington was waiting for her at Judge Lloyd's house. A rotund man in his mid-fifties, he had uneven patches of red hair sprouting from his balding head. His eyes were thin green slits on a podgy red face. Like Flaherty, he smelt of nicotine, his pin-striped suit stretched to breaking point across his stomach. 'Inspector Swanson, good of you to come,' he said, looking her up and down, grimacing as he struggled with the heat.

Chessington went over the details. Judge Lloyd had failed to turn up to his first hearing that morning. He had last been seen leaving the court's car park late the previous evening. His car was in the garage and there was no sign of a break-in. His bed was unmade even though his cleaner had been in earlier that day.

Swanson walked alone through the house. An unusual amount of forensic and crime scene officers busied away in each room. The house was large, clean but cluttered. Lloyd was unmarried and it seemed his passion for antiques had gone unchecked. Swanson thought the unmade bed was of little significance. Some of Lloyd's belongings sat on an intricately carved wooden dressing table. Inside a marble bowl, Swanson found two gold watches and a rose-gold ring. She picked up the larger of the two watches, surprised by its weight, and placed it onto her thin wrist, enjoying the look of the oversized watch face.

'Nice piece, that one. About six months' salary, I would guess.' Swanson felt Chessington's bloated hand on her shoulder. 'Looks good on you,' he said.

'Remember that at Christmas time, sir,' replied Swanson, as she returned the watch to the bowl.

'You've been in front of Judge Lloyd before, Swanson?'

'Yes, sir.'

'Any thoughts as to why he may have disappeared?'

'Paperwork? Miscommunication?'

'No, no,' said Chessington, shaking his head. 'I've spoken to his secretary. I know them both well. She phoned him at seven this morning and when there was no answer she called me.'

'That was a bit dramatic, wasn't it, sir?'

'That's just it – Lloyd is so organised and professional that something as ordinary as missing a phone call becomes extraordinary.'

Swanson licked her lips and sighed, noticing how Chessington's gaze lingered on the movement of her tongue. 'I presume we have something more, sir.'

'He's a judge, Swanson. The fact that he is missing is enough. Find Keane and meet me back at the station as soon as you're finished here.'

Sergeant Joseph Keane was outside interviewing Judge Lloyd's neighbours. Swanson had never worked with him before but had seen him around the station. He was attractive, in an obvious way, and Swanson couldn't help noticing the silver wedding ring on his left hand. 'Ma'am,' he said, as she approached.

'Keane. Anything of interest?' Swanson asked, trying to soften the rasp of her voice.

'Nothing of use. One of the neighbours saw Lloyd arrive at approximately nine forty-five last night, alone,' said Keane.

'Give those reports to Flaherty, you're working with me now,' she said. 'And call me Swanson, for Christ's sake.'

'I hope I'm not speaking out of turn, ma'am, but why are we putting so much energy into a missing persons case?' asked Keane.

'You're not speaking out of turn. He's a judge,' replied Swanson, echoing Chessington's earlier words.

Keane smiled a half-smile. Swanson noticed his bottom row of teeth were crooked, the front four teeth overlapping as if fighting for space. Somehow, he carried off the look. She looked away, conscious that she'd been staring at him.

'I know he's a judge and everything but there was no sign of a forced entry,' said Keane.

'He's a judge, Keane. Apparently, that's all we need to know for now.'

In the judge's garage, two officers were dismantling a large saloon car. 'Were all the locks intact?' she asked the pair.

'Intact and unlocked,' said George Reilly, one of the white-boiler-suited forensic team.

'Makes sense. Why lock your car when you're in the safety of your house?' The air was heavy with diesel and Swanson was about to leave when she saw a piece of paper by the left rear tyre. She picked it up with the finesse of a conjurer. It was a flyer for a meeting of Lenity, a zero tolerance opposition group. She pocketed the piece of paper with a practised snap of her fingers.

Reilly was dusting the walls for fingerprints. 'Waste of time, naturally. Have you seen our fingerprint database? Ninety-nine percent of it is serving police officers and sentenced criminals,' he said.

'Maybe you'll find a print from the remaining one per cent,' said Keane.

Reilly looked at Swanson, then at Keane. 'It's a possibility, son,' said Reilly, as he continued dusting.

The car had been stripped and reassembled. 'If there is a case here, then I think the car may be key,' said Swanson, running a hand over the vehicle.

'No forced entry, so maybe someone accompanied Lloyd in the car?' suggested Keane.

'That obvious?'

'That easy,' said Keane.

Swanson showed Keane the piece of paper. 'What do you think?' she asked.

'The meeting is tonight.'

'Exactly, Keane,' said Swanson. 'Guess where we're going later, after I've reported back to Chessington?'

Chessington's desk was piled high with papers and legal texts, sharing the area with three half-empty coffee cups and an ashtray brimming with discarded cigarettes. Swanson had been waiting for twenty minutes. Keane was in the outer office researching Lloyd's work colleagues. Swanson played with some of the papers and uncovered a silver watch. It was heavy, with elaborate swirls carved deep into the silver; a much cheaper version of the watch she had seen in Lloyd's bedroom.

Closing her eyes, adrenaline flooding her body, she placed the watch in her trouser suit pocket. The stealing had started years ago, way before she'd joined the force. Despite this, she still experienced a delicious thrill every time she took something which didn't belong to her.

Seconds later, Chessington walked through the office doors. His eyelids hung low on his round face as if he'd recently woken up. He groaned in agony as he sat down. Swanson held her breath to avoid breathing in his body odour. 'Found it then?' he asked.

Swanson stood straight, her muscles tight. 'Sir?'

He pointed to a large stack of papers to her left. 'Judge Lloyd's last fifty cases. I want you and Keane to go through each one in meticulous detail.

'What exactly are we looking for, sir?'

'Motive, Swanson.'

'I'm sure we will find motive in every case, sir.'

'That's why you have to check every detail. There will be leads there, Swanson. The others are looking at the older cases but we have more of a chance with the most recent ones.'

'You flatter me, sir.'

For the first time since entering the office Chessington looked directly at her. 'What's your problem, Swanson? I'm giving you the lead of the investigation.'

Swanson sat down without asking. 'This is just grunt work, sir. You know it.' She pointed behind her. 'Anyone can go through old court cases. If we're going to investigate then let me investigate.' She softened her voice and looked directly at him, her hand reaching for the procured watch in her trouser pocket.

'Inspector Swanson, you're so sensitive,' he said, with a little humour. He pulled out a piece of paper from inside his desk drawer and handed it to her. It was a ransom note. Chessington liked his little games. It was his way of maintaining authority, and for now she let it slip.

'Interesting,' she said, after reading.

'Interesting?'

'It must be some sort of joke. Whoever sent this must know their demands are ridiculous. How did we receive it?'

'Courier. We're questioning the driver but he doesn't know anything. Forensics are checking for fingerprints. Should know within the hour.'

'What do you think?' asked Swanson.

The note was typed on a crisp piece of white A4 paper

folded horizontally into three sections. It demanded the release of every single person circling the city in the pods, including those nearing the end of their journey. The note was unsigned. There was a seventy-two-hour deadline.

'I imagine they want someone in particular set free. Quite a clever trick not to single out one specific person – it means we have hundreds of potential motives,' said Chessington.

Swanson thought it an obvious move. 'We could start looking at the cases involving the most recent convicts. If your theory is correct then I imagine they would only really be interested in those beginning their journey,' she said, meaning those who were still alive.

'Perhaps. It could be an organisational thing, the NZA or Lenity?'

'Neither has engaged in criminal activity before,' said Swanson, thinking of the Lenity flyer she'd found at Lloyd's house.

'No, maybe not. Let's concentrate on the convicts. Look at everyone in the first eight days of their journey to begin with. There are five still alive at last count.'

Swanson jumped up. 'Thank you, sir,' she said, heading for the door.

'Wait,' shouted Chessington.

Swanson opened the door then looked back, raising her eyebrows.

'Have you seen my watch?' asked Chessington, lifting papers off his desk in a frenzied motion.

'Sorry, sir, haven't seen it,' she said, not looking back as she left the office.

Chapter Three

The girl sat on the window ledge staring out at the pods. The outline of her thin body blurred, her figure fading then glowing back into life. Reg McClusky rubbed his eyes and hauled his fragile body off the sofa bed. His stick-like legs clicked as he stood upright. He was thirty-four, with severely receding brown hair and a body so devoid of flesh that he'd acquired the nickname of *Rickets* within the tower block. His arms and legs jutted out from a concave frame like gnarled twigs.

'Where is the other one?' he asked the girl, lighting his first cigarette of the day. The visions usually came in pairs, mother and daughter. The girl momentarily glowed, amber like the flash of fire from the lit match. She did not respond. McClusky left her to her sightseeing and returned to his bedroom to get dressed.

He was late for his meeting. He already had two strikes so he ran through the crowds, a fading cigarette drooping from his dry, thin lips, knowing a third non-appearance would lead him to the pods. Sunlight flared off the glass prisons and he was drenched in sweat by the time he collapsed through the church hall's door.

Lynette was about to start the meeting. 'Hi, Reg,' she said, her voice full of mock welcome. 'Join us when you're ready.'

McClusky took a seat within the circle. Lynette had started her introductory speech, thanking everyone for attending and inviting the group to share their experiences. Tim Summer raised his hand as he did every week but Lynette ignored him and asked Louise Vickers to speak instead. Louise was a voluntary. McClusky remembered her gruelling tale of addiction following the death of her husband. Dressed in a light yellow dress, she had a similar build to McClusky, save for the slight bulge of her chest. She had fine brown hair which looked dry and brittle. Her pale face was pitted with tiny splotches of red. She trembled as she stood as if, McClusky thought, aroused. 'I'm afraid,' she stammered in a high-pitched squeal. 'I had a drink of alcohol this week.'

A period of acute silence fell over the group, followed by numerous gasps of shock and dismay.

'Christ, you'd think she'd shot somebody or something,' mouthed McClusky.

Once the hysteria died down, Lynette got to her feet. In her early fifties, she wore large, circular rimmed spectacles and McClusky guessed she was about five stone heavier than was healthy. McClusky closed his eyes, a perfect vision of Lynette playing in his mind. She was on her knees, begging for mercy as McClusky held a knife to her throat. He savoured her imagined pleas, before slicing the bloated flesh of her neck.

'Thank you for sharing, Louise,' she said, waking him from his daydream. 'How did it make you feel afterwards?'

Louise thought about the question as if considering some great metaphysical conundrum and replied, 'Bad.'

McClusky snorted.

Louise looked at him, eyebrows furrowed. 'Guilty, I suppose. And perhaps a bit scared. I thought I'd let Graham down,' she said.

Graham, Louise's dead husband, no longer cared, thought McClusky.

'And did you manage to stop after one drink?' asked Lynette.

Louise thought again. 'Two glasses of red wine.' She hesitated. 'Large glasses. But I threw the rest down the sink.'

'Well done, Louise,' said Lynette, and began clapping. Soon McClusky was the only one in the room not applauding. 'You had a lapse but you didn't let it control you. In a way this is a very positive experience for you.'

A large smile filled Louise's face at this insight. 'Yeah, I guess you're right,' she said, tears flowing.

McClusky felt like crying as well. Unlike Louise, he was a compulsory. He sat through another hour listening to similar stories. Occasionally, he would close his eyes and imagine what he would do to the group. He devised numerous heroically complicated punishments for them. He saw with perfect clarity what they would look like after he had finished his handiwork; but more than that, he could imagine their pain. He felt, from the outside, the effect of each inflicted wound. He could sense the ripples of anguish surge through Lynette's obese being as he sliced her. It made him smile, and when he opened his eyes he saw a haze of red.

'And do you have anything to contribute this week, Reg?' asked Lynette.

McClusky sighed. He stared back at the overweight woman, the blood surging through his body. He shut his eyes for a second and flashed them open, refreshed. 'Nothing new this week,' he said.

'Okay. Maybe next week,' said Lynette. She kept her eyes focused on him as if expecting him to respond.

McClusky looked away.

Outside, the sun was at its highest. It was McClusky's day off so he ambled through the crowds and headed towards the river. He felt a presence near him. It was not the women. He looked behind him, searching for the familiar figure of the man. By the river, groups of youths gazed at the pods, stoned beyond imagination. They sat in small groups on picnic blankets, huddled together, unified by their wonder. The local workers walked by as if nothing unusual was hovering above them. McClusky didn't like to look at the pods. It was too easy to picture himself within the glass capsules, which he supposed was the point of the imposing prisons. He sat down near a young couple who were sharing a bottle of red wine. The woman sipped at her drink, a maroon droplet falling onto the side of her mouth. Her partner laughed and kissed the spilled drop.

McClusky lay back. He stayed beneath the sun for three

hours until his unprotected scalp started to burn. As he walked back home, he felt the skin of his arms and legs crack and tear.

His flat was empty. He ran the bath until it was full of cold water and took off his clothes, noticing in the bathroom mirror the bones of his rib cage straining against his flesh. The water cooled him and for a second he felt as if he were floating. After drying himself, he rubbed after-sun on his scalp, arms, and legs. Lighting another cigarette, he made up the sofa bed and took a last look out of the window, glancing first at the crystal domes and then down to the street below. On the pavement he saw the outline of a man. Next to the man were the two shadowy images of the women. McClusky drew the curtains and stumbled towards his sofa bed. He pulled the sheets over his burning skin and closed his eyes, but could imagine nothing.

Chapter Four

It was dusk by the time Swanson and Keane reached the church hall where the Lenity meeting was to take place. The circling pods were illuminated now and they coloured the night sky like overgrown Christmas decorations. The church, Corpus Christi, was in Sector One, near the valley area where the pods started their journeys. Swanson glimpsed the occasional movement within the glass capsules.

Swanson had sat through similar meetings numerous times before. The police attended them as a matter of course. Lenity meetings were a guaranteed way of finding future prosecutions, even though there was nothing illegal about the gathering. Free speech was enshrined in the law. As a citizen, you were free to say, but not do, what you wanted; sometimes citizens found it difficult to separate the two.

The church hall was used for sport during the day and the cold draught which billowed through the cavernous area failed to extinguish the reek of day-old sweat. They sat at the back, Swanson's coat wrapped tight against her body; Keane was squashed up against her, such was the large attendance.

Swanson scanned the room, having no idea what she was looking for. A thin man in his early twenties made his way to a wooden lectern at the front of the hall. His hair, which was blonder than Swanson's, looked ethereal in the dim lighting of the hall.

'Thank you all for coming,' he began in a nasal drawl. 'This is a wonderful turn out. As most of you know, we have a demonstration planned for this Saturday. We are only nine months away from the Mayoral elections and now is the time to make the powers-that-be understand we are serious. I will be passing out a full itinerary for the day. Those of you who have signed up know where you will be stationed. I see a few new members in the crowd and if you are still interested at the end,' he stopped at this point to laugh, 'then please come and see me and I will show how you can show your support.'

'Student,' said Keane, with a dismissive sneer.

They sat through an hour of uninspiring speeches. Swanson noticed a few familiar faces in the crowd, including a senior figure from the public defender's office. Some of the audience sat wide-eyed, lost in an almost evangelical zeal. Swanson had been a secret member of such an organisation as a student. She had attended the meetings but never participated in any demonstrations. Like now, she had always sat at the back, non-committal and unsure of her beliefs. She had since helped convict a number of her former comrades, none of whom recognised her.

'Anything?' she asked Keane once they were outside. It was late, close to lightsout, the night sky lit only by a sprinkling of stars and the glare of the occasional pod.

'This is clearly low-level. I can't imagine Lloyd has anything to do with that lot. They're going to wave a few banners, annoy a few tourists, and go back home to their parents. If he is, or was, involved with any opposition groups I would have thought they would have been a bit more intelligent than this.'

'Why do you think the note belonged to the judge?' asked Swanson.

Keane looked at her, his face inches from hers. 'The kidnapper?'

'It's possible.'

'I don't think there was anyone capable of abduction at that meeting. I would be surprised if they can all tie their own shoelaces.'

'Let's not make any assumptions about anything or anyone just yet,' said Swanson. They walked along the river bank. Wood fires were being extinguished and smoke drifted above the glass-like water. 'I'll see you first thing tomorrow at the courthouse,' she said as they reached the station.

Keane hesitated. 'I know a little place still open,' he said. 'I thought you might like to join me for a drink.' He stood with his hands in his pockets like a nervous schoolchild. 'It might not be your scene, though.'

Swanson didn't hesitate, remembering his wedding ring. 'Don't stay up too late,' she said, turning away from him and walking up the stone steps that led to Sector One's central police station.

She was stopped at the entrance by the journalist she'd

exchanged looks with earlier that day. 'Inspector Swanson, may I have a minute of your time?'

Swanson sighed. 'What is it, Jane?'

Sutton worked for a left-wing online publication. Swanson felt as if she spent at least part of each day in conversation with the woman. 'There has been no press release, but I understand Judge Lloyd is missing?'

Swanson was not surprised that the story had leaked. Stone-faced, she gave her standard response. 'No comment.'

'Are you treating his disappearance as suspicious?'

'No comment.'

The woman adjusted her glasses. 'Could you tell me why you attended a Lenity meeting this evening, Inspector?' she continued.

'Standard police business,' said Swanson, opening the station door. 'If there is nothing else?'

'One more thing,' said Sutton. 'Who was that attractive man you were with? A date?'

Despite herself, Swanson smiled and shut the door on the journalist.

She didn't stay long. She picked up the files on the five convicts from Chessington's desk and placed them in her holdall. They were available electronically but she liked the tangibility of the paper. The open plan office was empty. She had already stolen two things that day but the opportunity was too great to ignore. Checking again that she was alone, Swanson searched through the various desks for anything of interest and alighted on a framed picture on Gardner's desk. Alan Gardner was close to retirement and had never been promoted beyond the rank of constable. The photo showed a smiling Gardner with his family; what looked like his four children and seven grandchildren. Swanson shook as she picked up the picture. She swivelled three hundred and sixty degrees on the spot and placed the frame in her holdall.

Lightsout kicked in as she drove home. Only minimal electricity use was allowed during the hours of ten p.m. to six a.m. The city darkened in an instant, only the car headlights and the shining pods giving illumination.

Her father was still awake back at her flat, a small apartment in Sector Eight. He sat in the living room, reading by candle-light. He had a long face with a strong, prominent jaw. His once blond hair was now white. It sprang from his head in various random directions. 'Good evening, beautiful,' he said, looking up from his book. 'Don't mind me, I'll finish this page and I'll be off to bed.'

Swanson kissed him on the head. 'Don't be silly, Dad. You don't need to go anywhere.' He had been living with her for the last year since his retirement. 'What are you reading?' she asked.

'Some uninformed nonsense.'

'As usual,' she said.

'Quite. Join me?' he asked, pouring himself a glass of red wine.

'Why not?'

The wine looked black in the half-light of the candles. 'Tough day?' asked her father.

'The usual,' replied Swanson.

'I hear Judge Lloyd has gone missing.'

'Now, how the hell do you know that?'

'Still have a few contacts, you know,' said her father, drinking deep from his glass. 'I taught him. Precocious sort but highly dedicated.' Her father was a retired professor of law. He still went to the university every day. 'I believe he wrote quite a convincing thesis against the policy of ZT as an undergraduate, would you believe? I'll check my records if it would help?''

'Didn't everyone you taught oppose ZT?' asked Swanson. 'Eventually?'

'Obviously not enough of them,' he replied. 'You could pick any subject, Kate, and academics would disagree over it. As you know, there were solid reasons for its incorporation. The city was a different place following the Flux. There were areas too dangerous to go near. There was so much crime that a zero tolerance policy sounded like a good idea. The initial policy reduced crime, so the logical step, for some, was to extend its reach. I read a hundred new theses a year on the subject. Always new insights.'

The financial crisis preceding the Flux had lasted for two decades, the catalyst a breakdown in trade agreements between member states. Her father had told her they had been difficult years, but had followed what was perceived to be a cyclical pattern. The downturn lasted longer than was expected but there had been a general belief that things would change for the better.

'It proved one thing,' he told her one night, long ago when she had been a gangly teenager eager to learn.

'What's that?'

'That economists didn't, and don't have, even the

faintest of grips on their subject, on reality itself.'

'Oh, Dad.'

The Flux had effectively been instantaneous. Within forty-eight hours the world's markets crashed and the world stopped trading. The city suffered energy crises for years. Only the rich arable land on the outskirts of the city, and the alternative energy supplies, had kept it alive for the first years of the Flux.

The City was its own world now, almost entirely self-maintained.

Swanson's history books told her that the implementation of ZT had been a gradual process. It had started with a zero policy on carrying firearms and weapons. The initial benefits were all-encompassing. Swanson remembered watching video footage in high school of amnesty week, where thousands of firearms were surrendered and destroyed by the city.

Initially, zero tolerance meant life imprisonment not death. The policy was successful, greatly reducing the amount of people who carried weapons. The council began extending the scope of ZT to cover more and more crimes but it appeared life imprisonment was not the deterrent the council believed it would be. Prisons became overcrowded to the extent that it was costing more to house convicts than it had previously cost to manage the criminal population. It was the perfect opportunity for the council to introduce the death penalty, and the pods were born.

Her father pushed himself from his chair. He was still a towering figure, despite the stoop he had acquired in old age. He walked to the kitchen and returned with another bottle of wine. Swanson placed her hand over her glass as he continued his lecture. 'For a time, the city was virtually clean. No one could have envisaged where it would lead, what with the pods and everything. Well, you know my thinking on all that. So what has happened to our young Judge Lloyd? The university is alive with rumours. Suicide, elopement, government conspiracies.'

Swanson laughed. 'Are you responsible for any of those rumours?'

'Possibly. I hear it's all being taken quite seriously.' As he leant towards her, she saw the blood lines which decorated the whites of his eyes, and the spots of maroon which discoloured his teeth and lips.

'You know I can't discuss the case, Dad,' said Swanson, getting to her feet. She moved her hands towards the newly opened bottle but was too slow.

'Good try,' said her father, filling his glass.

'Goodnight, Dad,' she said, kissing him again.

'Goodnight, pumpkin.'

She lit the oil lamp in her bedroom, a treasured gift from her mother, which flickered into life. Her room was sparsely decorated: dark carpet, double bed, wardrobe and chest of drawers. Swanson sat on her bed looking out the bay window. In the shadows she saw the outlines of the pods. Reaching under her bed, she took out a large antique box. She adjusted the numbers on the small padlock and opened the lid.

Every time she opened the box, she was reminded of her mother. The stealing had started after her death. What started out as a taunt, an act of rebellion, was now part of her life, as necessary as breathing. Stealing was a release for her, and had been ever since the day her mother had died. While her teenage friends had been busy drinking or getting high, Swanson's youth was spent stealing. It was an almost physical thing now, her own form of addiction, a way of rebelling against a society which had stolen her mother away.

The irony of working for the police was not lost on her. Her father had been shocked, if not dismayed, when she told him she was joining the force. She had feared he would see it as a betrayal but he was more confused than anything. 'Why, after everything that happened with your mother, would you join them?' he'd asked.

She hadn't been able to articulate it then, and struggled now. It was a kind of calling. At the time, she'd wanted to protect the city. Now, she thought it had all been a subconscious thing, a perverse way of honouring her mother. Maybe if she'd been the arresting officer, she would have been able to help somehow.

Maybe the opportunity would present itself again.

From the holdall she retrieved the gold pen she'd procured from the lawyer Dave Legg, Chessington's watch, and the photo frame from Gardner's desk. She placed the three items in the box, and sealed it shut.

Chapter Five

She left early the next morning, the sound of her father's snoring reverberating around the flat. An ash-fog had spread over the river and the pods were hidden by the cold grey clouds. Her walk was brisk, her coat pulled tight against her.

She thought about her father as she walked, and the increasing amount of empty wine bottles she had to recycle. He'd started drinking around the same time she'd started stealing, his own response to their loss. She'd been a teenager then but remembered the time as if it was yesterday. The bang on the door in the middle of the night, the Special Investigation guards dressed in full regalia, her Dad's pleas as they dragged her mother away, the look on her face, the pitiful resignation in her eyes, the touch of her hand on Swanson's hair before she was handcuffed.

Keane was waiting for her at the south-west entrance of the courthouse. His face was covered in an uneven sprinkle of stubble, his eyes bloodshot.

'Good night?' asked Swanson.

'Too good,' replied Keane, his hoarse voice as harsh as Swanson's.

The courthouse was one of the older buildings in the heart of the city. It had survived a number of riots and years of civil disobedience unscathed. A tall, white-brick building, it swamped the centre of Sector One. From the heart of the building sprouted a vast glass dome which stretched towards the clouds. The dome was a modern addition, designed by the same architects who had created the pods. Within the dome was the Supreme Court, where all ZT cases were heard. The pods travelled over the building early in their journey, the glass capsules insignificant compared to the imposing dome of the courthouse.

They walked through the maze of corridors until they reached Judge Lloyd's office. A petite lady dressed in brown greeted them. 'Sarah Natal,' said the woman, offering her hand. 'I'm Judge Lloyd's personal assistant.' Her voice was light and steady, almost a monotone. Swanson noticed her smile as she shook hands with Keane.

Natal showed them through a set of glass doors to Lloyd's office. It had the same carpet as the judge's bedroom. At one end of the office stood a large oak desk which was clear except for a small lamp with a glass lampshade. The office was swamped with bookcases which stretched from the floor to the ceiling. Hundreds of books were arranged in perfect lines on the custom fitted units.

'Miss Natal, may I call you Sarah?' asked Swanson, sitting down.

'Sure,' said Natal.

'Sarah, I know this must be a strange situation for you but can you give me some details of Judge Lloyd's movements on the day of his disappearance?'

Natal sighed as if bored. 'It was like any other day. He worked in his office until nine as always. He said goodnight and that was the last I've heard from him.'

'How did he get home?' asked Swanson.

'Car, I presume.'

'How did you get home?' asked Keane.

Natal brightened up at the question. 'I walked home. I live close to the courthouse, in a little apartment block near the river in Sector Two.'

Keane returned her smile.

'Do you both usually work until nine?' asked Swanson.

'Every evening. You wouldn't believe the paperwork. The judge always leaves at nine, dead on. He normally takes files home with him.'

'He always leaves at nine?' asked Keane.

'Always. The man is pathological. He likes to be home before lightsout. He is the most precise, methodical, organised, and pedantic person I've ever met.'

'I expect it becomes a bit grating after a while,' said Keane, again offering a smile.

Natal's pupils dilated. 'It can be, but at least you know where you are with him.' She continued looking at Keane as Swanson spoke.

'I realise that Judge Lloyd may have made some enemies due to his position but do you know of anyone close to him who may hold a grudge? A colleague perhaps, or a lawyer?'

'He's surprisingly quite a shy sort of person,' replied Natal, still focusing on Keane. 'He doesn't really make enemies. Apart from the families and friends of those he has to sentence, of course.'

‘Has he ever received any threats or been directly confronted?’

‘Most of the families accept his sentencing. Despite the severity, I think they know he’s doing his job. Occasionally they come to the office to speak to him but I never let them in. It wouldn’t be fair to him.’ Natal crossed her hands in her lap. ‘What do you think has happened to him?’ she asked, looking at Swanson directly for the first time.

Swanson didn’t comment. They spent the next thirty minutes discussing Lloyd’s recent cases. There were a few potential leads but nothing striking enough to provoke any optimism. Swanson thanked the woman and headed out of the office.

In the reflection from the office doors, Swanson saw Natal hand Keane a piece of paper.

Chapter Six

Old Blue had been sitting in the side pews for half an hour when the police officers entered. He knew they would come although he no longer remembered why he had dropped the piece of paper at the judge's house. The female officer was Inspector Swanson. She had a statuesque presence which she tried to dampen with conservative clothes and tied-back hair. Her partner was no less striking. He was nearly as tall as Old Blue with dark hair and darker eyes. Together they looked like a celebrity couple trying to blend in with the natives.

People gravitated to him. They sat next to him as they waited for the meeting to begin, ignoring the empty spaces nearer the front. He didn't speak to them but still they came, men and women alike. He looked at them and they smiled, holding his gaze for as long as they were able.

Old Blue tuned out the words of the nasal young man who held the audience in such rapture. He had no interest in what anyone else had to say. At the end of the meeting, he remained behind, watching the officers leave. With the crowd diminishing, he walked towards the stage. To the left was a battered wooden door, with flaking red paint. He knocked twice, the wood hard on his knuckles.

Agatha Trent opened the door and smiled at him. The gesture was perfunctory – Trent's smiles always were. Old Blue made his way into a cramped side room and poured himself a coffee from a lone pot on a side table, the liquid lukewarm and bitter. He sat on one of the plastic seats arranged in a semi-circle and waited with five others for the nasal-voiced man to appear.

The nasal-voiced man was called Timothy Basle. He was the head of a small unofficial sect of Lenity which had been given the moniker Chapter 12. Basle looked as if his body had outgrown him. He struggled to carry his elongated limbs, which drooped from his torso. Up close, his face was riddled with acne scars. 'Thank you for your patience,' he said to the group. 'I am pleased to announce that we have been selected to assist in the first wave.' He carried a large holdall which he placed on the table next to the coffee pot with the mastery of an amateur magician. When he took the device out of the bag, Old Blue had to suppress a laugh.

'What is it?' asked Trent.

'The beginning,' said Basle. 'This is the first of many devices we will be using during the demonstration.'

'By the pods?' asked Trent, her voice squeaky with excitement.

'Not this time – there will be too much security. But the demo will give us the perfect distraction.'

Trent looked disappointed. Old Blue looked at the other

members of Chapter 12 who looked as nonplussed as he felt.

'From little acorns, I guess,' said Stephen Crampton, a middle-aged man whose son was due to go to the pods that Saturday.

'It's not the only device. I understand that most of the sections will have one and they will be deployed tactically throughout the target building.' Basle sounded desperate to appease them.

'Which is?' asked Old Blue.

'We will not find out until the evening before, Blue,' said Basle, with a slight tremble.

Old Blue already knew the target. After leaving the meeting, he walked back to the courthouse to report for work. He was already dressed in his navy-blue overalls. There was an increased police presence following the judge's disappearance. The queue at the entrance was longer than normal. Once inside, he walked to his store cupboard and pulled out his cart. He was on outside duty that evening and he walked to his destination at an even pace, never once looking at the other workers.

He had been working at the courthouse for two years. The ease of the application process had staggered him. The documents he had provided had never been verified. The monolithic building needed so many workers to keep it functioning that security was overlooked. He'd spent the seven months well, mapping the building until he knew every corridor and each room, from the grand dome of the Supreme Court to the smallest broom cupboard. And each step he took through the labyrinthine corridors increased his sense of injustice. On his day shift, he would take his breaks in the public galleries. There were only a few cases tried each week, which was a true testimony to the policy of zero tolerance. But still they came, mainly minor infringements, petty crime so meaningless that he wondered why the defendants had bothered.

The following morning, as his shift neared its end, he found himself near Judge Lloyd's office. He heard voices from within and bowed his head with a slow movement to the floor as the two officers left the room. They walked past him, scents of vanilla, musk, and rose hovering in the air. Seconds later, a third person emerged from the office. He knew the woman to be Judge Lloyd's assistant, Sarah Natal. She looked flushed and wore a wide smile. 'Hello, Blue,' she said.

By the time he reached home, he'd been awake for close to twenty-four hours. The reek of ripe, fresh sweat masked the sour tones of the dried sweat which covered his body. He lived in Sector Thirty-Two in a secluded summer house. The building was cocooned within a covering of overgrown trees and bushes. Inside, he opened the windows and stripped as the air filtered through. In the kitchen he prepared a large batch of scrambled eggs. He poured coffee and water into two separate cups and placed the completed meal onto a tray. In the study he lifted the Persian rug from the floor to reveal a trap door.

A wave of heat rose towards him, heavy with the

overpowering odour of vomit and excrement. He let fresh air flood the stairwell before moving down. A single nightlight lit the stairwell. At the bottom was a reinforced glass door, side panelled with thick cuts of steel. The door had six deadlocks and it took him several minutes to open it and enter the cellar. The cellar spanned the length and width of the house. He'd plumbed a small bathroom with toilet and sink but unfortunately there was little ventilation save for the three fans which he'd placed in the room. The smell was something he'd not anticipated.

The judge sat on the floor next to his bed dressed in a set of pyjamas two sizes too big. He looked up at the noise of the door opening and stumbled to the glass panel which held him imprisoned. Old Blue placed the meal in a double sided trap box. The judge stared at him through the glass. 'Nate, you can't solve anything this way,' he said. His voice was steady and assured. He kept his gaze focused on Old Blue.

Old Blue remained silent. He shut the trap box and pushed the food through to Judge Lloyd.

Chapter Seven

A light breeze accompanied them as they walked along the riverbank back to the station. Shards of grey cloud, pregnant with water, moved across the sky. Keane kept close to Swanson, his arm occasionally brushing against hers. She waited for him to speak. If she had to ask about Natal's note it would be the end of their professional relationship.

Like the courthouse, part of the police station was constructed of glass. Here the similarities ended. This was no monumental structure. Society's deterrent was found in the courthouse's imposing architecture, and the glass pods which glided across the city's skyline. The police station was an afterthought. Every time Swanson walked up its concrete steps, she was reminded how redundant society considered its police force. They were a dwindling necessity, becoming more and more like administrators; administrators with black caps. She'd wanted to quit so many times she'd lost count. Her initial zeal for signing up, her plans of changing the system from within, of ridding society of its ill whilst protecting the innocent, sounded more naïve with every passing day.

Curved panes of frosted glass loomed twelve storeys high. The glass was kept in place by ugly steel girders which curled around the structure like ivy. Thirteen concrete steps led to the station's entrance. Keane stopped at the foot of the stairs and turned towards her. 'I know you saw her give me that piece of paper,' he said. His eyes drooped and Swanson tried not to smirk. He looked hurt and slightly pathetic.

Swanson shrugged. 'Tell me about it.'

'It was her phone number, what else?' The boyish innocence had disappeared, replaced by an arrogant swagger.

'She must know you are married.'

Keane smiled and Swanson came close to smacking the smirk off his face. 'Does this happen to you often?' she asked, regretting the excitement and jealousy she heard in her voice.

'More than you'd imagine.'

Swanson walked up the stairs, desperate to know more but not willing to ask him how often he phoned the numbers. 'Keep the number, we may need it later.'

The station was swamped with officers. Lloyd's disappearance had led to unprecedented activity. Even those officers not connected to the case were visible busying away on future prosecutions.

Crime rates were low. Aside from fraud and organised crime which had its own special department, most crimes were of two variants: passion and desperation. For Swanson and her colleagues, the hardest part of their job was the burden of proof with its increasing amount of bureaucracy. The current mayoral council was less than a year away from re-election and could not risk any false prosecutions. A major kidnapping, if the Lloyd case was such a thing, was a welcome distraction. It would give her a chance to put her investigative abilities to the test. The fact that society legally killed its criminals was not something she could fight, however much she opposed the penalties administered for such menial crimes. Where she could make a difference was apprehending the real criminals. Those who posed a real threat to society, however unbalanced a society.

They sat opposite each other in Swanson's office and began working on the last five convicts, the prisoners who had just started their journeys on the pods. Occasionally Keane's foot touched hers and she wondered if he was doing it on purpose. Despite herself, she enjoyed his proximity.

'She's a very attractive lady,' she said, after twenty minutes of studying the cases.

'What's that?' asked Keane.

'Sarah Natal.'

'I guess so, if you like that sort of thing.'

'What do you mean, that sort of thing?' She knew he was playing with her but couldn't help responding.

'Nothing, really. She's just not the kind of woman I am normally attracted to.'

The obvious question hovered behind Swanson's lips but she left it there. Swanson had three of the five case files. The first convict, Simon Eagleman, was a drink driving case. Eagleman had been five times over the limit when he'd been stopped randomly by a uniformed office. The officer had taken a breath test from Eagleman and had then brought the man in for a backup blood test. Both tests had been positive. After all these years, Swanson still could not get over people's stupidity. A report had just appeared stating that Eagleman had died nine days into his journey. His file made for depressing reading. A drunk and a loner, he lived alone in Sector Seventeen and had no remaining family, and as far as Swanson could see, no friends.

'There's no way anyone wrote a ransom note for this loser,' said Keane, reading Eagleman's file. 'Why would anyone have wanted him rescued?'

Swanson could see nothing in his file which suggested Eagleman was a member of any opposition group. He'd been a teacher who had lost his job due to his drinking problem, which in turn had intensified his addiction.

'Let's go through the rest but I want you to visit the school where he used to work afterwards. We can't risk missing anything,' said Swanson.

The other two cases were Giles Thornton and Jeremy Mills who had been arrested for their part in an armed robbery. One other member of their gang had escaped. 'Possibility?' said Swanson, handing the files to Keane.

Keane glanced through the papers. Concentrating made him look more youthful. His forehead furrowed as his lips clenched tightly together. Swanson darted her head away as he caught her looking at him. 'You think the other member of the gang may want these two free?' asked Keane.

'Who knows, but whoever has written this note must know that no one will be set free.'

'Maybe it's a gesture,' suggested Keane.

'It seems a pointless gesture as Thornton and Mills will never know anything about it.'

'Perhaps they're part of a large organisation and this is a gesture from on high. A sign to their employees.'

'This isn't some dodgy cop show, Keane,' said Swanson.

'They could have worked together on a number of jobs for all we know. Obviously it's the first time they've been caught.' Keane threw the file back over at Swanson.

Swanson caught the file. 'Speak to Special Crimes, see if they know anything,' she ordered. 'What are yours like?'

'First one sounds interesting,' said Keane. 'Two months ago. Josephine Richardson, twenty-one-year-old girl prosecuted for petty theft. All procedures were met properly. During the trial, her father had to be restrained. In his report, Judge Lloyd said the father, Leon Richardson, came close to contempt.'

'Rather tentative,' said Swanson.

'This whole thing is rather tentative,' replied Keane.

'Okay, we should check out the father,' said Swanson. 'The last one?'

As Keane began reading, Chessington stormed into the office. As usual he was covered in sweat, his red hair matted to his bulging scalp. 'How are you getting on with those files?' he asked, not once looking at Keane.

'We ruled one out, sir,' said Swanson. 'We've probably ruled out another three from the information we have. We're looking at the last file now but I'm not sure if this is the correct approach.'

Chessington sighed. 'I would like you both to attend the Lenity protest on Saturday,' he said, changing the subject.

'That's a bit of a coincidence. This last guy here was a member of Lenity,' said Keane.

Swanson frowned at him, surprised by his naivety.

Chessington snatched the file from him. 'I presume you're talking about Jude Wesley,' said Chessington. 'If you're only just discovering this fact, Keane, then I think we should perhaps be looking for a new partner for Inspector Swanson.'

Keane's face reddened.

'Your sucking up didn't work so well that time, Keane,' said Swanson, after Chessington had left.

'Perhaps now would be the time to share the note we found with our esteemed boss,' said Keane in response.

'No, let's just get on with the hard work behind the scenes. He can apologise for your hurt feelings once we've sorted this case.'

Jude Wesley was indeed a former member of Lenity. He'd been discovered carrying a low calibre explosive towards the outer region of the pods, close to Sector Thirty-Two. When questioned in court as to his intentions, Wesley had replied, 'I intended to blow the monstrosity up.'

The son of two lawyers, Wesley had been a member of Lenity since his early teens. He'd had a surveillance note on his file since the age of sixteen and had been watched on and off for years. As an organisation, Lenity was scrupulously clean. Their manifesto stated an official abhorrence to violence of any kind. The meeting Keane and Swanson had attended the previous evening suggested this was still the case. The demonstration planned for the weekend was one of peaceful protest. Occasionally radicals like Wesley became frustrated with the organisation's peaceful ways and took matters into their own hands.

Both parents had attended Jude Wesley's trial. The mother worked in the commercial law division of a highly successful legal firm. The father, Charles Wesley, was a high ranking public defender.

'Maybe we should question that spotty youth from the other night,' suggested Keane. 'He looked like the type.'

'The type?'

'Yeah, the type. The type to write such a pointless ransom note.'

'The type to kidnap a high profile judge as well?'

'Probably not. But he must be reasonably high up in Lenity to be holding that meeting. If it wasn't him then at least he might have some useful information.'

'Really?' asked Swanson, eyebrows raised.

'What's your suggestion?'

'I'm not buying it. Even if Lenity has branched out into more controversial means of protest, it would destroy their reputation to support Wesley. It's ludicrous. No one wants Wesley released. It can't be about him.'

Keane sighed. 'So that's that?'

'You're quite sweet when you're angry, Keane. I'll question Wesley's parents and Richardson's father. You question that spotty guy from the meeting after you've visited Eagleman's school and spoken to Special Crimes.'

'Yes, ma'am,' said Keane, offering her a mock salute.

As Keane left the office, Swanson opened her reader. Chiding herself, she pulled up a picture of Charles Wesley. Jude Wesley's father had been the public defender she'd seen at the Lenity meeting.

Chapter Eight

The alarm sounded at six a.m. McClusky swiped at it with his right hand. Within seconds he felt the burning pain. It covered his whole body and centred its intensity on his scalp. Lighting a cigarette, he fell out of bed and stumbled towards the bathroom mirror. He retched at the sight of his naked body, his skeletal frame lacking any sense of humanity. His skull looked misshapen, his scalp pitted with patches of sun-scarred red. He pulled back his remaining hair, and gently probed the small blisters and peeled skin. Each touch sent delicious shivers through his body until the pain became too much and he was forced to rub Vaseline over his wounds.

He smoked six more cigarettes and drank a litre of coffee for breakfast. He looked out of the window without seeing anyone, his blistering skin enough of a focus for the time being. He changed without showering into a white, long-sleeved shirt and blue dungarees, and headed downstairs. The streets were already full of people. They shuffled past him as if he were invisible. Occasionally they would brush against him and the contact was enough to send his imagination into overdrive: the sudden demise of the suited businessman, the energy spilling from his body as his femoral artery was cut with a perfect slice; the despairing gulps from the female student as he grabbed her by the throat and squeezed. The encounters pushed him onwards, the snippets of suffering giving fuel to his empty body.

A larger security presence than normal had formed outside the factory and McClusky took his place in a disgruntled queue. Leonard, the old security guard by the gate, shook his hand as he did every morning. 'Morning, Reg. Sorry about this crazy stuff.' Leonard had less hair than McClusky, his perfectly shaven skull gleaming in the light. He glared at the other security guards as if disgusted by their presence.

McClusky imagined Leonard on a butcher's slab, rivers of fear and nerve-shredding pain flowing through him as McClusky took swipe after swipe at him. 'No, problem, Leonard. Have a nice day.' Leonard was the one person in the building who spoke to him. He either didn't know what the others knew, or didn't care.

McClusky clocked in and took his place in the assembly line. The mind-numbing job of sorting through metal sheets would be his for the next nine hours. The cavern-like factory smelt of tar and oil, and the heat from the machines simmered in the air. McClusky watched motionless as the metal objects drifted past him, each indistinguishable from the next.

At lunch, he sat alone in the canteen, chain-smoking and drinking coffee. Everyone else sat in huddled groups, talking and laughing. He thought it unlikely that every conversation was about him but he couldn't be sure. People would turn from his gaze, refusing to make eye contact. McClusky imagined them slaughtered where they sat; layers upon layers of pain overwhelmed him until he had to shut his eyes to control the sensation. He clenched his fists as the shared hurt rushed his body.

A blow dragged him from his reverie. McClusky opened his eyes into a blurred world. 'Sorry, Reg,' said Tom Miller, rubbing his elbow. Miller was often clumsy, especially when McClusky was around. The elbow connected with McClusky's temple and his vision had yet to fully return. Miller walked away, his steel-capped boot making perfect contact with McClusky's shin before he left. McClusky sucked in a half-anguished, half-ecstatic cry.

Throughout the afternoon, talk circulated about a drinking session after the shift. People talked openly in front of him although he was neither invited nor allowed to attend such gatherings. McClusky picked through the objects, his hands slick with oil and grime. His head itched and he smeared it with the black lubricant. The aroma of cigarettes and coffee filled the air but he had no access to either until the end of the shift. Miller walked past him and was so involved in whatever he was doing that he failed to kick him. Perhaps he would go and get drunk tonight; then Miller could learn the true nature of their relationship.

By the time the whistle sounded his fingers were numb and locked in position. He left the conveyer and headed outside for a cigarette. The first drag made him dizzy, more so than Miller's elbow. He waited fifty minutes before heading to the deserted changing rooms. The windows were open and cold air swirled within the steam from the showers. The room needed disinfecting. The reek of stale body odour, oil, perfumed sprays, piss and shit had mingled to create something so foul that it made him heave. He clawed off his overalls and shivered as he entered the showers, his burnt scalp and face covered in black patches. The windows were jammed open and the cold stayed with him despite the acid-like heat of the water. He lathered soap onto his body, sensing his fragility as his thawing hands traced lines over the bones of his body. After he switched off the shower, he dried himself in the chill of the open windows.

Miller, who was undressing, was waiting for him in the changing rooms. Pure, ripped muscle ridiculed McClusky, leaving him to consider how it was possible to build such bulk. Miller was putting on a show. He knew McClusky was watching and was luxuriating in his display of masculinity. 'What are you looking at? I thought you only liked women,' said Miller, wrapping a towel around his waist.

McClusky looked away, ignoring the inference. He thought about changing, his shame freezing him in position. He tried to imagine Miller in a situation of mortal peril but was too intimidated by his proximity. Perhaps this was the day. Miller had been threatening him for the last two years. Now that they were alone, McClusky wasn't safe. He closed his eyes and waited. Contemplating his own demise, he was filled with joy.

'Not today,' said Miller, smacking McClusky around the

head with the open palm of his right hand as he walked to the showers.

McClusky opened his eyes. The changing room was silent, as if frozen in time. Still shivering, he considered finding something heavy from the shop floor and punishing Miller for his delaying tactics but such actions were for the courageous.

He ignored Leonard's farewell as he left the factory. The night sky was cloudless and a multitude of stars glistened above him. Despite his layers, the cold coursed through him; it had reached his bones, the cold air rooted in his marrow. He walked faster, directionless, furious at his encounter with Miller. He passed the bar, Little Joe's, where they all drank; where one evening another lifetime ago, he'd also drunk. He stopped by the entrance, sensing the warmth and promise within the bar's doors. Even standing there was breaking his parole. If he entered, he would be in the pods within days. Through the frosted windows his colleagues were united in their revelry. Perhaps they knew about Miller's plan to wait for him in the showers and were laughing at him.

He hurried away, knowing any one of them would betray him without a second thought. He walked by the river back to his apartment. He'd been so enraged that he hadn't thought about being followed. Now the thought returned, and it was as if he'd wished the presence into existence. It wasn't Miller; Miller was only a threat at work. The knowledge empowered him as if he had ticked off a potential threat, albeit from a very long list.

Nevertheless, the presence accompanied him all the way home.

Chapter Nine

The public defender's office was in Sector Twelve of the city, three miles from the Supreme Court. The building was a monolithic brick structure badly in need of renovation. It was sixteen storeys high and painted a questionable shade of green. Tiny slits of windows were sprinkled across its façade, giving it the look of a prison. Swanson entered the foyer through a tired set of revolving doors, the glass chipped and unwashed. She was presented with a scene of chaos and confusion. As well as housing the public defender's office, the building was home to a number of other state-run offices including welfare and counselling services. Hundreds of people wandered around the beige carpeted ground floor, searching for information from randomly placed help desks. When Swanson asked a young woman working at one of the larger desks if she could meet with Charles Wesley, she received a humourless laugh in response. 'Do you have an appointment?' asked the woman.

Swanson stared at the woman, and flicked open her warrant card. 'I don't need an appointment,' she said.

The woman paused. 'I'll call him but I can't imagine he'll want to see you today. His diary is fully booked for the next three weeks.'

'He has no choice. Tell him it's about his son.'

Wesley appeared twenty minutes later. 'Inspector Swanson?' he asked.

Swanson stood and shook the man's hand. She had come across Wesley before but had no previous interaction with him. He looked impatient to leave. Swanson took a step towards the man, forcing him to step back. 'Can we go somewhere quieter to talk?' she asked, showing Wesley her warrant card.

'Listen, Inspector Swanson. I'm sure you have the finest motives for being here but I'm afraid I've fully explained my relationship with my son to your colleagues.' Wesley spat the word colleagues at Swanson as if it was a dirty word.

'I do apologise but you're going to have to go through it all one more time, Mr Wesley.'

They stood motionless, staring at one another, Swanson's gaze never once faltering.

'Fine, follow me,' said Wesley, turning his back and moving away. Swanson followed at a discreet pace behind him.

A woman, at least twenty years Wesley's junior, was waiting in his office. She smiled at Swanson, the warmth never reaching her eyes.

'Thanks, Rachel. Could you give me the office for ten minutes?' said Wesley.

The woman left the office in silence, her eyes fixed to the floor as she walked past Swanson.

Wesley took off his jacket and sat down behind his desk.

He pointed to the seat opposite but Swanson remained standing. She paced the office. It was in a similar state to Chessington's, pieces of paperwork filed everywhere in no particular order. On the noticeboard to Wesley's right was a list of upcoming cases which she presumed Wesley was working on. 'Please, Inspector, I've agreed to this discussion but time really is of the essence. If we do have to go through this all again, please can we get on with it?' He rolled up the sleeves of his shirt, revealing a large scar on his right forearm glowing red on his otherwise pale skin.

Swanson sat.

'Tell me what you want to know,' said Wesley.

Swanson picked up the file from her briefcase and opened it. 'Mr Wesley, following your son's arrest, your statement claimed that you hadn't had contact with him in six months?'

Wesley's face contorted into a mixture of bemusement and anger. 'Are you calling me a liar?'

'I'm just asking for confirmation.'

Wesley continued to stare. Finally he leant back in his chair. 'As I told your colleagues, I've had little to do with my son over the last few years. I'd seen him six months previously at a family get-together. It was the last time I spoke to him prior to his arrest.'

'May I ask why your relationship with your son was in such a poor state?' asked Swanson.

'Not that it's any of your business but we drifted apart because of his political ideals.'

'Which were?'

'Well, although we shared the same basic ideologies, in that we both intrinsically oppose ZT, I'm afraid Jude desired to take his opposition to the extreme.'

'He wasn't afraid to use violence?'

'Quite,' said Wesley. 'It had been ongoing for a number of years but as he became more and more militant I could no longer be a part of his life.' Wesley looked troubled by this admission.

'So you had no knowledge of his plans on the day he was arrested?' asked Swanson.

'Of course not. If I had known what he was planning then I would have intervened. Even if it had meant going to the police.'

'So tell me about your involvement with Lenity,' said Swanson.

'How is that relevant?' asked Wesley.

'Please just answer the question, and I can be on my way,' said Swanson.

Wesley sighed again. 'Fine. As you know, Inspector, Lenity is a zero tolerance opposition group. And as I'm also sure you're aware we are a peaceful group and abhor violence of any kind.'

'Yes, but what is your role?'

'I'm just a member. I attend meetings though hold no official capacity.'

'And you believe Lenity had no part in your son's plans?'

'Don't be preposterous,' said Wesley, his face turning red. 'No Lenity member has ever been connected to any form of violent protest.'

'Your son was a member of Lenity,' said Swanson.

'That may well be but he was acting independently. Did you find any connection between him and other members of Lenity?'

'Have you seen your son since he was placed in the pods?'

Wesley grimaced. 'You're very good at avoiding questions,' he said. 'No.'

'You know he has been in the pods for five days now?' After eight days, prisoners could press the suicide button. The button released a poisonous red gas into the pod. The gas was coloured to highlight the suicide, an extra show of deterrence for any would-be criminals.

'His mother informed me when he went into the pods,' said Wesley. 'I guess that was five days ago.'

Swanson closed her file. 'And your wife, Mr Wesley. Do her political ideals differ from yours as well?'

Wesley chuckled. 'In some ways, yes. Now if there are no further questions, Inspector, I must be getting on.'

'Thank you for your time,' said Swanson, rising from her seat. She didn't offer her hand as she was sure it wouldn't be taken.

Wesley's assistant was waiting outside his office. Again she looked at her feet as Swanson opened the door. Swanson introduced herself and the woman looked up.

'Rachael Stanton,' said the woman.

'How long have you been working for Mr Wesley?' asked Swanson.

'About eight months.'

'Do you know his son?'

'No,' said the woman. 'Obviously I've heard about what's happened to him. It's a horrible business.'

'Yes, it must have taken its toll on Mr Wesley. I imagine he was quite devastated by it all.'

'Yes, very much so. They destroy families don't they?' said the woman. 'The pods, I mean.'

'Yes, I guess they do,' agreed Swanson.

In another life, she could have been in Charles Wesley's position. Her thoughts on ZT were muddled. She'd never seen her mother in the pods. Her father had forbidden it. The last time she'd seen her mother had been that evening when the SI guards broke into their house. Her father had sent her away to relatives in the outer sector and to this day she still didn't know how long her mother had survived in her pod.

The pods had devastated her life but she'd never thought a direct opposition to ZT and the pods was a feasible approach. Her mother's crime was aiding and abetting a so-called terrorist, a woman called Thea Kendal, who had an arrest warrant out on her. It might have seemed natural to follow in her path, but her mother's fight had been futile.

Swanson decided as a young woman to take a different approach. ZT didn't eliminate crime. Bad people still did bad things. Would she have made more of a difference if she'd worked for the public defender's office? Once the public prosecution office decided to take a case to court it was almost a foregone conclusion. Part of her still thought she could make some form of contribution, though such optimism was ground out of her on a daily basis.

The journalist, Jane Sutton, was loitering outside the building. 'Inspector, a minute of your time?' went her familiar refrain.

'If I only had a penny for each minute, Miss Sutton,' replied Swanson, unsmiling.

'Can you give me any updates on the Lloyd case, Inspector?' asked the journalist.

'No.'

'It would really be in our readers' interest if you could give me some information. Your station has passed on all enquiries to you. At the moment I'm in the dark. Nothing to report, except speculation.' She paused. 'Were you here to see Mr Wesley?'

Swanson's eyes narrowed. 'Listen, Jane, there's simply nothing to report. Judge Lloyd is missing; we're looking at certain avenues.'

'And the ransom note?'

Swanson edged closer to the journalist. Like every other citizen, Swanson was subject to ZT. Officers were only allowed to use reasonable force. Unfortunately, it didn't extend to throttling journalists who annoyed her. 'Whether or not there is a ransom note is classified, Miss Sutton.' The growled intonation on *classified* left the journalist under no illusions as to what would happen should she decide to publish such information.

Sutton shifted from one foot to the other. 'Surely knowing that a high court judge has been kidnapped is in the public interest? Is Wesley involved?' The journalist scrunched her face up at the question, her glasses riding high on her nose.

'The ransom note is not of public interest at the current time. If the public knows there is a ransom note all the crackpots will be out claiming responsibility.'

Swanson began walking away and the journalist followed. In a more convivial tone, she asked, 'You must sense the unrest?'

'None more than usual.'

'A large protest is planned on Saturday coinciding with a podding. Zazen's council is hanging by a thread. People want a change. ZT, at least in its current form, is outdated.'

'Is that supposed to be a question?' asked Swanson.

Andrew Zazen was the city's mayor. His council had been continuously re-elected since ZT's inception, with some minor changes of personnel along the way. The opposing parties were fragmented – small bands of people who normally stood on an anti-ZT basis, with little thought given to any other policies. The only approximate democracy in the city was the mayoral election, where citizens had the choice between various shades of the same colour. Zazen had started off as a moderate. In the last election, he had fought the challenge of a radical colleague who wanted to extend the range of ZT to so-called 'moral' crimes. However, now he was in power, the whispers were that Zazen was considering this extension as well. Swanson shuddered to think how far the range of moral crimes could reach.

'If my readers know the judge has been kidnapped, it might balance out the argument.'

Swanson stopped. 'How long have you known me, Jane?'

Sutton smiled. 'For a time.'

'Your readers don't want a balanced argument. They want to interpret the information to fit their own twisted viewpoint. The ransom note is classified. I will let you know when it is not. Now if you can excuse me, I need to be elsewhere.'

'And does Charles Wesley have anything to do with the Lloyd case?

'No comment.'

Swanson drove back to Sector One where Jessica Wesley worked. The central zones of the city had prospered over the last two decades. The majority of the imposing skyscrapers which adorned Sector One were now close to full occupancy, after decades of standing empty. Only the occasional building was vacated, usually too damaged to be habitable.

Charles Wesley's wife, Jessica, worked for Kinsley-Jacobs, a commercial law firm based in the heart of Sector One. From the décor of the building, Swanson determined that Jessica Wesley was somewhat more successful than her husband, in monetary terms if nothing else. Her firm's offices took up the top six floors of a glass-fronted skyscraper a short walk from the Supreme Court. Swanson waited for Keane in the lobby of the building which was in stark contrast to the public defenders' office. Well-dressed business people strode across a white marbled floor whilst soft background music was piped out of the building's speakers.

Keane arrived ten minutes later than he should have. 'Timothy Basle is quite an interesting character,' he said, breathless, as he took a seat next to Swanson in one of the plush leather armchairs. 'PhD in political science, practically a member of Lenity since birth. One black mark on his copybook, though. He was briefly a member of an extreme left wing militant group during his first year at university. The group was shut down after promoting violent protest. The leader of the group came close to being prosecuted.'

'Did you question him about it?' asked Swanson.

'Yes, he tried to dismiss it. He's very nervous, generally. I think he fears authority. He gave me the usual non-violent spiel. I asked him if he knew the Wesleys and he hesitated before saying that he knew of Charles Wesley and the "terrible business" with his son. Not much else, I'm afraid. Flaherty called. Apparently there are rumours that Mr. and Mrs. Wesley have split up recently.'

This came as no surprise. 'Eagleman?'

'Date fixed with the school's head after this.'

'Thornton and Mills?'

'Special Crimes report that they are low level. From the post-arrest interrogation, it looks like this was their first crime.'

They shared the lift with three business women to floor fifty-six. Swanson eavesdropped on the conversation. She understood the legal jargon the women used but she was out of her comfort zone. They discussed contract law and indemnities and by the time the lift doors opened Swanson had switched off.

The firm's receptionist was much more welcoming than the one at the public defenders' office. 'Mrs Wesley's very busy at the moment, but I will call through to her. Please take a seat,' she said.

Five minutes later Jessica Wesley appeared. In Swanson's opinion, the woman was wearing too much make-up. Her cheeks were smothered in rouge, her eyelids painted blue, her lashes a thick black. It looked as if she were wearing a mask.

'Inspector Swanson,' said the woman, offering her hand.

Swanson introduced Keane.

'Please, follow me.' She led them through an open plan office where hundreds of cloned business people were busy working at their personal computer terminals. Cold, stale air conditioning billowed through the area. The sign on Wesley's office door stated that she was Senior Managing Partner. It was a corner office with an uninterrupted view of the domed Supreme Court building. The steel tracks which transported the pods were not visible.

'Please take a seat,' said Jessica Wesley. 'How may I help you? I should inform you my husband has called in advance so I have a fair idea of why you are here.'

'Thank you,' said Swanson. 'I appreciate your time. We just wanted to go over a few details of your son's arrest once more.'

Wesley clasped her fingers together. She had a healthier complexion than her husband; her skin, or at least the parts untouched by make-up, was lightly tanned. 'I'm happy to discuss the matter with you, Inspector Swanson, but could you tell me if this has to do with the case involving my son or if it has to do with any other case you may be working on at present?'

Swanson paused. 'What other case would you be talking about?' she asked.

'Nothing specific,' said Wesley. 'I'd like to be clear whether or not we are discussing the incidents involving my son's arrest or some other matter.'

'Would it make a difference if we were discussing another matter?' asked Keane.

'It wouldn't make a difference to my responses, but I would like to know what we're discussing. The fact is, as you're well aware, my son has been tried and convicted. He's currently five days into his death sentence. So it seems to me there is not much more to be gained from interrogating me about his so-called crimes.'

Wesley stared at them. Her demeanour was hard to read. She was used to being in control and was clearly not going to be deceived.

'We're investigating another case,' said Swanson. 'I'm afraid I can't go into details at the moment but there is a possibility that your son is involved directly or indirectly.' It was clear the woman had heard about Judge Lloyd's disappearance. It was likely that news of the ransom note had also leaked, and a woman of Jessica Wesley's intellect would hardly miss the connections.

'Go ahead,' instructed Wesley.

'Your husband claims that he was no longer on speaking terms with your son at the time he was arrested. Is this how you see things?'

'It's how things were,' said Wesley. She leant forward on her desk, dominating the space. 'Both of them have strong political convictions and they disagreed intensely about how far one should go for one's beliefs.'

'Your husband favours the non-violent approach?' asked Keane.

'Correct.'

'And your son?'

'Clearly his approach was somewhat different. You may have noticed he was arrested carrying explosives.'

'And your view?' asked Swanson.

'Not that it's relevant, but we live in a supposedly civilised society so we should behave in a civilised manner.'

'So you think your son was guilty?'

'My opinion is not relevant.'

'Have you seen your son in the pods?' asked Keane.

'I've said my goodbyes, Sergeant. It's what he wanted.'

'Thank you, Mrs Wesley,' said Swanson. 'We won't take up any more of your time.'

Wesley showed them to the elevator doors and handed Swanson her card. 'I'm sorry I couldn't be of any more assistance, Inspector Swanson.'

Swanson nodded as the doors closed, thinking to herself that Mrs Wesley had been of more assistance than she realised.

Chapter Ten

Swanson left Keane outside Jessica Wesley's office and headed for the pods. She sympathised with both parents, and understood what it was like to have a loved one in the pods. She didn't blame them for not wanting to speak to the police again. They would have endured enough of that when Jude was arrested, would have spent weeks talking to the state-provided psychologists. But the couple's reaction to her questioning suggested they were hiding something. Charles Wesley had been overly abrasive, Jessica Wesley too measured and composed.

She parked close to the Valley where the convicts' journey always began. The Valley was nothing more than a vast clearing of land, where thousands of people regularly gathered there to watch the poddings. A set of eight steel pylons stretched towards the sky. They were connected by thick, intertwined steel wires known as the tracks. The glass prisons dangled from the wires that circulated through the thirty-eight sectors of the city, interspersed at regular intervals with more of the triangular pylons. Three separate lines of tracks were used to hold the pods in case one line malfunctioned. They each followed the same route. In the valley and the central zones, they corkscrewed through the populated areas. Their path was designed for maximum viewing potential. As they left the central areas their path straightened out. On the outskirts of the city they acted as a makeshift perimeter, encasing the more desolate areas whilst maintaining a brooding presence for the population that dwelt outside the central zones.

Hundreds of miles of cables were in use, and thousands of personnel were needed for maintenance and security. It was a thriving industry. Viewing stations were available all along the route, each with its own small refreshment area. Non-denominational buildings of worship were positioned at regular intervals. It was not uncommon for the family and friends of the convicts to follow the route of their loved one's pod. Even now, Swanson saw two people watching one of the pods. They looked like the parents of the podded youth whose pod dangled only yards away, his hands pressed against his glass prison. Their faces held the same death-like expression she'd seen too many times before; a mixture of despair and impotence which was horrific to behold.

The convicted prisoners entered their pods in the Valley area before being dragged skywards along the thick steel tracks. To the unknowing, it looked like the beginning of a rollercoaster ride.

Swanson had watched countless convicts enter the pods. Thousands of spectators would jeer as they began their journey. Although there was only one outcome for anyone who began this particular journey, there always seemed to be a sense of misplaced hope as they entered their pod. It was as if each new convict thought they would be the one to survive the journey which in thirty days would return them to the very same point.

The pods moved slowly in the more populated areas and Josephine Richardson was only a thousand metres along the tracks. She was the latest podded convict and from her parking space Swanson could see her silhouetted figure in the distance. She followed the imposing cables to the piece of barren land beneath Richardson's pod. Her glass prison was half a mile above them and still rising. The pod had a flat base with a cylindrical dome which mimicked that of the Supreme Court's. Richardson was asleep, her prone figure curled into the foetal position.

Swanson had wanted to see the girl before she made contact with her father. It was the respectful thing to do, though looking at the sad and lonely figure above made her question her motives. She'd seen hundreds of convicts in her time, from serial killers to shoplifters, and every time she was reminded of one person.

She sighed and took one last look at Josephine Richardson and the line of pods careering off towards the horizon. She wondered how many of the convicts farther along the tracks were still alive, and how much longer Richardson would survive.

The Richardsons lived in Sector Twenty-Eight to the west of the valley. The pods reached this sector somewhere in the twentieth day. Red brick buildings dominated the area, built during the years following the Flux. Each building was indecipherable from the next. Only the grid-like street plan made it easy to find Richardson's house. She parked outside a building marked 'Block Seventy-Two.' The Richardson apartment was on the sixth floor and she made her way up flights of urine-soaked steps. Number sixty-one was first in a row of ten small apartments. Each door was painted a dark, racing-car green. The door was answered by a woman in her late fifties who had a bloated face with small, almost unblinking eyes. 'Mrs Richardson?' asked Swanson.

After examining her identification, Mrs Richardson invited them into the apartment. Swanson followed her down a poorly lit corridor, dragging her feet as if tethered to a large weight. In the living room, Leon Richardson sat on a battered leather sofa. A single naked light bulb dangled from the ceiling. The room was a dull white, the walls cracked and peeling. Five unlit candles were perched on a vinyl-covered sideboard.

Leon Richardson looked up at her, his stare as blank as his wife's. Most people were put on edge by the appearance of an officer but Richardson was passive. Only when Swanson mentioned his daughter's name did his eyes flicker with animation. 'How dare you mention her name in front of me?' he snarled, drops of spittle falling onto his grey stubble. When she explained the reason for their visit, the man struggled out of his chair towards her.

'Take a seat, Mr Richardson,' instructed Swanson, the vehemence of her growl-like voice enough to stop him. 'Now, I understand your anger,' she said, once he had placed his ample body back onto the chair. 'Please appreciate that I'm here investigating the disappearance of Judge Lloyd.'

'I hope he is rotting away in some ditch,' said Leon Richardson. 'How could he send my girl to the pods for such a meaningless thing?'

Swanson understood she was wasting her time, was intruding on the parents' grief. Reluctantly, she questioned the parents about their whereabouts on the night of Lloyd's disappearance. As she took a sample of handwriting from each, she looked away at Mrs Richardson's trembling hand.

Swanson met Keane back at the station an hour later. His meeting with Simon Eagleman's school had proved a dead end. 'As it said in the file, he was a drunk. No family. The rumour circulating the school was that he was sleeping with one of the cleaning staff, but it didn't get any more exciting than that. No one seemed to miss him, and I can't imagine anyone writing any ransom notes for him.'

'So where are we?' asked Swanson. 'Aside from the Wesleys?'

'You really think they have something to do with this?'

'They're withholding something. Anyway, what else do we have?'

'There's always Sarah Natal,' said Keane.

'You think she knows something?'

'Don't you?' said Keane. 'And she hated you,' he added with a smirk.

'I wasn't sure she knew I was in the room.'

'I could call her, suggest a date?'

'Is that wise?'

'Why not? If you know about it then it is officially police business.'

'And how are you planning on obtaining information from her, over an intimate glass of white wine? It's not ethical.'

'I'll wear a wire, it will be above board. And I prefer red.'

Swanson was not sure if her objections were personal or professional. She hadn't worked with Keane before. He was a fast riser, on some form of accelerated program with the force, and would be probably be her boss in ten years' time. She couldn't deny she was attracted to the man, but nothing like that would affect the way she conducted her professional life. 'Fine,' she said. 'Call her.'

Keane turned on the speakerphone and called Natal. Swanson tried to hide her fascination, and reluctant admiration. Keane was confident, directing the conversation expertly to his own ends.

'I'm not sure your partner was too keen on me,' said Natal, her voice a luxuriant hush.

'Don't worry about her, she gets a bit jealous when there's another beautiful woman in the room,' replied Keane, smiling at Swanson, who tried in vain to control the colour in her cheeks.

'So you really want to get together? Isn't it a bit dangerous?'

'What's life without a bit of danger? You live alone don't you? Perhaps you can cook me dinner?' suggested Keane.

Natal laughed on the other end of the phone, a confused, excited yelp. 'God, you're forward.'

Swanson was bemused by the exchange. She understood they were both toying with one another but it was not a game she was used to playing. Swanson had spent most of her life single. She'd had flings but nothing which lasted more than a few weeks.

Keane placed the phone down after agreeing to meet with Natal that evening. He held his hands up and shrugged his shoulders.

'Get that smug look off your face,' commanded Swanson. 'We've plenty of work to do before your *date*.'

Chapter Eleven

'Who the hell was that?' asked Old Blue.

'Jealous?' Sarah Natal was lounging on a cream-coloured sofa in Old Blue's living room, wrapped in a pale green silk dressing gown which only half covered her body. He saw the wildness in her eyes. It was a look which in a former life would have unnerved him. A lustful hunger shone through her, close to becoming uncontrollable. She shared a story similar to the others; relevant to Old Blue's. He considered her response. Clearly, she wanted him to be jealous but he had not felt that type of emotion for years.

'We agreed not to be exclusive, Sarah.' The words grated as he said them.

She moved from the sofa, her dressing gown falling open, and crept towards him. 'You're allowed to be jealous, though,' she whispered, climbing onto him. Close to weightless, she wrapped her thighs around his waist. She nuzzled her mouth into his neck and began the ritual.

Afterwards she lay across him, dwarfed by the expanse of his body; her legs, clammy with moisture, locked tight with his. 'So when can I see him?' she asked, seemingly unable to play along with the pretence that the last thirty minutes had been anything other than a prelude to that question.

'You don't want to see him,' said Old Blue.

'You're wrong. I want to see that bastard suffering.' She had disentangled herself and was straddling him, her brow furrowed. She looked more confused than angry.

He knew her well. Despite her rhetoric, she wouldn't be pleased to see the judge in his current state. 'When the time is right,' he said, and moved to get off the bed.

She clenched her thighs around his legs and pushed her hands onto his chest. 'Show me now,' she insisted, so sincerely that he stifled a laugh. He grabbed her arms and twisted her over, gripping her throat with his large right hand, holding her prone on the bed. She looked up at him, fully surrendered, and a shiver of disgust ran through him to see the desire in her eyes. He let her go and walked to the bathroom to urinate before showering.

Ten minutes later, he heard the front door slam. He stood naked in the cubicle, drip-drying in the mild draught from the open bedroom door. The judge should have been fed two hours ago but he couldn't face it. Musty heat billowed through the cellar, each particle of air packed dense with an indecipherable odour; something riper, deeper than body sweat. He could smell the judge's blood, the fear which ripped through him every time Old Blue opened the trap door.

He dressed and made himself a meal of black coffee and dry toast. Now was not the time for indecision. The plan was on track, save for his queasiness over the smell. The echo of Nathaniel Jacobson, of who he once was, warned him not to deviate in his operation. Now that everything had started, time was limited. He downed the coffee in one swift motion, the black liquid burning his throat. He coughed and poured dry cereal into a large, white, ceramic bowl and filled a glass jug with water. He placed the meal onto a wooden tray and carried it to the trap door. He placed the tray next to the trap door and grabbed a scarf from the cloak room which he wrapped tight against his mouth and nose.

His footsteps echoed as he made his way down the stairs. As his eyes adjusted to the darkness of the cellar, he made out the blurred figure of the judge collapsed on the stone floor behind his glass-fronted prison. He didn't rush. He was not a man prone to hysteric assumptions and presumed the judge was asleep. He knocked on the glass panel but the man didn't move. He placed the tray in the glass trap door and pulled it down shut. The noise reverberated around the cavern. Old Blue saw himself reflected in the glass, the scarf wrapped tight against his mouth, his eyes glaring back at him as if he was a stranger. 'Get up,' he shouted, his voice sending further reverberations around the dungeon.

As the judge stirred, Old Blue felt his heart quicken. The prisoner pulled himself upright and stared out at him. 'A little bit late for disguises don't you think, Nathaniel?' he said, his voice weak.

'Your lunch,' he replied.

'Ah, always a treat.' Lloyd didn't move towards the food. He stared at him, defiant. He looked gaunt. An unhealthy-looking grey beard had appeared on his face, and his hair looked like it was falling out. Old Blue could make out patches of dampness on his pyjamas and decided he would give the judge a change of clothes at dinner time.

'I don't know if you are planning on keeping me or if you are planning to starve me to death, but dry cereal and water will not keep me alive for long.' Lloyd bent towards the tray and tumbled over. On the floor, he gulped at the water and forced handfuls of the cereal into his mouth.

Old Blue turned and left the room. At the top of the stairs, he slammed the trap door shut and ripped the scarf from his mouth. The smell lingered; he sensed it seeping through the floor boards, threatening to interfere with his plans. He already felt rushed and urgency resulted in mistakes.

An hour later he was in Sector Twelve in a bar called Little Joe's. He'd spent many days and nights in the establishment. Little Joe's was spread over four floors but only the ground floor was open during the day. The basement was a large cavern of a room. Uneven wooden floorboards stretched across the interior, covered in a fine carpet of an ash-like substance which he suspected had been placed there on purpose to create atmosphere. A number of elevated wooden tables and chairs were spread randomly across the floor; to the side wrinkled brown leather sofas were pushed up against the wall. Drink was cheap in Little Joe's and the clientele was a disparate one. To one side of the room, a group of students poured drinks from large jugs of brightly coloured liquid. On the overlarge tables, couples and groups of business people enjoyed Little Joe's 'legendary' burgers. At the bar, which stretched the length of the ground floor, loners drank from glass bottles or pitchers of lager. Old Blue took his place at the bar and ordered a glass of lemonade, trying his best to ignore the mild odour of stale beer and disinfectant which hung in the air. Twenty minutes later the pair walked in.

Their daily rituals were more precise, and predictable, than that of the judge. Every work day, they arrived at the bar within five minutes, either way, of six o'clock. The men, in their early thirties, wore jeans and t-shirts. They were freshly showered, their hair still damp. The tallest of the pair, Glen Thurrock, led the way to the bar and ordered two beers. Within minutes they had both finished their drinks and the second man, Simon Wilson, whose curly hairstyle reminded Old Blue of a mop head, ordered a second round. Their night would be as predictable as their choice of drink. Sometime around seven they would order some food, most likely burgers, and by eight they would move on to harder liquor. By nine they would be on one of the upper floors trying their luck with the various young women who frequented Little Joe's in the evenings. By midnight they would be on their way home, sometimes alone, sometimes with female companions. Little Joe's was open twenty-four-seven, and save for work and sleep, these two men spent most of their time in Little Joe's hospitality.

He watched from a distance. He knew where the men worked, where they slept. He could pinpoint their whereabouts at any given time, such was their ludicrous predictability. He finished his lemonade and moved across the bar to where they stood. He ordered himself a beer. Oblivious to his presence, they continued their mindless chatter.

'Is that Lucy girl coming tonight?'

'I hope not.'

'Keeps your options open though?'

'I guess.'

Only their height differentiated one man from the other. If he closed his eyes and simply listened, he was unable to tell them apart from voice alone. They talked in simple, abbreviated, sentences.

'You looking forward to Friday?' said one of the men.

'As always,' said the other.

'Should be a good one. Payday and all that.'

'Yeah,' said the second speaker. 'We should get a little extra stuff. You know, to celebrate.'

'To celebrate the end of the month?'

'Yeah, why not?'

Old Blue drained his lemonade and left. The pods drifted low in this sector, and he could easily see the inhabitants. They sat huddled in their prisons, staring into nowhere. It had been a political decision to make the tracks so visible in this stretch of the city. To the west, the pods ran high, almost out of sight. The pods tracked low in Sector Twelve, because Sector Twelve had the highest level of crime.

He made one last detour before returning home.

Chapter Twelve

At lunch they went over the plan for Keane's meeting with Natal. 'Now, you're sure about everything tonight? I'm taking a big risk on you so don't let me down.' She'd considered calling off the operation numerous times since Keane had first suggested it. It wasn't the sort of risk she was used to taking and something about Keane's eagerness unsettled her. In the end, only the thought that her growing personal feelings for Keane were clouding her judgment had prevented her from aborting the plan.

'Don't worry about me. Let's just hope she knows something.'

'And that you can get her to share it,' said Swanson, regretting the words as they left her lips.

Keane chose to play dumb on the innuendo and took a swig of coffee before flicking through his case files.

Keane was silent as Swanson drove them to Natal's residence, glancing at his watch every couple of minutes. He'd applied too much aftershave and Swanson opened her window to let in some air. He was dressed in a sharp black suit, with a pastel striped shirt. His hair was slicked back with more gel than was necessary. It highlighted the definition of his bone structure, the clearness of his large eyes.

The back seat was filled with an large bouquet of long-stemmed white roses and Swanson wondered if her partner was overdoing things.

Natal's flat was close to the river, and the road to her apartment followed a line of pods. For most of the journey, they hung directly above Swanson's car. When manoeuvring around corners, she would catch mirror images of the glass domes; would occasionally catch shadows of the ghost faces within.

'Let's check your wire once more,' said Swanson, parking two streets down from Natal's apartment.

'Jesus Christ, I'm wearing four of the things. I've more chance of a pod falling on me than all of these failing,' he said, wiping away droplets of sweat from his brow.

'Just for me,' she said. She'd made Keane wear four separate microphones and he'd chosen the most minuscule, and potentially unreliable, models.

'Fine, testing, one, two. Are you playing with me?'

Swanson was laughing.

Keane talked to her as he walked to the apartment, his voice a whisper. It was a one-way conversation, Keane having refused an ear piece. 'So how come you're not married, officer? I'm sure you must have an endless supply of admirers. Do you have a *significant other*, or are you playing the field? Play the field, Swanson. That's my advice. Whilst it's legal. Christ, I'm here.'

'You look amazing – these are for you,' Swanson heard him say to Natal, minutes later. 'I love your dress. Black. Classic.'

'Thank you,' said Natal. 'Wow, these are beautiful. I didn't expect these.' The distant sound of Natal's voice sounded genuinely surprised.

Swanson sat back in the car and listened as Keane worked. The back of her neck was sticky against the leather of the driver's seat. Keane's smell lingered; with the doors and windows shut the smell overtook the interior. Despite herself, she kept the windows shut.

Natal was generous with the wine. The alcohol relaxed Keane, and it sounded as if his nervousness had disappeared. Natal was an attentive host, and Keane was an equally attentive guest. An hour into the date, Natal invited him into the dining room. 'Well, a dining table in my kitchen,' she said to Keane.

Swanson admired the way Keane worked. Halfway through dinner, Swanson knew more about Natal than she did about most people. She'd been raised in the outer regions of the city and wanted to go into law but didn't make the grades in school. Instead she worked as a clerk and covered the three areas of criminal law, having held positions both at the public prosecution and defender's office as well as working for Judge Lloyd.

‘Do you like working for Lloyd? Sounds like a hell of a job,’ said Keane. The question sounded reasonable, a natural progression of their conversation.

The line went silent for a few seconds longer than Swanson had expected. ‘It’s okay,’ said Natal. Her voice had dropped in tone, heavy with emotion. ‘Sometimes it gets too much. You see lots of things you wish you could erase. Heart-breaking stuff. Lives are destroyed by what goes on in there.’

Again, the line went silent until Swanson heard a mumbled sound that sounded like gentle sobbing.

‘It’s okay,’ said Keane, his own voice muffled as if he was covering up his mouth. Swanson pushed her earpiece further into her ear. She could hear more noises, wet and squelchy.

‘Stupid man,’ she mouthed.

She continued to listen, horrified at what was happening. Natal’s breathing became heavy and slow. Swanson cursed herself for not insisting that Keane wear an earpiece, and considered barging through the door and dragging him out of the situation as if he were an errant child. ‘I’ll just pop to the bathroom, the bedroom is through there,’ whispered Natal.

‘Get out of there,’ Swanson shouted, alone in the car.

‘I’ll explain everything,’ whispered Keane, as if answering Swanson’s call. ‘I know this all looks suspect but I’m sure she knows something. Maybe you should stop listening now.’

Swanson considered the myriad breaches of ethics and morality the three of them were committing. Swanson herself was now an accessory, yet she couldn’t stop listening.

Her own body became flushed as she heard them move to the bedroom. Despite herself, she pictured the scene as Natal's breathing intensified: Keane's naked body hovering over Natal, the woman staring up at him brazen and wanton. She pictured herself in the same position, a ripple of heat surging through her body. It was possible her attraction to Keane was stronger than she'd first envisaged.

The sound of Natal moaning tore Swanson from her reverie. She ripped her earpiece away, disgusted with herself. She started the car, her face still red, and left Keane to his investigations.

She sped through the city fighting her feelings of guilt. Keane was in the wrong, so he should have to face the consequences. If Natal was so enamoured with him then she could drive him home; Swanson flushed hot at the obvious thought that Keane would stay the night.

Her father was drunk again. He sat in the half light of the living room sipping from a large glass which brimmed with single malt whisky. 'Busy day catching criminals?' he slurred as she stormed through the door.

'Don't start, Dad.' She took her coat off and stood before him, hands on hips.

'Oh dear,' he said, bowing his head in contrition.

He was drunker than usual and she went straight to her room. She took out her reader and searched for records on Sarah Natal.

Chapter Thirteen

Old Blue had worked hard to stamp out Nathaniel's presence. He crept up on him during times of calm. Once the judge had been fed and everything was quiet, once he had fed himself and was ready for bed, Nathaniel would nudge at his consciousness. It was not a two-way conversation. Old Blue understood that he was Nathaniel; that Nathaniel remained within him. Old Blue was Nathaniel's creation. He'd created him to do what was necessary. Nathaniel Jacobson had found it surprisingly easy to change his identity. He'd cultivated a couple of well-connected contacts and had soon become Blue Lessing, with back up documentation to prove his new identity.

Old Blue knew his place but wondered if Nathaniel knew his.

He was asleep the second he lay on the bed. He didn't dream, the dark void of his subconscious impenetrable. When the door-bell rang an hour later, he returned from the darkness in an instant, alert and as ready as he had been before sleep.

It was still dark and it took a while for his eyes to adjust. His mind worked hard as he made his way downstairs. Everything looked in place. The trap door was still covered by the faded Persian rug and there was no sound from below. The bell rang again, three insistent rings, each one longer than before. He moved to the window and looked through a gap in the curtains. A silhouetted figure was waiting for him on the porch.

'What the hell are you doing here, Sarah?' he asked, opening the door.

'That's a nice welcome,' said Sarah, barging past him. She was dressed in a short black dress. Her face looked drained and her hair was a mess. She walked into the living room and slumped down on the sofa.

'Have you just got out of bed?' he asked her.

'You could say that,' she replied.

He sat next to her and breathed in her unwashed smell. Her lips were curved into a cocked smile. Old Blue checked her eyes to see if the smile was true. Her blank eyes gave away little detail. 'I've just spent the evening with that policeman.'

'Which policeman?'

'The good looking one, from the office that time. Keane.' Her smile increased in intensity. Teasing. Mocking.

He looked at her with disdain. 'Is there a reason you have woken me to tell me this frankly uninteresting news?'

'But it is interesting,' she said, and snaked her body across the sofa closer to him. The ripeness of her odour wafted towards him, masking a fainter smell of aftershave. She lifted his striped dressing gown and placed her hand on his leg, her flesh warm, the skin of her fingers smooth.

'Don't play games, Sarah. Either tell me or don't.'

She shuffled away from him, her lips pouted. 'Fine,' she said.

They sat in silence for two minutes, Sarah flashing him the odd mocking smile. 'Okay,' she conceded, and made her way back to him, manoeuvring between his arms. 'They think it's a suicide.'

'The judge?'

'Yes. He told me straight off. Complete waste of time on their part.'

Old Blue thought about this development. 'And what did you tell him?'

'Nothing.'

'Sarah, they're not all as stupid as they look. Tell me everything you said to him.'

'He wasn't investigating me, for Christ's sake. He just wanted me. He's married. If anyone found out about us he'd be in trouble.'

'You don't think sometimes, Sarah, do you? Maybe he isn't married.'

'He was wearing a wedding ring,' she said. He waited a few seconds for her to fully consider the situation. 'He's married,' she insisted. 'I can tell.' She raised her eyebrows in a knowing way, as if that was all the explanation necessary.

Old Blue pushed her away and sat on one of the armchairs. 'Tell me everything you told him.'

'I didn't tell him that much. He asked about my past and my family. I told him about my plans to become a lawyer and how I'd ended up a judge's assistant.'

'Did you explain why you didn't become a lawyer?'

'Give me some credit.'

'You're not giving me much reason to, Sarah. All they need is one excuse to do some thorough research into you.'

Sarah pushed herself away from him and sat on the sofa opposite. 'Those details are sealed away. Our friend has seen to that. They can't make a connection.'

'Don't underestimate them,' said Old Blue. 'What else?'

'He asked about my family and I made up some stuff. Same stuff I always say. Same story I told you.'

'You didn't stick with that version for very long with me.'

She moved back towards him. 'That's because I trust you,' she said.

'Shower,' he ordered, pushing her away.

After she had showered and joined him in bed, he told her about Thurrock and Wilson.

'It's all moving quick now,' she said.

'I can't hold the judge in the cellar forever,' he said. 'So are you ready to do it?'

'I'm ready. But I want to see the judge first.'

He sighed. For all her bravado, he didn't think she would handle seeing her former employer in captivity very well. Even he didn't enjoy his daily excursions into the cellar. It was more than the stench. The transformation of the judge was all consuming. Sarah might think she hated the judge now, but her humanity might get the better of her once she saw what had happened to him. 'Let's get these two out of the way. Once we have them then I will show you the judge.' His words were final. Sarah relented and fell asleep.

He'd met Sarah at the courthouse, not long after he'd started working there as a cleaner. He'd noticed her watching him. She was hard to miss. When he'd found out she was Judge Lloyd's assistant, he'd tried to avoid her. Then one day, she sat next to him in the staff canteen. This in itself was not unusual. Since his transformation, he had become accustomed to people looking at or approaching him. For someone trying to remain inconspicuous it proved problematic. 'I know who you are,' she said, not looking up from her food.

Her words were unthreatening. If anything, they sounded hopeful. 'I haven't had the pleasure. I'm Blue,' he'd replied.

A few days of gentle play followed that initial meeting. Sarah had refused to tell him who she believed him to be, and he'd never volunteered the information himself. He needed to hear something from her first. They slept together after a week, and after two she'd told him her story.

He didn't enjoy the tale. As a student, she'd been seeing a married man a few years older than herself. Following his wife's mysterious death, the man had been arrested on a murder charge and subsequently sentenced to the pods by Judge Lloyd. He'd managed to keep his relationship with Sarah secret but she had attended court on the day he was sentenced. She was still adamant that the man was innocent.

'Why assist Judge Lloyd?' he had asked her.

'I'm just biding my time. Waiting for an opportunity. I think I've been waiting for you, Blue.'

His plans had been in their infancy then. He'd thought at

the time that it would be helpful to have a conspirator and she'd proved to be useful. Lately, however, Sarah had become a nuisance and worse, a risk. Sleeping with the policeman, Keane, was the culmination of a number of ill-considered decisions which jeopardised their shared ambition.

She slept soundly next to him, her breathing light. Her usefulness was wearing thin. Once Thurrock and Wilson were accounted for, he would have to reconsider her necessity.

Chapter Fourteen

Swanson spent the night submerged beneath the covers. In the morning, she dragged herself to the bathroom, her limbs heavy. A rhythmic thudding filled her head and she bent double towards the toilet basin and dry retched.

Her father didn't look hungover. He sat at the dining table eating a bowl of muesli, a fresh pot of coffee at his side. 'Morning, sleepy,' he said, not looking up from his newspaper.

Swanson was unable to speak. She poured some coffee and slumped down opposite him. Images of Natal and Keane haunted her as she ate. It was these imagined visions of her colleague which had troubled her through the night, not her own complicity in the act. She had no idea what to do next. Her brief research on Natal had not given her much additional information and she had emailed Flaherty, instructing him to conduct a detailed report on Natal's past. She didn't want to report Keane over the incident but not doing so was in itself grounds for dismissal. As if sensing her unease, her father put down his paper.

'What's the matter?' he asked.

'Just work problems.'

Her father sighed, and returned to his paper. 'Are you still attending tomorrow's extravaganza?' he asked, from behind the broadsheet.

The following night was the annual legal professional dinner. It was the first time Swanson had been invited and she'd completely forgotten about it. 'I'm not sure I have much interest in spending a ludicrously decadent evening with a load of legal bores,' she croaked.

'You do realise I will be there,' he said.

'Present company excluded, obviously. It seems such a waste of time. Not to mention money and resources.'

'It is technically government business.'

Swanson took a large swig of coffee, the oily liquid singeing her throat. 'I should arrest everyone there,' she said.

'Let me guess, abuse of natural resources? Nice idea, although I am not sure we should apply a policy of zero tolerance to it.'

'I thought you would argue that abuse of natural resources should be the only reason to apply zero tolerance,' said Swanson.

He smiled. 'Some days I do.'

Swanson took the long route to work, walking between the concrete tower blocks in her sector until she reached the riverside. The cobbled pathway was busy with commuters walking into the central zones. A smoother, parallel path hosted the cyclists who dashed past their more sedate colleagues in a blur of effort. Swanson's pace was so slow she was barely moving. She hoped it would give her time to gain some clarity on the situation. Instead, her mind processed more and more elaborate images of Keane and Natal in various compromising positions. A large man in work overalls barged past her and woke her from her daydream. She upped her pace and headed for work.

Keane was at his desk working on the Lloyd files as if nothing had happened. When he noticed her presence, he looked up. His face was inscrutable though his eyes were once again bloodshot. He didn't say anything, perhaps hoping she would be too embarrassed to mention the previous night. She was about to tell him exactly what she thought when Chessington shouted over.

Swanson followed her superior to his office, her mind drifting to the stolen watch which was beneath her bed. Chessington walked without speaking. He sped through the corridors, forcing Swanson into the occasional skip to keep up. He stopped outside his office. 'Heads up, Swanson. Luce is in the office, with some politico by the name of Hanson.'

'What's going on, sir?

'You'll find out.'

Chessington introduced Swanson to Trent Hanson, the Mayor's chief assistant. Hanson sat next to Chief Superintendent Luce, the Head of Sector One police. Neither man rose from their seat or mouthed a greeting.

'As of zero nine hundred hours this morning, a convicted prisoner has escaped from the holding zone,' began Luce, once Swanson was seated.

Luce pushed a file towards Swanson. 'Oscar Garner. Conspiracy to destroy public property and illegal possession of firearms. Arrested carrying explosives which we believe he intended to detonate near the tracks.'

Swanson looked at a photo of the escapee. 'Any political links?' she asked.

'Affiliated to Lenity. On arrest he said he was working on his own,' answered Luce. 'Under interrogation it was discovered that he is something of an explosives expert.'

'Any link to Jude Wesley?' Swanson hadn't come across Garner during her research on Wesley but the cases had an obvious resonance. From the brief notes in the file, Garner had a similar profile to Wesley. Both held extreme political views, and were introverted with violent tendencies. Both were arrested carrying explosives towards the pods.

Trent Hanson spoke for the first time since Swanson had entered the office. 'No connection to Wesley. We had Garner under surveillance prior to his arrest. He'd published a number of inflammatory articles which went just short of incitement.' Hanson flashed a smile, void of humour.

'We?'

'SI. Our surveillance on Garner had been part of a wider project on a number of subversives; a splinter group of Lenity who are seemingly tired of their pacifist ways. We don't believe Jude Wesley was one of their number. He was working independently.'

Special Investigations were the council's so-called intelligence bureau. They were distinct from Swanson's police force. Reporting directly to the mayor, they worked solely on the city's security.

Swanson glanced at Chessington. 'Why am I here?'

'Considering your ongoing investigation into the

disappearance of Judge Lloyd, we thought it prudent you head,' he paused, considering his words, 'the search for Garner.'

'You think there's a link here between the escape and Lloyd's disappearance?'

The empty smile appeared once more on Hanson's face. 'It would seem rather coincidental otherwise,' he said.

'We're not jumping to any conclusions,' interrupted Luce. 'Clearly, there is a potential link. We'd like you to continue your investigation on Lloyd and cross-reference it with Garner's disappearance. Gather what you can from the holding zone. SI will head up the investigation into the escape itself, as a potential terrorist is now on the loose and this has obvious implications to the city's security. They will liaise with the holding zone's security staff on the details of the escape. Your remit is to find Garner.'

Swanson looked over at Chessington, who refused to give her a response. The division of labour made little sense. 'I'll need to see all the SI files on Garner and your surveillance operation.'

Smirking, Hanson placed a piece paper marked *Secure Document Release* in front of her. 'Sign this,' he said. 'You can read cleared aspects on the way.'

'This has to remain confidential, Swanson,' said Luce. 'Even within your department.'

'I'm working with Keane on the Lloyd disappearance. He'll need to know.' Her skin flushed as she mentioned Keane's name. She was unsure if this was because of anger or embarrassment.

Hanson stood. 'You must understand, Inspector Swanson,

how sensitive this is for the Mayor's office. The public will find out sooner or later about Garner's escape, but the less people know about this the better. Keane will have to sign the same documents. Any leak of what is said in this office is an immediate criminal offence. I appreciate your understanding.' He left followed by Luce.

'What was that?' Swanson asked Chessington.

'That was politics. There's a car waiting for you downstairs. You need to leave in the next ten minutes.'

'What shall I tell Keane? I don't want to commit an "immediate criminal offence."' At that moment she couldn't stand the idea of being in the same room as her partner, let alone visiting the holding zone with him.

Thankfully, Chessington gave her an out. 'Leave him to work on the Lloyd case for the time being. Go to the holding zone alone.'

Keane was not at his desk when she returned so she left him a note and took the lift down to the underground car-park. A minivan with black-out windows was waiting for her, the driver of which, absurdly, was wearing dark glasses. Swanson slid open the side door of the minivan, momentarily fearing Hanson would be there waiting for her. The back of the van was empty and she eased herself into one of the faux-leather chairs.

'Ma'am,' said the sunglasses-wearing driver, handing her a file.

Swanson read the file as the van pulled away. Many of the pages were blanked out. SI loved their secrecy. Swanson had once applied for a position with them early in her career but had never even reached first interview, something her father had blamed on himself.

She struggled to find anything of significance in Garner's file. He'd been a lay preacher at a church in Sector One. His arrest had caused quite a stir amongst the evangelical congregation, some of whom were still under surveillance by SI. Garner had managed to break through the security fences surrounding the pod tracks with a huge bag of explosives and had been close to one of the steel pylons by the time he was picked up by SI. Swanson wondered why they had let him get so far. He'd been tried by Judge Lloyd but so far it was the only link between the two men.

Out of curiosity, Swanson scanned the document to see who had defended Garner during his trial.

She was only mildly surprised to see the name of Jude Wesley's father, the public defender Charles Wesley.

Chapter Fifteen

The van made its way out of the central zones. Prior to the Flux, the inner ten zones had served as an amalgamated business area which housed workers numbering over one million. Although there had been numerous developments since that time, many of the office buildings on the periphery of the central zones stood vacant, hollow monuments to a different time. The farther out you travelled, the more the office blocks were used as cheap shelter by poorer citizens. As a matter of course, the police steered away from such buildings.

They passed little hives of activity, industrial and business zones where corporations used mayoral funding to start new businesses. A lone voice called to her from the front of the van, offering his opinion. 'They're just going to build it all up again and wait for it to crash. It's all been done before.'

Swanson decided to humour him. 'How old are you exactly?'

The driver laughed. 'You don't need to have experienced it to see what will happen. The only difference now is the tighter criminal legislation. It's the civil laws they should have sorted. Mark my words, we'll get to a brief moment of perfect prosperity then down it will tumble again.'

Swanson had heard the cyclical argument many times before. How in many ways the Flux mirrored the American stock market crash of the nineteen thirties. In the thirties there had been a recession following the market crash. However, the Flux developed into something much worse.

It started with the markets crashing, a reaction to a worldwide trade war sparked by the dissolution of numerous agreements between the world's superpowers. The impact was intensified by the public's lack of faith in the private sector and governments which it blamed. Within days banks were closed, savings disappeared and inflation spiked so much that money became worthless. Something that had been unimaginable to most was now tangible. Looting and rioting became widespread in the world's major cities. Martial law was implemented in the City, and the journey to ZT and the pods began.

Now that decades later the city was finally recovering, the doomsayers were all too ready to say how easily it could happen again.

'It's a different world now,' said Swanson.

'Is it? We may have turned a corner on crime and enjoy economic stability but it would take a nudge, nothing more, and people would tear those things down,' said the driver, pointing to a line of pods in the distance.

She didn't argue. Many of her colleagues shared the same conviction. Despite the oppressive nature of the laws, and their methods of enforcement, the authorities had always sought to recruit pragmatic citizens to the force. It was true that some of her colleagues revelled in their power, but Swanson found the majority of her colleagues to be level-headed. Even when supporting the notion of zero tolerance, most were sympathetic to those it affected. The majority accepted ZT as a necessary evil, would have something in its place if only they knew what.

Swanson shut the divider which separated her from the driver.

Her thoughts returned immediately to Keane and the previous night. The whole idea had been dubious from the beginning but there was no way she could have predicted what would have happened, however hard she wanted to blame herself. She was still in a state of shock about the whole incident. Keane had gone beyond recklessness; his behaviour, negligent at best, came very close to being criminal. She knew that one word to Chessington would result in Keane's suspension and possible dismissal. It would also possibly result in her own suspension, and she guiltily considered if this was a reason for her silence. She would need to talk to Keane when she returned, find out what was so important about Natal that he had to stay the night.

Two hours later they reached the holding zone. A brick wall, eighty metres high, surrounded the compound, which was five miles in diameter. The van was ushered through steel gates, the driver directed to park in a secure parking space.

Someone knocked on Swanson's window. A towering

figure dressed in khaki fatigues stared through the pane. 'I'll need you to exit the car, Ma'am,' he said, as she wound down the window.

Swanson stumbled as she left the car, her legs weak from the journey.

'I.D.,' said the guard.

The driver had been summoned, and stood next to her by the side of the car. 'Security always this tight or just recently?' he joked.

The guard didn't acknowledge the comment. 'Through to the next section. Keep your I.D. with you.'

The next section was a mile away. They drove along a solitary track surrounded by overgrown vegetation. Tall wooden poles poked out from long-stem grass, with the sign: DANGER, MINEFIELD. Swanson was aware she knew nothing about Garner's mode of escape and wondered if any detail would be forthcoming. It was evident that he hadn't walked out.

They endured two more checkpoints before reaching the centre of the compound. At each one they were asked for identification and the car was searched. The central compound was guarded by a second wall, higher than the outer perimeter. Towers were situated every fifty metres along the wall, with armed guards facing every direction.

At the entrance to the main compound they were frisked by a female guard. 'I need you to wait over there,' she said to the driver. 'We have no access permissions for you.' The driver was led to a prefab hut by two guards, still wearing his ridiculous looking sunglasses.

The woman walked Swanson through a brick tunnel. They passed six locked steel gates before reaching the centre compound where Swanson was handed over to another female guard. 'Angela Chadwick,' said the woman, offering her hand. 'You must be Inspector Swanson. Apologies for the rigmarole of security.'

'I understand,' replied Swanson, shaking the woman's hand.

'If you would follow me, I have arranged an appointment with the warden. As you can appreciate, his time is rather limited at the moment.'

'Have you been here all day?' asked Swanson.

'We all have,' replied Chadwick.

'What can you tell me about the escape?'

Chadwick smiled. 'Nothing, Inspector Swanson. Any questions will be answered by the warden.'

Swanson sat in a sterile waiting room and flicked through the file on Garner. After twenty minutes, Chadwick brought her a lunch tray. 'You must be hungry after your journey,' she said. Swanson thanked the woman and placed the tray to her side. Something had been troubling Swanson since she'd first entered the outer perimeter of the holding zone. From the large oval-shaped window in the waiting office, she realised that the pods were not visible in any direction.

A door opened. 'Inspector Swanson, please join me. Dominic Patterson. I'm the warden of the holding zone.'

Patterson was young for someone in his position, close to Swanson's age. He had a pleasing smile and looked relatively calm considering the situation.

'Thank you for coming to see us,' he said once they were seated. 'I believe you're also investigating the disappearance of Judge Lloyd at present.'

'That's correct, Mr Patterson.'

'What do you need from me?'

'Some details on Garner's escape would be a good start.'

Patterson gave her a practiced smile, multiple creases in the skin surrounding his eyes suggesting he was older than Swanson had first believed. 'Naturally, we have our own team working on the escape and we're liaising with SI. The details are a bit sketchy at the moment.'

Swanson ignored the brush-off. 'I've already seen the mined area, so I imagine he must have had help. Is that the case?'

Patterson shook his head again, smiling. The gesture reminded her of the condescending way she'd been dealt with by Hanson. 'We don't know.'

'It took me three hours to reach your office, Warden, and you're telling me you don't have an idea how he escaped?'

'It goes beyond embarrassment, Inspector. Believe me when I say many people will pay for these mistakes, myself included. There's an eight-hour gap in our surveillance of the prisoner.'

'How can that be?'

'The last footage we have is of him exiting exercise yard two. He proceeded into the main compound area via entry 7C which leads into the back of the kitchens.'

'Surely your video footage captures him there?'

'The CCTV in that area malfunctioned as he entered.'

Swanson laughed. 'That's convenient. How long did it malfunction?'

'A matter of minutes. We only noticed on playback. As I said, eight hours later.'

'Where could he have gone once inside?'

'It was only the cameras along the 7A corridor which were down. There's the kitchen area and a main gathering area which houses over one hundred prisoners at a time. We have no footage of him entering either area.'

'He vanished?'

Patterson held his hands up.

'Show me,' said Swanson.

Chapter Sixteen

The gathering area had been locked down. It was a vast space, occupied by numerous cordoned-off sections: television areas, board and video games, table tennis and pool, even a small library. 'You've questioned the prisoners?'

'Working through it. Hard to motivate them into answering.'

'What about your officers?'

'SI is working on that independently.'

'Have you been questioned?'

'What are you insinuating?' asked Patterson.

'Nothing, I just want to know you're cleared.'

'Naturally I was the first to be cleared.'

'You must see that Garner had inside help?'

'I don't know anything for sure at the moment. SI has questioned the two guards who were monitoring CCTV. We have over three hundred staff here, Inspector. It's like a small town.'

'I'll need all records of interviews with guards and staff. Plus I want to see log books recording who went in and out of the prison in the twenty-four-hour period prior to Garner's disappearance, and the period since his escape. What can you tell me about Garner?' asked Swanson.

'I doubt I can tell you much more than your file does,' said Patterson.

'What was your opinion of him?'

'We monitored his behaviour during his incarceration; nothing special to report.'

'He wasn't due to be podded for eighteen months.'

'That's correct.'

'Is there any reason for such a delay?'

'As you know, Inspector Swanson, we have different quotas for different types of offences. Due to the potential severity of Garner's offence, the council wished to schedule a time where his podding would be most feasible and didn't conflict with the podding of others.'

'You mean Jude Wesley?' asked Swanson.

Patterson folded his arms. 'I remember Jude Wesley. Yes, I guess they committed similar offences. They would not be podded close to each other.'

'Did they know each other in the holding zone?'

'Not that I am aware of; I'll have to check my records for you.'

'Who was Garner friendly with?' asked Swanson.

'His cell mate was Alex Dempsey.'

Swanson searched for her notes. 'There's no mention of Dempsey. Is he still with us?'

'He's due to be podded in a month's time.'

'Crime?' asked Swanson.

'Active solicitation,' replied Patterson.

Swanson raised her eyebrows in question. 'He was a pimp?'

'Quite.'

'Can I question him?'

'Yes, we have him waiting for you in an interview room.'

'How do the prisoners spend their time, waiting so long for their execution?'

'They have relative freedom,' replied Patterson. 'We run a tight, secure holding area, with the exception of today's debacle, but we try to make it as bearable an environment as possible for the prisoners. However, many end up doing periods in solitary confinement. They know they're going to die so they have no reason to behave.'

'How do you mean?' asked Swanson.

'It stands to reason. They all have their death dates. They know it's irreversible. So why not cause a fight with another prisoner? Why not try to escape? Why not commit murder? What difference can it possibly make?'

'I'm sure you have other punishments,' said Swanson.

'Unfortunately, yes. We try to show the prisoners that they can spend their last days on earth enjoying worthwhile pursuits but we do have certain... physical deterrents should they step out of line. Either way, eighty percent of prisoners can't be trusted. We can't let them mingle.'

'But Garner and his cell mate, Dempsey, were deemed fit?'

'Each prisoner spends a month in solitary confinement to begin with, whilst they're fully assessed. If cleared, they're released into the holding zone. Garner and Dempsey were both cleared. We always partner the prisoners with one another.'

Swanson tried not to think about her mother, hoping that somehow the women's holding zone was different. 'And what sort of activities did they pursue?' she asked.

'We have lots to offer. Garner had a penchant for black and white films. Dempsey has become something of a squash player since his incarceration.'

'When you give a prisoner freedom, do they ever break the rules?'

Patterson held his hands out. 'Of course, Inspector, you can only guess so far as to any man's motives. Two weeks prior to their podding, all prisoners are placed back into solitary confinement and put on suicide watch.'

'Suicide watch?' asked Swanson.

Patterson sighed. 'We can't risk prisoners committing suicide before they face the pods. It wouldn't go down well with the Mayor's office.'

'That's your only concern?'

Patterson didn't answer.

'One final question,' asked Swanson. 'Do you know who presided over Alex Dempsey's prosecution?'

'That's one thing he did have in common with Garner.'

'Judge Lloyd?' asked Swanson.

'How did you guess?'

Swanson checked her phone as she was led to a small room where Dempsey was waiting. Five missed calls from Keane were listed but no voicemail message.

Two armed security guards stood either side of the door

and Swanson was only allowed access once she'd verified her identification with both of them. Swanson presumed the intense security was a reaction to the day's events.

Dempsey sat behind a square wooden table. His hands were handcuffed and chained. Both his ankles were strapped to a steel plate screwed into the floor. His scalp was fully shaven and a small tuft of brown hair stuck out from his chin. His face was as white as the sheet of paper she held listing Dempsey's crimes.

It stated how he was caught offering prostitution services in Sector Twelve near a bar called Little Joe's. Swanson sat opposite the man and Dempsey glanced downwards to his left as if he could see something on the floor which no-one else could.

'Thank you for seeing me,' said Swanson, after introducing herself.

'Not my choice,' replied Dempsey, not looking up.

'We all have a choice, Mr Dempsey.'

Dempsey adjusted his position. The rusted chains which held his legs in position jangled from the motion. He turned to face her, his eyes yellow with malnutrition.

'Not if I want my bones in working order for my last few days on earth.'

'Okay, tell me about your former cellmate, Garner,' asked Swanson.

'What's to tell? I've been here eight months now, seen them all come and go. He's one of those deluded political types. He only ever became animated discussing his situation,' Dempsey considered, 'or should I say, *our* situation.'

'Go on.'

'He loved to moan about the conditions here, and the Mayor. Obviously, he hated ZT but he said it wasn't a personal thing.'

'That's why he planned to bomb the tracks?' asked Swanson.

'He said it was just a matter of time. If it wasn't him it would be someone else. Once the first bomb was detonated, the whole cruel edifice would crumble. I'm paraphrasing, naturally. He said his passion was political. He was religious as well; prayers every night before bedtime.'

'How did he escape?'

Dempsey laughed. The hollow sound reeked of sickness and he coughed; a thin, grating, noise escaping from his throat.

'Did you know he planned to escape? Did he have collaborators? Did he ever talk about anyone coming to rescue him?'

'Listen, the other guy asked me all this bullshit, why don't you talk to him?'

'What other guy?'

'Your pal from SI.'

'Not my department,' said Swanson, leaning back in her chair. 'Did you ever meet a man called Jude Wesley?'

Dempsey's pale face flashed briefly with animation. 'I knew Wesley. Nut-job. He's in a pod now.'

'Did he know Garner?'

'Cut from the same cloth. Yes, they were identical, spouted the same nonsense.'

'Did they gain any support? Within the holding zone?'

'What do you think? They were preaching to the

converted. They didn't work together, but knew of each other. In fact, they seemed to be at awful pains to avoid one another.'

Swanson leant in. 'Are there many escape attempts?' she asked, softening her voice as best she could.

'They are otherwise known as suicide attempts,' replied Dempsey. 'Though the guards here are well trained.'

'In what way?'

'You must have noticed how many of the convicts in those wonderful pods of yours are nursing injuries, bullet-holes to the flesh. The guards know where the non-fatal areas are and they know how to manipulate them. You know what I mean?'

'Can you tell me anything?' whispered Swanson.

Dempsey leant forward as best he could, his movement restricted by the chains. He looked over at the two armed guards who stood motionless, staring into the distance. 'They say it's an inside job. It has to be, I guess. What I know is someone in here has friends in high places.'

Swanson smelt the decay on Dempsey's breath. Up close his skin was pitifully dry, pockmarked with spots; flakes of dry skin coated his prison uniform.

'Tell me about your prosecution,' said Swanson, leaning back to escape the air surrounding the unwashed prisoner.

'I was guilty. It was a foregone conclusion.'

'Who was the judge?' asked Swanson, although she already knew the answer.

'Some old guy, Lloyd; same as Garner's, same as lots of guys in here I guess. No one cares about the judges, Inspector. They can only hand out one sentence; they can't make you not-guilty.'

'No one resents them?'

'Not really. The police maybe.' He lowered his eyes. 'No offence, and possibly the lawyers, but the judges do as they're told. They have no leeway. They can only guide a jury then have to give the same sentence to each convicted criminal.'

Swanson was not convinced. She strummed her fingers on the desk. 'How do they treat you here?' she asked.

'If you do what you are told,' said Dempsey, 'it's just about bearable.'

Chapter Seventeen

Keane had left a message on her phone. 'Swanson, we need to talk. I need to explain.' He hesitated, and with what sounded like a laugh, added, 'I would have appreciated the heads up about your visit to the holding zone. Please call.'

She was at once stunned, angered, and amused by his message. Somehow, he was coming across as the injured party. She pressed redial then hung up before it had a chance to connect.

Giles Bracken, the holding zone's Head of Security, showed her to the area where Garner had escaped. Bracken reluctantly played her the various CCTV cameras and went through all checks and procedures with her. He led her through to the common room area where Garner should have been on the day he disappeared. Guards were stationed throughout the room and as Swanson walked through the area she was surprised that the prisoners gave her little more than a cursory glance.

The majority of prisoners were immobile, huddled in small motionless groups: one group sat slumped before a flat screen television, another two or three inmates gazed at books, some went through the pretence of playing board games. Only a few of the inmates showed any animation. Two young boys, surely no more than eighteen, were playing table tennis with the occasional burst of enthusiasm, and one elderly man paced the room with a manic intensity. They were very much in the minority.

'Most of them are on one thing or another,' said Bracken, in explanation. 'Some form of tranquillisers. It's a kind of mercy.'

'Was Garner on any medication?'

'I presume so. You'll have to check with the doc. As far as I'm aware the majority are on tranquillisers and the dose increases as they approach their death date.'

Swanson watched the men and tried to imagine how anyone in that state could have had the wherewithal to stage an escape, especially one as elaborate as Garner's. Yet Dempsey had sounded and looked lucid so the drugs were obviously not compulsory.

Bracken led her through to the kitchen area where civilian chefs were preparing the day's meals.

'Why don't you have the prisoners cook?'

'You can't really make the prisoners do anything. There's nothing in it for them. We offer incentives, treats and what have you, but they don't care. On the other hand, we're limited as to the level of punishment we can offer. You can't really threaten them with anything worse than death.'

Swanson made a mental note to request the files of all civilian workers in the prison. Her phone vibrated and she ended Keane's call without answering.

'All staff are Level A security cleared,' said Bracken, as if reading her thoughts. 'And each one has been interviewed.'

Swanson nodded. 'Was Garner much trouble for you when he was here?'

'Kept to himself.'

'What about Dempsey?' she asked.

'What about him?'

'I just spoke to him. He seemed pretty lucid. Quite chatty.'

'He's been in solitary since Garner's disappearance. Not on anything.'

Beyond the kitchen area they passed through a labyrinth of secured doors until they reached the prison cells. The area was brightly lit, the walls of the corridors painted lemon yellow. Each cell had a large glass-fronted entrance so the prisoners were visible within.

'It prepares them,' said Bracken. 'They get used to people viewing them.'

'I assume they're fed, though?' she replied.

Bracken ignored her. 'You could call this our death row,' he said, pointing to a small block of four cells. 'Due to be podded within the next two weeks.'

Swanson recognised one of the death row inmates. Crampton, the petty thief she had seen sentenced only days before, was curled up on a mattress, wearing the standard velcro prison jumpsuit. His feet were bare and for some reason this bothered Swanson. 'How can he be here so soon?' she asked.

'I think there was some mess-up with his original court

appearance. He's been in the holding zone for nine months. It was decided he should be podded immediately. Not my decision, naturally, but I guess it's another small mercy.'

'You'd think,' said Swanson.

'If it were me I'd want it over with.'

'You could at least get him a blanket.'

'Against policy,' replied the guard.

The death row area was overly clean, like a sterilised hospital ward; the lingering aroma of bleach masking an underlying stench.

A stout muscular man in a white overcoat greeted them. 'I'll pass you over to the doc now,' said Bracken, offering his hand.

'Dr Winters,' said the man in the white coat, his voice half an octave higher than Swanson had expected. 'I see you've met our death row inmates.'

'They look cold,' said Swanson.

'They can't feel anything, Inspector,' replied Winter.

'Drugs?' asked Swanson.

'I'm afraid it's the only way. The alternative would be rather too disturbing.'

Swanson followed the man into his office, unable to erase the vision of her mother lying in her own cell, drugged and freezing as she awaited her death date.

'I've been working here for five years now, and I've never known anything like it.'

'You're talking about the escape?'

'Yes, whatever it was.'

'It's never happened before,' said Swanson.

'Well quite – I think Mr Bracken there fears for his job. A travesty, for everyone concerned.'

'Do you administer all the prisoners' drugs personally?' asked Swanson, ignoring Winters' last comment.

'Not personally, obviously, but I manage their prescriptions and monitor the doses.'

'How many of the prisoners choose the drugs?'

'80 per cent, at least. It is not always optional.'

'Do you have to keep them so docile?'

'We found, to our cost, it's the only way. Suicides are down forty per cent in the last decade.'

'And the prisoners actually choose this?'

'As I say, Inspector, they're closely monitored and rewarded for good behaviour.'

'What about Garner, was he well behaved?

'He didn't choose drugs.'

'What sort of physical and mental function would he have had at the time of his escape?'

Winters shivered as if the question had caused him some form of physical pain. 'Are you asking me if I think that Garner had some assistance with his escape?'

'Your opinion would be welcome,' said Swanson.

'Obviously it's not my area of expertise, but there is no way I could see him staging the escape on his own, even if he wasn't taking any drugs. It would be impossible.'

This was the first honest thing she'd heard that day. 'Do you have to treat many gunshot wounds?' she asked.

'Peculiar question.'

'Just something that was mentioned to me earlier.'

'Ah, the escapees,' said Winters. 'Yes, unfortunately some of the prisoners aim for friendly fire, rather than face the pods. Who could blame them? We try to manage their fears. We offer medication; we force them in the last few weeks, but they know what's coming. I don't think that what happens in the pods is really comprehensible unless you, or maybe someone close to you, is facing that eventuality. So yes, Inspector, I have to treat the odd gunshot wound. The prisoners try to escape, and the guards cannot take the risk.'

'Are the wounds ever fatal?'

Winters sighed as if he wanted to tell her something. 'They are very rarely fatal. Occasionally a prisoner bleeds out, but normally we can patch them up.'

It was past midnight by the time she reached home. Ten minutes into the journey back, and the pods were visible once more. A stab of melancholy hit her as she saw the tracks loom up on the horizon, the glass prisons reminiscent of the cells she'd seen in the holding zone. The van stopped at a crossing next to a deceased prisoner's pod. The pod hung low from its cable which dangled from two holding towers. It looked unsteady as it swayed in the breeze. The corpse within followed the dance of the glass capsule, the cable emitting a high pitched whine as it was teased by the wind.

The unreality of the prison had disorientated her. She thought about the prisoners with their gunshot wounds, and the amount of drugs being pumped into the veins of the hapless convicts. She tried not to think about the women's holding zone.

At home in bed, she was about to fall asleep when Keane

called. She sent the busy signal to him but he called once more. She stared at her phone for two minutes before switching it off.

Chapter Eighteen

Swanson waited for Keane in her office. She'd thought about little else since leaving the holding zone. If she was going to report him, then she had to do it now. Sleeping with Natal had never been part of the plan. It was a step Keane had taken upon himself. Her doubt over whether her concern was professional or personal was the only thing to have stopped her reporting him so far.

'I can explain,' said Keane, sitting down. He still smelt of the cinnamon-tinted aftershave he had covered himself with before meeting Natal.

'Unlikely, but go ahead.'

'I had to gain her trust – I'm sure she knows something. If I hadn't gone ahead with it then she would never have confided in me.'

'Ignoring how limp an explanation that is for the time being, what has she confided in you?'

Keane folded his arms, the sleeves of his shirt crumpling. 'Okay, nothing at the moment. But she is not going to divulge something straight away. It's going to take time.'

'So how many times do you think you will have to sleep with her?'

Keane ignored the question.

'While we're at it, are there any more women we can arrange for you to sleep with in case they might know something about Judge Lloyd's disappearance?'

'Don't be like that,' said Keane, something close to a smirk growing on his face.

'Knock the smile off, Keane,' said Swanson. He tried to match her glare but soon looked away. 'I am seconds away from losing my patience. Tell me you have something more concrete to work on or I'm reporting you to Chessington.'

The threat galvanised him as if he'd only just realised the potential trouble he was in. To his credit, he didn't try to threaten her for her complicity and it was perhaps this which made her relent. 'I could tell she was lying to me. Little things which suggested she was retelling a story she had invented. I told her that our working theory was that Lloyd had killed himself. That stopped her in her tracks. Something crossed her face then, I swear it. I spent all of yesterday looking into her. Naturally, the records are insubstantial but I know she is lying to me. Let me meet her again and I'll prove it.'

'But did you have to sleep with her, Keane? What if we end up arresting her? You think she is not going to mention your evening together?'

'All I am saying is that she's hiding something. She can lead us somewhere on this. Please.'

Swanson looked at the file of papers on her desk. She had an ever-increasing mound of paperwork to sign. It was what her job had become, signing off on correct police procedure. Anybody could do it. By the time a case reached the court it was practically guaranteed to be a successful prosecution. Only a mistake in procedure or an abstract application of the law could save the accused. And now that she had a rare chance to work on a proper case, she was hesitating. At least Keane was trying, taking risks, albeit extreme risks. 'You're not going to meet her again. Not yet anyway. We'll set up surveillance on her. In the meantime, read through this.' She handed him the file on Garner.

'Is that all?' asked Keane, relieved.

'I'll call you when I need you.'

She waited five minutes and visited Chessington. He yawned as she sat opposite him, not bothering to place a hand over his mouth. His bloated face drooped, the voluminous bags beneath his eyes a black-purple colour.

'I think SI are holding back some information on Garner's disappearance,' said Swanson.

'I thought I was clear: your job is to find Garner. SI are investigating the actuality of the breakout,' said Chessington. He sounded tired or bored. Swanson glanced at the new watch on his wrist.

'I can't do one without the other. The escapee had to be aided by an insider. The place is a fortress,' said Swanson.

'All I know is that there have been two high profile disappearances and I'm getting it in the neck from Luce so we need to get working.'

'Garner knew Jude Wesley, sir.'

'That's not what SI are saying.'

'I know, sir. I was here when Hanson came out with that crap. But Dempsey, Garner's cellmate, told me they knew each other and he has no reason to lie. Apparently, they tried not to acknowledge one another whilst in prison.'

'And?'

'The kidnapper wants the podded convicts released and Wesley is one of those at the start of their journey. Like Garner, he had access to high-powered explosives. Garner is sprung from prison a day after the ransom note arrives. Hanson mentioned something about a subversive group SI have been investigating. It would be useful to have access to their files, sir. And I think we need to put security on Wesley's pod.'

'I'll speak to Hanson. They're a bit prickly on access. In the meantime, I'll assign security to Wesley's pod. You should know that we're already adding extra security to the sentry posts in Sector One.'

The sentry posts were scattered along the perimeter of the tracks. Just like in the holding zone, they were heavily manned by armed guards. 'Are you expecting something in particular, sir?'

'Just that bloody Lenity demonstration which is coinciding with a podding. With Lloyd's disappearance and now this breakout, we need to be prepared.' Chessington yawned again and Swanson stood up to leave.

'You know Charles Wesley was the public defender for Garner, sir?'

'I can read, Swanson. Listen, I wouldn't go down that road if I were you. Charles Wesley is a senior defender. His name is bound to crop up on lots of cases.'

'Sir,' replied Swanson, not ready to get into an argument yet.

Back in the main office, she updated Keane.

'Shouldn't I have been in that meeting?' he asked.

'Don't sulk. What have you been working on?'

'Looking through Lloyd's old files. I'm sure if you started cross-referencing every case he's presided over you could arrest half the city on suspicion. I'm hungry, take me to lunch?'

'You need to absolve yourself of your sins first,' replied Swanson.

During the drive, she told Keane about her thoughts on Charles Wesley. 'His name links everything so far.'

'Perhaps Lloyd's kidnapping wasn't random. He presided over both Garner and Wesley's trials – maybe they have no intention of letting him go,' said Keane.

'Whoever is behind the disappearances has some pretty big support, but we need to focus on the disappearances as separate at the moment.'

Garner's former church was situated in Sector One. St Christopher's was a pre-flux building, its red brick exterior one of the oldest in the city. Its architecture was grandiose in comparison to the small Chapel of Corpus Christi where they had attended the Lenity meeting. An imposing steeple rose into the afternoon sky, a shaft of sunlight glistening off a triangular stained-glass window which depicted the Virgin Mary. Despite it being a midweek mass, the church was almost full. Swanson and Keane sat at the back on the wooden pews and listened to the priest, Father Annerley, finish his sermon.

The congregation was varied, men and women of all ages. Many of the weekday churchgoers were business people who had been given permission to attend mass during the day by their employers. It was something the Mayor's council actively promoted. Funding was available to allow employees to attend church during the week. Spiritual input was favoured as a means to mental well-being; Swanson saw the policy for the vote-grabbing opportunity it was. Even as a police officer she was allowed to attend mass during the week.

Annerley's voice boomed in the cavernous space of the old church. Dressed in a white robe with an embroidered purple crucifix, he instructed the congregation to be vigilant in the current climate. He went just short of mentioning Judge Lloyd. 'Go in peace,' Annerley instructed, as an ancient organ struck up the opening chords to an ancient hymn. Annerley walked up the aisle flanked by the procession of four altar boys who swung a golden chalice filled with incense. The bitter scent invaded Swanson's nostrils. Gradually the congregation exited, as one by one they shook hands with the priest.

'Christ, how long are we going to wait?' whispered Keane, as the queue extended down the aisle.

Swanson looked at him wide-eyed. 'Do you think that language is appropriate?' she asked, eyebrows raised.

'Sorry,' said Keane, mimicking the sign of the cross.

Swanson shook her head and repressed a smile.

Ten minutes later a middle-aged woman dressed in a floral print approached them. 'Inspector Swanson?' she asked, looking at Keane. Keane pointed to Swanson. 'Oh, sorry, Inspector. My name is Clare Mason. I'm Father Annerley's personal assistant. Would you care to wait for the Father in the vestry? It normally takes a while for him to say goodbye to everyone.'

They followed the woman back down the aisle towards the altar. Mason was almost as tall as Keane. She walked down the altar in an awkward mechanised walk. At the end of the aisle she stopped and genuflected before a giant wooden crucifix.

The vestry was a sparse uncarpeted room, its only furniture a sleek mahogany desk and three hard-back wooden chairs. Above Father Annerley's seat was a smaller version of the crucifix they had just seen in the church. 'Please take a seat,' said Mason. 'May I get you both a drink? Tea? Coffee?' The woman's face twitched as she spoke, her chin jabbing forward on each word.

'Nothing for us,' said Swanson. The woman nodded and backed away.

Annerley entered the vestry twenty minutes later. He had taken the time to change his robes and was now dressed all in black. He stood at the entrance of the vestry and looked at the police officers, waiting. Reluctantly, Swanson stood, staring at Keane as she did so. Keane followed her lead.

Swanson made introductions. Annerley sighed and waved at the chairs, signalling for them to sit. He shouted for his assistant.

'Yes, Father?' said Clare Mason, sticking her long neck around the vestry door. 'Black coffee,' said Annerley.

'Yes, Father.'

'So,' said the priest, turning his attention to Swanson and Keane. 'How may I help you both?' The scent of incense hung around him. Swanson doubted it ever left him.

'Thank you for seeing us, Father. I believe you've been informed that your former deacon, Oscar Garner, has escaped from the holding zone?'

Annerley shook his head. He was a long-limbed muscular man, removed from the stereotypical vision Swanson had in her head of a priest. 'Terrible man. Shameful,' said Annerley. 'Somehow he managed to deceive us all. He should have been put in the pods months ago.'

'I take it from your response, Father, that you have not heard from him since his escape?'

'Of course not,' said Annerley impatiently. 'He will not return here and if he did you would be the first to know, as I told your colleagues. A dangerous man like that should be locked up and podded immediately. He has no friends in this house of God, Inspector Swanson.'

'I appreciate your perspective on the matter, Father Annerley. Do you know of anyone he was close to? Who perhaps shared his political leanings?'

'There is no one in this church who shared Mr. Garner's "political leanings,"' said Annerley.

'How can that be?' asked Keane.

'As I am sure you're already aware, such beliefs are simply not compatible with the Church's.'

'Did you know Garner was a member of Lenity when he worked here?'

'Of course I didn't know,' said Annerley, a genuine anger to his voice. Swanson was not sure if the man was angry for being duped by Garner, or if something else was bothering him.

'So he never discussed his beliefs with anyone in this church?' asked Keane.

'Are you listening to me, officer? He wouldn't dare spout such nonsense in the presence of my congregation. The church wholeheartedly endorses zero tolerance. It's our Christian right to live within a law-abiding community. Anyone who is preposterous enough to think otherwise does not have a place within these walls.'

People had flocked to religion since the inception of ZT. The Church was seen as a moral vanguard: as ZT had become more prevalent and strict, so had the religious teachings.

'Why would Garner spend so much time in the church, having the beliefs he did?' asked Swanson.

'As I've told you, he was the ultimate deceiver. Not only did he not mention his political ideals, he pretended he was wholeheartedly in line with the Church's teachings. He would assist me in mass. I shudder to think of the blasphemy he committed in the face of God. He will pay for his sins in this life and the next.'

Swanson found it hard to have sympathy for anyone convicted of carrying dangerous explosives with intent, but she had some sympathy for anyone who had worked alongside Father Annerley. 'We'll need a list of your active congregation,' she said.

'If you wish. The numbers go into the hundreds. But I can assure you that no one here has helped Oscar Garner escape. Miss Mason,' said the priest, his voice impatient.

'Yes, Father,' answered his assistant, dashing into the room with a large cup of coffee.

'Please get the officers a list of our active parishioners. If there's nothing else, officers, I have important matters that I must see to. Good day.'

They followed Mason into her office. 'I'm sorry Father Annerley was a bit stern with you,' she said. 'It's just his way. He can be abrupt at times and the whole thing with Mr Garner has thrown him somewhat.'

Mason downloaded the requested information onto a small data stick which she handed to Swanson. 'Naturally, this is private information,' said the woman.

'Did you enjoy working with Mr Garner?' asked Swanson.

'He seemed a nice man. He was very helpful, in fact. Always at the church, helping with mass and the various groups – but something changed about a year ago.'

'Oh?'

'He was late for mass a few times and he even missed a couple of prayer meetings he was supposed to take.'

'How did he explain his absences?

'He didn't really, didn't even apologise. Fortunately, word never reached Father Annerley. We managed things here in the office. There are plenty of other lay preachers waiting to fill such spots.'

'Was there a trigger for this behaviour?'

'I don't know about that, but there were rumours,' said Mason.

Swanson could tell the woman was enjoying telling her little tale. 'What rumours?'

'I believe that there were, how should I say, one or two sightings of Mr Garner in places he shouldn't have been.'

'Such as?' said Swanson.

Mason lowered her voice. 'There was talk amongst the parishioners that Mr Garner has been using the services of…'

'Yes?'

'Scarlet women,' said Mason, her face turning its own shade of red.

'Prostitutes?' asked Keane.

Mason shuddered. 'Yes,' she said in a high pitch squeak. 'Please be quiet. It would upset Father Annerley.'

'Thank you for your time, Miss Mason,' said Swanson. 'Please call me if you hear anything about Mr Garner.'

'Is he a danger?'

'I wouldn't worry. I don't think he would be so foolish as to come back here, but you hear any word of him, however vague, please let me know.'

Chapter Nineteen

Swanson breathed deeply once they were outside the building. The aroma of incense clung to her clothes.

'Very welcoming organisation,' said Keane. 'Is there anything in Garner's file about him going to prostitutes?'

'No, but it's interesting that his cellmate was convicted for solicitation.'

'The priest talks a good game. Do you really think he had no inkling about Garner's left-wing leanings?'

'I don't think that man has much appreciation of people at all,' said Swanson. 'From what his assistant said, I would be surprised if he knew anything about Garner whatsoever. One thing I do find intriguing is how the parishioners knew Garner was going to prostitutes.'

Keane kept close to her as they walked back to the car, Swanson acutely aware of the casual way he kept invading her personal space. There was no defined red light district in the city, but some areas were watched by the police. Although prostitution itself was not illegal, soliciting, as Garner's former cellmate Alex Dempsey knew, was a criminal offence. The use of prostitutes was rife in the city; despite the moral concerns of the state, it had remained outside the scope of the criminal system.

Swanson had a number of sources who worked on the game; good informants, some of whom had provided vital information in successful prosecutions. They drove to a new-build block of flats in Sector Two where one of her informants, Nicole Petric, lived. 'You wait here,' she told Keane, parking outside. 'Take a closer look at the list Mason gave us. See if any names are familiar.'

Swanson had known Nicole since her first days as an officer. She'd been introduced to her by her former partner. They had been working on a case involving one of Nicole's clients who had been suspected of assaulting his wife. Swanson had stayed in contact with the woman ever since.

A light shone from Nicole's hallway. Swanson knocked on the front door, repeating the action when no one answered. She heard an exchange of voices within the flat and eventually Nicole opened the door. She looked at Swanson, at first confused as her eyes adjusted to the light of the day.

'Oh, Kate,' she said. 'I'm a bit busy.'

'Sorry Nicole, I need to speak to you now,' said Swanson.

Nicole sighed. 'Come in.'

Swanson stepped into the hallway, a blast of dry heat hitting her.

Nicole had covered herself with a cotton dressing gown. 'I have a client,' she said.

'Tell him to go, Nicole. I'll wait in the living room.'

Ten minutes later, Swanson heard the front door slam shut. Nicole's possessions were spread randomly throughout the small living room. An oversized flat screen television hung from one of the walls, dwarfing everything else. Swanson handled a cheap brooch, but laid it back down before Nicole returned to the room.

Nicole had changed into grey sweatpants and top. 'You could have given me some warning,' she said.

'Sorry, Nicole, there was no time.' She showed the woman a picture of the escaped prisoner. 'Have you seen this man before?'

Nicole shook her head. 'Who is he?'

'His name is Oscar Garner.'

Nicole pursed her lips. 'Not one of mine.'

'I need you to do some digging for me,' said Swanson. 'Garner could be very dangerous. We believe he has previously used the services of some of the girls.'

'So has half the city,' said Nicole.

'He used to be part of the church, St Christopher's in Sector One. He was a lay preacher there.'

'Ah, the church. Rich pickings.'

'Really?'

'Those hypocrites are the worst. I know a couple of girls who have recruited from St Christopher's congregation.' Nicole searched her handbag and opened a battered-looking address book. She tore out a piece of paper and handed it to Swanson. 'I know this girl works that area. If she didn't deal with him, then I'm sure she knows who has.'

Swanson took some money from her pocket and handed

it to the woman. 'Thank you, Nicole,' she said.

The woman smiled shyly, and pocketed the money. Swanson knew better than to ask her how things were. She showed Nicole a picture of Judge Lloyd.

'I've seen him in the papers. He's that judge who's disappeared?'

'That's right. Any dealing with him?'

'Can't say I've seen him before. I'll keep an ear out, though.'

'Thanks, Nicole.'

It was only a short drive to the address Nicole had given her. Natasha Hulbert, street name Clarissa, lived in an almost identical new-build block of flats less than five minutes from Nicole's. 'You can join me for this one,' Swanson told Keane. 'What did you find on the list?'

'A veritable who's who,' replied Keane. 'Half the police force. The Mayor's office feature. It seems everyone has the religion bug.'

'Anyone from the case?'

'That spotty youth, Timothy Basle from the Lenity meetings, and Garner's cellmate, Alex Dempsey, despite being incarcerated. And…' He hesitated.

'Sarah Natal?' asked Swanson.

'The very same,' said Keane.

'Oh, and one more. A Mr Astor Lloyd. Otherwise known as his Honour, Judge Lloyd of the Supreme Court.'

Hulbert answered the door within seconds, wearing jeans and a tight fitting T-shirt. A scent of vanilla hovered around her. She flashed Keane a welcoming smile which abruptly faded once Swanson produced her identification.

'Natasha Hulbert? May we come in?' asked Swanson.

'Do I have an option?' Hulbert led them through to a small kitchenette area. 'What is this all about?' she asked, not bothering with any further pleasantries.

'Listen, Natasha,' said Swanson. 'You're not in any trouble. We just need to ask you a few questions about St Christopher's Church.'

'I'm not the religious type.'

'Yeah, we gather,' said Keane.

Swanson glared at her colleague. 'We understand that you may have some clients who attend that church?'

'I don't divulge names. Bad for business.'

'I am not asking for a list of names. Yet. I am looking for one man in particular.' Swanson showed the woman a photo of Garner. Hulbert did her best to hide it, but Swanson saw recognition in her eyes.

'Oscar Garner,' said Swanson.

'I know who it is,' said Hulbert. She lit a cigarette and sat down.

'Was he one of your clients?' asked Swanson.

'Let's just say I knew him. Why the concern now? He's been prosecuted hasn't he? I didn't know anything about that, before you ask me. He was just another trick from the church. It was as big a surprise to me as anyone when he got arrested for that thing he did.'

Swanson told Hulbert about Garner's escape.

Hulbert dragged hard on her cigarette, her cheeks inverting and thin lines breaking out on her face. 'Do you think he's dangerous?'

'No, I don't think you are in any danger, Natasha. I'm just trying to find some more information about Garner. Did you happen to go to his trial?'

'God, no. I told you, he was nothing to me.'

'So, you wouldn't even know the judge who presided over his trial?' asked Keane. 'Now how the hell would I know that, darling?'

'What can you tell us about Garner?'

'He was a shy type. Very inexperienced – pathetic, really.' She stubbed out the cigarette and lit another, her hands trembling slightly as she inhaled.

'Did you ever feel threatened by him?'

'By Oscar? Don't make me laugh. He was like putty in my hands.'

'So why the concern now?' asked Keane.

'I just don't want anything to do with an escaped convict.'

'Did he ever mention anything unusual to you?' asked Swanson.

'He liked to talk more than… well, you know.'

'What did he talk about?'

'Some politics or something. I never really paid much attention.'

'Think hard,' said Swanson, extenuating the deep growl of her voice.

'He would talk about the pods, I suppose. How unjust it was. He would sometimes say how much he hated the people in the church. How they were supposed to be caring when all they really did was support the travesty of zero tolerance. Quite funny really, when you consider what happened to him.'

'Hilarious,' said Keane. 'Did he mention any groups or any other people?'

'He was always going on about some organisation, Lenity perhaps. He kept saying that one day there would be a change for the better. It sounded so far-fetched. To be honest, I just tried to get him out of here as fast as possible, that's why I did my best to shut him up.'

'When was the last time you saw him?' asked Swanson.

'A couple of weeks before he was arrested.'

'Did you notice anything unusual?'

'Nothing more than normal. I suppose he was a bit agitated, a bit more talkative. He tried to kiss me goodbye.'

Swanson nodded. 'As if he wouldn't see you again?'

'Possibly.'

'What about this man?' asked Swanson, producing a photo of Alex Dempsey.

Hulbert laughed. 'I know him. Funniest thing ever when he was arrested.'

'How's that?' asked Keane.

'He was always trying to recruit girls, providing security when none of us needed it. I couldn't stop laughing when he got arrested.'

'Even though he'll die?' asked Keane.

'I don't make the rules.'

Keane stood up, surprising Swanson with his anger. 'I need a list of all your clients,' he said.

'You have no right to ask for that,' said Hulbert. 'No way.'

Keane leant towards the woman, placing both hands on

the kitchen table. 'I have every right. It's a matter of city security.' He glared at the woman who cowed back in her seat.

'We won't show anyone the details, or use your name. It would be very helpful and beneficial to us if you could give us a list of your clients past and present,' said Swanson. 'You can ask the other girls about me. I'm not here to cause any trouble for you.'

'Who can I ask?' asked Hulbert.

Swanson didn't want to give over Nicole's name, in case Hulbert blamed her for the questioning. 'You can trust me, Natasha, just ask around,' she said.

'I presume I don't have any option,' said Hulbert. She picked up a small reader in the corner of the kitchen and made a couple of clicks on the touch screen, then stormed off, cigarette in hand, and returned thirty seconds later with two sheets of A4 paper. 'Please, don't mention my name,' she said, handing the papers to Swanson.

'Thank you, Natasha.'

Swanson ordered Keane to drive back to the station. She cross-checked the list of names Hulbert had given her with those they had acquired from the church. A number of police officers were on both lists.

'Anything of interest?' asked Keane.

'She certainly takes on all sorts. There is one familiar name.'

'The suspense is killing me,' said Keane.

'Your buddy with the PhD. The spotty student from the Lenity meeting.'

Keane considered for a moment. 'Timothy Basle?'

'He's on the current client list. I'm surprised he never mentioned this to you during your meeting.'

'I guess he's not the sharing type,' replied Keane. 'He works in a bookshop close to here – shall we make a detour?'

Chapter Twenty

The shopping mall was less than five years old. Like the majority of the modern buildings it was a sterile place, immaculately clean and devoid of any personality. The shops were arranged in identical boxes along the varied floors. Citizens flocked to the mall despite anything of consequence being available on the city's intranet.

Swanson found a space at the top of the multi-storey car park which stretched into the clouds. Four convicts hovered in their glass prisons. Surprisingly, each one was standing as their pods glided over the streets of the central zones.

Basle's bookshop was on the second floor of the mall, flanked on either side by a woman's fashion store and a boutique cosmetics shop. Covers of the latest bestsellers flashed from the visual screen of the shop window. Inside, soft classical music was piped through invisible speakers, no doubt scientifically chosen to induce impulse buying. Swanson stopped by the political section. She had seen the cover of one of her father's books. *The Conflicts of Deterrence* by Professor Swanson. One hardback version of the book was connected to a shelf by a thin steel wire. People rarely bought paper versions of books. The cost was prohibitive. Below the book was a barcode where consumers could download the electronic version of the book onto their readers. Swanson hadn't seen this particular title for a long time. It was used as a standard textbook at the university but she was surprised to see it for sale in a commercial setting.

Keane glanced over her shoulder, his face inches from hers, the heat of his breath prickling the skin on her neck. 'Famous relation?'

Swanson shut the book. 'My dad.'

Keane picked up the tome. 'Heavy stuff.'

They wandered through the makeshift store. Basle stood behind a small shop counter reading from his electronic reader. He produced a hankie from his pocket and blew his nose, not looking up at the approaching officers.

'Mr Basle,' said Keane.

Basle finished reading and then looked up, unable to hide his dismay at seeing Keane once more.

'This is my colleague, Inspector Swanson.'

'What now?' asked Basle in a nasal drawl, which took Swanson back to the Lenity meeting. Up close, Basle's face was pitted with spots, with deep scarring on his cheeks and around his neck. Swanson could only imagine what his teenage years had been like.

'You've been a bit of a naughty boy,' said Keane.

Basle switched off his reader.

'Do you know Oscar Garner?' asked Swanson.

Basle scratched his neck, drawing a speckle of blood from one of the open spots.

'I'm sure you're aware that I know Garner. He was one of the lay preachers at my church.'

'Do you know what happened to him?' asked Swanson.

'He was arrested, possession of explosives or some such thing.'

'Carrying explosives with intent to use,' said Swanson. 'How well did you know him?'

'Hardly spoke to the man.'

'Even though he clearly shared your political ideals?'

Basle shook his head. 'I find that rather insulting.'

'Why? You both oppose ZT.'

'My objection is political, Inspector Swanson. I am a respected member of Lenity. I oppose violence of any sort.'

'Yes, I saw your meeting the other day. You're quite high up in Lenity for someone so young,' said Swanson. 'Wasn't Garner a member of Lenity also?'

'I believe so, but clearly he was a radical. We attract that sort. It's understandable really.'

'But you're not a radical, I presume,' asked Keane.

'As I told you last time we met, no,' replied Basle.

For the first time, Swanson saw a colder side to the young man. 'How do you know Natasha Hulbert?' asked Swanson.

Basle was clearly not adept at hiding his feelings. His pitted face flushed red. 'I don't know what you mean.'

'You know what we mean, Timothy. You may know her as Clarissa,' said Keane, showing him the picture of the prostitute.

'There's nothing illegal in anything I may have done.'

'No one is suggesting that, Mr Basle. We're just interested in how you knew her in the first place.'

Basle sighed and looked around him. He tried his best to turn his nasal voice into a whisper. 'She's always around the church. Lots of people use her,' he hesitated, 'services.'

'Did Oscar Garner pass on her details to you?'

'I hardly spoke to Garner,' reiterated Basle.

'What I have trouble reconciling, Mr Basle, is that both of you are members of Lenity, what we could call a left-wing organisation, and both attend or have attended St Christopher's – which, if my chat with Father Annerley is anything to go by, is a church fully in support of ZT.'

'Your point?' asked Basle.

'Surely two people who shared such conflicting views with the church they attended must have known each other quite intimately.'

'The church is made up of many different people with many different views,' said Basle. 'You're allowed to believe in God and oppose ZT. Just because the overall majority support ZT doesn't mean that everyone in the congregation feels the same way.'

'Why not go to a less hard-line church?' suggested Swanson.

'Unfortunately, they're far and few between. There will always be some conflict between parishioners and the church's teaching. For many, Mass is just a get together. Half the congregation doesn't have any firm religious beliefs.'

'So, tell me once again, how well did you know Oscar Garner?'

'I didn't know him to talk to,' said Basle.

Swanson changed tact. 'What about Mr Garner's cellmate?' She showed Basle a picture of Alex Dempsey.

'I knew of him. He used to hang around the church, unsavoury sort.'

'Did *he* introduce you to Hulbert?' asked Keane.

Basle rubbed the coarse skin of his forehead. 'That would be illegal, officer.'

'What about Jude Wesley?'

Basle paused, his growing confidence momentarily disturbed. Swanson could tell he knew Wesley and that he was scared of lying. 'Just tell us what you know,' she said. 'It won't go any further.'

'Again, I knew of him.'

'Did you know that he was friends with Garner?'

'The Wesleys go to the church so I am sure they met each other but I don't know if they had any special relationship.'

'You're moving in some interesting circles, Mr Basle,' said Swanson. 'Judge Lloyd is also a parishioner of St Christopher's?'

'It's a large church. What's this all about?'

'We'll be in touch.'

'I look forward to it,' said the man, opening his reader.

'He's lying,' she said to Keane, outside the shop.

'He's clearly hiding something,' agreed Keane. 'But I can't think of anything other than food at the moment. Too late for breakfast now I guess. Brunch?'

They found the food court and were about to order when Swanson received a call from Chessington. 'There's been a sighting of Garner at a demonstration in Sector Three. I will send some patrol cars over but I want you and Keane there now,' he said.

'Who called it in?' asked Keane, as they drove to Sector Three.

'Anonymous. They're trying to track the call. The description of Garner was accurate.'

Keane shook his head. 'Do you really think Garner is going to show his face at a demonstration the day after his escape from prison?'

'No, of course I don't, Keane, but we have to follow it up. You're very tetchy when you haven't eaten.'

The demonstration was outside one of the manned pylons staged along the tracks. Twenty or so people were holding various placards. A convict hovered above them in their glass pod; it was the figure of Josephine Richardson. The girl was still lying on the base of the pod, holding herself tight as if trying to avoid the attention of the demonstrators below.

The amount of demonstrations had increased in the last year, in line with the forthcoming elections. However hard they protested, Swanson knew they were still the minority. 'Wait in the car,' she instructed. 'We don't want to get them jittery.'

Swanson scanned the faces of the demonstrators who were walking in circles shouting anti-ZT slogans. She recognised one or two from the Lenity meeting. Garner was not there. As she stood watching, a suited businessman stopped and engaged her in an conversation. 'Too good for them,' said the man.

‘What’s that?’ she replied.

‘The pods, too good for them.’

Despite herself, Swanson continued the conversation. ‘How could it be much worse?’

‘They should execute them. Clear and simple, on the day of conviction. Save all this messing about.’

‘What, without the prolonged starvation and everything?’

‘Jesus, you’re one of them?’

Swanson walked away and sat down next to a lone woman who was drinking from an aluminium hip flask. The girl smiled at her. Wrapped in multiple woollen layers, she looked as if she was still in her teens. ‘Been here long?’ asked Swanson.

‘All morning,’ said the girl, her voice as light as the air. ‘Are you here to join in?’

‘Just watching,’ replied Swanson, trying to match the girl’s easy voice. ‘Are you protesting over the girl in the pod? Or is it a general thing?’

‘One or two of the demonstrators know the girl up there. The rest are here for support.’

‘Why was she podded?’ asked Swanson.

‘Why are any of them podded?’

‘I was hoping to see a friend of mine here today,’ Swanson continued. ‘I don’t know if you know him?’

The girl smiled helpfully, her face open and innocent. ‘What’s his name?’

‘Oscar.’

The girl thought for a second and her face dropped.

'Oscar who?' she asked, her voice losing some of its warmth and innocence.

'Oscar Garner,' replied Swanson, hardening her own tone.

'Who are you?' asked the girl.

Swanson flashed her warrant card. 'We had a report of Mr Garner being here.'

'Ha,' said the girl. 'He's in the holding zone.'

Swanson was momentary surprised that the girl didn't know about the escape. 'Did you know him?' she asked.

'Everyone knows of him. He's a hero.'

'And you know nothing more?'

'I know that he almost made it.'

'By almost made it, you mean he nearly detonated a bomb which could have killed innocent people?' asked Swanson.

'That was never his objective,' argued the girl, her welcoming innocence giving way to fierce passion. The sound of the argument attracted the other demonstrators. A tall man in a bright fleece jacket wandered over and looked down at Swanson. 'What's going on?' he asked the girl.

'Police,' she replied.

'What do you want?'

Swanson had noticed a growing trend of aggression towards police officers. With the increased demonstrations, some citizens had lost their fear of the police and it was clear these hard-line demonstrators were not bothered by her presence. Swanson showed the man in the fleece jacket a picture of Oscar Garner. 'Have you seen this man recently?' she asked.

'I wouldn't tell you if I had.'

Swanson stood and stared at the man. 'You realise obstructing a police officer is a criminal offence,' she said, emphasizing the word criminal so the man was left in no doubt as to her meaning.

He stepped back. 'I told you, I haven't seen him,' he said.

As he spoke, Swanson saw Keane barging through the gathered crowd. His jacket was open and his handgun was visible.

'Oh look, the cavalry has arrived,' said the man, to the amusement of his fellow protestors.

'Just before I go,' said Swanson. 'One of you called in the sighting of Garner. So either he was here and you have a traitor amongst your ranks or he wasn't here and one of you is guilty of staging a hoax.'

'Let me guess, that's criminal as well?' said the man.

Swanson snapped a photograph of the man on her mobile phone. 'Yes, it's a criminal offence.'

'What the hell was that all about?' she asked Keane when they were back in the car.

'What?' said Keane.

'Why did you walk over with your gun showing? You think I need protecting?'

'No, I was just bored. I thought you could do with some support.'

'What do you think they were going to do to a police officer in a broad daylight?'

'Jesus, Swanson. I just walked over.'

'Don't ever do that to me again,' said Swanson.

'Yes ma'am,' said Keane.

They drove back to the police station in silence.

Chapter Twenty One

The following morning, Swanson purchased a drink from the small coffee shop near the station. Outside, the area was spotless; not a trace of litter. CCTV cameras hovered above, following her and the other citizens. They were omnipresent, only slightly less conspicuous than the pods.

Ten minutes later, she was in Chessington's office. Her superior sat glum-faced behind his desk, rubbing his eyes. A day's growth of red stubble sprouted from his face, his checked shirt was unbuttoned, and a cotton tie hung loose around his neck. 'First of all, don't forget the legal ball tonight,' he said. 'This bloody thing has taken on even more significance with the Lloyd disappearance and the breakout. Be prepared for numerous questions on both subjects. Deflect them as best as you can. We have a number of leads, nothing confirmed yet but we're close to a breakthrough, so on, so forth. You know the drill. Second, I want you to take Keane.'

'What?' said Swanson, a little louder than intended.

Chessington scratched his chin, an idle gesture, as if he'd

lost track of what he'd said. 'He's up and coming, Swanson. Well connected, too. Some of the top guys have requested his presence.'

It was the first Swanson had heard of Keane having any connections. 'Anything else?'

'Yes, there is, Inspector,' said Chessington, raising his voice, his narrow eyes bulging into life then fading back into his pudgy face. 'Regarding Jessica and Charles Wesley.'

'What about them? They have a clear link with Lloyd's disappearance.'

'I would steer clear if I were you. They're not involved. Jessica Wesley has been in contact with Luce, suggesting that you are harassing her family.'

'Hardly. Any news from Hanson or SI?'

'Listen, you have to take this seriously, Swanson. You do not want Luce on your back.'

'No, sir. Hanson?'

'He reiterated his story about a splinter group. Top level security so he can't share details at the moment.'

'How convenient.'

'Just get on with it, Swanson, and think about what I said.'

Swanson returned to her office. It was typical Chessington behaviour: controlling, disrespectful, incompetent. It was pointless conducting any investigation if he'd managed to reach his own conclusions without her input, and if SI were refusing to play ball. She packed her holdall and left the office, stopping at Keane's desk to inform him he was to attend the ball with her that evening. He didn't look remotely surprised. She imagined he'd already had his tuxedo dry-cleaned.

'What time are you picking me up?' he asked, not looking up.

'I'm not.' Swanson stared at him until he looked up. It was as if he'd forgotten what happened the other evening at Natal's, the chance she was taking with him. 'What are you working on?'

'Doing some more research on Timothy Basle. Going to speak to some of his acquaintances. Find out how well he really knew Garner and Jude Wesley. You?'

'I'm off to see your girlfriend,' said Swanson, noticing with satisfaction the hint of colour in Keane's cheeks.

She decided to walk. The business district of the city was laden with row upon row of identical office buildings. The skyscrapers were covered with mirrored windows which on closer inspection held the intricate waves of solar panels. Swanson saw her reflection on every side. A multitude of busy employees was working inside the glistening buildings and she shuddered at the thought of their hidden eyes spying on her as she checked her appearance.

The courthouse was as imposing as ever, its glass dome centre dwarfing even the tallest office building. Swanson walked through the checkpoint with no opposition, two khaki dressed guards lowering their gaze as she rushed by. She was used to the labyrinth of corridors and weaved her way expertly to Judge Lloyd's office. A plump woman in her fifties sat at the desk usually occupied by Sarah Natal. She looked up at Swanson. 'May I help you?' she asked.

'Sarah Natal,' replied Swanson, not returning the smile.

'No,' answered the woman, confused.

'You misunderstand. I'm looking for Ms Natal.' Swanson emphasised the 'Ms,' her voice a luscious snarl.

'Oh, sorry, I'm a temp. I think Ms Natal is the judge's secretary. She called in sick this morning, I believe. Can I help?' The woman's politeness was infuriating.

'Did she mention how long she'd be away from the office?'

'I've been asked to cover until Friday. Can I take a message?'

Swanson left the office without answering and headed towards Natal's flat in Sector Two. The office buildings soon dwindled as she moved into the more residential area. The pods were more visible here, and Swanson sensed a different set of eyes focused upon her.

She stopped outside Natal's tower block, standing in the same space where her car had been parked the two evenings ago. She moved towards the building and pressed the electronic buzzer before she'd had a chance to think about what she was doing. She tried two more times before pressing random buttons until someone allowed her access to the building. If anything, her rage intensified as she ran up the five flights of stairs to Natal's corridor. The air inside the building was coated with a faint muskiness as if the place suffered from latent decay. Swanson knocked on Natal's door. When there was no answer, she began pounding, harder and harder until her knuckles hurt. She acted outside of herself, as if her rage from the other evening was dictating her movements.

The noise of an opening door stopped her. An elderly woman peered out from the door next to Natal's. 'I don't think she's there, do you?' said the woman, looking at Swanson kindly, with gentle amusement.

Swanson stared at the woman, for a moment confused. 'I'm sorry,' she said.

'I think the door can take it. Aluminium or some such thing. Why don't you come in for a cup of tea?' suggested the woman.

The gesture was so unexpected and generous that Swanson felt close to tears. 'Maybe that's a good idea. Thank you very much,' she said.

'My name is Abigail,' said the woman, offering Swanson a seat. The woman looked like she was in her eighties. Her skin was light brown, a permanent tan resulting from too many years in the sun. Deep lines were carved into her face and her skin hung loose from her neck. 'Can I get you a tea, or something else perhaps?'

'Tea would be lovely. My name is Kate.'

As the woman made tea, Swanson scanned the room. The white walls were adorned with large abstract paintings. A red cloth sofa filled the space of the living room and candles were scattered throughout, on the wooden floorboards and shelves. By the window stood a large telescope which was pointed towards the pods which hung almost level in the distance.

'I'm afraid I'm a bit of a snoop,' said Abigail as she

returned with a tray. 'My husband died many years ago and since then I haven't had much energy for anything other than spying.' Her laughter was melodic.

Swanson noticed the thick leather-bound book by the telescope. 'Do you keep records?' she asked.

'Oh,' said the woman, momentarily lost in a private memory. 'The book. Well, I'll let you in on a little secret. I decided some time ago to record all the pods which pass by. I've been doing it for nearly twenty years now. I've recorded each and every person. I have books and books in my office.'

'Why?' asked Swanson.

'I think it's important,' replied the woman, pouring the tea. 'It's not the only thing I record.' For the first time, Swanson noticed a flash of blue in the older woman's eyes as she spoke. 'For instance, I believe you were here the night before last. I saw you sitting in your car. I saw your friend leaving your car. Have you lost him?'

'Who?' asked Swanson.

'Your friend who was here the other night.'

Swanson didn't answer immediately. She was trying to decipher if there was a hidden threat to the woman's words, or if her snooping broke any laws. 'No, he's returned,' she said.

'I'm sorry. It's none of my business. Do you know Miss Natal as well?'

'Yes, we're acquaintances,' said Swanson, deciding now was a good time to show the old woman her warrant card.

'Ah, police. I thought it was just a matter of time,' said the woman.

'Oh, really?'

'It's just that I've been keeping a record of Miss Natal's comings and goings lately. Listen to me, I must sound like a silly gossipy old woman. I just like to imagine things, I don't mean anything by it.'

Swanson sipped her tea, which had a crumpled mint leaf floating on its surface. 'Why record her comings and goings?'

'Just a bit of fun really. She lives such an interesting life.' The woman sat forward and hushed in conspiring tones. 'Lots of men, you see. Lots. Never seen your friend before, though.' Abigail was clearly enjoying herself. She leant further forwards, a malicious grin spreading across her face, causing it to break into a spider web of wrinkles. 'Again, none of my business but I noticed he was wearing a wedding ring.'

I bet you did, thought Swanson. 'A long story. This tea is lovely, by the way.'

'Thank you,' said the old woman, her face losing some of her previous light now the conversation had turned to more mundane matters.

'Maybe you should consider a career with the police,' suggested Swanson.

Abigail tilted her head back, her laughter filling the room. 'I'm just an amateur. I presume you can't tell me any more about why you're so keen to see Miss Natal.' The woman poured more tea into Swanson's cup.

'Nothing serious. I got a bit fed up earlier. I was told she was at home and having traipsed all the way over here I was bit annoyed to find out she was not in.'

'Understandable. Have you tried her boyfriend?' asked the old woman.

Swanson sipped at her tea again. 'I thought she had lots of boyfriends.'

'She does,' said Abigail. 'But there's one she sees more than the others.'

Chapter Twenty Two

Abigail's description was detailed. 'A very large man, I would place him in his mid-fifties. He has grey hair and beard and two of the most piercing eyes I have ever seen. Ice blue, quite remarkable. I used the zoom feature on the telescope to get close. I was hypnotised by them. Such lovely eyes. I would have taken a picture but my rule is to only take pictures of the pods. Am I in trouble?' she asked.

'Not yet,' said Swanson. 'How often have you seen them together?'

Abigail hesitated. 'He used to come to the flat quite often but he hasn't been around much recently.'

Swanson remained silent, waiting.

'I have followed her on a few occasions. It gets me out of the house.' The old woman looked into her lap. 'I don't mean anything by it,' she said again, as if it justified her actions. 'I don't have much else to do and her life, well, it seems so very interesting.'

'So you know where this man lives?'

'No, but I've seen them together a few times. I wonder if

his feelings for her might be waning. I don't think she will get him to marry her.'

'Oh, really?' Swanson bit her lip to hide her amusement.

'Yes, when they meet he has this permanent scowl as if he is counting down the seconds until she leaves.'

'And what about her, what does she feel?' Although she was humouring the woman, Swanson had a genuine desire for the answer.

'Besotted,' said the old woman, folding her arms. 'Absolutely besotted. All these other men, well it's a rebound thing I guess. It's him she wants. You can see it in her eyes.'

Abigail showed Swanson into her office which was little more than a desk and chair surrounded by four fitted bookcases filled with journals identical to the one by the telescope. Swanson scanned the dated journals and alighted on one from five years ago. Swanson lifted the volume. 'Christ, these are heavy,' she said. 'May I borrow this one?'

'Will I get it back?'

'I promise,' said Swanson. She hesitated, nervous. 'Where do you keep your older journals?' she asked.

Abigail showed her to a further library in her spare bedroom. Swanson ran her fingers over the books, searching for a particular date. When she found the journal in question she pulled it gently from its resting place, her hands shaking. 'May I take this one also?'

Abigail looked at her kindly, as if they were sharing a secret. 'You can keep that one,' she said.

'Thank you for all your help,' said Swanson, by the front

door. She left Abigail her card with instructions to call as soon as Natal returned.

Swanson scanned the crowd as she walked home, looking for a large grey-bearded man with blue eyes. It was not the worst description she'd ever been given. Twenty minutes into her walk and she had only encountered four men with beards, none of which had been grey. Clearly, it was not a look currently in fashion. She called Keane to update him on her meeting with Abigail, fighting the urge to tell him he was a 'rebound thing'.

'You think Natal is missing now?' asked Keane.

'No, but she could be shacking up with this bearded guy. I'll leave the rest of the investigations on this one to you. I presume you still have her mobile number?'

'No answer.'

'Oh dear, she can't have been that impressed. Keep trying. I'll see you tonight at the dinner. I will be accompanying my father.'

She hung up and rewarded herself with a brief smile.

Chapter Twenty Three

Jane Sutton was waiting outside Swanson's block of flats. It felt like she saw the journalist more than her work colleagues. Swanson walked to the doors of the building trying her best to ignore her.

'Inspector Swanson, may I?' asked Sutton, pointing her hand in the air like a schoolchild trying to attract the attention of her teacher.

Swanson sighed. 'What?'

'No need for that, Kate,' said Sutton, smiling. 'Are there any updates for me?'

'Nope.'

'Rumours are that a prisoner has escaped from the holding zone. Oscar Garner.'

'Are there indeed? You should print that, Jane.'

'Is that an official statement?'

'What do you think? I'm quite busy, Jane, so if there's nothing else?'

'What happened at the demonstration over in Sector Three yesterday?' Sutton continued.

'Are you following me, Jane? You seem to be everywhere I am.'

'You leave a trail of goodwill behind you, Inspector. My sources update me. You were questioning demonstrators about Oscar Garner.'

'It's classified. Now, if there's nothing else?'

'Does this have anything to do with the church?'

'Does what have anything to do with the church?'

'Judge Lloyd's disappearance, and the escape of Oscar Garner?'

'I'm sure you would like it to be about the church. Your readers love a bit of conspiracy theory.'

'Why did you question Father Annerley yesterday?'

'Classified.'

'I can still report it,' said Sutton.

Swanson edged towards the journalist. 'What are you going to publish?'

'You questioning the demonstrators about Oscar Garner. You questioning Father Annerley. I can let my readers put two and two together, or you can tell me.'

'What is it you want to know, Jane?'

'I know Oscar Garner has escaped from the holding zone. I am surprised there's been no press release yet.'

'Not my department,' said Swanson.

'So why were you questioning Father Annerley?'

'Garner is a former parishioner, a lay preacher.'

'Do you think the church has helped him escape?'

Swanson pursed her lips. 'Jane, you can print what you want about my investigations but if you print anything about Garner escaping, you'll be arrested.'

'I have a possible name for you, Inspector.'

Swanson paused. 'Okay, I'll play along.'

'Someone you may not have come across yet.'

Swanson raised her eyebrows.

'I get the first call when Garner's disappearance is official?'

'Give me the name and we can talk.'

'Jackson Sharpe.'

The name sounded familiar. 'Go on.'

'Retired lawyer. Very good friends with Judge Lloyd,' said Sutton.

'Is there a point to this, Jane?'

'It's just a rumour, but you may not be aware of it.'

Swanson figured she knew what was coming. 'Enlighten me.'

'They were involved.'

'Involved? As in seeing each other?'

Sutton nodded.

'You're sure about this?'

'They were very secretive. I only know because of one person.'

'Who is going to remain nameless, I presume? Okay, Jane, thanks for the information. I'll get back to you.'

Her father sat on a lounge chair reading a legal text, a large tumbler of brandy on the table before him. He was already dressed in a black tuxedo with a red bow-tie and cummerbund. 'Do you know something I don't?' asked Swanson. 'It's barely gone lunchtime.'

'No point changing twice in a day,' replied her father. 'Too much work to be done.'

Swanson shook her head. In her room, she removed her shoes and lay on the bed, taking a guilty pleasure in being away from work. She called Flaherty and told him to check on Sharpe. Something about what Jane had told her made her uneasy. It was another secret she could do without.

She took out the first of Abigail's journals from her holdall and gasped after opening the cover. Each entry was accompanied by a large colour photo. Swanson flicked through the journal, amazed at the clarity and unsettling beauty of the images. These were more than casual amateur efforts, even to Swanson's untrained eye. The photos pierced the protective layer of the pods as if the photographer was sharing the capsule with the captives. Swanson returned to the first page. The first of the two photos was a sweeping shot of the pods as they looked from Abigail's window. Coils of thick black cable stretched above a background of redbrick buildings. Two pods visible. The first was some way in the distance, travelling towards the camera lens. The other pod was more central and held the blurred figure of a prisoner within their glass jail.

The second photo was a close-up image of the same prisoner. A man who looked to be somewhere in his late fifties. He was naked save for a loin cloth. He stared towards the lens as if posing, his face gaunt, his eyes hollow and confused. Beneath the photos Abigail had recorded the following:

I call this man 'Stanley.' He has been in my view for two days now. Like the others he is pretty static by this point. I imagine he is too tired to express his fury. He sits and looks out of the glass. Sometimes he stares right through it as if he is in the same room as me. I will light his candle this evening as he passes out of sight. As always, I wish him luck.

Swanson scanned through the other pages, each presenting her with two photos and Abigail's mostly repetitive contribution. Each face held the same deathless gaze and Swanson wondered how many pictures Abigail had taken to reach the perfect image. She stopped when she saw a face she recognised. Jemima Ferrington had been prosecuted for a number of theft offences stretching back over ten years. She was a career criminal who embraced zero tolerance as a challenge. She had been caught by chance, a bag snatch at a bar when an off-duty officer had been standing nearby. Ferrington had been unrepentant and Swanson couldn't blame her. She was guilty and nothing she had to say would change that. The woman had walked silently into her pod as if the prospect of the glass prison was merely another obstacle to overcome. Abigail's photo recorded the change in the woman. The arrogance and defiance had been obliterated. The woman in the photo had been reduced to a lost little girl. She sat in one corner of the pod, holding her legs. Her grey jumpsuit was torn and her breasts fell onto her knees. Swanson shut the book with a shudder.

She couldn't yet bring herself to open the second journal.

Chapter Twenty Four

The dinner was as decadent and repulsive as she had feared. Swanson had never been in the State Hall before. It was situated on the second floor of the Courthouse, a level of the building with such limited access that usually only the highest security-checked people were allowed within its hallowed interior. Even tonight, each guest had to pass through a metal detector; the khaki dressed SI guards selected for their smiling faces and supplication to their superiors. Swanson and her father were ushered through the large steel entrance with apologetic grace by one of the guards who, although smiling, never once looked them in the eyes.

The hall was swamped with round tables, covered in fine silk cloth. Her father pecked her on the cheek and headed for the high table where special guests and dignitaries sat. Swanson thought about Judge Lloyd and wondered if his presence would be missed. Flaherty had done some initial digging on Lloyd's relationship with Jackson Sharpe and was finding it difficult to find any confirmation. Swanson had instructed him to meet with the man.

The room had the feel of a wedding reception, and Swanson's heels clicked on the hardwood floor as she made her way to her table, some distance from her father's elevated position. Keane was waiting for her. He was clean shaven and looked fresh and alert in his tuxedo. He rose from his seat and welcomed her, introducing her to the rest of the table. Swanson knew most of the fellow guests, mainly low-level lawyers and administrative staff from the courthouse. She sighed inwardly, shaking the hand of Dave Legg, the defence lawyer whose gold pen now lived in the box under her bed.

'Inspector Swanson, you honour us,' he said, his mouth contorting into a conceited smirk.

'Glad of the invite,' she said.

During the seven course dinner, conversation rarely veered away from the law. While Keane flirted expertly with everyone on the table, Swanson resigned herself to polite smiles and more red wine than was good for her. By the time the after-dinner speeches began, there was barely a sober person in the ballroom. The Lord Chief Justice began the speeches with a muted acknowledgement of Judge Lloyd's disappearance. Apparently, the police were very close to a breakthrough. Oscar Garner was not mentioned.

Swanson noticed that after insisting she attend the ball, Chessington had failed to appear. She had imagined that he would have taken his place with the other bigwigs at the top table.

At long last, the speeches finished. The consumption of alcohol had affected the majority of guests. Swanson laughed to herself as the dancing began. It was a pitiful sight, drunken middle-aged men and women dancing like teenagers. Swanson kept a dignified distance by the bar where she was soon joined by her father. 'Red wine?' he asked.

'I suppose one more won't hurt.'

'It will definitely hurt me in the morning but I'm sure you'll be fine,' he said. 'So how are you enjoying your first legal ball?'

Swanson took a heavy drink. 'About as much as I'd expected.'

'That much? I guess you must have really enjoyed the speeches. What did you think of my little number?'

'Oh, I hadn't realised you'd taken to the stage,' said Swanson.

'Quite right,' said her father. 'Anyway, I must be off. I'll see you soon – more networking to do.' He walked onto the dance floor, shuffling his feet in mock imitation of the other dancers.

The party circled around her as if she were invisible. It suited her fine. Her position at the bar was the perfect spot to assess everyone else. She watched the varying social interactions with a detached amusement. Through years of experience she was able to analyse each subtle movement of body language, the flirting and the subservience to hierarchy. And amongst the mass of happy people, she couldn't help but notice Keane. He ambled through the throng shaking hands and kissing cheeks as if he were the host. He made everyone feel special, made them the most important person in the room. Swanson had to marvel at his expertise.

Everyone he spoke to seemed entranced by what he had to say. It was a gift, one that Swanson lacked.

'Hey, boss,' said Keane, walking somewhat unsteadily towards her.

'Keane, how are you?'

'Great, I thought these things were supposed to be a bit dry,' he said, drinking white wine from an oversized glass.

'I guess it's what you make of it,' replied Swanson.

'Yeah, you're probably right. Have you been questioned yet over Lloyd and Garner?'

'The odd query here and there. You?'

Keane shuffled towards here. 'The rumour mill is in full bloom, boss,' he slurred. 'You can't imagine the theories I've been hearing.'

'The rumour mill is in full bloom?'

'It's an expression,' insisted Keane, absently touching her right arm. 'Anyway, let's forget about all that, we're off duty after all.' He ordered two more glasses of wine from the bar. Once the drinks arrived they toasted the missing Chessington. Keane glared at her, his eyes unsteady, and whispered, 'you know they have rooms here, don't you?'

It took a few seconds for Swanson to realise what he was suggesting. Part of her wanted to take him up on the suggestion, to accompany him to the nearest hotel. What harm could it really do?

Out of the corner of her eye, she saw her father approaching the Chief Super. The sight brought her back to her senses. 'I think it's best if we both forget you just said that,' she said.

'Just saying,' said Keane.

Swanson took the glass of wine away from him. 'And I think that's enough for tonight.'

Keane stared at her, struggling to keep his balance. He went to raise an objection but seemed to lose his train of thought. 'See you tomorrow, then,' he said, and headed back onto the dance floor.

Swanson made her way over to her father, who was by now involved in a ferocious debate with two of the most senior officers from her station.

'As usual, Luce, you don't know what you're talking about,' he roared, at the elder of the two officers.

Chief Superintendent Luce looked at her father with detachment. He was standing next to Luke Campbell, his second in command.

'The problem with the police is that you view it all from a numbers angle. You don't care about legality or morality, all you care about is how many people you can get up in those godforsaken pods of yours.'

Both Luce and Campbell laughed, but neither looked happy. 'I thought you were retired, Swanson. Yet every time we have one of these things, you're here bending my ear. I know your viewpoint on everything. You've been sharing it with me for the last thirty years,' said Luce.

Swanson moved towards the three men. Her father's face was reddening, a mixture of alcohol and anger. 'Ah, Inspector Swanson, come join us. I hope you can shed some light on your father's rather old-school arguments,' said Luce.

'Good evening, sir. I think this is one discussion I would be wise to avoid,' said Swanson, working hard not to slur.

'Quite right, too,' said Campbell.

'Okay, Dad, let's get you out of here.'

'So soon?' said her father. 'I've only just started to enjoy myself. I was hoping Luce or Campbell were going to finally give me some answers and not the same old tosh they give me every time I see them.'

'Goodnight, Swansons,' said Luce, walking away with his subordinate in tow.

Her father's tirade continued during the taxi drive home. 'Buffoons. I wouldn't trust them as door security. They're too stupid to understand. Those two idiots can only see figures. Prosecutions. It's all a numbers game for them, and so it should be, but they should be judged on how few people they send to the pods, not how many.'

Sometimes he forgot that his daughter was part of the same regime he detested so much.

As if reading her mind, he stopped and turned towards her. 'You know I don't mean you, darling, don't you? If the force was run by people like you then my opinions would be redundant by now.' He smiled, his upper lip slightly crooked. They'd never talked in detail about why she had decided to join the police force. His disappointment, and possible disapproval, had remained unspoken. She could tell that part of him had a vague grasp of her reasons, but it was not something he wished to pursue. His rage was easing and Swanson could see that his eyes were glazed with moisture. 'I'm sorry,' he whispered, pulling her close to him. 'I'm such an old idiot.'

'You're okay,' said Swanson. 'They'll probably promote me out of pity.'

At the flat, Swanson helped her father up the stairs. She could smell the red wine on his breath, and the lighter citric smell of the aftershave he had used ever since she was a child. They were reassuring in their familiarity but they couldn't mask the newer smell, the musky odour of old age, which had accompanied her father for the last couple of years. His body felt feeble under her arms, and as he tried to put the key into the front door his hand trembled.

'Nightcap?' he suggested as they entered the living room.

It was pointless objecting. He poured two ludicrously large measures of brandy into oval-shaped glass tumblers.

'I must say that my behaviour at these events is quite consistent. It wouldn't surprise me to find that there is a sweepstake on when I will finally crack.' He laughed at his own predictability. 'They provoke me, you know,' he said, winking.

'Oh, I know, Dad. I know.'

They sat in silence, sipping at their drinks. Swanson kept thinking about Keane's proposition. He'd been almost as intoxicated as her father was now, and would no doubt regret it tomorrow. Part of her had been flattered, whatever his state, but she couldn't help thinking about Natal, and the wedding ring on his finger.

Outside, black clouds rolled through the sky, blanketing the stars. Swanson slept fitfully, her sleep pitted with thoughts about Jessica Richardson and Jude Wesley, and how they must view the impending weather. Perhaps it was a distraction, or a melancholy reminder of the beauty of the world they were soon to depart. She dreamt of Jude Wesley, huddled in his glass cell, his face occasionally replaced by that of her mother's.

Sometime in the night, her phone rang, and her instant reaction was that Keane was following up his request. Despite herself, her heart sped up in anticipation. She was disappointed to hear Chessington's voice.

'Sir?' she questioned.

'Get to the office. We've made an arrest on the Lloyd case.'

Chapter Twenty Five

Sarah Natal appeared in the living room clouded by a mist of heavily scented perfume. 'What do you think?' she asked, running her hands up and down the sides of her body. She was wearing a tight-fitting dress with a thin black choker wrapped around her slender neck. Her long auburn hair was tied into plaits so the flesh of her shoulders and neck were fully on show. Old Blue had to confess she looked striking, close to irresistible in the outfit. He told her as much, knowing he had to feed her compliments to ensure the job was completely properly.

'A little drink before we go?' she suggested.

'There'll be plenty of time for that when we're there. We need to be on time. We can't afford to be too early or too late.'

They arrived at Little Joe's at eight o'clock. It was the last Friday of the month, payday for the multitude of factory workers for whom Little Joe's was a favourite destination. Old Blue had been deliberating about whether or not he should attend with Sarah. He had weighed up which was more plausible, Sarah going alone to the club or arriving with him and ditching him once she found a better offer. Reluctantly, he had decided on the latter.

The ground floor bar of Little Joe's was busy but not yet full to capacity. The chairs and tables had been placed to one side, the customers standing together in groups, some swaying to the blaring music. The factory workers were in high spirits, and drinks and conversations were flowing. Sarah locked arms with him as they walked in. The crowd didn't stop but he sensed a subtle change of atmosphere as if some of the men had stopped talking for an instant, such was the distraction of Sarah Natal in the figure-hugging dress. Customers made a clear path for them as they walked to the bar. He was dressed in a tailored suit. In comparison to the mainly younger clientele he was overdressed but he knew his clothes suited him. He ordered drinks from a nervous girl, a student who looked overawed to be serving them, as if he reminded her of her father and Sarah reminded her of the popular girls in school. He had noticed that Thurrock and Wilson, the tall one and the curly-haired one as he now distinguished them, had watched them enter. They were still at their usual place by the bar, off to the right some fifty or sixty metres from where he'd ordered his drinks. Once again he shuddered at their predictability. He turned his back on them so that they could get a better view of Sarah Natal.

'Don't look over,' he warned her. 'Have you noticed them?' He'd spent an hour describing Thurrock and Wilson to Sarah, to the point where she'd got bored and tried to encourage him to indulge in other forms of pleasure. 'This is important,' he'd told her and his preparation had proved to be a success.

'I can see them,' she said. 'I've looked over once but I can feel them staring at me now. They're talking and laughing.'

Old Blue wondered if he was the reason for their laughter. He was much older than Sarah Natal and knew that he was not the type of man people would expect her to be with.

'They probably think they've got a chance with you, seeing me here,' he said, instantly regretting his words. He sounded jealous and needy and couldn't afford to display any signs of vulnerability.

Sarah didn't react, as if she hadn't been listening.

They stayed at the bar an hour or so, Sarah flirting outrageously with any man who walked near her. It was amusing to see how these men crumbled in her presence. Even those with partners blushed as she spoke to them, scared that their wives and girlfriends would see the desire in their eyes.

As planned, they staged a mock argument at ten o'clock. Ever the actress, Sarah took to the role with a fitting theatricality. She flung out her arms in an exaggerated gesture, throwing what remained of her glass of vodka and lime directly into his face. He wiped the alcohol away and walked slowly across the ash-filled floor. He didn't look back, either at the still-shouting Sarah Natal or at Thurrock and Wilson, whom he sensed were watching from the bar.

Back at the car, he imagined Sarah fulfilling the plan. She

would have ordered herself a drink and walked over to the two men; or more likely, would have manipulated the situation so they bought her a drink. The rest he could only guess at. If the plan worked out she would return with the men at one a.m. whilst the bar was still at its busiest.

At midnight he crept into the boot of the large people carrier. Although much more spacious than the tight confines of Judge Lloyd's boot, he still found himself struggling for space. He pulled a blanket over his body, flattening himself out, and hoped the bulk was not as noticeable as it felt. Four hours later, Sarah returned.

A number of thoughts had played through his mind in that time but he'd felt unable to move in case someone saw him leave. The plan had been as meticulous as possible but there were a number of variables which he was unable to account for.

He was relieved when at last he heard Sarah's footsteps on the cobbled path next to the car. Her voice was loud and high pitched just as they'd planned.

Old Blue unsheathed a large hunting knife. He hoped he wouldn't have to use it, but the three main variables were about to enter the car and he had to be sure. Sarah opened the passenger door. The two men were giggling like nervous schoolboys.

'Here, let's take these,' said Sarah.

'What are they?' said one of the men. Old Blue thought it was Wilson but he couldn't be sure.

'They'll help us get into the mood, if you know what I mean,' said Sarah.

'You're full of surprises you, aren't you?' slurred the other man, presumably Thurrock.

'Right, you boys get in the back,' said Sarah. 'I don't want one of you being jealous about the other one sitting in the front.'

'Oh come on,' said Wilson. 'He won't mind.'

'No, both of you in the back,' said Sarah. 'You can wait your turn.'

Old Blue felt the two men thump down into their seats. Already the car was filled with the noxious fumes of alcohol and nicotine.

'Where do you live again?' said Thurrock. His slurred voice had taken on a more discordant tone, as if he was struggling to give voice to the words which troubled his brain. Five minutes later Sarah Natal opened the boot of the car. Old Blue jumped out as quick as his bulk would allow him. He opened the door and leant into the back seat, handcuffing the two drugged men for safety.

'How did I do?' asked Sarah. She looked remarkably good for all of the night's exertions. Her make-up was faultless and only the slight drunken intonation of her voice suggested she'd been out all night. He fought back his anger at having to wait in the car for much longer than had been planned.

'You did great,' he said, kissing her hard and full on the lips. A tinge of red lipstick clung to his mouth as he broke the embrace.

He left early the following morning. He'd gagged the two men in the same cell as Judge Lloyd. They were currently tied to chairs but he would set them free later that afternoon. They needed time to adjust to their surroundings. The cell was divided into two and he'd placed the two men into a separate half from Lloyd though the three could still speak to one another. He would leave it to Lloyd to explain the situation. Between the three of them they would figure out what was happening and perhaps acceptance would make it easier on everybody.

He arrived at the church hall where he had attended the Lenity meeting earlier in the week. The splintered door was locked as always. Timothy Basle answered this time, the nasal-voiced leader of the section. The man stammered a greeting but he ignored him, walking straight past him as if he wasn't there. Agatha Trent and Stephen Crampton were the only other members present.

'Thank you for coming,' said Basle. 'There has been a slight change of plan.' Crampton sat up tensely in his chair. It was his son who was going into the pods the following day. Old Blue saw the heartbreaking look of hope etched onto the man's face.

'I'm sorry Stephen,' said Basle. 'There's no plan to stop the podding, I'm afraid. Just a slight change to where the bombs will be set off.' Crampton sat back in his seat, deflated.

Old Blue was part of the group for two reasons. One, the bombing would cause a distraction from his more important side project. The police would spend less structured time focusing on

Judge Lloyd's, and now Thurrock and Wilson's disappearance, if they were side-tracked by a more threatening incident. Secondly, he owed someone very senior in Lenity a debt of gratitude. The person in question had created this unofficial sub-group: Lenity only supported peaceful protests but a growing number of members who had become disillusioned with their impotency. The leader of this group had assisted Old Blue and now he was returning the favour.

Basle outlined the five areas where the bombs were to be detonated. Crampton and Trent gasped when they found out the destination of the last bomb.

'If we're going to bomb there, why can't we bomb the pods? It doesn't make any sense to me,' said Crampton.

Basle cleared his throat. A long, bulbous, green vein pulsated on his bony right hand as the man coughed into a handkerchief. 'I'm just following orders, Stephen. Our aim is to cause as little damage as possible. Think of it as a warning shot. Something to make them sit up and consider.'

Crampton laughed, humourlessly. 'Consider? We know they're going to go through with it. Let's bomb the pods and rescue my son.' The man was close to tears. In another lifetime, Nathaniel Jacobson would have comforted the man, but Old Blue was too practiced in his new role; he sat motionless in his chair. He was given a location to be when the bombs were detonated. He didn't really understand the thinking behind it. He was supposed to measure casualties and to make sure there was no police interference before the bombs were due to be detonated. He accepted his instructions with good grace and left Trent, Crampton, and Basle without a goodbye.

Chapter Twenty Six

Swanson sat in the kitchen, drinking as much black coffee as she could stand. From the window, a pod came into view, the glass capsule empty. This in itself was not unusual. An empty capsule was as much of a deterrent as an occupied one.

She called Keane, shuddering at her unprofessionalism. It was no comfort that the majority of her colleagues would be as hungover as she was. Keane answered on the twentieth ring, his voice at once guttural and fragile. 'Hello?'

'Chessington has made an arrest. Meet me outside the station in twenty minutes.' She hung up before he had time to object. It was four a.m. on Saturday morning and the city was deserted. Above her, the pods followed her course. It was a peaceful sight, each glass capsule alone and distinct, all following their preordained paths lazily across the night sky.

She waited outside the police station for fifteen minutes. When Keane arrived, he was dressed in the previous night's clothes. 'Don't,' he warned.

'Tell me you've a change of clothes in there,' said

Swanson, feeling both smug and guilty at her hypocrisy.

'What the hell is this all about? Give me ten minutes to have a shower.'

'Five.'

Swanson waited twenty more minutes outside the locker room. She felt too nauseous to face Chessington alone. Keane looked better for his shower. He'd changed into standard trousers and a crisp shirt which he must have kept in his locker for such emergencies. Only his bloodshot eyes betrayed the previous night's excesses.

If Chessington was pleased with himself he was hiding it well. He looked as bad as Keane, sitting at his desk staring intently at a file. 'How was the party?' he asked.

'Fine, sir,' said Swanson. Her stomach rumbled, as she waited with dry mouth to be offered a seat. Keane said nothing.

Chessington threw the file he was reading across the desk. 'Sit. Richard Beck. Wrote the ransom note. Handwriting checks out. Former member of Lenity but "disbarred", his word not mine, four years ago for what he calls extreme views. He has admitted to kidnapping Lloyd but at present refuses to tell us his whereabouts.'

Swanson picked up the file which turned out to be an A4 piece of paper with Beck's name, address and photo on it. She glanced up at Chessington who nodded his head. 'He just walked in off the street?' she asked.

'Yes, we would probably have ignored him if it hadn't been for the handwriting sample. I've done a preliminary interview with him but now it's over to you. He hasn't been charged yet. If he knows where Lloyd is then I expect to hear the location the next time we speak.'

The room was stifling. Swanson's head was heavy, a dull thud beating just behind her eyes. As they went to leave, Chessington stopped them. 'And if you ever turn up in my office in such a state again, Keane, it will be the last step you ever take in this department.'

Keane mumbled a conciliatory 'sir,' and they both left the office, Swanson grateful both to be out of the heat and to have missed out on a reprimand.

They went to the canteen for coffee. Keane was more animated than in Chessington's office. 'This is bullshit. There's no way this guy knows anything. So, he wrote a ransom note. We knew that was rubbish anyway. I should still be in bed.'

'I agree. Let's go tell Chessington,' said Swanson.

'Funny. I suppose I owe you an apology for last night.'

'I'm surprised you remember anything.'

'I think I possibly made a few ill-advised proposals, as it happens.'

'You know how to make a woman feel special, Keane.' Despite herself, she hoped he was joking.

Keane turned his palms up. 'Got to play the percentages.'

'I suppose zero is a percent,' growled Swanson, pouring the last of her coffee down her dry throat.

Richard Beck slouched in the interview room. In his thirties, he had a pale angular face with large hazel eyes which lent him a mournful look. When he saw Swanson and Keane enter the room, he turned to them with a smile which revealed two rows of small, uneven teeth. Swanson made the introductions.

'Why turn yourself in?' she asked.

'It didn't look like my demands were going to be met.' He was well spoken, sounded educated.

'You know you will go to the pods for this, whether or not you have anything to do with Judge Lloyd's disappearance,' said Keane.

Beck shrugged his shoulders. 'I know how your antiquated system works. It must be at times like this where it really backfires on you.'

Swanson slouched in her chair, mirroring Beck. She knew exactly where this was all heading even if Keane didn't. 'How's that?' asked Keane.

'You don't really have much to bargain with now, do you? As I'm going to the pods anyway, you only have two options open to you.'

'Which are?' said Keane.

'Meet my demands and see Judge Lloyd again.' He paused for effect. 'Or don't.'

'So, you want us to free all the prisoners in the pods and you'll tell us where Judge Lloyd is?' asked Swanson.

'After a time period,' said Beck. Swanson raised her eyebrows, suggesting he continue. 'Three days.'

Keane laughed.

'I assure you that the Judge will be provided for during this time,' said Beck.

'Do you know Charles Wesley, or Jessica Wesley?' asked Swanson.

Beck scratched his chin. 'I know Jude Wesley is in the pods. Relation?'

'He's their son. What about Sarah Natal?'

Beck hesitated. 'I know of her, yes.'

'What do you know?'

'She is Lloyd's assistant. That's as much as I know.'

Swanson shook her head and suspended the interview.

Beck lived in Sector Twenty-Nine, to the east of the city, on the thirty-first floor of a grey tower block. His one-bedroom flat was dank and heavy with the smell of unwashed clothes. A metallic dining table pushed against the far wall of the living room was covered with anti-establishment leaflets. Amongst the standard Lenity pamphlets, Swanson found material she was unfamiliar with. Nameless articles promoting forms of uprising which came close to being criminal. She ordered Keane to bag the literature for further study. Beck's bedroom contained a teak-framed single bed. The mattress was covered by a child's duvet cover. On the carpeted floor were the remains of Beck's last seven or eight meals.

'Nice,' said Keane, producing a number of pornographic magazines from a chest of drawers next to the bed. 'It seems our man likes the larger lady.'

Swanson sighed. It was a pitiful sight and reinforced her assertion that Beck had no direct part to play in Lloyd's disappearance. In another world, it would have been considered a cry for help. In her world, it was a suicide sentence. The magazines were bagged, and Keane boxed up an ancient-looking laptop to take back to the station. Swanson called Chessington and gave him her verdict.

'You think someone put him up to this?' asked Chessington.

Swanson wanted nothing more to do with Beck's fantasy world but a sorry-looking flat was not reason enough to give up on him as a suspect. 'I don't think Beck has the wherewithal to stage a kidnapping on his own. He's either deluded or working for someone.'

'But why turn himself in?'

'We'll question him again later, sir. He can explain some of the literature he's studying at the moment.'

As they were leaving, Swanson noticed a prescription note pinned to the fridge by a cow-shaped magnet. 'Painkillers,' she said, handing the note to Keane.

'Serious stuff,' said Keane.

Instead of driving back to the station, Swanson made a detour to Natal's flat. She saw Keane's face drop as he realised their destination. 'What's that cliché, Keane? Something about returning to the scene of the crime?' She parked in the same spot as the other evening; her body flushed at her mixed memories. She phoned Flaherty and instructed him to obtain a medical report on Beck, then informed Keane of her visit to Natal's flat the previous day and her meeting with Abigail Thompson.

'Fantastic, I'm glad we're working as partners on this.'

Swanson snorted. 'I think you blew that slightly when you slept with our material witness.'

'In your opinion.'

'Whether she is or not is irrelevant. You went against everything I stand for and you are moaning about me going back? Christ, Keane, you're lucky to still be on the force.' Keane stopped moving.

'Don't sulk,' said Swanson.

'If we're going to continue working together then you're going to have drop this,' he said, still not moving. 'I made a mistake – get over it or I'll have to make a transfer request.'

Swanson considered his words. Although she didn't appreciate the ultimatum, she knew he was right. 'Okay, but I reserve the right to mention it in the promotion of humour.' She held out her hand which Keane shook, his eyes not meeting hers. 'Have you made any contact with her since?'

'Still not answering her phone.'

There was no answer at her flat, so Swanson knocked on Abigail's door. The old lady answered immediately as if she had been expecting their call. Swanson remembered the telescope and imagined Abigail had been watching them. 'I hadn't thought I'd see you again so soon,' said Abigail. 'And you've brought a gentleman friend with you, how nice.' She ushered them into the living room. 'I've made tea.'

Swanson introduced Keane, knowing that the old woman would recognise him from the other night. 'May I pour you both a cup?' She looked hopeful.

'I'm afraid we can't stay long,' said Swanson.

'I understand. I suppose you would like an update. Unfortunately, there's nothing to tell. She hasn't returned since yesterday. Is she a missing person now?' Abigail's voice was full of mischief.

'Please, just call me as soon as she returns.' Swanson gave her another copy of her business card.

'Crazy old biddy,' said Keane, once they had reached the relative safety of outside.

'You should perhaps watch what you say,' said Swanson. 'Sometimes the walls have ears as well as eyes.'

They stopped for lunch at a greasy spoon close to where Natal lived. Swanson ordered a fried breakfast which she regretted as soon as it was placed in front of her. Bacon, sausages, eggs, and baked beans floated on a thin film of grease. She sliced into the yolk of the egg, releasing a thick yellow river into the plate, then crossed her cutlery and sat back in her seat. Keane smirked and sipped his oily coffee. Swanson went into detail about her previous meeting with Abigail. She told Keane about the large, bearded man Abigail had seen Natal with. Keane looked unfazed.

'Not jealous?' asked Swanson.

'She didn't strike me as the one-man type.'

'Did she discuss anyone else with you?'

'No one apart from Lloyd. She was quite torn up about him.'

'Is there any chance she was trying to make you think that?'

'I guess. She did talk about him a bit.'

'But no mention of a bearded man?'

'I think that was something I would remember. I take it you've done a background check on her.'

'Everything she said to you checks out.'

Outside, Swanson phoned Lloyd's office. The temp answered. Natal was now not due in until next week at the earliest. 'She's called in?' asked Swanson.

'Yes, I spoke to her this morning,' answered the temp.

'How did she sound?'

'Okay, a bit croaky maybe. She was only on the phone for ten seconds.'

Swanson hung up and the phone rang again immediately. It was Chessington.

'Sir?'

'You need to get to the holding zone. Alex Dempsey is dead.'

Chapter Twenty Seven

The metal sheets rolled endlessly down the production line. McClusky was more agitated this morning than normal. He'd risen late and had only managed one cup of coffee before leaving for work. He'd chain-smoked his way to the factory but his hands had yet to stop shaking. It was still three hours until lunch. The factory was in turmoil. Two of the employees, Glen Thurrock and Simon Wilson, had not turned up for work and as such the factory was not running to full capacity. Tom Miller walked from workstation to workstation, a distracted look on his face. It was only a matter of time before he would pay him a visit.

When the supervisor did make his way over he was short and to the point. 'McClusky, you're working an extra hour before lunch and an extra hour at the end of your shift.' There was no pause for objection, not that McClusky would have dared.

He tried to ignore the time as he worked through the metal sheets. Oil clung to his hands like a second skin, and mixed with the sweat on his brow, dripping into his eyes.

When lunch finally arrived he scrubbed himself clean and lit a cigarette. His pigeon chest heaved as he sucked in the fumes, his hand shaking each time he lifted the burning object to his lips. He ordered the largest black coffee on offer and found a table on his own.

The canteen was alive with conversation. Thurrock and Wilson had still not appeared and the rumour mill was already spouting out nonsense. McClusky knew they were talking about him. He had once been an acquaintance of the two men; before the incident. He would never have called himself a friend but they had abided him then. The close-knit groups looked over at him drinking his coffee accussingly. After drinking another coffee, he ordered a jacket potato from the surly woman behind the canteen. He savoured a third cup of coffee, feeling normality return.

On the next table one of his co-workers, Zack Layton, turned to him and smiled, dead-eyed. 'Where were you last night, McClusky?' he asked, to the amusement of his colleagues.

McClusky ignored him and prodded at his jacket potato. A lump of congealed cheese dripped off the rubbery skin and McClusky had to force the food into his mouth.

'Don't ignore me, McClusky,' Layton continued. 'You better not have been in Little Joe's. You know you're not allowed alcohol.' McClusky closed his eyes and sipped on his coffee. He pictured himself jabbing his fork into Layton's eye. The pain would be instant and would spread an almost incomparable panic through Layton who would convulse in sightless fear. Layton would be unable to comprehend that a fork was sticking in the jelly of his eye and McClusky gloried in the imagined incident, a delightful swarm of pain shivering down the left side of his body. 'Fuck you, then,' said Layton, returning to the giggling group.

The afternoon shift dragged by. The monotony was interspersed with unwelcome interventions from colleagues who felt it acceptable to question him about the two men who had seemingly disappeared. McClusky kept silent at all times which seemed to further enrage his fellow workers. By the end of his shift he'd imagined the slayings of practically every person in the factory.

He waited fifty minutes for the others to finish showering. Miller was waiting for him in the changing rooms as before. He was already half undressed, a thick red towel wrapped around his waist.

'What is it with you, McClusky? You wait until I go in the shower every day. Can you not get enough of this?' he said, pulling the towel away from him and revealing his genitals.

McClusky called Miller's bluff by sitting down on one of the changing room benches and slowly removing his grime soaked work clothes.

'You're sick, McClusky, sick,' said Miller and walked naked to the showers. McClusky pictured the man falling, slipping on one of the tiles and cracking his skull on the hard floor. He imagined burrowing his hands into the man's wounds as he screamed for mercy. The pain would fill every nerve in Miller's body. He waited until Miller had finished showering and brushed past him as he walked to the shower.

'Don't touch me,' said Miller, moving his arm away and then returning a sharp left elbow to McClusky's shoulder.

McClusky staggered at the blow and stumbled towards the shower room. Miller was not the man who'd been following him and he regretted aggravating him. He showered as quick as he could but the oil stuck to his body and it took numerous washes to remove the worst of it. And still it clung to him, an invisible layer, cloaking him, blocking his pores so his skin was unable to breathe properly.

Thankful that Miller was not in the changing rooms, he changed and walked towards home, chain-smoking as he went. He stopped outside Little Joe's. From the interrogations he had received all day, it had become apparent that Thurrock and Wilson had visited Little Joe's the previous night and had not been seen since. It was all too easy to picture them lying in an alleyway, dead from choking on their own vomit. The disappearance had done little to dampen Little Joe's appeal to its diverse clientele.

McClusky stood on the street opposite, noticing through the windows that the place was heaving with the workers who had just finished their shifts. He moped outside, smoking cigarettes, like a young child desperate to play with the big children. He was about to leave when a woman tapped him on the shoulder. She was little more than a girl, seventeen or eighteen at most. McClusky knew her for what she was immediately. She wore a short black leather skirt and absurd-looking fishnet stockings. She had a tight cropped white t-shirt, two sizes too small for her, and her face was plastered with over-enthusiastic make-up. Her lips, cherry red, pouted towards him as she asked him if he wanted any company. The girl introduced herself as Clarissa and led him away to her flat which was two streets down from the bar.

Prostitution itself was not a criminal offence within the city. To engage with a prostitute was considered a civil misdemeanour which would result in a number of hours of counselling. It had been suggested in the press that this by-law was to protect the council. In particular, it was whispered in hushed tones that the Mayor had a certain penchant for ladies of the night. McClusky's wasn't breaking his parole but it was unlikely that the factory would allow him any more time off work for counselling.

The woman lived in a bedsit. A large double bed took centre stage, draped in red sheets. A small kitchen area held a portable stove and a rusty kettle. Clarissa's clothes were arranged over a single brass bar which hung on one of the walls. A freshly painted door led to a small bathroom with a toilet and sink. Clarissa asked him to wash himself, and he struggled to position himself within the cramped confines of the bathroom which smelt as if it had recently been covered in bleach. He stripped mournfully, not understanding fully how he had found himself in this position.

The woman was semi-naked when he returned. McClusky looked longingly at her body, a shiver of disgust flowing through him. He was pretty sure no one had seen him leave with the woman and she must have had so many gentlemen callers that it would be difficult to maintain a link between him and what he intended to do with her.

'Why don't we have a drink?' said the woman. She

poured two large tumblers of whisky and offered him one.

The cheap alcohol smelt worse than the woman's bathroom. He winced as he held it to his nose, then laughed. 'You shouldn't offer me this,' he said, and handed Clarissa his glass of whisky back.

She gulped both drinks, her face contorted as the liquid rushed her throat. She flashed him a grin and asked him to join her on the bed.

McClusky stood, glaring at her. All it would take would be one drink, probably one sip of the whisky the woman had gulped down. Without it, he was worthless. His desires, forever out of reach.

He threw some notes at her from his back pocket. He dressed and left her lying there.

Outside, he sensed the man's presence. He now understood who was following him and why.

'Why don't you get it over with?' he shouted into the air as he reached his building. He turned around but couldn't see anybody in the vicinity. He ran up the stairs instead of taking the lift and collapsed in a heap on his living room floor. He didn't even have time for his last cigarette of the day.

Chapter Twenty Eight

'I would stop answering the phone when Chessington rings,' suggested Keane as they headed out of Sector One. 'He just seems intent on giving us more work.'

Swanson was driving and didn't respond.

'You met Dempsey when you went to the holding zone without me?' questioned Keane.

'You're still upset about that?' Her head was still beating and she regretted not having eaten at the cafe.

'I'm just pleased you saw fit to bring me along this time.'

'Yes, I questioned him about Garner. He seemed decent enough for a…'

'Pimp,' interjected Keane. 'Hulbert didn't seem so taken with him.'

'I didn't say I was taken with him, Keane. I said he seemed decent enough.'

Chessington had sent over a preliminary report which Keane was reading. 'Dempsey hung himself, apparently.'

Swanson considered. 'That can't have been easy in that place. Even their clothes are fastened with Velcro. Any more details?'

‘Something about electrical wire. He was working alone in one of the rooms. The last person to see him was a prisoner by the name of Ramsey Minton.’

‘That name sounds familiar,’ said Swanson.

Keane swiped the touchscreen a few more times. ‘Ramsey Minton, Christ,’ he said. ‘He’s been incarcerated for fifteen years.’

Swanson remembered the man now. He’d been arrested all that time ago for multiple murders.

‘Why the hell hasn’t he been podded yet?’ asked Keane.

‘Maybe they were waiting for the right moment, an anniversary or celebration.’

‘How long did Josephine Richardson have to wait before she was podded? Two weeks?’

‘The world’s not fair,’ agreed Swanson. ‘Check one thing for me, Keane.’

‘Dempsey’s defence?’

‘Let me guess, Charles Wesley?’ said Swanson.

‘Bingo.’

They reached the holding zone an hour later. They followed the same arduous procedure Swanson had endured on her last visit and were finally led to the warden’s assistant, Chadwick, who led them through to the waiting area as before. She offered them both a drink, which they declined.

‘As you can imagine, Mr Patterson is even busier than last time,’ said Chadwick, unease in her voice. She lacked the warmth Swanson had experienced on their previous meeting. They waited for fifteen minutes before Patterson summoned them. ‘Good to see you again, Inspector.

Sergeant. Please take a seat, both of you.'

'Thanks for your time,' said Swanson.

Patterson nodded. 'Terrible business, naturally,' he said. 'But then, these things are all too common; however hard we watch them and assess them, they somehow find a way.'

'Can you give us more detail?' asked Swanson.

'Dempsey managed to dislodge some electrical wire from the skirting boards in one of the computer rooms. He strung it around his neck and connected it to the door. I think the pictures on your reader demonstrate what happened next.'

'Was there anything suspicious about his death?'

Patterson visibly tightened. 'His suicide?'

'Any reason someone might want him dead?' asked Keane.

'Society wants him dead,' said Patterson. 'He was going to be podded within the next couple of months. I can't see why anyone would have reason to end his life beforehand.'

'Perhaps for the pure enjoyment,' suggested Keane. 'I believe Ramsey Minton was the last person to see him alive?'

'We've checked with Minton. He had nothing to do with it. He'd seen Dempsey an hour before in the library. Our security cameras show Minton in the library when Dempsey took his life. This is a suicide. Surely there's no reason to think this is related to Judge Lloyd's disappearance or Oscar Garner's escape. You must understand, I have already answered the same questions for SI. Perhaps you should cross-reference?'

Swanson was not surprised SI had been there first. 'May we interview Mr. Minton?'

‘Take a seat outside and I will see what I can do,’ agreed Patterson, with a heavy sigh.

‘Why hasn’t Minton been podded yet?’ asked Keane, as they stood to leave the office.

‘That’s out of my hands.’

‘But fifteen years is ludicrous.’

‘He’s something of a trophy prisoner.’

‘How do you mean?’ asked Swanson.

‘They could pod him now but it’s all about timing. I wouldn’t be surprised if Minton faces the pod a week before the elections. What better time for the Mayor to show his firmness? What better way to prove the pods are a force of good than by sending a convicted serial killer into them?’

‘Won’t people question why he had been in here for fifteen years?’ asked Keane.

‘People think that the holding zone is a living hell anyway. The picture would be painted as this: he’s been in purgatory for fifteen years and now that he has considered the atrocity he has committed, he is ready to pay the price. You didn’t hear that from me, obviously,’ said Patterson.

‘You don’t think he should be here now?’ said Swanson.

‘That’s not my decision,’ repeated Patterson.

It was ninety minutes before they were able to see Minton. A guard led into the same interview room where Swanson had questioned Dempsey. Unlike Dempsey, Minton wasn’t cuffed or chained to the floor. He was a relaxed figure, slouched back in his chair and dressed in the standard prison jumpsuit. His plump face was half hidden by a grey-black beard, his thinning hair tied back in a ponytail. He smiled on seeing Swanson, a lascivious grin spreading across his wide face. Swanson momentarily thought about the grey bearded man Abigail Thomson had mentioned seeing with Sarah Natal. Minton's eyes, however, were not a sharp blue. They were dark brown and lifeless.

'More guests,' he proclaimed in a booming voice. 'I feel so privileged.'

Swanson made the introductions. Keane folded his arms and glared at the convicted prisoner. Minton glared back and observed Swanson, his eyes moving up and down the parts of her body he could see.

'Mr. Minton, I believe you were the last person to see Mr. Dempsey alive.'

'Yes,' said Minton. 'I saw him leaving the library about an hour before he was found.'

'Did he say anything to you?'

'We had a general conversation. He had a taste for noir fiction which I share.'

'Was he carrying any books?'

'He checked out a couple.'

'Strange thing for a man about to commit suicide to do.'

'You think? I've seen hundreds of suicides in this place. Very hard to spot one without the benefit of hindsight.'

'What can you tell us about Dempsey? I imagine you know most people here quite well.'

'Yes, I'm a man of the people,' agreed Minton with his oversized grin. 'He was a good sort, and, as I said, had a strong taste in fiction. Never any trouble. He stayed away from fights.'

'You think it was suicide?' asked Swanson.

'Whoa, Inspector, some very forward questioning.'

'Our time here is limited.'

Minton lent forward. 'Let's put it this way, officers. Dempsey didn't want to kill himself, and no one wanted to kill Dempsey before your visit the other day, and now all of a sudden one of those two things isn't true.'

Swanson ignored the accusation. 'Did you know his former cellmate, Garner?'

Minton looked up at the ceiling of the small interview room. 'Ah, Garner, the free bird. He spent a lot of time in library as well. Highly intelligent man, actually, although completely indoctrinated.'

'You didn't share his beliefs?' asked Keane.

'Unlike the majority of these fools, officer, I deserve to die. He had a point about the severity and the application of ZT. Though justice is blind, as they say.'

'Did you ever hear any talk?'

'Talk? It's all I ever hear. What is it that you're both investigating? I have already spoken to your colleagues. I must say your questions are a bit more direct.'

Swanson decided to humour the man. 'What did they question you about then?'

'They seemed to be preoccupied with my movements. They wanted to know if I had been anywhere near the area where Dempsey hung himself.'

'Why do you think that is?'

'I assumed they suspected me of having something to do with his death. It wouldn't have bothered me if they had.

What are they going to do to me? But then I started to think that maybe they wanted to make sure I hadn't seen something.'

Swanson nodded and encouraged the man to continue.

'That's all I can tell you. I love conspiracy theories as much as the next man.'

'We're investigating the disappearance of Judge Lloyd. Did you hear anything about that over here?'

'Dempsey told me about your questions. Obviously, many of the men here have been sentenced by that man. I'm sure none of them wish him well.'

'What about Jude Wesley?' asked Swanson.

'Similar character to Garner, except not as intelligent. That boy came from a privileged family and he fucked things up for himself. Garner was trash but made something of his life. Wesley blew it.'

'Why do you think you haven't been podded yet?' asked Keane.

'You guys crack me up,' said Minton, flailing his arms back in an exaggerated gesture causing twitchy responses from the two armguards at the door. 'I know my worth. They're going to pod me one day in spectacular style. But in the meantime, I have my uses. I know how this place works. I have information on every prisoner who has been here in the last fifteen years. They keep me alive for moments like this, so dumb officers can ask me dumb questions.' He leant forward, searching for a physical response from Keane.

'Thank you, Mr Minton,' said Swanson, standing.

'Yes, thank you Mr. Minton,' agreed Keane. 'Be seeing you shortly.'

Minton nodded, any trace of humour wiped from his face in an instant.

It took them over an hour to be released from the holding zone, enduring three car searches. 'That was unnecessary,' said Keane, as they drove back through the rush hour traffic.

'I imagine they're making some point,' said Swanson. 'Do you think it was suicide?'

'People manage to kill themselves before they get to the pods. Who wants to go through that indignation?'

'Maybe someone helped him,' said Swanson.

'You think Dempsey knew something?'

'I don't know.'

'Minton's a funny character,' said Keane. 'Acts like he has more power than the warden.'

'He certainly has more of a free reign, definitely more than Dempsey. My guess is he has a lot of pertinent information we haven't managed to get from him yet. What's clear though is we need to meet with SI. That politico Hanson, is getting in the way. It makes us look like fools. We're both working on the same case.'

'I was interviewed by them,' said Keane.

'SI?'

'I was offered the position, turned it down.'

'You humble us, Keane,' said Swanson. 'I'll bite. Why did you turn it down?'

'When it comes down to it, they're glorified bodyguards. I wanted to do some police work.'

'Make a difference and all that nonsense?'

'Something like that.'

A call came in from Jane Sutton. 'Even when you're not here, you're a pain,' said Swanson.

'Now, that's not nice, Inspector Swanson. I have some information that might interest you, and as you have been so forthcoming,' said the journalist, sarcastically, 'I thought it only fair to share.'

'I'm not interested.'

'It's regarding Jessica Wesley, and her son Jude.'

Swanson sighed. 'Meet us at the police station, one hour's time.'

Swanson called Flaherty as they drove to Sector One. 'Did you meet with Sharpe?' she asked.

'He's just left the station.'

'And?'

'Not much use, I'm afraid, ma'am. I tried subtlety, then I just came out with it,' said Flaherty.

'You asked if they were lovers?'

'Something along those lines, ma'am. Sharpe smiled but didn't say yes or no. He did say he hadn't seen Judge Lloyd in the last two years, started getting a bit agitated about his workload.'

'Okay, ask around a bit more. See if anyone else knows anything about their relationship.'

It took them a further two hours to reach the station. Sutton was waiting at the front of the building. She was wrapped in a long rain coat, her hair pinned neatly back in a bun. She was dressed for a special occasion, and for the first time Swanson could remember the journalist looked like she was wearing makeup. When Swanson introduced Keane, she understood why. 'Tell me what you've got, Jane. I've had a long day.'

'I want something in return.'

Swanson shook her head and began walking up the stairs. 'Your Jackson Sharpe exclusive has proved less than useful, Jane.'

'You'll find it useful, I promise,' said Sutton.

'Tell me what you want,' said Swanson.

'Can you tell me why you visited the holding zone for a second time today?'

'A suicide. We thought it might be relevant to Judge Lloyd's disappearance. I presume you've seen the press release about Garner? It's now official, you can print it.'

'Can you tell me who the suicide was?'

'Not at the moment.'

'What about the details of Garner's escape?'

'The full details are still classified, Jane,' said Swanson, realising she knew little about the actuality of the escape herself.

'You're not really giving me anything, are you?'

'Listen, if the information on Jessica Wesley is of significance, then I'll give you the exclusive on the Judge Lloyd's disappearance.'

'And the breakout?'

'If there's anything forthcoming, then yes.'

Sutton tilted her head. She smiled briefly at Keane and for second seemed to lose her train of thought. She shook her head as if shaking sense in to it. 'I have strong sources suggesting that Jessica Wesley will be running for the council in the next election.'

'Really?'

'I thought that would be interesting enough for you, Inspector. The suggestion is she will be representing Lenity.'

'Lenity is not political, at least not in that sense,' argued Swanson.

'No, but they have a great number of supporters. No other party can stand up to Zazen's council. You see for yourself the unrest, the growing amount of demonstrations.'

'That would be wonderful for you, I presume. Circulation would go through the roof.'

'City needs a change.'

'Okay, thank you, Jane. I'll keep you updated as promised. We might have to sit down one day soon, have a little chat in more detail.' Swanson was keen to know how Sutton was always one step ahead of her.

Sutton nodded. 'Inspector. Officer,' said the journalist, lingering a little bit longer than necessary.

'You do have a way, don't you, Keane,' said Swanson as they walked into the building.

'How's that?' asked Keane.

'In all my years of knowing that woman, I have never seen her wear makeup. She was plastered in the stuff.'

'It's a blessing and a curse,' said Keane smiling.

Chessington was in his office, slumped behind his desk, his face devoid of energy.

'Sit down, both of you. What news do you have for me?'

Keane ran over the details of Dempsey's suicide. Chessington looked unimpressed. He scratched at the random growth of ginger stubble on his chin. 'How is this related to Garner or Lloyd?'

'We think that Garner may have let slip some information to Dempsey.'

'So it wasn't suicide.'

'Impossible to prove otherwise, but the timing is suspiciously coincidental.'

'So whoever broke out Garner also had Dempsey murdered?'

'Working theory.'

'What else?'

'Sarah Natal,' said Swanson.

Chessington raised his head. 'What's Sarah Natal got to do with anything?'

'Sir, we've both questioned Natal,' said Swanson. 'Quite thoroughly,' she added, looking at Keane. 'Now the woman has disappeared.'

'Disappeared?' said Chessington.

'Not as in missing, sir. She's taken time off work and is not answering our calls.'

'Understandable.'

'Maybe so, but we think she's withholding something from us and she was effectively the last person to see Lloyd alive.'

'Look into it, for Christ's sake,' said Chessington. 'What's happening with Richard Beck?'

'I have no doubt he wrote the ransom note. But as I said on the phone, he hasn't got the wherewithal to kidnap the judge, and from what we can ascertain he doesn't have the contacts. No link to either Garner or Dempsey. We found a lot of painkillers at his house. Records from the hospital show he has terminal cancer.'

'Nothing to lose then?'

'Exactly, I would like to speak to Charles and Jessica Wesley again. And SI.'

'SI?'

'They're running their own investigation and it's getting in the way, sir.'

'They have to look after the council's security.'

'Sir, I'd like a meeting with Hanson.'

'They'll let you know when they need to talk to you. My hands are tied. And why the Wesleys? I've warned you already about them.'

'They have a son circling the tracks and Charles Wesley was the public defender for Garner and Dempsey.'

'It all sounds coincidental. If you're going to speak to them again then be careful.' Chessington looked down at the mound of paperwork, the signal for them to leave the office.

'What now?' asked Keane back in Swanson's office. 'Are we holding off on the Wesleys?'

Swanson was sure Chessington was holding something back. 'I want you to look into Lloyd's contemporaries some more,' she replied. 'Catch up with Flaherty and see if you can find anything more on Jackson Sharpe. Maybe quiz some of the other judges.'

'Livermore is his senior judge.'

'Start with her then.'

'And you?'

'I'm going to find out what SI are hiding,' said Swanson.

Chapter Twenty Nine

Three blocks from the central police station, Swanson was waiting for the overhead train which circulated around Sector One. Before boarding she called Judge Lloyd's assistant Sarah Natal once more. It went straight through to voicemail. 'Miss Natal, Inspector Swanson again. I would appreciate you calling me at your earliest convenience, it's a matter of great urgency.' The train appeared and Swanson boarded. It was mid-afternoon and a scatter of people boarded with her. Six minutes later she disembarked and walked a short distance to the town hall.

Unlike many public buildings, the town hall was a new build, less than fifteen years old. Flights of concrete steps led to the grandiose main entrance which was guarded on either side by two giant sculptures, one of a lion mid-roar, the other an artist's impression of the pods. The pod sculpture was an idealised snapshot of the city. The concrete pods meandered across a fantasy city like a fairground ride; only the prisoners conspicuously absent from the vision.

Security cameras were spread across the facade of the

building. Swanson looked around and saw them at the top of lampposts and the surrounding buildings. They were oversized, much larger than modern technology made necessary.

Swanson passed through the first security gate with a flash of her warrant card, but her progress through the warren of corridors and offices was soon halted. Two guards dressed in the camouflage SI uniform asked her for identification. They were polite but stern in refusing her access to the inner sanctum of the government building.

'I have an appointment with Trent Hanson,' she lied.

The more senior of the guards swiped his reader. 'Mr Hanson doesn't have any appointments today,' he said.

'Then tell him I'm waiting for him.'

'Take a seat,' he replied. It seemed that all she had done for the last few days was to wait for men.

The town hall housed the offices of the Mayor's council, including the Mayor, Andrew Zazen, as well as being home to SI. Swanson was running a risk being there.

The guard returned forty minutes later. 'Come with me,' he said.

Hanson's office was in the mezzanine. It had the highest security clearance and the guard accompanying her in the lift had to leave one floor before they reached the top. Two more guards greeted her on the top floor, both dressed in plain clothes.

Hanson sat behind a clear glass table which was big enough for a boardroom. He spread his arms wide and flashed a humourless smile. 'Inspector Swanson, sit. You should really have called ahead.'

'I need some answers,' said Swanson.

'I take it Chief Inspector Chessington knows you're here?'

'I'm sure he will.'

Hanson smirked. Swanson wondered how much media training he'd endured to perfect the gesture. 'Keep it short,' he said.

'I need some more information on the surveillance work you carried out on Garner, and details of this so-called splinter group.'

'I have provided you with all the information that is relevant. Anything else is classified. As you know, SI investigations have a higher security clearance.'

'I'm not interested in any terrorist investigations you're working on. My job is to find Judge Lloyd, and Oscar Garner. If Garner was a member of some form of splinter organisation then I need information on them. I can't see why I am being denied access.' Swanson linked her hands together to control her anger.

Hanson paused. He looked at the reader on his desk and swiped through some pages, studying the visuals as if they were unravelling the secrets of the universe. 'I can give you some details,' he said, finally. 'You may only share these with your superiors and your colleague, Sergeant Keane.' He placed a drive in his reader and downloaded the information. 'We're still running a number of surveillance operations. The data is highly sensitive, even considering the breakout at the prison. Garner was not considered enough of a security risk to be watched at the holding zone. We were as surprised as anyone when he escaped.'

'Am I under surveillance?' asked Swanson.

'That's a strange question, Inspector.'

'Your officers seem to be one step ahead of me. Why is that?'

'They are privy to the same information as you,' said Hanson, handing her the data stick.

Swanson softened her voice. 'Can you give me a list of those under surveillance?'

'Some are on there, but the information is readily available to your clearance. The names of those in the splinter group under investigation will remain classified.'

'Are they linked to any other organisations?'

'Such as?

'The church?'

Hanson laughed, the first genuine sound she had heard from the man. 'The church?'

'What are the links to Lenity then?'

'We suspect the splinter group has former links to Lenity, but don't think Lenity as an organisation is directly involved. I would steer your investigations away from them.' Hanson clicked his fingers together, and it was all Swanson could do not to rip them from his arms.

'But if they are a splinter group from Lenity, surely they still have links with Lenity?'

'You're overthinking it, Inspector. Furthermore, it's not your concern.'

She wanted to ask how she was supposed to find Garner with such lack of clarity, but stopped herself. 'Did you interrogate Garner once he was first arrested?' she asked instead.

'Yes.'

'What did he tell you?'

'Are you going to read the file, Inspector?'

Swanson glared at him.

'Unfortunately, as he was in the holding zone, our questioning techniques were, how shall we say, somewhat hindered. But as I stated, we didn't think he was of value to anyone. It's all assumptions, Inspector, and I'm sure you hate those.'

'Am I to deduce that he was potentially taken from prison to stop him talking?'

'Possibly,' said Hanson. 'Or they may have wanted to find out what he'd already said.'

'Why didn't they have him commit suicide?' asked Swanson.

Hanson shook his head. 'You're very cynical,' he said.

Swanson considered asking him about the Wesleys but decided to keep that line of investigation to herself for the time being. 'One last thing, sir: is there any pertinent information you hold on Lloyd which may be of use to me?' She wondered if he knew about Sharpe.

'Nothing, I'm afraid. I would be happy to share anything I have on Judge Lloyd. The man is clean. The only black mark against him was his bachelor status, but I guess we can't all be lucky in love.'

Swanson didn't need to view her own file to understand the implication. 'Thank you for your time,' she said.

As she went to leave, Hanson stopped her. 'A bit of career advice before you go, Inspector.'

‘Sir?’

‘I wouldn’t advise you going behind Chief Inspector Chessington or Superintendent Luce’s back again.’

‘Thank you, sir, noted.’

Outside, Swanson realised that Hanson had not once mentioned Richard Beck or the ransom note.

Chapter Thirty

'They've picked a fine day for it,' said Keane.

They stood in the Valley, where the prisoners entered the pods. It was the day of William Crampton's journey which would coincide with the Lenity demonstration. Crampton was the petty thief Swanson had helped prosecute on the day of Judge Lloyd's disappearance. With no objection on either side, Crampton had been fast-tracked to the pods.

The sky was a perfect blue, the air still and tranquil, save for the excited voices of the thousands who had gathered to see the guilty man suffer his death sentence. The Lenity demonstration had increased the turnout. Hundreds of their supporters walked the barren land, some waving placards calling for the abolishment of zero tolerance. The demonstrators intermingled with right-wing factions, and it was difficult to decipher who supported what. It should have stopped surprising her many years before, but Swanson still couldn't understand the voyeurs who attended the poddings to cheer on the ceremony. She could understand the friends and families of the victims wanting to be present. It was a natural human condition, if a distasteful one, to seek retribution. The pods had always been part of Swanson's life, and she noticed that the majority of people in the crowd were the same age or younger than her. She thought about her father, at his despair at the changes he had seen in his lifetime. Maybe that was what made her feel so uncomfortable. Her generation, and the younger ones below her, knew no other way. They were cheering for what they perceived as a valid response to a crime against society.

Crampton was led to a large circular area covered in small stones. A barrier surrounding the area was respectfully observed. Khaki-uniformed SI guards leant against the barrier, looking solemnly into the crowd. Police snipers looked down from discreet locations, prepared should anyone consider breaching the barrier.

In front of the circular area was the glass pod which was to be Crampton's final home. Dressed in his prison jumpsuit, Crampton's legs were chained with crude leather straps, making each step slow and painful. He had not shaved since his conviction and his beard was full.

Crampton stopped at the centre of the circle. Judge Livermore sat on a chair to the man's right, flanked on either side by armed guards. Livermore stood to face Crampton for the last time. She had presided over his conviction so it was her role to conclude Crampton's sentence. Keane had met with the senior judge the previous afternoon. He'd questioned her about Judge Lloyd, and Livermore had had only good things to say about the man. She'd said he was unassuming, quiet, gentle. Keane had questioned her about his relationship with Jackson Sharpe but Livermore had not been forthcoming.

Placing a black cap on her head, Livermore read out the sentence.

Swanson was tired of the ceremony, the crowd, the pomp as a guilty man was forced to suffer one last indignity before having to endure the last painful days of his life. She had attended too many of these occasions. She looked at those members of the crowd who were baying for blood, their faces contorted in rage. The young man who was about to be starved to death had stolen a bottle of vodka.

It was impossible not to think of her mother. How her father would have witnessed such a ceremony, would have endured the sight of his wife chained and led into the glass prison. They'd never talked about that period. The closest her father ever came to it was during moments of extreme intoxication, when his words were inaudible and laced with tears. Her father preferred to focus on the times before her mother's arrest. She'd had a keen intellect, an academic like her father. Her views had been more radical than his. She'd been a vehement opponent of ZT, and it was this which led to her eventual downfall.

A guard pushed Crampton to his knees, a false show of redemption. He was then dragged to the pod by two more of the khaki-uniformed guards. He didn't resist. All prisoners were heavily sedated before they began their journey. The guards threw him into the glass prison where he lay, foetal and unknowing.

The pod was hoisted into the air by the thick steel tracks.

The crowd grew strangely silent, as if the enormity of what was happening had just occurred to them. Even those full of anger were still. They looked in awe as the pod was dragged upwards through the pylons. It swayed in the air, the glare of sun reflecting off the glass and making it painful to look at.

'Look,' said Keane, pointing into the distance.

Swanson looked away from the sight of the man she'd help kill to look at the crowd. 'What am I looking at?'

'Over there, Charles Wesley,' said Keane.

Swanson squinted and made out the figure of Wesley in the distance, mingling with colleagues. Half the city had come out to see the podding of the junior gang member so his presence wasn't that surprising.

'I'm going to go and speak to him,' said Keane.

'Good luck,' said Swanson. 'It'll take you hours to get through that crowd.' Five miles along the track, Charles Wesley's son was nearing the end of his life. He was seven days in now and it was only a matter of time. Wesley must have considered this as he watched William Crampton dangling overhead.

Keane headed off towards Wesley. He showed his warrant card and people moved out of his way but still his journey was a slow one. The crowd dispersed as he divided them and then regrouped, reforming, becoming one as they restarted their cat-calls and vented their anger either at the prisoner or at the society that had placed him in the pods. Halfway across, Wesley spotted Keane coming towards him. He looked at Keane and then towards Swanson and started to edge away.

Swanson turned away, deciding for the time being she no longer cared about Charles Wesley. She had effectively put Crampton into the pod. After the initial arrest, she had questioned him and filled in the forms which had been given to the prosecution lawyers. She had attended the courtroom where the case against him had been proven, was present at the sentencing, the mitigation, and had said nothing to stop it happening. Of course, there was nothing she could have done but at times like this she suffered from her hypocrisy. She was no different to the man in the pod. Only this week, she'd stolen three items. Would no doubt steal again in the next few days.

A flash of violet-red caught her eye to the left, followed by a high-pitched whistle which tore through the air and silenced the crowd. A blast of air pushed at Swanson's eardrums and it took her a few seconds to understand what had happened.

From her vantage point, she concluded that the bomb had been detonated approximately a mile away. A safe distance from the crowd but close enough to the line of pods, and the surrounding buildings, to be a severe risk to the population.

Seconds later, panic spread throughout the massed group of people. Swanson moved into the stone circle, which was still heavily guarded. Outside the circle, the uniformed police tried to maintain control but were overwhelmed by the amount of people. The crowd moved through them as if they weren't there, scrambling over the exit barriers to any other place they could find.

Swanson closed her eyes as she saw a young woman fall to the ground. Helpless, she heard the sound of crunching bones as the crowd continued regardless, using the fallen body as a stepping stone to freedom. She looked in vain for Keane. He was nowhere in the melee of flesh. A five-year-old boy fell to the ground yards from her. Swanson was about to help when the boy was plucked from the floor by a young woman.

Another explosion stunned the hurrying crowd. The blast hit Swanson's back, a gust of warm air almost lifting her from her feet. A fireball tore through the sky close to where the Supreme Court and the Central Station were located. The crowd were now wild animals, darting in random directions, screaming to avoid the danger.

Above her, the pods continued to move serenely onwards. Crampton leant against a glass pane, watching the scenes in wonder.

An hour later, Swanson moved from the valley area with the armed guards. The crowd had thinned making it possible to assess the damage. Bodies were scattered across the expanse, although fewer than she had feared. She went to a man lying on his side, his right arm bent back at an improbable angle. He was conscious, his face contorted with pain. Close by, a woman was kneeling over the body of an eight-year-old girl. Swanson eased the crying woman to the side as she looked at the girl. She recoiled at the unnatural way the girl's head dangled to one side, her right eye socket pierced and bloody.

A subdued silence hung in the air, where only minutes before thousands had been assembled. Stragglers gawped in disbelief or scurried about trying to help the wounded. Five further explosions echoed around the city, spots of colour flashing from different areas. Sirens whined in all directions. Swanson's phone vibrated in her pocket. She looked at it as if it were some foreign body. A number of text messages were on the screen, from headquarters and Chessington, plus a missed call from Keane. She called her partner, grateful for his immediate answer.

'You ok?' she asked.

'I think so. You?'

'Yes. Bit shocked. We need to get back to the station.'

'I'll head there now,' said Keane. 'You sure you're ok?'

'I'm fine. See you there.'

Swanson waited for a skeleton rescue crew to arrive, one from each emergency service. She helped as best she could but there was not much else she could do. Back at the police station, she could try to piece together where the explosions had occurred and how serious they were. She called headquarters and Chessington's mobile but no one picked up.

When she reached the station she understood why.

Chapter Thirty One

Old Blue didn't know the precise location of the bomb. He was standing two streets down from the central police station which he'd been told would be a safe enough place. Wrapped in a rain jacket, which blended with the grey of his beard, he could sense people looking at him. The noise from the crowds in the Valley, gathered to watch Stephen Crampton's son's entry into the pods, filtered through to where he stood. The noise increased in intensity as the time approached. No doubt Crampton would be in the Valley, crying as they led his son away.

He tried not to dwell on it, his attention drawn to one of the pods which had drifted across its tracks and now hung directly in his line of sight a hundred and fifty metres away. It hovered above a glass fronted office building like a surrealist rooftop decoration. A woman was inside, naked. She waved to him as if he was some long lost friend. It wasn't a crime to engage with the prisoners but it was frowned upon. He nodded his head, the smallest of gestures. The woman pushed her ample body against the glass prison, her large breasts squashed against the pane, as if his acknowledgement had moved something within her. She was too far away for him to be sure but he thought she had smiled at him. Seconds later her capsule filled in an explosion of red smoke.

No one else had seemed to notice: life moved on as if nothing extraordinary had just happened. Sometime later the noise from the Valley area grew to a crescendo; a cacophony of protests and delight.

It was a matter of seconds from happening and he steadied himself. He didn't hear the first bomb – it was too far away, but its impact filtered through. The noise by the Valley subsided for an instant and then grew exponentially, the panic and fear swelling as the second, third and fourth bombs were detonated. The people close to him froze; dazed by the change in atmosphere they could sense but not understand. Seconds later, the bomb was detonated inside the police station. The pressure of the explosion surged through the air and he was glad he hadn't been situated any nearer to the building. A snapshot of silence preceded the explosion, replaced by a piercing, whistling sound which mutated into a deeper, thunderous noise. The sounds of crashing glass and screams of complaint were initially dampened by the explosion but soon he could hear the cries easily enough.

He walked back to the police station to assess the damage. People tumbled out of the building, tripping over themselves to get to safety. The building remained intact, though the large glass windows had been completely destroyed. Tiny fragments of glass were scattered all around the pavement in front of the building whilst thick, black smoke coursed through the holes in the structure. The occupants found their way out, some slicing themselves open on loose fragments of the sharp material. The fire service arrived within minutes and he made himself scarce. Despite the supposed intentions of Chapter 12, the sub-section of Lenity, there seemed to have been fatalities at the police station. It had been naïve of them to think otherwise. He walked to his agreed meeting place. Sarah Natal was waiting for him, perched on a decrepit-looking moped. The vehicle had been purchased for the event, it being the quickest way to escape the centre of the city. He let Sarah drive, clasping his hands to the side of the bike, not wanting to touch her.

The following day, they drove the moped to her flat in Sector Two. The people carrier was parked in the car park. It had become too dangerous for her to return to the flat but she had insisted on taking her belongings with her.

'Thirty minutes,' he said, as he got off the moped.

He stood staring out of the flat window as Sarah packed. The interfering neighbour next door had already bombarded them with a number of awkward questions and he was keen to get out of the place. He was sure the police would have the flat under surveillance by now.

Sarah had packed two oversized suitcases and a large holdall big enough to have been used in a bank robbery. 'Jesus,' he whispered, under his breath.

Sarah's neighbour stopped them again. 'You both look so

tired,' she said. 'Why don't you come in for a quick cup of tea before you have to leave for wherever it is you're going?' she said, darting looks at him.

Sarah thanked the woman politely and he did his best to smile. They packed the goods into the people carrier and returned to their house, Sarah driving the scooter and Old Blue the car. The streets were awash with people. The bombs had been placed strategically throughout the central part of the city to create as much of a disturbance as possible. The citizens stood around in the street, unsure how to proceed. From that point of view the bombs had been a success, but he wondered at what cost.

It took them fifty minutes to reach Sector Thirty-Two. News of the bombings had already spread to the area. He noted the looks of concern on the citizens as he drove through the side streets back to the house. It was as if they were waiting for the bombs to reach them.

The smell had intensified. He had left some of the windows open to try and rid the house of the foul, stale air but the plan had backfired somewhat. The fumes from the cellar had leaked to the outside and he feared that it was only a matter of time before someone complained about the stench emanating from the house. Sarah had bought a box full of various air-fresheners at the supermarket and they walked through the house, filling the house with the artificial fragrances. He carried one can of pinewood and one can of lavender. He sprayed the two cans at once, the cold liquid from the spray trickling down his thick fingers, burning mildly into his skin.

'You said after Little Joe's that I could see him,' said Sarah. They were at the front of the house, savouring the relative freshness of the air, gazing at the mud banks of the lake which stretched before them.

'You've smelt it in there, Sarah. Do you really want to go into the cellar?'

'I'm the same as you,' she said. 'I know this is your plan but I need to be a part of it. They've hurt me too.'

She wasn't the same as him. They weren't even closely comparable. Yet once the cloud of air freshener had seeped out of the house he reluctantly led her into the cellar. They both wore filtered smoke masks which he'd purchased from a local bicycle shop, secured in place with thick bandanas, but the protection proved to be close to useless. With the addition of the two new men, the smell from the cellar had intensified in its pungency. It had become an almost visible problem, lingering within the close confines of the room.

Both Thurrock and Wilson, the two factory workers, looked asleep. They had vomited against their gags, drips of putrid matter dripping down their necks onto their clothes. Wilson's wild curly hair was matted with the stuff, which was tinged with blood. Old Blue ripped the fabric from their mouths, worrying that they had choked. He smacked both of them hard on the cheeks and they came to. The taller one, Thurrock, tried to return to sleep but he slapped him again, the sound of flesh on flesh echoing in the cellar. Sarah sat transfixed, staring at Judge Lloyd who was lying on the other side of the prison to Thurrock and Wilson. It looked as if he had aged twenty years in the last few days. His hair was falling out and his body was wasting away. He gazed back at Sarah, but didn't recognise her.

'It's me, sir,' said Sarah. 'Sarah Natal, your assistant.'

Lloyd moved towards the glass barrier between him and Sarah. Old Blue watched as the old man lifted his hand.

'I don't understand,' said Lloyd, his voice a faint echo of its former self.

Sarah stared at the man, a look on her face Old Blue had never seen before, so full of hatred that he had to look away. 'In all this time, you never once remembered who I really am,' she said to Lloyd.

'What do you mean, Sarah?' Lloyd's voice was little more than a whisper.

'Simon Akers,' said Sarah.

Lloyd furrowed his brow. 'Akers?'

'Must we do this now?' said Old Blue.

'Yes.' Sarah glared at him. 'I want to hear it from him.'

'I remember Mr Akers,' said Lloyd.

'You remember killing him?'

'What's this about, Sarah? Akers murdered his wife.'

Sarah shook her head. 'He didn't kill his wife. He loved me.'

Confusion spread across Lloyd's face. 'You were Akers' lover? I don't remember your name in the evidence.'

'I changed my name, you old fool,' said Sarah, spitting against the glass.

'Sarah, I was only doing my job…'

'Enough,' said Old Blue. He untied Thurrock and Wilson at gunpoint. The shackles had dug deep into their skin and both wore red rings on their wrists. Sarah continued staring at Lloyd. Old Blue pulled down the divider separating the two men and the judge.

'Meet your new friends,' he told Lloyd, who still looked stunned by Sarah's revelation. 'I'm sure you have some things to discuss.' He left three dinner trays for the men and dragged Sarah away. He slammed the cellar door shut, pulled over the rug, and tried to pretend nothing existed beneath it.

Chapter Thirty Two

The station had been the main target. The front windows were destroyed. Clouds of smoke billowed through the gaps where the panes of glass had once been. The building had been evacuated. A number of Swanson's colleagues meandered aimlessly outside, paramedics treating the static. Flaherty, the newbie constable, sat on the pavement, wrapped in a silver-foil blanket. He shivered and rocked himself in a slow rhythm, his eyes staring into the distance.

One of the surrounding buildings was still on fire and the emergency services were working hard to make the area safe. Chessington sat in the back of one of the ambulances, his face and clothes covered in blood. A paramedic was treating a thick gash to his right eye.

'No need to fuss, Swanson,' he said, as she moved towards him. 'It's just a flesh wound. I was lucky.' She had seen three bodies taken from the station already.

'The bomb was detonated on the seventh floor. A small explosion, probably a homemade nail bomb, but those in the immediate vicinity didn't stand a chance,' said Chessington.

'Fortunately the fire service were quick to the scene. They seem to have stopped it spreading. We still have detainees in the holding cells, including Beck.'

Swanson grimaced. 'Are we not evacuating them?' she asked. The smoke had crept into her lungs, deepening the gruffness of her voice.

'Not yet. We have a small crew down there. They're sealed off from the rest of the building so they face no immediate danger. We'll go down there when we get the all-clear.'

The acrid smoke clung to her clothes. It invaded her pores, seeping further into her body. The heat was claustrophobic. It emanated from the buildings, leaving a dense pressure building in her ears. Chessington stood up once the paramedic had finished. Long, crude stitches sealed the cut on his head.

'We had a phone call minutes before the first bomb went off,' he told her. 'It was declared a hoax. As you know, we get them all the time, especially when someone is about to enter the pods.'

'Has anyone taken responsibility?' asked Swanson.

'Not yet, but you don't do something like this without wanting to let people know why.'

Swanson thought about Charles Wesley. How he had turned and run once Keane had spotted him in the crowd. She struggled to believe it was a new Lenity tactic. They'd never so much as shouted in anger since their formation. But if Wesley's son was aggressive enough to carry explosives, why not his father?

Keane arrived, his torn shirt exposing the flesh of his arm. He shook his head on seeing Swanson. His eyes returned to the ground as he moved towards her as if wanting an embrace. 'I can't believe what I've seen,' he said.

'You'll have time enough to think about that later,' said Chessington. 'Now we've got jobs to do.'

One of the fire officers walked over and introduced himself as Chief Rosendale. He removed his yellow protective helmet to reveal a smooth black skull which glistened with sweat. 'It's all clear but I can only allow key personnel back into the building. There's still a lot of smoke and the fifth floor is as far up as you can go until we've stabilised it. That could take a few days. I need the station completely clear in the next two hours. We're going back through the whole building to secure the structure.'

'Right,' said Chessington, 'you two go into the cells and start arranging the evacuation. I'll call Sector Two to see if they have space. For the time being, Beck's our priority. Get him out first. They may be coming for him, for all we know.'

The smoke was denser inside. Despite her mask, Swanson's eyes streamed with tears within seconds. She struggled to see her way forward as she followed Keane down to the holding cell. A crew of three were managing the situation. Noise echoed from the stone walls. Prisoners screamed for freedom, demanding calls to their solicitors, and tried to make bargains with their captors. Swanson spoke to Sergeant Yates who was in charge of the area. 'We need to evacuate,' she instructed him. 'Prepare the inmates and your officers. Once we have the clearance from Sector Two we're going to take the prisoners up one by one, starting with Richard Beck.'

Yates nodded and shouted orders to his colleagues.

Richard Beck sat on the bed in his small holding cell. He looked smaller than she'd remembered. 'Everything okay?' she asked.

He looked up at her, his face drained of colour. 'What's happening?' he asked.

'Nothing to worry about now, we'll be taking you out of here soon.' She coughed, the smoke stinging her eyes and burning her throat as she tried to expel it from her body.

Keane patted her on the back. 'Go up and get some air,' he said.

'I'm fine.'

Chessington joined them, stumbling into the holding area. 'We have a van upstairs waiting. We're going to have to go to Sector Four. Two is overrun and three isn't answering. Start with Beck.'

'Kneel, and interlock your hands behind your back,' Swanson said to Beck.

Yates opened the door and edged towards the prisoner, cuffing him in a fast, sharp movement and hauling him to his feet. Keane and Swanson guided Beck up the stairs. They shone their torches into the gloom of the stairwell revealing a swathe of grey smoke. Taking small steps, they inched closer to the surface. It was slow and laborious but their efforts were rewarded when they reached ground level. Jets of warm air billowed in from the broken windows. Swanson began coughing again but was grateful to be able to breathe the semi-fresh air. Keane guided Beck into the waiting police van where he instructed one of the junior officers to watch him.

Soon the van was full with prisoners. The fire officers began boarding up the broken windows and Rosendale locked the two front doors. 'No one is to go back in there without my permission,' he said.

Swanson followed the police van as it drove to the Sector Four station, Keane in the passenger seat. The city's streets were full of people, many of whom shared the same dazed look as her partner. 'Are you going to tell me what happened?' she asked Keane.

'Isn't that self-evident?' Keane replied.

'With Wesley?'

'I still had him in my line of sight when the first bomb went off. Unlike everyone else he didn't seem to react. He hesitated after the explosion before moving off. I tried to follow him but there were too many people in the way. I stopped following him to help out.'

Swanson decided not to ask for any more details yet. It was clear from his face that whatever he'd seen had shaken him.

Progress through the city was slow. Cars had been abandoned in the roads and large snaking traffic jams had formed. Reports suggested that all the explosions had been similar in scale to the one at the central police station. The bombs had been detonated in five of the eight central sectors of the city but the aftermath had spread everywhere. They drove past pockets of activity where buildings were on fire and shop fronts had been smashed. Opportunists had used the distraction of the bombs to begin looting despite the consequences should they get caught.

The pods continued their journeys regardless. None of the explosions had affected the tracks. A specialised patrol team was dispatched along the perimeter and no reports of any damage had been submitted. Swanson wondered if the circling prisoners would find some hope in the scenes playing out beneath them.

'You think Charles Wesley has something to do with this?' asked Swanson.

'The bombings? God only knows. He didn't seem surprised. One thing for certain, Beck's not involved.'

'What makes you say that?' asked Swanson.

'You've met him. That man can barely breathe unsupervised, let alone stage something as intricate as setting off numerous explosions at practically the same time throughout the city. Also,' he added as an after-thought, 'he's been in prison for the last couple of days.'

'We need to interrogate him as soon as possible. I'm sure someone has put him up to writing the ransom note.'

'Why?'

'That's what we need to find out. He's dying anyway. Maybe someone offered him some money to write it.'

'Some form of distraction?'

'Possibly. We need to speak to the Wesleys again, and find Sarah Natal.'

'Natal?'

'It's not a coincidence, is it, Keane? Judge Lloyd goes missing, Natal goes missing, Garner escapes, Dempsey dies, then the bombs go off.'

'You can't think she's responsible?'

'No. You need to listen a bit more carefully. I think those bombs may have knocked out what remaining sense you have. I never said she is responsible, only that we need to talk to her.'

'So you did,' said Keane, flashing the briefest of smiles for the first time since the explosions.

The Sector Four station was a smaller version of the central office. Swanson supervised Beck's transportation from the van to his new holding cell, giving strict instructions to the new duty sergeant that Beck was not to share with anyone else. The officer, Sergeant Irvine, looked at her as if he doubted her authority, but didn't go so far as to question her.

Chessington ordered her and Keane to one of the meeting rooms where Chief Superintendent Philip Luce was waiting. Luce didn't speak as they entered. Swanson tried her best not to think of the embarrassing incident with her father at the legal ball.

'Okay everybody, sit,' said Luce. 'Give me your updates,' he ordered.

Chessington ran through the procedures that had been put in place. 'Central office, Sector Two, and Sector Five stations are closed for the time being. Sector Three is up and running as are Four, Six and Seven. It's likely that the central office will be shut for two months.'

'What about the bomb threat phone call?' asked Luce.

'We're working through the recording now,' said Chessington. 'No one has come forward yet.'

Luce placed the palms of his hands onto the desk table. His fingernails were chipped and uneven. He stared at Swanson.

'Where are we on the Judge Lloyd and Oscar Garner cases?'

'We still have Richard Beck in custody, as I am sure you're aware. We're working on a number of leads including Lloyd's secretary, Sarah Natal.'

Luce raised his eyebrows at this revelation and ran his hand through his still-immaculate-looking grey hair. 'Why would that be?'

'She has been absent from work for the last three days,' said Swanson. 'She hasn't answered any of our calls since we spoke to her about Judge Lloyd.'

'Please tell me this is not all we've got to go on at the moment,' said Luce.

Swanson decided not to inform him of her meeting with Abigail and the mysterious large man she'd seen in Natal's company.

'We're also speaking to Mr and Mrs Wesley,' said Keane.

Luce continued looking at Swanson as if Keane wasn't there.

'Their son was arrested for weapons possession and is currently circling the pods,' said Keane, defending himself.

'How far into his journey is he?' interrupted Luce.

'Nearing his personal end, I would suggest,' said Keane. 'Charles Wesley is a member of Lenity and his wife works for Kinsley Jacobs, the law firm.'

'The plot thickens,' said Luce. 'I'm very aware of Mr and Mrs Wesley. They both have some very powerful allies, especially Mrs Wesley, so you need to be very careful when talking to them.'

Chessington, who had remained quiet, broke his silence.

'We know that Lenity have never previously gone in for any violent intervention but as their son was caught carrying explosives we thought it was a good line to investigate.'

Luce broke his glance away from Swanson and turned towards Chessington. 'Yes, perhaps,' he agreed. 'But these are hardly results, are they? We have a city in chaos. We need a show of force. Officers in the street. The rule of law is close to disappearing and no one has any idea who's responsible. The first thing we have to do is find out whether there is a link between the disappearance of Judge Lloyd and Oscar Garner and these bombings.'

'Of course they're linked,' said Keane.

'How can you be so sure?' said Luce.

'It's obvious.'

'It looks obvious, I agree, but that doesn't help us in any way. Here's what I propose. We're going to go through each of Judge Lloyd's last two hundred cases. I want to see who has been prosecuted, who is in the pods, who was in the pods, who is about to go into the pods. I want you to speak to their families, their friends, their enemies. I want to find out whether Lloyd's disappearance is just a ruse, whether Beck's threat is viable or just fantasy. Arrest anyone who mentions Garner. Search for connections with Lenity, or more importantly, links to splinter groups.'

Chessington shook his head. 'We don't have the resources for that sort of search,' he said. 'You may not have noticed but our numbers are depleted at the moment.'

Luce stood up. 'SI will work with you. Make it happen,' he said, leaving.

Swanson wished she'd asked him about Hanson and SI's investigations.

'I wish you hadn't mentioned Natal,' said Chessington. 'Luce doesn't believe in things like hunches anymore. We need to get this search organised. I'm going to head it up and I want you two to continue work on Beck, the Wesleys and, if you wish, Natal. Though you may also have to attend the searches.'

'What about this splinter group?'

'Christ, Swanson. I don't know anything about such a group apart from what little Luce has shared with me. That's over to SI.'

Swanson drove Keane home. He told her to pull over next to a small, newly built terraced house. 'Come in with me,' he suggested. He leant towards her, close enough for her to smell the sweat on his neck.

'I think you should spend some time with your wife, Keane,' said Swanson. 'She must be worried about you.'

Keane smiled, a sheepish expression which looked to Swanson both embarrassed and sorrowful.

'I don't have a wife,' he said.

Chapter Thirty Three

The city was awash with panicked citizens. They ran aimlessly, trying to avoid further explosions. McClusky had been close to one of the explosions. The pressure of the detonation had surged through the air and he was glad he hadn't been situated any nearer to the centre of the blast.

As he headed home, he recalled the snapshot of silence which preceded the explosion, almost instantly replaced by a piercing whistle which mutated into deeper thunder. The bomb had exploded within the central police station. McClusky remembered his time within those same walls: seventy-two hours of questioning, punctured by brief snippets of sleep and the odd meal.

McClusky had watched the occupants tumble out of the building, tripping over each other to get to safety. He'd laughed internally, savouring their panic as if it was his own. He'd only retreated when the fire service arrived.

As he walked through the crowds, he sensed once again that he was being followed. It had become a nagging constant, a mental addition he carried with him, not knowing if what he felt was real. He passed Little Joe's. A group of revellers were in the streets, still swilling from glass tumblers. The news of the bombings had filtered through to them but the alcohol dulled their senses so, if anything, they looked excited by the commotion travelling past them.

McClusky loitered on the fringes of the groups, both disgusted and envious of their condition. A sullen man dressed in a plain T-shirt spoke to him as if he were normal. 'You'd think, of all places, you'd be safe here in the city,' said the man, as if stumbling upon a piece of newfound wisdom. 'Here, let me buy you a drink, buddy.'

McClusky scratched a thin patch of hair behind his temple, bursting a blister. As warm liquid oozed down his ear, he considered if one drink would really hurt. He nodded to the man, who promptly retreated to the bar.

Anticipation swelled within him as he fantasized about the courage the drink would give him. Maybe after the drink he could find Tom Miller. Now would be the perfect time, with the city in chaos; he could wreak his revenge, knowing how hard it would be to be detected.

He was gone by the time the man returned.

Retreating from Little Joe's, lest his newfound friend spot him, McClusky dragged his arm against the coarse brickwork of a nearby office building, shivering in delight as the jagged edges tore the skin from his meagre flesh. A trickle of blood dripped down his fingers and left a trail on the concrete pathway beneath his feet. The heat of the sun burnt the back of his neck and he took off his hat to allow the rays to penetrate the blisters on his scalp. He sensed his own anger, a pot of bubbling rage within his stomach which he couldn't access, and cursed himself for not accepting the offered drink from the stranger.

'Is that you?' said a voice in the distance.

The piercing female voice was slurred, panicked. He was close to his flat now and chose to ignore the question, which he presumed wasn't for him; but the sound came nearer.

'It is you, isn't it?' she said, this time less panicked, more accusatory.

By now, his arm was soaked with blood and he smeared it across his face and onto the boils on his scalp.

'Stop! You owe me some money,' said the woman.

McClusky, remembering the voice, stopped and turned. 'I don't owe you anything,' he said.

'You just left me,' said the prostitute he'd encountered the other evening.

'I think you did quite well out of our little transaction,' said McClusky. 'You were paid for nothing.'

'I was only half-paid,' said the woman, 'and I could've found another client while you were busy getting scared.'

McClusky pictured himself striking the woman with the back of his hand. No one would notice or even care.

'Christ, what have you done to yourself?' said the woman, noticing the blood smeared across his face and arms. 'Did you get caught by the bombs?'

McClusky was amazed by the change in the woman. She'd gone from accusing zealot to concerned citizen in a matter of seconds. 'Are you following me?' he asked.

The antipathy returned. 'Why the hell would I be

following you? You're a freak. I work this area. If anything, you're following me.'

He retreated.

Back in his flat, he bathed his wounds in a cold bath. A tear in his flesh caused his arm to throb and fresh scabs wept on his scalp. In the living room, he drank coffee and smoked cigarettes. As the pain from his altercation with the wall subsided, he stubbed out one of the burning filters onto the fresh scar of his arm, savouring the pain and fading out the prostitute's words.

Outside his window, the man waited.

Chapter Thirty Four

Swanson had asked him why he still wore his wedding ring which she now regretted. In retrospect it sounded insensitive and rather obvious. His wife had died two years ago. Swanson wished she'd checked up on his background more when Chessington had put them together. How hard would it have been to speak to his former colleagues?

Despite her humiliation, he'd still insisted she accompany him inside. She'd come close to accepting before telling him she had to get back to her father.

Her hands were still shaking on the steering wheel. She had already called to check that her father was okay. He'd watched the events unfold from their flat, glass in hand, and told her not to rush home on his account. It took another hour to reach her flat. Breakdown trucks had started clearing the streets of the abandoned vehicles but the city was still a mess. The journey gave her time to think and as time progressed she became more and more convinced she'd made the right decision about Keane. It was an added complication she didn't need at the moment.

Her father gave her a fierce hug as she walked through the door. He reeked of alcohol, his cheeks cherry red. 'You're okay?' he asked.

'Yes, I'm fine.' They talked briefly about the bombings. 'What are your thoughts, Professor?'

He took another sip from his large wine glass which was now filled with an amber liqueur. 'It's very interesting that no one has come forward. You would have thought someone would be desperate to claim this as some sort of victory. In a perverse way, you have to give them credit. How many bombs were there? Five? Setting off one bomb in this city must be incredibly difficult. Setting off five all at the same time, in different locations, that takes some organising.'

'I guess it does,' said Swanson. 'Do you think Lenity could have had something to do with it?'

'I doubt it. Officially at least. They're cleaner than clean, but there are always hardliners in any organisation. Some splinter group, perhaps? Do you have intelligence on their members?'

'We have a library full of files,' said Swanson.

'I expect mine is the biggest file of all,' said her father.

'We have a wing devoted to you.'

'Good,' he said, with a crooked smile.

'I need to get to bed, Dad,' she said, kissing him on the cheek.

'I think it's all changing, Kate.'

'For the better?'

He kissed her goodnight once more. 'Let's hope so.'

She showered before going to bed, remaining under the

steaming hot water for twenty minutes, scrubbing the smoke from her skin. In her bedroom she took out the box from under her bed and removed one of the books she had taken from Sarah Natal's neighbour, Abigail. She flicked through the pages looking at the photos.

Each entry held a terrifying snapshot. It was hard not to empathise with the imprisoned souls. Swanson still felt overwhelmed at how Abigail had captured the loneliness and despair in her photographs.

The most horrifying were the pictures where the prisoners were already dead. In a way, it was surprising that more of them hadn't succumbed to the suicide button. They clung grimly to life when clearly there was no future for them. Swanson closed the book and tried to fall asleep. She thought about what her father had said to her, that the city was changing. She dwelled on Keane's persistence and the revelation that his wife had been dead for the last two years and it was a long time before sleep finally took her. What rest she had was fitful and by five the following morning she was ready to return to work.

After a rushed breakfast of scrambled eggs and toast, she drove to the pods. All leave had been cancelled and there was a large police presence throughout the city. Swanson placed the blue lights on the roof of her car to save being pulled over at the checkpoints. Keane was waiting for her at their agreed rendezvous. He smiled on seeing her as if their experience with the bombing had brought them closer.

They were in Sector Sixteen, where Jude Wesley's pod currently resided. It made its slow way along the tracks close to the riverside. Wesley was lying on the floor of his prison, his face squashed against the glass floor. 'Is he alive?' asked Swanson.

'He hasn't pressed the button,' said Keane, 'but I haven't seen him move.'

'It's early for him to die from any other cause,' she suggested.

'It happens, though. Sometimes their bodies just give up.'

They walked through the shadow of the pod. 'We could look closer,' said Keane.

'How's that?' asked Swanson.

'We have the power to stop the pods if we want, don't we?'

'I'm sure that would go down well. Anyway, we would need to get a warrant and the judges would be reluctant. Let's give him a few more hours and see if he stirs.'

They had lunch in a small cafe by the river, their eyes rarely moving from the glass prison. The latest report Swanson had received from Chessington suggested that there had been nine fatalities, six of which had been at the police station. The other four bombs had been detonated in under-populated areas, confirming that the main target was the police station.

'I forgot to tell you, I found some more information on Jackson Sharpe,' said Keane, sipping an iced tea. 'Apparently he and the judge were in some form of on-off relationship at university.'

'That was forty years ago. And since?'

'A long romance, Swanson. They never shared a place. It seemed to be an official, unofficial thing. I managed to speak to Sharpe. Almost broke down crying when I mentioned Lloyd. He said to me that Lloyd should never have become a judge. Not in this society anyway,' said Keane.

'When did he last speak to Lloyd?'

'He is sticking with the story he told Flaherty. Not for two years. Apparently they had an argument, but he was not forthcoming over the details.'

They sat in silence for a time until Keane blurted out: 'It wouldn't surprise me if someone has claimed responsibility for the bombings.'

'What do you mean?'

'The council and SI are probably withholding the information.'

It had crossed Swanson's mind. 'You really think they'd withhold something like that from us?'

'I think they would withhold it from you and me, yes. They may well have told Luce or someone higher up.'

'We can't investigate without that information,' she said.

'We can investigate, but not very effectively.'

Swanson struggled with her lunch, a green-pea risotto, but Keane seemed to have recovered from the shock of the previous day and devoured his triple-decker club sandwich. They avoided discussing Keane's wife, as Jude Wesley's pod drifted farther and farther away from their line of view. Swanson paid for the lunch and was about to follow Wesley's pod when she received a phone call.

'Inspector Swanson?' came the nervous voice on the other end of the line.

'Speaking.'

'Inspector Swanson, this is Abigail. Do you remember me? I'm Miss Natal's neighbour.'

'Yes, Abigail, of course I remember you. How are you? How can I help?'

'Inspector Swanson, you told me to call when Miss Natal next came back to her flat.'

'Is she there now?' asked Swanson.

'Yes, she arrived about ten minutes ago.'

'Is she alone?'

'No, she is with that man I mentioned. The large one with the beard.'

'Your girlfriend's back,' said Swanson.

'Which one?' replied Keane.

Abigail was waiting for them at Natal's block of flats. Waving from her window, she shouted something inaudible to them.

'She's gone, I'm afraid,' said Abigail, when they reached the flat. The frail woman was shaking, evidently excited by the turn of events. 'I tried my best to stop them. I offered them both a cup of tea but they were in a rush.'

'Did they take anything with them?' asked Swanson.

'Yes, it was as if they were going on holiday. They had two large suitcases and the man was carrying a couple of rucksacks.'

'Contact Chessington about getting a search warrant,' said Swanson to Keane.

They moved into Abigail's apartment. The telescope still

pointed out towards the pods. 'You didn't by any chance…'

'Yes,' Abigail beamed. 'I managed to photograph both of them.'

The large man Abigail had described was in his fifties. Swanson had never seen him before. From the pictures, she estimated he was somewhere between six foot two and six foot four, broad and solid. He indeed had a silver beard as Abigail had described. She had taken several photos of the pair. In none of the pictures were the pair touching. Natal was carrying one of the suitcases. The man was pulling the larger suitcase and carrying three rucksacks, one draped over his shoulder, two in his right hand. Abigail had taken a picture of them placing the luggage into a people carrier. The number plate was clear from the picture and Keane called it in.

'Have I been useful?' asked Abigail.

'You've been incredible,' said Swanson, shaking hands with the old woman. She downloaded the photos onto her phone.

'We'll keep you informed but please let us know if Ms Natal returns or if her friend does,' said Keane.

'I don't think either of them will be coming back anytime soon,' said Abigail.

'Did you hear any of their conversation?' asked Keane.

'Not much. They were preoccupied with getting the luggage out of the house.'

'Any talk of destination? Any place they were planning to stay?' asked Keane.

'No. The man seemed a bit disgruntled. When I offered them tea he ignored me.'

‘What did Ms Natal do?’ asked Swanson.

‘She was quite polite. She said they were in a rush but thanked me for the offer. I asked her when she would be back next because I hadn’t seen her for such a long time.’

‘What did she say to that?’ asked Swanson.

‘She smiled and said not to worry.’

They checked the photo of the man back at Sector Four and circulated the image to the other stations. They couldn’t find any records, and the facial recognition software didn’t produce any results. Swanson phoned Natal’s office again. The temporary secretary informed her that Natal was now on annual leave and wouldn’t be back for two weeks. They showed the pictures to Chessington who was not impressed.

‘All this says to me is that Judge Lloyd’s assistant has some sort of penchant for older, heavy-set men.’

Keane smirked.

‘Don’t go there,’ suggested Chessington. ‘There’s absolutely nothing to go on here.’

‘She’s on annual leave now,’ said Swanson. ‘She hadn’t mentioned this to us before.’

‘So what?’ asked Chessington. ‘We didn’t put any restrictions on her movement. It’s quite conceivable that she’s just upset regarding Lloyd’s disappearance. You’ll need to come up with a bit more if you want me to sign off on a warrant to search her flat.’

Swanson was about to object, when a siren began wailing somewhere beneath them.

Chapter Thirty Five

'What the hell is that?' asked Chessington, getting to his feet. The siren was a continuous high-pitched tone, different to the fire alarm they were used to at the central station. They rushed out of Chessington's office only to find the Sector Four officers still working at their desks as if oblivious to the wailing.

They were told by one of the secretarial staff that the sound came from the holding cells. 'It always goes off when there's a problem, however minor. Rarely anything serious.'

'"Rarely" does not fill me with confidence,' said Chessington.

Keane had already radioed down. 'No answer,' he said.

Swanson took the lift with Chessington whilst Keane ran down the stairs. 'This place is a shambles,' said Chessington. He sounded nervous, his normal stubborn authority somehow diminished in the new location.

The door to the holding cells was locked, and a security guard dressed in a drab uniform made them show their identification before allowing them to enter. 'What's happened?' demanded Chessington.

The siren stopped. The building sounded too quiet. 'Suicide attempt,' said the guard.

Chessington shook his head and ran towards to the cell. 'Do you know which one?' asked Swanson.

'One of the prisoners from central office, I think. Not sure of the name,' replied the guard.

Swanson followed Chessington to the doorway of cell four where a man's body lay on the stone floor. From his left arm ran a sea of dark-red blood, patches of which had splattered the white walls of the cell. The station's medical team were working on him but it looked as if they were too late.

Richard Beck's blank face drooped limp on the ground, his eyes lifeless. To his right was a razor blade doused in blood.

Chessington turned white. 'I need an explanation,' he said, the words coming out as a whimper rather than a command. The medical staff continued working, ignoring his request. Their silence returned the colour to his face, his cheeks reddening in an instant. He grabbed the nearest police officer, pulled him out of the cell and up against one of the stone walls in the corridor. 'What the hell has happened?' he growled.

'He had a razor blade,' said the officer, who dwarfed Chessington in size.

'What the hell are you talking about? He was fully checked before we came here.'

'It's possible his cellmate let him have it,' said the officer. 'Though obviously we checked him too.'

'His *cellmate*?' said Chessington, incandescent with rage. 'His fucking cellmate? Who's in charge here?'

'Sergeant Thompson.'

'Get him now.'

Thompson was a portly man similar in shape and complexion to Chessington – only his mop of brown hair, styled sometime in the last twenty years, differentiated the pair. He ambled towards Chessington and stared directly into his eyes. 'Sir?' he asked.

'Please tell me that Beck didn't have a cellmate.' The words were laced with threat.

'What were we supposed to do, sir? We've taken all your prisoners and all those for Sector Two.'

'You were under strict instructions.'

'Sir, there was nothing I could do about it.'

Chessington breathed in deeply. 'I'm afraid that decision may have just cost you your job. You're suspended. Report to your senior officer. You two, sort this,' he instructed Swanson and Keane, before walking away, no doubt to inform Luce that Beck was dead.

'Asshole,' said Thompson.

'Listen, mate, you're the one who's messed up,' said Keane. 'You realise he was the chief suspect in Judge Lloyd's disappearance?'

'What was I supposed to do?'

'Listen to your orders,' said Swanson.

They returned to the cell. Beck's body was still dripping blood. The incision on his wrist was deep and jagged as if he'd had trouble with the first, lethal incision.

'Where is his cellmate?' Swanson asked Thompson.

The sergeant looked as shell-shocked as Chessington had moments earlier. 'He was rooming with Ian Muir. We've moved him next door.'

'How long had they been sharing?'

'Nine hours.'

'Why is Muir here?'

'Drunk driving.'

'Are you sure?' asked Keane.

'Course I'm bloody sure,' said Thompson.

'We need his file now,' said Swanson.

'Can we take him away?' asked one of the paramedics.

'No, you can't take him away,' said Swanson. 'Have I entered amateur hour here? This is a crime scene. Get forensics. Let's make sure it was a suicide.'

Muir was alone in the cell next door. 'Funny how he gets a cell to himself,' Keane said to Thompson who flashed him a sarcastic grin. Muir sat in one corner of the cell, his head between his legs. He looked up as they entered. A line of dried vomit made its way from his chin onto his white t-shirt.

'What happened?' said Swanson.

Muir wiped his mouth, his hand shaking. 'I don't need to tell you anything. I know what's going to happen to me. Maybe I could say I killed him. I'm going to the pods anyway.'

'Maybe you could, or perhaps we could come to some agreement?'

'What do you mean? What sort of agreement?' asked

Muir, perking up.

'You'll still be going to the pods, but we can arrange it for you not to have any ceremony.'

Muir curled his lower lip. 'What does that mean?'

'Tell us what happened and one evening we'll set you on your journey. You won't have to face the crowds. Your family won't have to go through that particular humiliation.'

Muir scowled, his face ageing with each gesture as fresh lines of wrinkles erupted on his face. 'It's not the greatest bargain in the world, is it?'

'It's all I've got. Do you have any children?' said Swanson.

Muir considered. 'Fine. I don't want anything to do with it anyway. That man's a nutcase. He'd been spouting on for God knows how many hours about justice, morality and other such rubbish. Though, saying that, I had to agree with some of his views on zero tolerance.'

'I bet you did,' said Keane.

'Just tell us what happened,' said Swanson.

'He started getting more and more agitated. He was banging on the doors, kicking the bed. One of the guards came in and calmed him down. The next thing I know he's lying on the floor, blood spurting out of his arm. Some of it hit me in the eye, disgusting. I might have caught something.'

'Where did he get the razor from?' asked Keane.

'Beats me.'

'You didn't bring it with you?' asked Swanson.

'Didn't have time to pack.'

It was two hours later and they were gathered in Chessington's office. 'That's Judge Lloyd done for,' said Keane.

'How's that?' asked Chessington.

'As Beck's taken his own life there's not much hope of him saving Lloyd's is there?'

'We need to find out who put him up to this. There must be a reason for him writing the ransom note,' said Swanson.

'And then committing suicide?' asked Keane.

Chessington interrupted. 'What about this Muir chap? What do we have on him?'

'He's just a nobody,' said Swanson. 'A labourer over in Sector Seven. Probably drink-drives every evening. It was just a matter of time.'

'No political connections?'

'Nothing.'

'But was he carrying a razor blade?' asked Chessington.

'I don't think so,' said Swanson. 'The blade's off to forensics but my guess is Beck had it with him all the time.'

'Christ, how thoroughly do we check these people?' said Chessington.

'They're all going to the pods anyway,' said Keane, smiling.

'Either way, I want that sergeant out of a job. I told him not to put anyone in with Beck.'

'Sir, I'm going to pass this on to Flaherty if that's okay with you?'

'What are you going to do?' asked Chessington.

'I'm going to see the Wesleys again.'

'And Sarah Natal?'

'I would like to talk to her, sir, as you know, but I'll make the Wesleys a priority for the time being.'

'Fine, you find Flaherty and tell him. I'm going to try and explain this to Luce.'

Flaherty was in the main office which was overrun with officers from the two non-functioning stations. He looked awkward as Swanson approached him. 'What are you working on?' she asked.

'Some of Judge Lloyd's cases,' he said.

She threw the Muir file on his desk. 'Work on this.'

'Muir. Is he the guy who was in the cell with Beck?'

'News spreads fast,' said Swanson.

'Ma'am,' said Flaherty, 'there was one other thing. We had a report of a missing persons case just before the bombs went off. Two men, last seen in a nightclub a few days ago.'

'Names?' asked Swanson.

'Thurrock and Wilson. They both worked for a manufacturing plant in Sector Nineteen.'

Swanson glanced at the pictures on Flaherty's reader. They were an odd pair, one much taller than the other. The smaller man had a mop of curly hair which made him look like a cherubic child. 'Okay, cross-check them with Muir. He worked in a similar place. Then cross-check them with anything else we've got going on. Aside from that, Flaherty, this is your priority.'

'Also, Ma'am,' said Flaherty, as Swanson was turning to leave. 'I've been doing some more research on Wesley, Charles Wesley.'

'And?'

'It seems that he comes from a very wealthy background. A kind of aristocracy.' He pulled out a slim file from his desk drawer.

She read the file as she walked. The Wesley dynasty was significant and following the death of his father, four years ago, Charles Wesley had inherited a vast sum. She showed the file to Keane, who didn't seem too impressed.

'What does this tell us? Lots of wealthy people keep working.'

'That's true enough,' said Swanson. 'But imagine what you could do with that sort of wealth, especially if you had certain political motivations.'

'You really think he had something to do with the bombings?'

'If he wanted to organise it then he had the sort of money that could make it happen, and his son never told us where he got the explosives from. I think we need to interview Jude Wesley again. I think now we have enough reason to suspend his journey.'

Chapter Thirty Six

'Jesus, I hope it doesn't come in threes,' said Keane.

They were standing on a cobblestone path looking across the river where Jude Wesley's pod dangled from its wire. They had obtained a warrant from the judiciary to question Jude Wesley but had quickly realised this was never going to happen. As before, Jude Wesley's body was lying on the floor of his prison but this time he wasn't asleep. The pod was filled with red gas.

A small crowd had gathered opposite the pod. The sight of the vapour was nothing new. The majority of prisoners pushed the suicide button days before they came close to starvation. Each prisoner was given three opportunities to confirm their decision before the toxic cloud was released into the pod. The council claimed the button was humane, installed as a way to alleviate the suffering of the prisoners. Opposition groups had counter-argued that it was simply another way of demonstrating control and highlighting the deterrent nature of the pods. The sight of the red gas was a powerful symbol, arguably more powerful than the pathetic specimens some miles farther down the tracks who grew too weak to reach their own release buttons.

'We'd better contact his parents,' said Swanson.

'I think they're automatically informed as soon as the button is pressed,' said Keane.

'Let's take them our condolences,' said Swanson. It gave her no comfort having to break the news to them but she was keen to gauge their reaction.

They visited Jessica Wesley first. The employees of her upmarket law firm were busying away as normal, but there was a clear tension in their reaction to the officers' presence. Swanson introduced herself to the smiling receptionist she had seen a couple of days earlier.

'I know who you are, Inspector Swanson,' said the woman. It was clear from her voice that despite the smile she was less than pleased to see them return. 'Mrs Wesley is upstairs in her office with her husband. She's asked not to be disturbed.'

'Please inform her that we are here,' said Swanson.

'I've been told not to disturb her.' The smile had vanished. 'You must know what has happened. Can't you leave them alone on a day like this?'

It was a reasonable request but if the Wesleys did have something to do with Lloyd's disappearance, Swanson figured now was the best time to approach them. 'Call her,' she said. At times like these, the guttural rasp of her voice was an asset.

Swanson and Keane sat in the armchairs of the reception for twenty-five minutes before they were finally summoned.

A stern-looking man in a drab grey suit greeted them. 'Mrs Wesley will see you now. Please follow me.'

They followed the man into the elevator and across the same office space they'd passed through a few days before. This time the staff stopped their work, glaring as if they were to blame for what had happened to Mrs Wesley's son. Swanson kept her eyes forward and followed the man into Wesley's office.

Charles Wesley stared out of the office window. His wife, Jessica Wesley, sat behind her desk. Immaculate in her business suit, not a single hair out of place, her makeup was as pristine as the last time they'd met. Charles Wesley turned to face them as they entered. In contrast, he was a wreck. His shirt collar was unbuttoned and Swanson could see patches of sweat beneath his shirt.

'Thank you, Simon,' said Jessica Wesley, to the man in the grey suit. 'Inspector Swanson and Sergeant Keane, how may we help?' The woman was less cordial than on their last visit. Her voice was neutral, business-like, with the faintest hint of impatience. She didn't offer them a seat. They stood before her desk like errant schoolchildren before a weary headmistress.

'We're sorry to bother you on such a day as this,' said Swanson. 'Please accept our sincere condolences.'

Charles Wesley pretended to laugh. His wife said nothing. Her hands were interlocked and placed on the desk in front of her.

'You would have been visited by two other officers today. It is protocol to be informed in person of a death. I realise there is no perfect scenario, and that you already know, but I thought it might be easier to hear the details from somebody you've already met.'

'Thank you,' said Jessica Wesley, her face blank.

'Officially, we have to explain a few things to you,' said Swanson. 'Some of them will not be easy to hear.'

Charles Wesley darted towards the desk. 'Can't you leave us alone? You people are monsters. We know what's happened to our son. There's nothing else you can tell us.'

'I'm sorry, sir, it's just procedure. I will inform you of what happened and what will happen. I'm sure you're probably aware of everything that I will say but I have to say it for legal reasons.' Swanson told them about the suicide button which she called the release button. She described the red smoke that currently filled their son's prison, how it had taken his life instantly and that he would not have suffered. Finally she informed them that their son's body would continue its journey through the city until it had completed the circuit.

Charles Wesley started howling and fell to his knees. The sounds from his mouth were guttural and wild, interspersed with deep, heavy sobs like a child in mid-tantrum.

His wife made no move to comfort him. She looked down on him and for a moment it was as if she was disgusted with his show of emotion. 'So, my son's corpse will travel around the city like some horrific puppet show,' she said. 'Tell me, Inspector Swanson, do you see any sanity in that? How much deterrence do people need in this damn city?'

Swanson's thoughts on the matter were irrelevant. She

placed her card on the lawyer's desk. 'Again, I'm sorry for your loss. If you have any further questions please contact me.'

'What is your real motive in coming here, Inspector Swanson? Don't give me that rubbish again about being a familiar face. I've only known you for a few days. I've only met you for twenty minutes. You're not familiar to me. I know you have some lurid ideas about Jude being involved in recent events but do you really think it's appropriate to visit us on the day of our son's death?'

'We're going now,' said Swanson.

Jessica Wesley stood up. 'I've listened to you,' she said, raising her voice, 'now you'll listen to me. This is harassment. Pure and simple. I'm not just some sub-human you can force your will upon like the people I'm sure you arrest on a daily basis. I know how this system works, however much I may dislike it. So please don't treat me like an imbecile. If you feel the need to question me again then I suggest you bring a warrant for my arrest. Good day to you both.'

Outside, Keane stopped her in the street. 'What was that about?' he asked.

'What do you mean?' said Swanson, annoyed with Keane's tone.

'We didn't even ask them any questions.'

'We didn't need to. I wanted to see their reaction to the news.'

'They seemed pretty upset to me,' said Keane.

'What are you getting so defensive about? Someone had

to officially break the news to them and that's what we did. I took the opportunity to get some confirmation on the state of the Wesley's marriage.' She had wanted to ask about Charles Wesley's inheritance but the timing had obviously been wrong.

'I'm glad it was worth it,' said Keane.

Swanson shrugged and began walking away.

The city was still awash with people, the threat of a second wave of bombs apparently not a concern. Chessington called to inform her that Richard Beck's sister, Sandra Thorn, had been to the station and was currently at the man's flat packing up his belongings. He suggested Swanson and Keane pay her a visit. Swanson decided to go alone, instructing Keane to visit the courthouse and discover Sarah Natal's current location.

Beck's sister was busy packing books into cardboard boxes by the time Swanson arrived. She was three years Beck's senior and from her demeanour, sensible clothes, and the easy way she moved around the flat organising things, the woman was clearly the more forceful of the two siblings. She smiled at Swanson's introduction. She had a pronounced bone structure; her chin jutted out a half centimetre too far, giving her face a crooked look.

'I haven't seen Richard for six years,' she told Swanson. 'We were brought up by our mother who passed away ten years ago. We never had much in common, I suppose. He used to come to the house on special occasions, Christmas and the children's birthdays. But he always drank too much, until it reached the point where I told him he was no longer welcome. He was becoming a bad influence, you see,' she continued, as if feeling the need to defend herself.

'Would you describe him as an alcoholic?' asked Swanson.

'Look at this place,' said the woman, pointing to the disarray. 'I don't remember the last time I saw him when he wasn't intoxicated one way or the other. Sad, really. From what our mother said, our dad was the same way. He died when I was about three, just after Richard was born.'

'What was Richard like at school?' asked Swanson.

'He was a bit of a loner. He wasn't very academic though he did like to read. He always had his head in a comic or a book. Always alone.'

'What about his political affiliations?'

'I've been flicking through some of these pamphlets, Inspector Swanson. Some of them horrify me. I knew he opposed zero-tolerance but he's not alone in that is he? I didn't know he'd reached these sort of extremes.'

'You knew why he was arrested?'

'Yes, your colleague told me. He claimed he kidnapped a judge or something?'

Swanson nodded.

'Surely you didn't believe him? He was a fantasist, Inspector Swanson. He could barely keep his own life together. The idea that he could kidnap someone, anyone, let alone a judge, is laughable, I'm afraid.'

'Have you heard of a man called Charles Wesley?' asked Swanson.

'No, should I?'

Swanson changed tact. 'You know Richard had been diagnosed with terminal cancer?'

'Not before, no. I suppose that sums up our relationship. He couldn't even tell me that.'

'Is there anyone you can think of who would have asked him to write that note?'

'Why would anyone have asked him to do such a thing?'

'Never mind.' Swanson thanked the woman. 'I'll send an officer over to help you finish the packing.'

Outside she called Keane. 'Any news?'

'Not really. I spoke to human resources and they confirmed Natal is on holiday for two weeks. She was under no obligation to give a destination and didn't.'

'But she's expected back?' asked Swanson.

'Apparently so.'

'Okay, meet me back in two hours. I'm going to get Flaherty to do some more digging.'

On the way back Swanson passed the central station. A small group of fire officers were busy working on the building under the supervision of the fire chief, Rosendale. Swanson reintroduced herself. 'How does it look?' she asked.

'It's structurally sound. We're just running final checks. You'll need to send in the cleaners, and builders for that matter,' said Rosendale, pointing to the boarded up windows. 'But I'd imagine you'll be back in there in the next couple of weeks.'

'I've left some things in my office. Would it be safe to go in now?'

'Which floor?' asked Rosendale.

'Floor seven.'

'I'll walk you up.'

The acridness of the smoke still lingered. The electricity had been cut and the chief lit the stairwell with a high powered torch.

'Thank you,' said Swanson, when they reached the seventh floor. 'I can find my own way from here.'

Rosendale handed her a torch. 'I'll wait here, twenty minutes maximum, then we need to go.'

Swanson made slow progress through the smoke-damaged office until she reached her desk. She placed everything she could find into her holdall, and shone her torch towards Chessington's office. The smoke loitered and the residual heat made her claustrophobic in the dark. She shone her torch onto Chessington's desk, revealing soot-covered files. Not knowing what she was looking for, she flicked through the documents. She sat at Chessington's desk, and went through each drawer in turn, her heart fast with excitement. She hadn't taken anything for days now, not since Lloyd's disappearance. Her abstinence put her on edge.

Her allotted time was nearly up. The drawers were even more disorganised than the top of Chessington's desk. Random pieces of paper, travel cards, expense accounts, even fast food wrappers were piled one on top of the other. She was about to leave when she came across a small notebook.

She flashed her torch onto the handwritten entries and placed the notebook into her pocket.

Chapter Thirty Seven

Swanson coughed, the rasping noise sounding as if it had been scraped from her throat. She could still taste the smoke. It clung to her clothing and skin, its intensity such that she wondered if it would ever leave her. She was in a waiting room at Lenity headquarters, Chessington's diary safe in her pocket. The ramshackle nature of the building stood in sharp contrast to the marbled hallways of the town hall. As if in provocation, the pods swooped low in this area, the tracks dipping down in line with the top of the office block. Inside, the base carpets and cheap furniture reminded Swanson of the public defender's offices. Lenity was a registered charity. As such, it seemingly had a much more relaxed work policy; the dress code was certainly more casual, with the workers wearing cheap-looking jeans and ill-fitting tops. Although it had many supporters, Lenity was an openly left-wing organisation and as such was treated with suspicion by many citizens. Working at Lenity was a declaration of intent which was unacceptable to the general establishment and as such was a serious obstacle to future career advancement – with a few notable exceptions, such as Jessica Wesley.

Lenity's central mandate was the abolition of ZT. Swanson had always been dismissive of how they could run as a serious political party when their concerns were so singular. Her appointment was with Lenity's head of operations, Avril Bruckman, who surprised Swanson by meeting her at the front desk. In her late forties, Bruckman was dressed only slightly better than her underlings in a cheap-looking navy suit. 'Welcome, Inspector,' she said, holding her hand out. She led Swanson to an open-plan cafeteria which overlooked the tracks. Swanson could see the sleeping figure of a convict in a pod almost directly in front of her.

'You sure you wouldn't prefer to speak somewhere more secure?' asked Swanson.

'Let's start here and see how we go.'

'Thank you for meeting me. How many employees do you have working for you?'

'We have fifteen full-timers and a small army of volunteers.' Bruckman was soft-spoken but Swanson sensed steel behind her words. 'How can I help you today, Inspector?'

'Obviously, this is just routine.'

Bruckman kept perfect eye contact as she spoke. 'I'm sure it is, but I have already spoken to your colleagues.'

Swanson grimaced. 'I'm working on a different case.'

Bruckman nodded as if she knew exactly what Swanson was talking about.

'It's an awkward question but I'm afraid I have to ask it. Can you offer any insight into the recent bombings?' said Swanson.

'No offense taken, Inspector, but naturally we know nothing about the bombings. I'm sure you're aware we're very proud of our peaceful protest standpoint. We oppose violence of any type. I understand from the reports that many innocent people have been hurt. Many were our members. It's heartbreaking and it's not something we would ever condone.'

'Of course not,' said Swanson, thinking of Garner and Jude Wesley. 'I understand that is your guiding principle, but some of your members are not so strict on its adherence.'

'I'm afraid this is a case of a few bad apples, Inspector. I'm sure in your line of work you understand that.'

'It must be difficult to raise funds in such a climate,' continued Swanson.

Bruckman shrugged her shoulders.

'Where do your donations come from in general?'

'We welcome donations of all kinds, all sizes.'

'Do you have any serious financial benefactors?'

'All donations are confidential. I'm sure you appreciate that.'

'Again, I must ask and apologise for doing so but do you as an organization know anything about the escape from the holding zone of Oscar Garner?'

Bruckman folded her arms. 'I've heard about the escape but nothing more.'

Swanson changed tact, trying to catch Bruckman out.

'What can you tell me about Jessica and Charles Wesley?'

'Nothing that you don't already know, I am sure,' said Bruckman, unflustered.

'They're big supporters of yours?

'I can't talk about individual supporters. It's safe to say they've been public in their support for us, especially considering the travesty which their son is enduring.'

'Their son was arrested carrying explosives, similar to the ones detonated yesterday.'

'The boy was not mentally strong, but did he deserve to die? Is it reasonable that his parents must face the agony of his corpse trailing across the city?'

'I apologise, Miss Bruckman, we're not here to talk politics. Can you tell me if you had any dealings with Judge Lloyd's office?'

'None more so than any of the other judges. We work close with the judiciary, trying to get our point across. You look confused, Inspector.'

'Sorry for being flippant, but I wonder why you bother.'

'True, their hands are tied by legislation but they can influence people. All great works have to start with a single step.'

'Perhaps,' said Swanson.

'Is that all, Inspector? I am extremely busy.'

Bruckman walked her to the front door of the building. The casually dressed workers ignored them both as they passed through the corridors. The notebook procured from Chessington's office weighed heavy in her inside jacket pocket. 'One more thing, Miss Bruckman. I understand that

Lenity may be represented in the next election?'

If the woman was surprised by the question, she didn't show it. 'I'm afraid that's just a rumour. We are not really equipped to become a political party. I think we would be a bit too one-dimensional for most voters.' She smiled and held her hand out again.

A bitter wind stung Swanson's skin as she left the building. She couldn't believe that Bruckman had anything to do with the bombings. Despite the occasionally violent alumni, Swanson understood that the organisation chiefly consisted of peace-loving members. They were fighting for less violence, not advocating more.

At home, she poured herself a large glass of red wine from her father's bottle and took it to her bedroom. Her father was asleep on the sofa, a half-filled glass of wine on the table in front of him, a legal textbook by his side.

Swanson flicked through Chessington's notebook, finding nothing of interest within. Chessington was clearly more methodical in his diary keeping than he was at organising his work environment. Each day had been recorded systematically. Entries included everyone he'd met, cases he'd worked on, and instructions given to subordinate officers. She could see nothing non-work-related within the leather volume.

Once again, she slept fitfully, her mind racing with thoughts of Judge Lloyd, Oscar Garner, the ensuing bombings and the image of Richard Beck lying in his cell, the jagged scar on his wrist leaking blood. She woke early and after showering discovered that her father was still asleep on the sofa. He was drinking too much, she knew, and she was avoiding what that meant. She nudged him softly. His flesh was clammy, the pale skin on his arm coarse and wrinkly like the crumpled up clothes he was still wearing. 'Dad, go to bed,' she whispered. The old man looked at her in confusion, nodded his head and stumbled off to his bedroom.

She was at the station by six a.m. Today was the first day of the searches, as ordered by Luce. The station was awash with police officers and SI personnel. Chessington was leading the searches and had set up a number of teams. Swanson was dismayed to discover that she was in one of the first squads to be sent out. Absently, she checked for Keane's name only to find he had been assigned to another squad.

Luce had ordered that anybody who objected to the questioning should be brought immediately to the station.

'We need to cut this off at the source,' said Chessington. 'Be polite but thorough, and remember that anyone you meet today could be responsible for Judge Lloyd's disappearance, the breakout at the holding cell, the bombings, or all of the above. You know what to look for.'

Chapter Thirty Eight

Swanson's squad consisted mainly of riot police, more used to controlling the crowds during the podding ceremonies than questioning suspects, and a handful of SI guards who had been brought in especially for the searches. A patrol wagon waited outside for them. Swanson took a seat towards the back of the van, her body wedged between two muscular officers dressed in full riot uniform. She kept her head down and didn't join in the banter.

The testosterone in the vehicle was almost visible. The men grunted and jeered, ridiculing one another with playful put-downs. She didn't know if they were aware of her presence, or if they were playing up to it, or simply didn't care.

The searches would take months. The warrant application had been made jointly by Swanson's department, Special Crimes, and SI. Trent Hanson had signed off on his own section. The warrant effectively gave carte blanche to the investigating teams, limiting them very little as to whom they searched, and how thorough those searches could be. The initial lists had focused on the families of podded prisoners, former suspects, including but not limited to anyone who had ever been arrested in the city, and citizens currently under surveillance. Chessington had told her that she and Keane should attend one day of the searches as a courtesy to the other groups.

The van stopped outside a university building in Zone Four. It was a sleek, chrome-fronted block of flats, and Swanson was surprised when she read the sign: *Student Halls of Residence, Mary Williams Campus.* The name on the warrant was Daniel Chapman.

Chapman was a third-year politics student in her father's former university. He had been questioned over an inflammatory political literature he had published for a second year thesis, but it was standard stuff. Anything with a remote possibility of inciting violence was normally brought to the attention of the police for a routine check, and the questioning of the man had gone no further than a gentle warning.

This information had clearly not been passed on to the rest of her colleagues.

She followed in dismay as a team of eight guards stormed the building, taking the stairs to the fourth floor where Chapman was residing for the final year of his studies. She reached the floor just in time to see his door kicked down by one of the guards. Swanson had seen raids on suspected terrorists go ahead with less violence and more professionalism. Wielding assault rifles, the guards screamed at the five students in Chapman's room. The lead guard, whom Swanson presumed was from SI, screamed Chapman's name over and over again, an absurd mantra which sent the students into a panic. Each was grabbed in turn by the other guards, dragged to the floor and cuffed.

Swanson stood at the entrance of the room, incredulous. 'Which one of you is Daniel Chapman?' she shouted, the deep resonance to her voice surprising everyone in the room, even the chanting lead guard.

One of the five students looked towards her from his position on the floor. 'Me,' he mouthed. Swanson checked the man's ID, and instructed the guards to free the other four students.

She let the lead guard interrogate Chapman. He was questioned about his whereabouts on the day of the explosions, and what he knew about the bombings.

Unfortunately for Chapman, he'd been at the demonstrations on the day of Crampton's podding. The lead guard took this as an opening and bombarded the student with more questions, despite the fact that, in Swanson's estimation, over eighty thousand people had been present in or around the valley area on the very same day.

'If I had anything to do with the bombings, why would I go to the poddings?' argued Chapman, his face red from the exertion of being cuffed and manhandled. 'The bombs were detonated metres from where I was standing. I could have been killed. I'm only a student.'

The guard ignored Chapman's protest as if he hadn't spoken. He gave him a producer, a form demanding his appearance at one of the central police stations every day for the next month. 'Non-appearance is criminal,' instructed the guard, releasing Chapman from his handcuffs. 'Even one missed appointment will result in a criminal prosecution.'

Outside, Swanson called Keane. He sounded as if he'd been having a similar experience.

'Oh, we're all having a fantastic, fruitful time here,' he said. 'Nothing like a bit of police brutality to get the juices going. How much longer will we have to suffer this?' he said.

'Let's just get through the day. I'll speak to Chessington later. I think we've only been put on duty for lip service for Hanson and Luce. We'll be back to our investigations by tomorrow.'

'What do you think Judge Lloyd would say if he knew what we were doing?' asked Keane.

'Hopefully we'll get to find out,' replied Swanson, hanging up.

The rest of the day followed a similar pattern of forced entries and brutal interrogation. Over half of the listed people were not present, and were rescheduled for other times. Laughably, they were put at the end of the list so they wouldn't be visited for weeks. It was symptomatic of the rushed and reactionary way the searches had been organized. With no real precedent for what they were doing, the ensuing chaos was inevitable.

By early afternoon, her team had made five arrests. Considering there were over forty teams operational that day, and weeks if not months left of the searches, the arrest rate did not sound sustainable. Within days the holding cells at the police stations would be overrun unless the arrests were processed smoothly: questioning and releasing suspects was fast going to become a necessity.

In the afternoon, they talked to three separate families of deceased convicts. At one point she came close to intervening. An elderly man whose son had been podded three years earlier reacted badly to some of the questioning, and attacked one of the SI guards. Within seconds he was face down on the carpet of his meagre living room floor, four armed rifles pointed to his head. The guards' enjoyment was self-evident. Eventually they freed the man, and outside the building Swanson berated herself for not intervening.

During the last search of the day, at the detached townhouse of a businessman formerly accused of embezzlement, Jane Sutton appeared. Swanson was almost pleased to see her. 'You must be following us,' she said.

'You hardly make yourself inconspicuous, do you?' replied the journalist. 'Speeding through the city in your grandiose riot van. I expected a knee-jerk reaction to the bombings, but this is preposterous.'

Swanson was not in a position to disagree.

'Your central office has recorded forty-two arrests today. Where do you plan on holding all the prisoners, especially as the Sector One police station is down at the moment?'

'I expect there'll be a quick turnaround,' replied Swanson.

'Are you questioning suspects on Judge Lloyd's disappearance, and that of Oscar Garner, or is this just some mad search for would-be terrorists?'

'There are no suspects, Jane. These are just routine inspections.'

'Routine?' laughed Sutton. 'It looks more like you're on the war path. I guess you've heard the latest from the Mayor's office, the new draconian extensions they want to add to ZT?'

'What do you want me to say, Jane?'

'You're just doing your job, I guess? Is that right, Inspector?'

The words stung Swanson as she returned to the office. Not for the first time in the last few days, she doubted both her ability as a policewoman and her rationale for being one in the first place. All she wanted to do was solve the case on Judge Lloyd and Oscar Garner. She wanted no part in the ongoing searches. Sutton was right, they were a knee-jerk reaction, and the journalist only knew the half of it.

She had arranged to meet Keane for a drink after the shift. His day had gone as badly as hers. 'By the end of the shift, I didn't know who we should be questioning,' he told her. 'My list of suspects, or the SI and riot guards. I have legitimate grounds to arrest all of them.'

'Day one, and they're already getting carried away with their newfound power,' agreed Swanson. 'Meanwhile Judge Lloyd and Oscar Garner are still missing. Anyway, we're off duty now,' said Swanson.

Keane went to the bar and bought them two more drinks. Swanson let the warmth of the alcohol spread through her. Soon the worries of the last few days eased. Keane kept glancing at her and had started holding her gaze for longer than was comfortable.

'Tell me about your wife,' said Swanson.

'There's not much to tell,' replied Keane, returning his gaze to the table. 'I don't mean that,' he corrected. 'She passed away two years ago, a long-term illness. I'm afraid to say it was a relief by the end. She was clinging on to life, and I couldn't bear to see her struggle anymore.'

Swanson knew she should respond with something positive, but at that moment it was beyond her. She empathized with Keane, had suffered the death of her mother and its aftermath, but had no words in her repertoire to offer. Keane was slurring. As he edged nearer, Swanson told him it was time to go home.

'Let me walk you back,' said Keane hopefully.

'Not tonight, Sergeant,' said Swanson, understanding the statement left the slightest hint of potential.

They were leaving the bar when Keane pointed over to someone in the crowd drinking alone. 'That's Jackson Sharpe,' he whispered.

The man was huddled over a pint glass of dark beer. By the look of his ruddy complexion, it had not been his first. They walked over and Keane introduced Swanson to the man. Sharpe looked at him as if he were a complete stranger. After staring at them both for a couple of seconds, his face broke into a smile of recognition. 'Sit,' he commanded. He ordered a round of drinks from one of the waitresses. 'Are you stalking me?' he asked, in an amused tone which didn't match his sullen appearance.

'Just a happy coincidence,' said Keane.

'You are Swanson's daughter, aren't you?' said Shape.

'That's right,' said Swanson.

'He was my university lecturer. Crime and ethics or some such nonsense.' The man slurred and gulped at his drink. 'How is the old… man?'

'He's fine,' said Swanson, wondering if Sharpe had developed his drinking habits whilst under her father's tuition. 'He taught Judge Lloyd as well, I believe,' she continued.

'Subtle, Inspector. Get to it, what do you want to know?'

'From what I hear, Mr Sharpe, you and the judge were very close.'

'From what you hear, Inspector?'

'That is until two years ago.'

'You are very thorough, Inspector. So your question is why the fall-out?' Sharpe had a pleasant voice, deep and kind. Swanson could imagine him in court.

The waitress returned with the round of drinks. Sharpe grabbed his pint and took two large gulps. 'I guess it is,' said Swanson.

'He is an infuriating man, Inspector. Extremely able, which I guess is obvious, but too sensitive by far.'

Swanson sipped her drink and exchanged looks with Keane.

'There was a case, two, three years ago. I don't remember the details. Caused a mighty commotion. Astor was getting berated by colleagues over something or other. I suggested he retire early. He disagreed and we had a falling out.'

'And that was that?' asked Swanson.

'That was that,' agreed Sharpe.

'A lifelong friendship destroyed over a falling out about retirement?'

Sharpe picked up his drink then thought better of it. 'Of course not,' he said, a little louder than necessary. 'It was the straw that...' he drifted off. 'You know what I mean,' he concluded.

'Let's get you home,' said Keane.

'Leave me be,' said Sharpe.

Keane called a taxi for the man. They waited in awkward silence for it to arrive, Sharpe occasionally staring at them with an unsteady gaze. Then out of nowhere he said, 'I am sure this is not of use, but Astor told me once about a threat he received.'

Swanson looked at Keane. Sharpe was clearly not in the most lucid of states but she wanted to hear what he had to say.

'I hadn't thought about it for a few years really. It happened at the time we were having problems. He laughed it off at the time, said it was made in the heat of the moment. The only reason I mention it now is I saw the man who threatened him today. Bit of a big shot actually.'

Sharpe sipped his drink. The memory seemed to have sobered him somewhat. He looked at the two officers who were eagerly looking back. 'Oh, that public defender guy. Wesley, that's it. Charles Wesley.'

Chapter Thirty Nine

They came after midnight.

They knocked at the door but McClusky had no time to answer it before they ripped it from its hinges. His flat was a haze of cigarette smoke and he struggled to decipher the men who filtered into his room.

'Reginald McClusky?' one of them asked.

The man looked superhuman, his body bulked by layers of armour. McClusky stared blankly, unable to process what was happening.

'Reginald McClusky?' repeated the man.

McClusky didn't know the right answer to the question. He stood before the man, gawping at the rifle he was holding. The man was accompanied by at least five others. They circled him, each with their own gun.

'Do yourself a favour and answer the question. Are you Reginald McClusky?'

As McClusky nodded, the butt of the man's rifle came crashing towards him, striking him hard on his temple. It was not a savage blow, but hard enough to knock McClusky off his feet. The smoke-filled room faded out of vision and for the briefest of seconds he faded into nothing.

A throbbing pain in his right leg robbed him of his slumber. One of the other men was kicking him hard on his thigh. 'Jesus Christ, you've pissed yourself,' he said. They were busy dismantling his flat. His bed, settee and dining table with its single chair were on their sides. They looked odd from his position on the floor, alien in feature. The men mumbled to one another as they attacked the flat, only fragments of their conversation audible to McClusky.

'How can he live like this?' asked one of the voices. 'Look at him. He looks close to death,' said another.

The blow to his temple had disorientated McClusky. The haze of smoke and the flashes of red in front of his eyes suggested he was in a dream. He listened more intently to the voices of the men, trying to discern who was speaking. His first thought was that Tom Miller had rounded up some of his cronies to teach him the lesson he'd been threatening him with for the last few years.

Then he thought of the person who had been following him. But it couldn't be him; McClusky knew he would come alone.

'Who are you?' he mouthed, a droplet of blood dribbling down his chin from where he had bitten his tongue.

He tried the same question again but couldn't hear his own voice.

'Mortimer. Read him the warrant,' said one of the men.

'What the hell for?' replied another voice.

'Let's just make sure we're protected.'

So they were police. A distant voice began reading legalese to him. Something about an all-encompassing search warrant. McClusky closed his eyes and laid his head on the threadbare carpet. He let the noise wash over him as he moved in and out of consciousness. An indeterminate time later, a gloved hand reached across his throat.

'Get to your feet,' said one of the men.

McClusky sagged in the arms of the police guard. 'Just hold him up, Mortimer.' The guard grabbed him under his arms and shoved him unceremoniously onto the sole dining chair.

'What do you want?' said McClusky, unsure if the words had left his dry mouth.

'Where were you on the twenty-third of April?' asked the guard he now knew as Mortimer.

'What?' replied McClusky, still dazed.

Mortimer's gloved hand smashed against his cheek. He heard one of the other guards laugh. 'Steady, Mortimer.'

'I'm going to ask you once more, *sir*,' said Mortimer with a joyless chuckle. 'Where were you on the day of the bombings?'

'I was out,' said McClusky, a dry gasp escaping from his throat.

Mortimer sighed. 'Out where?'

'I was walking somewhere in Sector One. I heard the explosions and I ran home.'

'Can anyone verify that?' asked Mortimer.

McClusky thought back to the day. He couldn't tell the officer about the man who had offered him a drink at Lazy

Joe's without risking his parole conditions; the same went for the prostitute who had accused him outside his flat.

'No,' he replied.

'Come on. Let's leave him. We've done our questioning. Look at the state of the creature. He's not capable of anything.'

McClusky smiled to himself. He wanted to say something witty, something like 'if you only knew,' but couldn't summon the strength.

Mortimer didn't want to leave. He sat staring at McClusky, his face contorted. The lower half of his face trembled in rage. 'You've read what he's done,' he said. 'We can just say he resisted.'

McClusky had seen that type of look many times before, most recently from Tom Miller. He locked his body into a still position and tried not to make eye contact.

'What do you say, McClusky? Shall I put you out of your misery?'

The guard was shaking now. McClusky knew one word or one movement would set him off. His body shook too, such was his concentration on sitting still. Time in the room stopped. The remnants of cigarette smoke circled around his face and he was about to cough when one of the guards pulled Mortimer away.

'For your records, sir,' said one of the other guards, handing McClusky a piece of paper with the warrant on it. The rest of the crew laughed as they retreated from the flat, leaving the front door open.

Chapter Forty

They considered going straight to Charles Wesley but it was too late and Sharpe's information too insubstantial. Instead, they reconvened the following morning at the station. Swanson met with Chessington and informed him they were no longer taking in part in the searches. 'My time could be spent more constructively elsewhere,' Swanson suggested.

Chessington sighed in resignation. 'We've made more arrests in one day than the last six months.'

'Anything linking in with Lloyd or Garner?'

'Not as yet,' replied Chessington. 'Keep me informed of any more unilateral decisions you intend to make.'

'Call Charles Wesley,' she instructed Keane, back at her office. 'I want to see him on his own.'

'What about his wife? Remember what she said about us needing a warrant to question her.'

'Well, we're not questioning her, are we?'

Keane called Wesley's office, only to be told that the lawyer had taken compassionate leave.

Swanson called his home phone number but there was

no answer. 'Let's pay Mr Wesley a visit,' she said.

A small group of demonstrators had gathered outside the station. The amateur group ambled around the front steps, occasionally chanting a protest slogan. Home-made banners advocated the abolishment of zero tolerance and the pods. Swanson ignored the chants and cat calls as she walked to her car. The group had clearly formed in reaction to the bombings. They would disband sooner or later. She had to restrain Keane from engaging with them. 'Don't they know we lost officers? It's not us they should be protesting against,' he said, as she dragged him to the car.

Charles Wesley had two registered properties. They tried his townhouse first. It was based in an exclusive gated community in Sector Two. It took them five minutes to get through security, much to Swanson's annoyance.

'Do you have an appointment to see Mr Wesley?' asked one of the security guards.

'We phoned ahead,' said Swanson. The guard called Wesley and discussed the situation with him. He reluctantly opened the gates and let them drive through. Wesley's property was detached and five storeys high. It had been built in the last five or six years though it was designed to look much older. Newly planted trees sprung from a perfectly manicured garden and various forms of rose bush lined the walk to Wesley's front door. The area had a plastic feel to it, a lack of warmth mirrored by the rest of the gated community, reflected in the layout of the neighbouring buildings with their sterile front lawns and identikit gardens.

Wesley looked worse than when they had met at his

wife's office. He wore black tracksuit bottoms, flip flops and a pastel green t-shirt. He hadn't shaved and spots of black and grey stubble decorated his face. 'Didn't my wife warn you not to harass us anymore?' he asked, as way of a greeting. He didn't invite them into the house.

'Mr Wesley, I do appreciate your situation. I know the last thing you want to do at this moment is to speak to us.'

'I don't think you do understand, Inspector Swanson. I've lost my son but I can't mourn for him yet. He's still circling in his damn prison. Can you even conceive of how it must feel to have someone you love pass away, but know they are still drifting around the city, a rotting corpse, when they should be buried? Just for the benefit of some lawmaker with some distorted, sick ideal. What sort of society could do something so monstrous?'

Swanson knew exactly how he felt.

'The last thing I want to do is trouble you, believe me, but we need to ask you some questions. I'm afraid if you don't let us in to talk to you now then you will have to come to the station with us; and however strongly your wife may feel on the subject I don't need a warrant for that.'

Wesley hesitated then stood aside and waved them in. The inside of the house was as immaculate and as sterile as the outer building. The walls were perfectly white as if recently painted. Large framed pictures adorned the walls, hung in perfect symmetry: abstract oil paintings in bright and vivid colours screamed out at them, contrasting with the blank walls. Wesley ushered them into the living room where a high-fronted double armchair faced two similar-looking single armchairs in the centre of the room. Aside from the furniture and two paintings, the room was bare. Swanson guessed that the minimalist design was stylised and in fashion, but she found it cold and uninviting. She took the offered seat on one of the single armchairs. Keane stood whilst Charles Wesley collapsed into the double armchair.

Swanson's eyes darted around the room looking for signs of Jessica Wesley. She was sure that the decor was down to her, but nothing else in the house suggested that the Wesleys shared the premises.

'Mr Wesley, I'll get right to the point. I need to know what your involvement was in the recent bombings.'

Wesley raised his eyebrows to comic effect. It genuinely looked as if he hadn't expected such a line of questioning. 'What? I know nothing about the bombings except that I was there, Inspector Swanson.'

'Where were you at the time the first bombs went off, Mr Wesley?' asked Swanson. Wesley looked up at Keane. 'You know that answer. Your esteemed colleague here was chasing me for some reason.'

'Why were you running?' asked Keane.

Wesley grimaced, as if the question caused him physical pain. 'It doesn't do my street cred any favours being seen in public talking to people like him.'

'People like me?' said Keane.

Swanson raised her hand. 'You're going to have to do better than that, Mr Wesley. You speak to police officers all the time in your line of work. If you do have *street cred* it's not going to be affected by speaking to us out in public. I think you ran because you have a guilty conscience.'

'Why would I be guilty?'

'You tell me. Look at it from our point of view. Your son was arrested carrying explosives. We receive a ransom note demanding the release of all the prisoners in the pods. Days later bombs go off.'

'Don't be so ludicrous,' said Wesley.

'This is a very nice house you have,' said Keane. 'You must be either very prudent or an extremely good investor to come by a place like this on your salary.' Keane walked around the room admiring the sparse decorations.

'I'm sure you're aware of my legacy, my wealth. So let's not play any of these silly games.'

'Again, Mr Wesley, look at it from our point of view. It would take someone very wealthy to organise the recent bombings. Someone with connections. Perhaps someone who works with known or accused criminals.'

Wesley shook his head, slowly mocking Swanson's hypothesis. 'I defend citizens, Inspector Swanson. Innocent until proven guilty. That proviso existed long before the council and their draconian zero tolerance. You forget I'm a public defender. If you think this circumspect evidence would even reach court you're very much mistaken. The city is full of wealthy people, full of people with connections to the underworld. Your own Chief Superintendent comes from a wealthy background. He has more money than I do and has much more interaction with criminals.'

Keane sat down next to Wesley and placed his face close to the grieving man. 'Yes, sir, but Chief Superintendent

Luce's son was not caught carrying explosives towards the pods, was he?'

'Right, I've had enough of this,' said Wesley, getting to his feet. 'Make your decision now. I'll come to the station with you if you wish, otherwise leave.'

'Okay, Mr Wesley. Thank you for your time,' said Swanson. She nodded towards the front door for Keane's benefit. 'If you do think of anything that could help us then please let me know.'

'Goodbye, Inspector.'

'Just before we go, sir. Could you tell me if you were ever in front of Judge Lloyd?'

'Many times,' said Wesley. They were standing by the front door. Swanson had her foot over the threshold, preventing Wesley from shutting them out.

'Did you win many cases?' asked Swanson.

Wesley's face reddened. 'I know your tactics, Swanson. They're so banal, pitiful really. As you're perfectly aware I never directly won a case against Judge Lloyd. But as I'm sure you're also aware the majority of cases that reach criminal court are foregone conclusions.'

'Judge Lloyd has had acquittals,' said Swanson.

'Yes, there is a four percent acquittal rate. The majority of which are technicalities.'

'But in all your time not one acquittal for you?'

'Not directly in front of Judge Lloyd, no,' echoed Wesley. 'Now if you don't mind.'

'Did this upset you, Mr Wesley? Perhaps provoke you into a confrontation with Judge Lloyd?' asked Keane.

‘What the hell are you talking about?’ replied Wesley.

‘We have reason to believe you made a direct threat to Judge Lloyd some time ago.’

‘Bullshit.’

‘A threat of extreme physical violence.’

‘Absolute nonsense. I’ve had some heated discussions with him, and many other judges, but I have never threatened anyone in my life. You must leave,’ insisted Wesley.

Swanson opened the door. ‘Sorry, one more thing. Where is your wife, Mr Wesley?’

‘At work.’

‘And when she finishes work?’

‘She will go home, I guess.’

‘To this house?’

‘I can’t see how that is any of your business, Inspector Swanson.’

‘No, sir, thank you.’

Chapter Forty One

Old Blue left Sarah to make dinner and rode the moped to Sector Sixteen. He sat outside the red brick building which he'd visited nearly every night for the last six years, his body slumped across one of the wooden benches on the grey, concrete forecourt. To his left a group of youths circled around on bicycles which looked too small for them. Mainly boys, they wore dark clothing decorated with bright, crudely designed motifs. Some wore baseball caps, others kept their heads warm with the hoods of their jackets. One of their number glanced over at Old Blue, a thinly rolled cigarette dangling from his lip. He went to say something to him then thought better of it.

Old Blue craned his neck so he could see the window where the man resided. He was not keen to return home. Sarah was waiting for him, as were the prisoners. He took some comfort from being on the bench, despite his motive for being there. Occasionally, he persuaded himself that he could see something else hovering in the window frame of the man's apartment, two phosphorous globes of light. As time went on, he concluded that they appeared due to the strain he was putting on his visual system by staring upwards for such a sustained length of time. Only now and then would he allow himself the pleasure of imagining they were something else entirely.

Sarah greeted him back an hour later. The windows of the house he now shared with her were now permanently left open, and a multitude of air fresheners were spread throughout the building. Plugged into the electric sockets, they sent small bursts of perfumed liquid into the air at regular intervals. In addition, Sarah had lit a number of scented candles and placed them at even intervals throughout the house. The flames from the candles flickered in the draught from the windows. The smoke merged with the air fresheners, creating random scents which defied categorisation. Yet they could not fully mask the stench of the cellar below which felt as if it had seeped into the foundations of the house, infecting the bricks and mortar irreversibly.

Sarah began pawing at him as soon as he walked through the door. Seeing the imprisoned judge had changed her, as he had predicted. He could see through her mock bravado to the insecurity which burrowed away at her. Originally, he had hoped to use her for the next stage of the plan, but she was close to useless now. His next target would prove to be a much harder proposition and he couldn't risk Sarah's unpredictability. Unlike the three men below, the target was not subject to a regular timetable. He had been watching him for the last two days, waiting for an appropriate time, but none had yet presented itself. Everything was coming to an end. It was only a matter of time before they were detected; such was the stink coming from the house. Tomorrow would be the last day. If he was unable to acquire his final target by then he would finish his scheme without him.

He set off early, trying not to wake Sarah as he went through the nausea-inducing process of feeding the inmates. Wilson raged at him as he placed the trays of breakfast into the double-sided slots, banging his fists against the soundproofed glass panels, his curly hair matted to his face. His colleague, Thurrock, sat resigned on the floor. Old Blue didn't need to reveal himself to the men. As idiotic as they were, he was sure they understood their predicament. Why he had taken them and why they were waiting in the cells with the judge. However, he was also sure that they didn't fully comprehend what lay ahead for them. The smaller of the two men, Simon Wilson, started crying. He scraped his nails against the glass, mouthing the word 'please' over and over. Old Blue looked away in disgust. Lloyd was curled up on the floor, his body pushed up against one of the walls. He passed the judge's tray through the opening and ran up the stairs. He snapped the trap-door shut, the wooden panel smashing hard against the floor. He was in such a rush that he almost forgot to lock the entrance. He paused, taking a deep breath of the fetid air. It was something he couldn't overlook. Sarah was too much of a risk. She was close to cracking and couldn't be allowed to visit the prisoners unaccompanied. He replaced the rug.

The relatively fresh air outside the house was a welcome relief. He sucked it in, his eyes closed as he savoured the warm, sticky air. He drove the people carrier into Sector Twelve where he replaced it with a light green hatchback he'd previously purchased. It was seven a.m. and the target normally left for work at any time between eight and nine.

He decided to buy a cup of coffee from a small coffee shop across from where he'd parked. The shop was surprisingly busy, filled with city workers and maintenance crews breakfasting. He walked through the entrance, not faltering, even after seeing the target he was hunting in the shop. The policeman was sitting at the back of the room, his face covered by a large broadsheet newspaper. The man looked up and stared at him, though nothing in his demeanour suggested he recognised him. He returned to his newspaper without incident.

Old Blue took a place two tables along from where the man was sitting. He ordered a large black filtered coffee from the anorexic-looking waitress, picked up a newspaper off the rack and pretended to read. It was a good opportunity but not a perfect one. A lot of people were present and he was unsure if it would be possible to coax the target towards his car. Would be able to take him away without being noticed?

He gulped at his coffee, which hadn't cooled, burning his tongue in his hastiness. The man had looked him right in the eyes but there had been no recognition. He doubted it was just the grey beard. The policeman had been responsible for numerous poddings in his time and Old Blue accepted that he was just one of many hapless victims of society's injustice. The thought didn't anger him. In a perverse way it made him question his decision to kidnap the man. The podgy, ginger-haired man had done his best at the time. To a certain extent, he had been Nathaniel Jacobson's ally.

Old Blue snapped into action: he left his coffee and walked over to where the policeman sat. He stood before the man who was still engrossed in his paper. 'Chief Inspector Chessington,' he said, 'I'm not sure if you remember me. I'm Nathaniel Jacobson.'

Chessington looked up from his paper. He hesitated before shaking Old Blue's hand. Old Blue watched intently as the man's eyes flickered then looked up towards the ceiling as he tried to recall the relevance of the name, Nathaniel Jacobson. He saw the information click into place on the man's round face.

Chessington shook the proffered hand. 'Mr Jacobson, good to see you again,' he said. His handshake was firm though his hand was slippery with sweat. The words and smile seemed genuine enough. 'How are you managing?'

'Fine, thank you. I thought it was you as I walked in, I wasn't sure. I don't mean to disturb you.'

'No, no please,' said Chessington. He folded up his newspaper and took a sip of his cappuccino. 'Can I get you a coffee or something?'

'No, thanks. I'm good.'

They talked away idly for a few minutes. He told Chessington he now worked in the courthouse as a cleaner. The information slipped out before he had time to control it. Chessington seemed to have a genuine interest in his welfare though he steered away from discussing the case. The conversation quickly narrowed to an end and he knew time was running out.

'It was good to see you again, Mr Jacobson,' said Chessington. 'You look very well and I'm glad things are working out for you workwise. I must dash – since the bombings, I'm having to work out of Sector Four police station and I'm not used to the commute.'

'I'm headed that way,' said Old Blue, spotting his opportunity. 'Please let me give you a lift it's the least I can do.'

'No, no, I'll be fine.'

Old Blue looked Chessington in the eyes. 'I insist,' he said.

After making sure Chessington was belted in securely, Old Blue started the car. He had practiced what he was about to perform many times before but never on a live subject. He'd planned to do it at Chessington's flat. Now, with him secure in the passenger seat, the job was potentially an easier one. With the car still running, he unbuckled his seatbelt. 'Sorry, I just need to get my sunglasses from the boot,' he told Chessington. The policeman didn't seem concerned.

He skipped to the back of the car and opened the boot. He unpacked the filled syringe from a white plastic box and cupped it in his right hand, his thumb on the plunger. No one was directly in his sightline so he decided to take the risk. He shut the boot quietly and moved back towards his seat with the syringe pushed flat against his right thigh.

'I'm sorry, would you mind looking in the glove compartment for me?' asked Old Blue, returning to his seat. 'They don't seem to be in the boot.'

Chessington did as asked, exposing the spongy skin of his neck as he leant forward to open the compartment. Old Blue thrust the syringe into the freckled flesh with one forceful practiced swipe. The needle stuck and he plunged the clear liquid into the Chief Inspector's neck. The man grunted and sat back in shock, falling almost immediately unconscious, his head falling hard against the passenger side window.

Old Blue sat back, pulling Chessington into a seating position with a forceful shove. The man's neck lolled to the left. Old Blue threw the used needle into the back seat and drove slowly away.

Chapter Forty Two

New demonstrations had begun appearing in random places throughout the city. The largest one they had seen so far had approximately fifteen participants. People were forming small groups, outside offices and factories, shop fronts, schools, and residential buildings. In some ways the effect was more powerful than a large gathering. With no prompting, and no subservience to a larger political ideal, these were genuine outbursts of objection; anger and fear at the bombings and what they represented.

Keane didn't say much as Swanson drove them back through the snail-like traffic. He occasionally looked over at her as if he was about to say something, then returned his gaze to the road.

'We need to speak to Jessica Wesley again,' said Keane. 'I want to know if those two still live together. They're hiding something. If they have split up then why not tell us?'

'Appearances? Pride?' suggested Swanson.

'Perhaps. But would they really care?'

'Maybe they've split recently and are trying to reconcile.'

She'd noticed that Charles Wesley was still wearing his wedding ring, unlike his wife.

'More likely there were legal issues,' said Keane. 'The sort of money Charles Wesley is packing would motivate anyone.'

The road approaching Sector Four ran parallel beneath the line of pods. Three of the pods were in view. Two of the domes were cloudy with red smoke. Between them was a clear pod which held the standing figure of a frail-looking man. The man stood looking out of his glass prison. He had stripped naked, his ample flesh pressed against the glass. It was a protest Swanson had seen many times before, as had everyone else in the city. People chose not to look, whoever the prisoner was.

As they walked into the police station Swanson could tell something was wrong. The other officers struggled to look them in the eye, keeping their distance. Even Flaherty looked concerned as he walked over. 'Luce wants to see you,' he said, 'both of you. I'm afraid it's urgent and he didn't look very happy. He's in there.'

Luce was waiting in Chessington's office. He was alone and was flicking through the poorly arranged files on Chessington's desk. The door was open and after knocking Swanson and Keane walked through without waiting for an invitation.

'Shut the door,' said Luce, not looking up from the paper he was reading. 'Sit.' Once again, Luce focussed his attention solely on Swanson as if denying Keane's existence. 'I have just returned from a very tiresome meeting,' he began.

'Jessica Wesley has contacts you can barely imagine. She has an almost direct line to the Mayor. You went to visit her on the day of her son's death?' Luce's voice was even but the anger lurking beneath his considered tone was clear.

'Her son, the bomber?' answered Keane.

Luce stood and grasped the table in front of him, his hands turning white from the exertion. 'Speak when you're told to fucking speak,' he said, for the first time looking at Keane. 'You have no idea the sort of shitstorm you've got yourself into.' Luce was renowned for his rage. Swanson pitied him for his lack of control and disliked him for his lack of loyalty.

'We felt it appropriate to give her the news of her son's death in person,' said Swanson.

Luce sat back down, his face flush with anger. 'Don't give me that crap, Inspector.'

'With all due respect, sir, the Wesleys are credible suspects in the bombings.'

'Credible, how?' spat Luce.

'For one, their son was caught carrying explosives towards the pods,' said Keane.

Luce shook his head. 'You just don't know when to keep quiet, do you boy?'

Swanson sensed Keane's agitation. She interrupted before he had a chance to respond. 'Sir, I'm sure you are aware Charles Wesley comes from an extremely wealthy background. You couple this with his political leanings and take into account the fact that his son was arrested, then they have to be taken seriously as suspects.'

'You need more than that.'

'Charles Wesley was the public defender on both Garner and Dempsey's trials. We have reason to believe he knew Richard Beck,' said Swanson.

'I guess you don't have much else to go on at the moment, do you?' said Luce. This was an accusation, not a statement of fact. 'I've met with the Mayor, and the head of Lenity. Lenity denies any responsibility for the bombings, and from my personal team's investigations, I'm confident that they didn't have anything to do with it.'

Swanson was bewildered that Luce had his own team. 'What do SI suggest, some phantom splinter group?'

'That is not your concern. Your remit is to find Judge Lloyd and Oscar Garner, two things you're failing to accomplish.'

'And if there is a link, sir, with the bombings?'

'If there is a link it will become evident. Trent Hanson has informed me of your little visit to his office. I'm ordering you not to go near Jessica or Charles Wesley again unless you have conclusive proof of their involvement. Stay away from SI as well. Any breach of that order will result in your immediate suspension.'

'Thank you, sir. Anything else?' said Swanson.

Luce flicked his hand as a dismissal, then picked up a file from Chessington's desk and started reading.

'We need to see Chessington,' said Keane, back at Swanson's office.

A file had been left on Swanson's desk, a small yellow post-it note attached. It was from Flaherty, the file on Sarah

Natal. 'Go and talk to Flaherty for me,' she instructed Keane. 'Find out what has been happening with the house searches; if any new information has come to light.'

She began reading Natal's file. The more she worked with Flaherty the more she was impressed by his work ethic and eye for detail. Natal's file was now thirty pages long. Swanson was sure that had she asked any of the other officers the chances were the file would have been a third of the size.

Natal had been Judge Lloyd's assistant for the last eight years. She was effectively a paralegal. She'd studied law at university and had taken some professional exams but had never fully qualified, which backed up the story she'd given Keane. Prior to assisting Judge Lloyd she had worked in the public prosecutions department. This was where her file became interesting. She'd worked at the office for ten years, ever since graduating, taking her professional exams under sponsorship by the department. She'd received glowing references from the department before moving to Lloyd's office but Flaherty had managed to delve deeper and had identified that there had been problems with her previous post. Swanson was impressed at how he had come by the internal information.

Two years before joining Judge Lloyd, Natal had made an accusation against one of her colleagues, Simon Featherstone. Featherstone was a senior prosecutor and Natal had worked as his personal assistant for three years. Natal had accused Featherstone of raping her but had waited six months before making the complaint official and taking the matter to the head of public prosecution, Denis Jenkins.

Swanson knew Jenkins. A sympathetic man, now in his mid-seventies, Jenkins recorded Natal's complaint but had never made it official by informing the police. Jenkins told her that she'd waited too long to make the complaint and that it would have come down to a 'his word versus your word' case which she would have been unable to win. He advised her to leave the matter alone and Natal had accepted his counsel at the time. Jenkins moved her to a different department and latterly arranged for her to work for Judge Lloyd. Swanson made a mental note to examine all internal complaints made against Simon Featherstone at some future point.

The file contained little else of interest. Natal came from middle-class parents, was well-educated. Nothing else traumatic had occurred in her life. Swanson flicked through her notes once more, cursing herself for missing one particular item. Whilst working for Judge Lloyd, Natal had spent six months at the public defender's office. She had completed the work experience under Judge Lloyd's instructions. He wanted her to understand both sides of the process, both prosecution and defence. In particular, Lloyd arranged for her to gain some invaluable experience with one of the senior defenders, a certain Charles Wesley.

Swanson found Flaherty in the canteen eating lunch with Keane. She ordered a coffee and sat down with them. Flaherty stood as she approached the table.

'At ease, Private,' she laughed. 'Good work on the Natal file,' she said. She showed the file to Keane, highlighting the passages on Natal's accusation and her work experience period with Wesley.

'Are we going to show this to Luce? Maybe he'll let us speak to Wesley again,' said Keane.

'Not yet. Flaherty, I want you to do some groundwork on the time period when Sarah Natal was working with Wesley. Find out which cases they worked on together and anything else you can about their relationship during that time and subsequently. Also, a thorough background check on Jessica Wesley would be helpful. But be discreet. Let's examine all these coincidences and see where it gets us.'

'Yes ma'am,' said Flaherty, getting up from the table.

'You can eat your lunch first,' said Swanson.

Flaherty picked up his half-eaten sandwich and took it with him.

'I've really messed up, haven't I?' said Keane.

'How's that?'

'If Natal has anything to do with the disappearances, or the bombs, then she's going to mention,' he hesitated, 'what happened.'

'Possibly. But at the time she wasn't officially a suspect. You're entitled to a private life. Admittedly it won't look good on your record but you won't lose your job over it. If we can find Lloyd or Garner, and especially if we can find who is responsible for the bombings, then I think your indiscretion will be overlooked. But Keane, if you ever do something like that again then I'll not cover for you.'

'Understood,' he said.

Swanson called Chessington's mobile but there was no answer. The following morning she understood why.

Chapter Forty Three

Swanson was summoned to the station at six a.m. Superintendent Luce took her to one side of the incident room and ushered her to one of the computer screens in Chessington's office. 'Chief Inspector Chessington has been offline since yesterday afternoon. I was supposed to meet with him yesterday evening at eight p.m. He was last seen in Sector One yesterday morning. This footage was sent to me an hour ago.'

CCTV cameras had recorded Chessington leaving a Sector One coffee house accompanied by a man. His companion was tall and heavy set, cloaked in a dark raincoat with a hood pulled over his head. It may have been coincidental, but the cameras gave no clear view of the man's face as they walked.

They stopped at a car and exchanged words. The man reached towards Chessington and placed his hand on the policeman's wrist. Luce zoomed in on the video footage, the assailant's hand grasping the pale, freckly skin of Chessington's wrist. Zooming out, Swanson watched the man look Chessington in the eyes. He mouthed some words and

Chessington took a seat in the passenger side of the car.

The man held a syringe. He shut the boot quietly and moved back towards his seat with the syringe pushed flat against his right thigh. As the video resumed, Chessington appeared to lean forward as if retrieving something from the glove compartment and the man thrust the syringe into the freckled flesh with one forceful practiced swipe.

'Tech are working on matching the image. This is the best we can muster so far,' said Luce, handing Swanson a grainy print-out of the man.

Swanson pulled up the picture of the bearded man Abigail had photographed with Sarah Natal. 'It's him,' she said.

Luce compared the photos. 'Could be. Where is Sarah Natal?'

'She's on two weeks' leave. We don't know where she is yet.'

Luce sighed, a deflated gesture. 'Let's get a missing persons order out on her.'

After debriefing the team, Swanson went with Keane to Chessington's flat. 'You would think a third missing person would make things easier,' said Keane.

'Maybe it will. Chessington was the leading officer on Garner's prosecution and Lloyd the presiding judge,' replied Swanson.

'So Garner and whoever broke him out of prison are retaliating?'

'Possibly. There's been no mention of the ransom note since Beck's suicide.'

Walking through Chessington's flat felt like an intrusion. Although Swanson had not seen eye to eye with Chessington on a number of things, she'd always respected his authority. She searched the living room and kitchen while Keane checked Chessington's bedroom.

'He must have a cleaner,' shouted Keane. 'This place is spotless, even the bed's made.'

A small room to the side of the living room served as Chessington's office. Swanson looked through the neatly packed files on the desk. She opened the desk drawers, feeling a guilty symmetry to when she'd taken the man's diary at the central station. She found nothing of interest. Some bills, old payslips, booklets on management style: a cleaner, less cluttered version of his work office.

Swanson imagined that Chessington's flat was a bastion of comfort and organisation for him, a place where he could escape the chaos of his professional life. Like so many of her fellow officers, Chessington's one true love was his work. Swanson felt ashamed that she didn't know anything about his private life; didn't even know if he'd ever been married or had a partner. The state of the flat suggested he currently lived alone. In the bathroom, a solitary toothbrush stood inside a chrome beaker on a sleek porcelain basin.

After two hours, the flat had been fully dusted for fingerprints.

'You okay?' asked Keane.

'I'm fine,' said Swanson. She thought about Chessington's notebook which at present was nestled in the box beneath her bed. At this precise moment another group of officers were searching through Chessington's office at the central station. Swanson doubted the notebook was common knowledge and even if it was, it was perfectly reasonable to imagine that Chessington would have had the notebook with him. Even if she had been the last person allowed to enter the building by Fire Chief Rosendale, she didn't think anything could connect her to the theft.

Superintendent Luce called from the Sector Four station. Swanson switched her phone to silent and placed it back in her pocket.

'I need to go somewhere,' she told Keane. 'I'll meet you back in the office in an hour.'

She ran back to her house, deciding that going by foot would be quicker than driving. Her father was out, no doubt involved in some mischievous protest somewhere. She retrieved the notebook from its hiding place and scanned each page. She searched in vain for anything of relevance. Her name was mentioned a couple of times. Keane was mentioned numerous times. Chessington admired her colleague but was also annoyed by his sometimes lackadaisical approach to things. Flaherty came in for some praise, Chessington stating that he was going to recommend the young officer for the fast track. She pocketed the notebook and caught a taxi back to the station. Sitting in the cab, she noticed six missed calls from Chief Superintendent Luce.

Keane was waiting for her in the lobby of the Sector Four station. 'Jesus, Swanson, where have you been? Luce is on the warpath. He says he's phoned you six times.'

'Oh dear, my phone has been on silent,' said Swanson, in her deepest growl.

Keane's eyes were bright and refreshed as if he'd had a good night's sleep in the short period since she'd last seen him. His appearance constantly mutated, she'd noticed. Within the hour he could easily revert to his bedraggled look, as if his demeanour was victim to his emotions and state of mind. She was not sure it was an ideal trait for a police officer to have.

She sat down next to him. 'I've been thinking more about Sarah Natal. Whether or not she's involved, it's possible that we have been looking at this whole case from the wrong perspective.'

'In what way?' asked Keane.

'We've made a huge assumption about the kidnapping of Judge Lloyd, and Garner, and whoever was responsible for the bombings. We've been working on the basis that everyone involved is against zero tolerance. That they're acting against those who implement or support it.'

'I think that's obvious,' said Keane.

'It would seem so, but perhaps that's what they want us to think. Look at Natal: she was failed by zero tolerance. Zero tolerance is only applicable to those who are found guilty. In her mind she was raped by a man who'd been responsible for the podding of more people than anyone else in this city, yet she couldn't even raise a case against him. So she was part of a society which rallies against any form of criminality, and she was working to support that system, yet somehow it conspired to allow her to be violated and not receive any justice. That's where her grievance manifested itself. Whoever this bearded guy is could have a similar grievance.'

'What are you saying, Swanson?'

'I am saying we shouldn't just look at those who have been prosecuted. Perhaps we should look at those who were failed in other ways by the justice system. The acquittals, not the prosecutions.'

Keane pursed his lips in thought. 'Hell, we haven't anything else to go on. Why not?'

'I'm going to face Luce. Find Flaherty for me. He mentioned a missing persons report earlier in the week. Two factory workers. We need to see if there's a connection.'

'Did it ever cross your mind that with one of our senior officers missing it would be a little foolhardy not to check that your phone was on silent or not?' Chief Superintendent Philip Luce was pacing his office. 'It's staggeringly incompetent, Swanson. Unless, of course, your phone was not on silent and you were just ignoring me?'

Luce had been Chief Superintendent for the last five years. In Swanson's opinion, he lacked even the faintest hint of charisma and she often wondered what it took for a man like him to reach such an elevated position. He sat down in his chair, leaning forward, his elbows pressed down on his desk. It was an awkward position and he looked uncomfortable.

'You are the most senior officer I have at my disposal. It's up to you whether or not that is a positive thing for me. I need a full report of our current standings. Aside from a missing terrorist, we have a judge and a senior police officer missing with no new ransom note. The only person who's claimed anything sliced his wrist open with a razor blade in our custody. All in all, it's not a positive situation.'

Swanson sat upright opposite Luce. Her superior's stale breath wafted towards her, forcing her to breathe through her mouth. Chessington's notebook was heavy, pushed up against her breast in her inside pocket.

'I'm giving you forty-eight hours, Swanson. The mayor has been on the phone eight times today. Can you imagine how embarrassing it is not to have anything to tell him?'

Swanson didn't answer.

'Forty-eight hours, or I turn this over to SI,' said Luce. 'Go.'

'Okay, tell me what you've got on those two men who disappeared.' Swanson was sitting in the canteen with Keane and Flaherty. Flaherty held a ring binder in front of him. With long, almost fleshless fingers he pulled the papers apart, tilting his head towards the report. Swanson couldn't help staring at his high forehead which lent his face an elongated look.

'Thurrock and Wilson were last seen in Little Joe's nightclub four evenings ago. They left at approximately four a.m. with a 'smartly dressed, striking brunette woman in her mid-late thirties.' By all accounts, they were highly intoxicated which was nothing new. The bartender said they were at Little Joe's nearly every evening, as were most of the workers at the local factories.'

'When were they filed as missing?' asked Keane.

'The next morning, after they had failed to turn up for work.'

'When did the report come through to us?'

'It came through to us the same day,' said Flaherty. 'The factory has a strict absentee policy. They're not, shall we say, highly skilled workers and there is a huge demand for their jobs. Any form of absence is frowned upon but the rule is if you're going to miss work you need to notify the duty plant manager a minimum of three hours before you start. The duty plant manager, Tom Miller, called it in when they failed to show for work. He told one of the officers that it was almost unheard of for anyone not to call in, that it was practically like resigning, and that for the workers in his factory resigning was not an option.'

'When did we first take it seriously?' said Swanson.

'About three days later. Miller kept calling and the families were getting worried. They're both single men. Thurrock has two living parents, Wilson an elderly mother.'

'They live at home?' asked Keane.

'They share a flat together. It's been searched and we've talked to the occupants of the building. No one remembers them returning that evening or since.'

'Worst case scenario,' said Swanson. 'We have a Judge, Chief Inspector Chessington, Garner and these two men missing and there's a connection.'

'I've gone through the database,' said Flaherty. 'Of

course, there are hundreds of cases where Chessington and Lloyd have been involved, and Garner relates to both Chessington and Lloyd, but Thurrock and Wilson do not appear on the database.'

'We need to go to the factory,' said Swanson.

Chapter Forty Four

The factory was part of a vast industrial estate out in Sector Nineteen. Dark, purple-black clouds hovered above as they drove towards the estate. The skyline was punctuated by pods against a background of dank industrial buildings. One of the pods moved along the tracks in the distance. The weather was such that the steel tracks that held the pod in place were obscured by the clouds, giving the impression that the glass dome somehow floated above the factory. As they approached, the pod became clearer. Swanson made out the form of a corpse on the glass floor. At this stage, the prisoner would be over twenty days into the journey. No residue of the red suicide gas was present, the prisoner's death likely a result of dehydration.

After enduring an elaborate security check at the factory gates, they were greeted by Tom Miller, the factory supervisor who had reported Thurrock and Wilson missing. A giant of a man, he towered over Swanson, Keane and Flaherty. He was dressed in his factory overalls, his thick neck covered in black grime. He didn't offer to shake their hands, for which Swanson was grateful. He showed them to a glass fronted office which overlooked the warehouse area. Blackened forklift trucks scurried below them, emitting high-pitched squeals at one another.

'You picked a right day for it,' said Miller. His dingy office was lit by a single fluorescent tube. A three-bar electric heater suggested, rather than provided, heat by a steel desk. 'You're here about Thurrock and Wilson,' said Miller, matter-of-factly. He had a heavy, drawling accent which seemed to elongate his words. 'Two of the best workers we've ever had here. I checked through their records the other day. Haven't missed a day's work in ten years.'

'I imagine you have a pretty reliable workforce,' suggested Swanson.

'Pretty good. The work here is valued. There's a lot of available overtime and good bonuses. I have about sixty applicants on a waiting list. People are rarely late and they never just don't turn up.'

Swanson accepted the explanation. Although unemployment was low outside the central zones, work was often menial and poorly paid.

'That's why you reported Thurrock and Wilson missing?' asked Keane.

'I didn't report them missing immediately, I asked around the factory. I called them both at home, no answer. I gave them until lunch time just in case they were nursing some form of unimaginable hangover and then I called it in.'

'So this is completely unexpected,' asked Keane.

Tom Miller leant back in his chair, enjoying the

spotlight. 'As I told you, they hadn't missed a day's work in ten years and I don't remember them ever being late. I knew something must have happened for them not to turn up. A day's absenteeism could result, or should I say would result, in them losing their jobs.'

'Have they lost their jobs now?' asked Swanson.

'This is a different circumstance, isn't it? Something has obviously happened to them.'

'So you've kept their jobs open for them?'

'Let's see what happens first, but as they've been missing for so long something strange must have gone on.'

'Any ideas what?' asked Keane.

Tom Miller held both palms up towards the ceiling like a child who'd lost his toy. 'Buggered if I know,' he said.

Miller gave them a tour of the factory floor. They received ear protectors to dampen out the harsh creaking of the vast metallic machinery which filled the space. The factory floor was awash with a multitude of competing aromas: gasoline, oil, body odour and ammonia hung in the air, almost visible in the fumes. Workers busied away at their stations on things beyond Swanson's limited technical knowledge. Some of the staff worked on the machinery, maintaining it as if it was the engine of a vast warship. Others sat on wooden benches sorting through small circular objects which came to them on a conveyor belt. All the workers were blackened with oil and grime. It would take them an age to scrub themselves clean after their shifts, and it seemed inconceivable that the stink of the factory ever truly left them.

They removed their headphones once they reached the relative peace of the factory canteen, though the drone of the machinery still lingered in Swanson's ears. The odour of the fumes remained on her skin and she found herself fantasising about a hot shower. She had been on the factory floor for less than five minutes. 'Tell me more about the two men, Thurrock and Wilson,' she instructed Tom Miller as they sat down for their lunch.

'As I told you, they're great workers. Always up for a bit of a laugh. Reliable, you know, I never had to check their work. I could trust them, which is more than I can say about a number of these people.'

'And what were they like socially?'

'Socially? Well, they liked to party. There are only a couple of bars around here and they normally headed off nearer to the centre.'

'Little Joe's was the place they frequented?'

'They all like Little Joe's,' said Miller, smiling.

'That's where they were last seen. Were you there on the evening they disappeared?'

'Not that evening, I was working night shift. It was the end of the month. It gets pretty messy on payday.'

'They left with a woman, apparently,' said Swanson.

Miller laughed. 'Look, I don't want to embarrass you but they often leave with women.'

'You're not embarrassing me, and I said woman, singular,' replied Swanson. She stared Miller directly in the eyes and he lowered his gaze. 'Would they normally just leave with one woman?'

'Depends on whether they both got lucky or not, I guess. I don't know what they get up to. '

'Have you ever been to their flat, Mr Miller?' asked Keane.

'I never really socialise with them much, with any of the workers. I go for a drink after work now and again but in my position I can't afford to become too close to them. You understand?'

Swanson scanned the canteen. The atmosphere was muted. Workers huddled in small groups, as if the police presence made them nervous. In one corner a thin man sat reading an oil-covered newspaper. Swanson had noticed him earlier, darting occasional looks at her. He looked up at her again from the newspaper, and quickly away as if he'd been caught doing something wrong. The man appeared ostracised from the rest of his peers, as if he was happy being alone, and everyone else was even happier not to have him at their table.

'Who's that?' asked Swanson.

Tom Miller looked up. 'Oh him, that's Reg McClusky.' Miller looked at her and paused. She could tell he was involved in some inner dialogue; his forehead was scrunched, thick lines carved into the fleshy part of his face. 'McClusky is just a poor loner really. He gets on with some of the more menial work and we tolerate him.'

After lunch, Swanson thanked Miller and arranged for Flaherty to take a full inventory of the staff at the factory. She wanted to know who was out with the two men that evening, and wanted everyone questioned. 'Oh, and find out about that McClusky guy.'

'Ma'am,' said Flaherty.

Outside, the blackened clouds had broken and rain poured onto the car. The pod she had seen earlier was now directly above their parking space. An involuntary shiver ran through Swanson as she looked up at the male prisoner within. The corpse looked down on her, his eyes fixed into a permanent stare, his rotting flesh squashed against the glass floor of his pod. Swanson looked away and handed the car keys to Keane. She pondered the conditions of the factory and the clawing fumes on her clothes as they drove to Charles Wesley's house.

Keane pursed his lips as if in concentration but said nothing. Ten minutes into the journey he finally spoke up. 'So do you think Chessington's hiding out someplace?'

'Like Thurrock and Wilson?' said Swanson, wishing it was that simple. 'Perhaps we should check Little Joe's?'

'Yeah, maybe he's still there, having a beer, while we're all out looking for him.'

'Let's go there after we see Mr Wesley again.'

'About that, Swanson. You're the boss and everything but do you really think it's the best idea? You heard what Luce said, about his connections with the Mayor and what have you.'

A torrent of rain bounced off the windscreen. 'What are you worried about, Keane?'

'If I remember correctly, Luce threatened us with our jobs.'

'You worry too much. Anyway, Charles Wesley's not

going to be telling anyone about the conversation we're about to have with him.'

After negotiating their entrance with the security guard, they parked the car and ran to the Wesley premises. The rain was so ferocious that they were drenched by the time Wesley answered the door. He rolled his eyes and shook his head on seeing them. 'You've been warned, Inspector Swanson,' he said. 'It seems you can't take friendly advice.' He didn't invite them in and was obviously enjoying the soaking they were receiving.

'Mr Wesley, do you remember working with a young woman called Sarah Natal?' asked Swanson.

Wesley stared at her, a hint of anger in his eyes. 'She used to work for me. What does this have to do with anything?'

'Please let us in, Mr Wesley, and we can talk about this in more detail.'

Wesley stood still. He was still wearing the same tracksuit bottoms she had last seen him in but had changed his t-shirt to a light grey polo shirt emblazed with a purple sports logo. He stood tall, his chest puffed out in an attempt to make himself look bigger.

'If we can talk about it here we can keep it unofficial,' said Swanson. 'Your private life is of no concern to me but your knowledge of Sarah Natal is.'

Wesley shook his head and allowed them to enter. 'You best make this quick. I'm seconds away from calling Philip Luce.'

'We won't take much of your time, sir,' said Swanson, shaking the rain from her hair. Wesley had clearly had a TV dinner the night before and had failed to clear up after himself. The half-eaten meal sat on one of the sideboards, its appearance destroying the aesthetic of the room.

'What can you tell me about Sarah Natal?'

'What's there to tell?' said Wesley.

'Anything would be invaluable. How long did she work for you?'

'Six months. She'd previously worked for the Public Prosecution Service and she wanted to see how the other side lived.'

'Was it a full-time position?'

'No, she was on sabbatical from the judiciary. She was going to work for one of the judges and he thought it would be better if she was able to see the two sides in action. as it were.'

'Which judge was she working for?'

Wesley shut his eyes and stretched his neck. 'Judge Lloyd,' he said. 'I'm sure you know this already, Inspector.'

'And what was your relationship with her, sir?'

'What was it like?' asked Wesley.

'What sort of relationship was it?' asked Swanson.

Keane shot her a questioning look. Wesley looked shaken. He paused, considering his response. 'I'm not sure what you think you know, Inspector Swanson.'

Swanson remained silent. It was possible she had accidentally stumbled across something.

'This is completely off the record. We were together on a couple of occasions,' continued Wesley.

'Together?' asked Keane.

'Oh grow up, man, you know what "together" means. But let me tell you, I wasn't the only one. She had a lot of *friends*. There used to be an orderly line outside my office door for her at times.'

'I assume your wife found out?' said Swanson.

'Yes, she found out.'

'Aside from all that, sir, can you tell me anything else about her? Did she strike you as overtly political in any way?'

'I don't know. I wasn't that interested in what she had to say. She seemed quite neutral. She'd have to be, working for Lloyd. I don't think they let anarchists in that building.'

'Do you not think it might have been prudent to inform us that you had an affair with Judge Lloyd's assistant a little bit earlier?'

'I don't see how that would have been relevant.'

'You know Chief Inspector Chessington is missing?'

Wesley lowered his gaze. 'I was sorry to hear that, but I can't see what this has to do with me.'

'Is there anything else you think we should know, now?' asked Keane.

'Does Sarah have something to do with all this? Christ.' Wesley fell back on the sofa and took a drink from a crystal glass filled to the brim with whisky. 'There were rumours of her making a rape claim when she worked at PPS. I only found out after our...'

'You think there was any substance to her claim?'

'I wouldn't like to comment on that at the moment.'

Swanson showed him a picture of the bearded man who

had abducted Chessington. 'Do you know this man?'

Wesley stared hard at the picture as if he was willing a memory to return to him. 'No, sorry.'

Swanson held his gaze. 'Thank you for your time. Sorry to have bothered you once again,' she said. They left Wesley on the sofa nursing his glass, and showed themselves out of his house.

An anonymous call appeared on Swanson's mobile as she walked to the car. She considered not answering. 'Yes,' she demanded impatiently.

It was a male voice, Swanson guessed forty to fifty years of age. 'Inspector Swanson, there is a disused factory in Sector Five, close to the river. I will send you exact coordinates. You may find something of interest within.'

Chapter Forty Five

'Who is this?' asked Swanson as the line went dead. The phone vibrated in her hand and a set of coordinates appeared on the screen. She punched them into the built-in sat nav and instructed Keane to drive.

The warehouse was in a former industrial estate close to the river in Sector Five. Swanson had never been there before and found it unfathomable that industries once thrived in such a location. It was a concrete wasteland interspersed with vast metallic buildings. A biting wind billowed through the zone, filled with decay, excrement and ammonia. The majority of the abandoned buildings in the zone were used by the homeless. There were no cameras and the area was treated as a no-go zone by the police and the authorities. It was probably the one place in the city where crime could go undetected and unpunished.

They found the specific building. A sign outside the building advertised the place as *Gosling Industries*. If such a company still traded, it did so far from such a hellish area.

Keane pulled back a sliding door, rusted metal staining

his hands. The building's innards were hollow. Steel girders held the crumbling building in place as water dripped through gaping holes in the roof.

'What exactly are we looking for?' asked Keane. Air whistled through the gaps in the structure. Swanson found signs of occupancy in the space: discarded food and drink containers, even a rotting sleeping blanket. She unclipped her gun, and nodded to Keane to do the same.

'Even the rats have left,' he whispered.

A spiral staircase in the southwest corner of the building led to a mezzanine area which overlooked the main factory space. Swanson led the way upstairs, slipping on one of the steps, almost losing her balance.

Upstairs, a line of offices stood derelict. Swanson opened one of the doors and gagged at the smell, which was heavy with urine, excrement, and something much worse.

'I guess this is why we're here,' said Keane, turning his face away from the sight of the disused room.

Swanson took a flashlight from her belt and lit up the office. The immobile figure of a man was sprawled across a desk. A puddle of dark liquid gathered close to his neck. It dripped off the desk and formed a second pool on the floor. 'Check your reader,' she instructed Keane, her gun still in her hand.

'What am I looking for?'

She flashed light onto the deceased man's face. His neck had been savaged. Deep incisions zigzagged across his throat as if someone had tried to hack off his head. The body was still warm. 'If I'm not mistaken,' she said, 'I think we've found Oscar Garner.'

They called it in. SI arrived ten minutes later, a fully armed response unit. Swanson and Keane held their hands up as the group scrambled their way up the spiral suitcase. Swanson instructed the lead officer to search her jacket pocket for identification.

Trent Hanson appeared once the crime scene had been secured. He wore a long overcoat, the bulge of a bulletproof jacket beneath. 'How long have you been here?' he asked Swanson.

'Thirty minutes or so.'

'Who called it in to you?'

'Anonymous. We're trying to trace the call.'

'Thank you for informing my officers. We can take over from here.'

Even in the gloom of the warehouse, the lack of warmth in the man's false smile was evident.

'How do you work that one out?' asked Keane. 'We were the officers at the scene and we're investigating this man's escape.'

'You've found him,' said Hanson, deadpan. 'Your cooperation is greatly appreciated. Please feel free to ask Superintendent Luce. Garner is a terrorist suspect and is therefore under our jurisdiction.'

Keane looked at Swanson, who nodded for him to check in with Luce.

'For fuck's sake,' said Keane, walking away.

'Have you verified it is actually Garner?' asked Hanson, still smiling.

'Obviously we haven't fingerprinted him. We matched

the picture on his file. The body is still warm. Can't have happened long ago.'

She accompanied Hanson to the corpse, pointing out the marks and entry wounds on the body. 'Signs of torture,' she suggested.

'Possibly. Let's not jump the gun.'

The SI officers cordoned off the area. Hanson made a few phone calls, requesting a road block for a three-mile radius, which sounded somewhat optimistic.

Keane returned and beckoned her over. 'I've checked with Luce. We have to hand it over. The call can't be traced.'

Hanson walked over. 'Again, officers, thank you for your cooperation. We'll take things from here,' he said.

Swanson nodded. 'Will you inform us of your findings?'

'Naturally,' replied Hanson. 'I'll make it my number one priority.'

Jane Sutton was waiting outside the factory. She looked over hopefully as Swanson walked out of the warehouse with Keane close behind. 'Do you have access to a police radio, Jane?' asked Swanson.

Sutton looked tired. Gone was the heavily made-up face Swanson had seen the other evening. Her tired eyes looked ready to close. 'Good try, Inspector. I know better than that.'

'What the hell are you doing here, then?'

'It's my job. Who died?'

'Please, let's not go through this again.'

'I thought I had an exclusive,' said the journalist, who was ignoring Keane.

'Who do you think the deceased is?' asked Swanson.

‘I know it’s Oscar Garner.’

‘Why the hell are you asking then?’ asked Keane.

Swanson touched his arm, his muscles tensing. ‘Miss Sutton here likes to play games. She’s asking for verification.’

They walked to their car, Sutton following like a stalker. ‘What I don’t understand is why they would go through the trouble of breaking him out of prison only to torture and kill him,’ she said.

Keane turned sharply towards the journalist. Swanson spoke before he had chance to speak. ‘No one has mentioned torture, Jane,’ she said, getting into the car.

‘Chief Inspector Chessington has not been answering his phone for some time now,’ said the journalist.

Swanson shut the door on her and started the car.

‘Sorry about that,’ said Keane. ‘To be fair, it was a good question. What did Garner know, and who wanted the information?’

‘We can let that be Hanson’s problem for the time being. I need a drink.’

‘Little Joe’s?’

‘You read my mind.’

Chapter Forty Six

He decided to keep Chessington separate from the others for the time being. As Old Blue walked down the stairwell, Chessington sat before him on the left side of the prison. The soundproof glass barrier divided him from the other three inmates. He had planned meticulously but wanted to be careful with Chessington; with the policeman's experience, he would likely foster some kind of escape plan if left with the others.

'You won't get away with this, Jacobson,' said the policeman, as Old Blue dished out the lunchtime rations. 'I understand why you're doing this. I don't condone it, but I understand. But you're going to get caught. I did my best for you before. I know you're a decent man. I can arrange something.'

He was not willing to engage the policeman in conversation. 'For God's sake, Jacobson,' Chessington shouted, as Old Blue walked up the stairs. 'What can you possibly gain from this?'

As he closed the trapdoor, he heard a further complaint

from Chessington. 'I helped you, Jacobson, why am I here?' It was two days since Chessington's kidnapping and Old Blue was growing restless. The house was close to uninhabitable and he'd yet to obtain his final target. He'd tried the night before but the man had changed his timetable.

To make matters worse, the two police officers he'd first seen at the Lenity meeting were getting closer. They'd visited the factory and he knew from his contact that their other avenues of investigation were leading them to the answers they needed. The bombings hadn't helped his cause. He hoped they would have proved to be a distraction but Swanson and Keane had somehow discovered a link. Tonight was likely to be close to his last chance of finishing the project.

He walked out into the front garden. Overgrown and badly maintained, it still held a certain beauty, the plants and bushes thriving in the untamed landscape.

Despite the dark clouds which hung above them, it was oppressively hot. Sarah stood next to him, looking into the distance. She was dressed in dark jeans with a light brown cardigan pulled over a black vest. With her hair tumbled loose onto her shoulders, she looked momentarily at peace. He walked towards her and placed his hands on her shoulders. He had not enjoyed the last few days with her but now their time together was nearly ended he felt a stab of tenderness. 'Sarah, you need to go,' he said.

'I want to stay until the end.'

'Nothing is here for you now. What would you gain from seeing what's going to happen? You've seen Lloyd punished for what he did to you. The rest is my concern. You have the documents, you can disappear. They're close to finding us, Sarah, you need to go.'

She grabbed him and held him tight. 'What will you do?' she asked.

'I'll be okay,' he told her.

They packed her belongings into the newly acquired hatchback and he drove her to the border of the city. Movements between the large conurbations were relatively simple and with her forged documents Sarah would be free to live a new life. She cried as he stopped the car some distance from the checkpoint.

'You'll be ok,' he said. She clung onto the front passenger seat as he pulled her out of the car, as if controlling a toddler mid-tantrum.

'I don't want to go,' she cried out. He ignored her pleas, slammed the passenger door shut, and dumped her bags by the side of the road. Driving away, he caught sight of her in the rear-view mirror, her sobbing figure curled up against her meagre belongings.

He couldn't hang around. His final victim was not at work today; it could be his last chance. Every month, the man attended a meeting. It was a prerequisite of the case, a procedural get-out clause aimed at helping the authorities justify their actions. Although he was sure it annoyed the man to have to attend these things, he knew it made no real difference to him; it was considerably easier to accept than being sentenced to the pods.

He waited outside the building and gazed up at the

window again. The lights were not there today and he slumped back on the park bench, disappointed.

The man left the building thirty minutes later, never once looking at Old Blue. He followed at a discreet distance in the car, playing the game. He was disappointed to find that being so close to the end gave him no joy. He hoped that he would get a sense of closure once the final target was back at the house.

His target was almost in as bad a state as Judge Lloyd. He'd always been a slight man, his body little more than bone. He walked absurdly straight, like a cartoon stick man. Old Blue knew he had been given the nickname 'Rickets', and he imagined that the man had suffered a lifetime of bullying, but his heart held not an ounce of sympathy for the pitiful balding creature. He waited in the car as the man attended his final meeting. The plan was in place; it was simple but effective. When the man returned home, Old Blue would simply walk up to the flat, knock on the door and overpower him. The hardest bit would be to get him back down the stairs. There was no lift in the block of flats but he was sure he could manoeuvre the man from the flat to the car.

Once the man had finished his meeting, he drove back to the flat and waited for him to return. He parked the car in the service car park, in a parking space less than twenty metres from the stairwell where the ground floor lift was positioned. He took a seat on one of the park benches away from the front of the building, just enough of a sightline for him to see all the comings and goings at the block of flats.

The man returned an hour later, his skeletal hand scratching away at his head. The man stopped at the entrance to the flats and looked around, as if surprised not to see Old Blue waiting for him.

Old Blue waited for ten minutes and took his normal seat beneath the man's apartment. He waited thirty minutes more before having to move.

Chapter Forty Seven

'We're going to try something new today. I'm going to go around the group one by one and I want you all to talk. Not very long, just a minute or two. But I want to know about your cravings and what you have done to overcome them.'

McClusky closed his eyes and shook his head. Every few weeks or so Lynette would come up with this master plan. The obese woman folded her arms, a smug look of satisfaction spreading across her face. 'So let's start to my left,' she continued. 'Tim?'

McClusky was thankful she'd chosen Tim. Once the man started, it was hard to shut him up. Tim stood. 'It's okay Tim, we can stay seated,' said Lynette.

'Lynette, everybody,' the man began. Like McClusky, Tim Summer was a compulsory. He'd been arrested one evening by the river, intoxicated. Tim had told the story on numerous occasions and the account was now so vivid in McClusky's memory that he thought perhaps he had witnessed it himself.

Summer had lost his son to the pods. His son had been

caught drink driving, two days after gaining his license. Tim Summer had been drinking by the riverbank, consoling himself next to the area where his son had pushed the red button in his pod. The way he told it, two policemen had stopped him committing suicide that evening. And although he hadn't committed any criminal offence, he'd been sentenced to compulsory counselling once a month for the rest of his life. 'As you know I've been clean now for seven years and this week, in truth, has been an easy one. I've had no real cravings so I've not really had to overcome them.'

'Wonderful,' said Lynette.

McClusky frowned. 'Is that it, Tim?' he said.

Tim smiled at him. McClusky had to listen to three other stories before it was his turn. Louise Vickery, the voluntary, had been on the drink again. She started crying once more, telling everybody how she succumbed to a glass of merlot one evening, lamenting her dead husband.

'Christ, it's not going to kill her,' McClusky said under his breath. When it was his turn, McClusky cleared his throat and was about to follow the line Tim Summer had taken. But as he spoke he found himself giving away more than normal. After all, it was close to ending now. The man was waiting for him and he'd decided to finally confront him. 'I was actually offered some alcohol this week,' he said.

The group gasped. Even Lynette was slightly taken aback. Everyone in the group knew that McClusky was a compulsory and by now the majority of them knew why. Not only was he a compulsory but drinking alcohol would be an immediate criminal offence and he would be in the pods within days. 'It's okay, I didn't take any,' he said, holding his hands up to prove his innocence. 'This woman, well, girl I met offered me a glass of whiskey. She didn't know anything about me.'

'Were you tempted?' asked Tim Summer, who unaccountably had started to shake.

McClusky wanted to be truthful. He wanted to say he hadn't been tempted by the foul smelling liquid, but had been tempted by the freedom it would give him. Downing the glass would have freed his inhibitions. 'The truth is, I don't really like the taste of alcohol. And the stuff she gave me looked and smelled so cheap the last thing I wanted to do was to drink it. So no, it wasn't a problem to overcome it.'

'Thank you, Reg,' said Lynette. She looked disappointed. Droplets of sweat glistened on her rumpled neck as she thanked him. McClusky closed his eyes, and slaughtered the woman with his imagination.

After the meeting, Tim Summer came to talk to him. He sounded excited by the evening's events. He kept moving from foot to foot. 'It's bullshit, isn't it?' he said. Summer was a slim man, close in height to McClusky. Whereas McClusky was merely bones, Summer had a thick layer of muscled meat on his body which made him look twice the size.

'What's that?' said McClusky.

'It's bullshit having to come here every week. Both of us don't like alcohol. Well, I say that, I don't mind alcohol but I'm never going to drink it again. It's like being in prison.'

'Not quite,' said McClusky.

'No, I suppose not. How's your work going? Anything interesting happen this week?' Summer asked.

McClusky instantly went on the defensive. 'Why, what do you know?'

'Nothing, nothing. You know, small talk, that sort of thing.'

'Oh. Actually, it was quite interesting. Two of the men from our factory have disappeared.'

'Really?'

'Yes, they went out partying one night and haven't appeared since.' In the brief exchange, McClusky said more words to Tim Summer than he'd said to any other human being in the last month. Since the disappearance of the two men, he had known for sure who was following him. The knowledge was liberating. McClusky was finally mastering the art of conversation. 'Yeah, the police were here yesterday speaking to us all. Trying to find out where they'd last been seen.'

'Strange times,' said Summer. 'What with the bombings and the men disappearing from your factory. Strange business.'

'Strange indeed,' said McClusky.

He walked along the river thinking about what Summer had said, the presence following him. He didn't know how the man played this trick, but he seemed able to maintain a presence even when not physically there. But this time it was different. The man was waiting for him, sitting on a park bench outside his building.

Normally, McClusky would have rushed through the stairwell and into the relative security of his flat but he stopped in the foyer of the building and waited. He didn't know whether it was Thurrock and Wilson's disappearance, or some sort of epiphany he had reached with the prostitute, but he knew today was the day he would meet the man who had been stalking him these last years.

Thirty minutes later, he opened the front door of his building and walked over to the man.

He was taller than McClusky remembered from the courtroom, and had certainly put on huge amounts of weight. He was gigantic, imposing and alert. He had a thick grey beard and eyes that McClusky didn't remember.

'Are you going to come with me?' asked the man McClusky knew as Nathaniel Jacobson.

'Yes,' said McClusky. 'Whatever it is you want with me just get it over and done with.'

'Come with me,' said the man, pointing to the passenger side of the car, like a friend offering a lift.

Jacobson drove for a while in silence. McClusky was desperate for a cigarette but dared not ask the man. Finally, Jacobson pulled over and stopped the car. 'Out,' he said.

The area was deserted save for the hum of the tracks above. Two of the pods were visible, both filled with rotting corpses.

'In there,' said the man, opening the boot.

McClusky clambered in and then looked up at the man, who smashed the bridge of his nose with his gloved fist. More blows followed until the world faded out.

Chapter Forty Eight

Swanson and Keane drove to Little Joe's in silence. Something troubled Swanson about Hanson's eagerness to take over the Garner murder; it went beyond professional one-upmanship.

Little Joe's was a multi-level bar cum nightclub in Sector Twelve. The pods were highly visible in this area, the prisoners still on the first stage of their journey. They loitered above the streets, a visible warning to the party dwellers below, the inhabitants of the glass cells in view. They sat huddled in their prisons, staring into nowhere. The visibility of the pods in this area was a political decision. To the west, the pods were high almost out of sight. The pods tracked low here in the east where there was a higher level of poverty; where there was a greater potential for crime. The police turned a blind eye to many of the activities in this sector. Swanson knew that on any given evening they could make numerous arrests. Being drunk and disorderly was not in itself a criminal offence, but drunk and disorderly normally went hand in hand with common assault and other crimes.

The ground floor of Little Joe's was covered with sawdust. Large flat-screen televisions were spaced out on the walls, playing endless reels of various sports. A few hardened regulars congregated at the bar, watching the activities on the screens.

Keane ordered some drinks and asked to speak to the manager. His warrant card provoked a startled response from the young barwoman who phoned her superior. Five minutes later a man walked over to their table and introduced himself as James Thatford, the Duty Manager. 'We've already spoken to your colleagues about the two men who have gone missing,' he said, by way of greeting.

'Yes, thank you, sir,' said Swanson. 'Were you here on the evening in question?'

'It's our busiest night. Yes, I was here.'

'Do you remember seeing Mr Thurrock and Mr Wilson?'

'Yes, they're regulars. They get here by six at the latest practically every evening. That particular night was payday so they were living it large.'

'Large?' asked Keane.

'Chasers with every drink. Drinks for the bar staff. Drinks for random women.'

'They stayed in this area all night?'

'They were talking to a woman. I hadn't seen her before. Good looking, brunette.'

Swanson showed the man a picture of Sarah Natal. 'Is this the woman?'

'She was striking, Inspector Swanson, but this place is dimly lit and to be honest there are hundreds of striking women. That could have been her but I couldn't possibly tell you.'

'You have no CCTV in here?'

'No.'

'Any reason for that?' said Swanson, knowing the answer.

'We respect our customers' privacy. It's not illegal,' said Thatford.

'Tell me about the rest of their evening?'

'I don't know for sure. I saw them up on level four at midnight. I only remember because they were doing a rather elaborate dance.'

'Was the woman with them then?'

'I don't remember. But they were seen leaving with her at four a.m. I was checking the tills at the time but some of the bar staff reported that. I believe your colleagues have interviewed everyone here.'

'Who is Linda Ashley?' asked Swanson, checking through her notes.

'She's working over there,' said Thetford, pointing to the nervous barmaid who had served Keane.

'Can we speak to her?'

'Why don't you come to my office, Inspector? You can speak to her there.'

Linda Ashley was in her late teens, a bird-like creature with peroxide-blonde hair.

'Hi Linda,' said Swanson. 'Please sit down, we won't keep you long. You told our colleagues you saw Mr Thurrock and Mr Wilson leaving with a woman on the evening they disappeared.'

'Yes,' said Linda. Her voice was high pitched as if she was permanently surprised. 'I can't be sure. It's all a bit hazy. I'd been working for twelve hours and I'd just seen this woman with them on and off through the evening. I only remembered because they sometimes buy me drinks, especially on payday.'

Swanson showed the barmaid the photograph of Sarah Natal.

'She definitely looks familiar. I can't really say though. I've seen her, yes I think I've seen that woman here before, but then again there are so many people who come here. They all start to look the same after a while.'

Keane rolled his eyes. 'The woman who was with Mr Thurrock and Mr Wilson. Do you remember if she came to the bar on her own?'

The barmaid fidgeted nervously in her chair. 'I don't know, I don't know, I couldn't say. I saw her chatting to some other men but I don't know if she was alone or not.'

'Okay, thank you for your help, Linda,' said Swanson. The woman stood up to leave. She had a short black skirt and matchstick legs.

'Before you go, have you seen either of these men here before?' Swanson showed the young woman a picture of Chessington, and of the man Abigail had seen with Natal.

The woman grimaced as she looked at the photo. 'I'm not sure, sorry.'

'Thanks once again,' said Swanson.

'Fancy another drink?' asked Keane. 'We could make a night of it. Perhaps retrace their steps.'

'Good try.' She smiled. 'We need to find some answers

soon or we're going to lose this case to Hanson.'

'Those fuckers? They almost shot us back at the factory. How are they going to sort this out?'

Flaherty called as they were about to leave the bar. 'Ma'am, I think you need to hear this,' he said. 'It's Reg McClusky, ma'am. Completely random but…'

'McClusky?' interrupted Swanson.

'The man you saw in the factory. The one who was sitting on his own.'

'Oh, yes,' said Swanson.

'Ma'am, McClusky has previously been before Judge Lloyd. Double rape and homicide, ma'am.' He paused.

Swanson froze. 'Continue, Flaherty,' she said.

'It's a bit of a complicated case, Ma'am. He was acquitted – diminished responsibility.'

'Acquitted?' asked Swanson, loud enough for a number of Little Joe's customers to look over at her. 'Who was the lead officer?' she asked in a softer voice, knowing the answer already.

'Chief Inspector Chessington.'

Swanson let Keane drive. She sat in the passenger's seat reading the notes Flaherty had emailed to her phone. A taskforce had been sent to McClusky's residence. They'd been told to wait for Swanson's arrival. She read the notes for a second time, trying to decipher how McClusky was involved in Lloyd's, Chessington's, Thurrock and Wilson's disappearances; how he could possibly be linked to Garner.

Six years ago, McClusky had gone on trial for the rape and subsequent murder of a mother and daughter, Laura and

Sally Jacobson. McClusky had been returning from a night out with his colleagues when he had seen the mother, Laura Jacobson, putting out milk bottles on the front porch of her house. He had subsequently managed to gain entry into the house.

What ensued made for harrowing reading. McClusky attacked both mother and daughter and bound them together by their wrists. Both women suffered horrific sexual assaults and died from multiple stab wounds.

McClusky admitted to assaulting and killing the women and was submitted for psychiatric evaluation. The reports proved inconclusive. Blood tests revealed that McClusky was highly intoxicated at the time of the incident. His bloodstream contained an almost lethal amount of an MDMA variant.

Following a thorough study, the defence counsel argued that McClusky was not a drug user or a drinker. They argued that he had never taken drugs before and that therefore, somebody must have slipped the drugs into the soft drinks he had been drinking during the night of the incident. Subsequent investigations discovered that McClusky was in fact a teetotaller who had never taken alcohol or any form of drug before. Even his colleagues had reluctantly acknowledged that fact. Chessington led an investigation into the people who accompanied McClusky that night. Drug use itself was not criminally illegal although selling drugs was. Chessington was unable to find conclusive proof of who spiked McClusky's drink that evening.

The prosecution went ahead. After lengthy deliberation,

Judge Lloyd ruled that McClusky could not be found guilty for his actions.

After rigorous tests, it was discovered that McClusky lived with a chemical imbalance in his body which made him prone to violent, and often sexual, outbursts. Until the age of thirty-nine he had always managed these impulses. He had never before risked taking alcohol or drugs as he had feared it would lead him to losing control over his dangerous desires. He had strived to remain sober and as a result had never acted illegally. Although he had committed the grievous acts mentioned in the case he couldn't be held criminally liable for his actions. It was a fundamental part of the law that the guilty party in a murder case must have not only carried out the action but must also have been responsible for his own actions. This was clearly not the case with McClusky. Lloyd found that the people who had spiked his drink were ultimately responsible for the assault and murder of Laura and Sally Jacobson. If a link could be found between the drugs found in McClusky's bloodstream and somebody planting those drugs, then successful prosecution was highly likely.

Lloyd had no other option but to acquit McClusky of the charges. However, he was given a minimum of six months psychiatric treatment in a secure unit and was subject to weekly urine samples, monthly blood tests, and would have to report to group counselling on a monthly basis for the rest of his life.

'Fuck me,' said Keane, as Swanson recalled the case file.

Swanson phoned Tom Miller at the factory. Miller

sounded pleased to hear from her. 'How can I help you, Inspector?' he asked.

'Is Reg McClusky in work today?' Swanson asked.

'No,' said Miller, perhaps a little too quickly.

'Where is he?'

'He's in one of his monthly meetings.'

'His group counselling meetings?'

'Yes, that's the one. You know he gets paid for a day's work every month for those. It's a liberty really.'

'Why didn't you tell me about him yesterday, when I pointed him out in the canteen?'

'Tell you what?'

'About his past, about his trial.'

'I don't know. Didn't want to assume. To be honest I thought you'd have known all about that. It was quite a big case.'

'Tell me, was he friends with Mr Thurrock and Mr Wilson?'

'McClusky's friends with nobody. You saw him. He's a sad waste of space.'

'And before?'

'What about before?'

'Before the incident. Was he friends with Wilson and Thurrock then?'

Miller went silent, only his shallow breaths audible on the other end of the line. Finally, the man spoke. 'He's never really had any friends here, he was just a bit more, what's the word… We put up with him, put it that way.'

'And were Thurrock and Wilson out with him on the night of the incident?'

Miller hesitated. 'I don't know who was out that night. It was a big crowd. We'd just completed a big shipment.'

'Were you out that night, Mr Miller?'

'No, as I told you before I don't tend to go out on those things much.'

'Think really hard for me, Mr Miller. Were Mr Thurrock and Mr Wilson with McClusky on that evening?'

'Look, I don't want to get anyone in trouble.'

'If you know something about that evening then we can talk about it later in greater detail. You're not going to get Thurrock and Wilson into any more trouble than they're already in. Were they out with McClusky that evening?'

'There was a big group of them. They went to Joe's. So yes, they would have been out.'

'Where does he take his counselling meetings?'

'I'm not sure. In fact, I have no idea. Somewhere central? HR may know. Do you want me to put you through?'

'Yes,' said Swanson.

One of the office temps gave Swanson details of McClusky's counselling meetings. Swanson contacted the centre but his meeting had been at one thirty, almost three hours ago. Swanson relayed all this information to Keane who was driving as fast as he could through the clogged city traffic.

'I can understand why he would want to get revenge on Thurrock and Wilson, if they had really slipped drugs into his drink, but why would he kidnap Judge Lloyd, or Chessington for that matter? Lloyd was the one who'd let him off, he gave him his freedom back.'

'I don't think McClusky's kidnapped anyone,' said Swanson.

'So why are we going to his house?' said Keane.

'I think he may need our protection.'

'Protection?' said Keane. 'I don't think that man deserves protection.'

Swanson shrugged.

McClusky lived on the fortieth floor of a large, grey-cladded tower block in Sector Sixteen. Swanson arranged officers at each entry point and at the bottom of the stairwell and elevator shaft. She led six of the armed response unit, and Keane, up to McClusky's flat. They walked in formation, the gunmen at the front and back of their small group.

It was a long walk. Swanson was out of breath by the time they reached McClusky's corridor. Her bulletproof vest was heavy on her slender frame and her skin had erupted into patches of sweat. They didn't bother knocking. One of the gunmen broke down the door and was followed in by the rest of the team.

McClusky was not there. His flat was even more depressing than Richard Beck's. A single mattress lay on the living room floor surrounded by hundreds of empty cartons of cigarettes. A huge bag of ground coffee stood on one of the work counters and a blackened saucepan, half-filled with congealed tomato soup, sat on top of the stove. His bathroom was covered in limescale and green mould climbed the walls and clung to the ceiling. Swanson opened his bathroom cabinet. It was empty save for a lone toothbrush and an industrial-size tub of after-sun cream.

Swanson arranged for the building to be evacuated and began searching room to room, starting with McClusky's corridor. Her team interviewed his closest neighbours. The verdict on McClusky was unanimous. He was a strange loner, always looked like death, had funny eyes, and was always staring. The room to room search would take hours so Swanson decided to head back to the station. She was about to get into her car with Keane when an elderly man stopped her.

He could have been anywhere between seventy and eighty-five. He was in good health, with a broad smile revealing well-maintained dentures. 'Oh, Inspector, one of your colleagues told me to speak to you. I think I saw the man you were looking for. That thin man, McClusky.'

'Yes?' said Swanson.

'I saw him here about three o'clock. He was hanging around the foyer area for a while. He looked a bit impatient.'

'Did you speak to him?'

'No, I was collecting my post and was waiting for the lift when he left.'

'Did you see anything else?'

'I confess I was a bit nosy, Inspector. The man looked so agitated that I thought I'd look to see what he was up to.'

'And?'

'A man was waiting for him. A huge man he was, both in height and girth.'

'What happened?'

'The thin man, McClusky, he walked over to this big guy and he just stopped. It was like the life had drained out of him. You could see his shoulders drooping. He walked over to the car and got into the passenger seat.'

'What type of car was it?' asked Swanson.

'Small car, green I think. I'm afraid I didn't get the number plate,' said the man.

'And they drove off?' said Swanson.

Swanson showed the old man the photograph of Chessington's abductor, and the old man nodded. 'That's him. Although the picture is not a very good one.'

'How's that?' said Swanson.

'It doesn't capture his eyes.'

Swanson had already pieced together what had happened. All she needed now was verification and an address. 'Christ, we've been stupid,' she said to Keane.

'Speak for yourself.'

'Come on, let's go.' Swanson ran to the car. She handed him the keys and rang Flaherty.

'The Reg McClusky case, Laura and Sally Jacobson, who are they survived by?' she demanded to know.

'Give me two seconds,' said Flaherty on the other line. She heard him typing fast onto the keyboard, each strike of the key as urgent and as fast as her heartbeat. 'Nathaniel Jacobson, husband and father.'

'What do we have on him?' said Swanson.

'I have a last known address.'

'Send it over to me now.' She gave the details to Keane who had already set off. 'Where was he on the evening his family was murdered?' Swanson asked Flaherty on the phone.

'At work. He came home to an open front door. Both the bodies were in the living room. I can only imagine,' said Flaherty.

'Best not to,' said Swanson. 'I need you to get everything you have on him.'

'I'm afraid he's gone off the radar in the last two years. We have no work address. All we have is the home address I just sent you.'

They headed back out towards Sector Nineteen. Nathaniel Jacobson's last known address was in the same sector as McClusky's factory. The sun had set and it was a starless night. The pods were lost in the gloom of the grey clouds. It seemed unlikely that Jacobson would be at the address. Swanson tried to empathise with Jacobson but it was almost impossible to put herself in his position. To lose his family was one thing; to lose them in such a horrific way was something else, something she didn't wish to dwell on. Worse still, the man responsible had been set free. She couldn't conceive of what it would be like to live in a world where the man who had tortured, assaulted and murdered your wife and daughter was walking free. There was no justice in abducting Judge Lloyd and Chessington, and even if Thurrock and Wilson were responsible for spiking McClusky's drink it was difficult to condone their abduction as a consequence.

But McClusky was perhaps a different matter. Swanson lived in a society where corporal punishment was the norm. Was it really a great leap for a citizen to take out his own form of corporal punishment? McClusky had admitted to the act itself. Swanson could see how Jacobson must have felt. Society had failed him, so he had decided to right that wrong. Of course, it was all conjecture at the moment. Even if Jacobson was responsible for the disappearance of these five men, it was unclear as to what had become of them. Somebody had also sent a ransom note for Judge Lloyd's disappearance but nothing subsequently. Although it seemed likely that the cases were all interlinked, it could be coincidental. And what was the link to Garner?

Keane pulled up outside Jacobson's last known address. It was a terraced house in a small cul-de-sac. They both drew their weapons and moved towards the front door. They should have waited for back-up but knocked on the door anyway. Swanson waited for twenty seconds before knocking again. A light came on in the hallway and her body tensed, rigid with anticipation. The door opened and a man in his twenties stood before them, dressed in blue boxer shorts and a white t-shirt.

'What is it?' He turned white when he saw the guns pointed at him.

The man had lived at the house for the last two years along with three other students. They hadn't seen either Nathaniel Jacobson or Sarah Natal before. The house was rented through a lettings agent and the man provided enough documentation to convince Swanson that he was not involved.

Back at the station, Swanson and Keane circulated pictures of Nathaniel Jacobson and Sarah Natal once more before being summoned to Luce's office. After a debrief from

Swanson, Luce agreed that Jacobson had probably abducted the five men and was holding them somewhere.

'For what reason?' asked Swanson. 'The last ransom note we had was for Judge Lloyd over two weeks ago and the person who wrote it killed himself.'

'We have to assume they're alive. Anything else is unthinkable,' said Luce.

Flaherty was waiting outside the office. He was not jumping up and down with excitement, as he'd done on that first day when Lloyd had disappeared.

'Ma'am, I was going through the court file again on the McClusky case. His name isn't on the document because he was in a supervisory role but guess who provided the research for the defence's case?'

'You're joking,' said Swanson, reading Charles Wesley's name on the file notes. 'Go with Keane and pick Charles Wesley up now. Tell him it's for his own protection.'

She picked through Flaherty's notes. Charles Wesley was senior counsel on the McClusky defence. He'd supervised the research on diminished responsibility which eventually led to the acquittal. When she had asked Wesley if he'd ever had an acquittal before Lloyd, he'd denied it. Technically, it wasn't his case but he'd definitely had an impact on the outcome. Swanson phoned Keane and instructed him to take backup. It was possible that Wesley was Jacobson's next target.

The station was buzzing but Swanson was uneasy. She was sure that something was missing. She couldn't believe that Jacobson had been working by himself. It would have taken a hell of a lot of organising to go dark in such a monitored society, and to survive for two years with no record was practically unheard of. Someone must be helping him. She put Jacobson's photos through all the databases again with no result. She played about with his picture, using software to estimate what his face would look like without his beard but nothing came up.

The man did not exist.

Chapter Forty Nine

Swanson read through the file one more time until the words stopped making sense. She rang her father to tell him she would not be home that evening and headed to the interview room. Keane was waiting for her, sitting opposite a very dishevelled-looking Charles Wesley.

'You must understand, Mr Wesley, everywhere we look your name appears – and I don't believe in coincidences,' said Swanson, sitting down.

'Don't be dramatic. It's not everywhere you look. Yes, I was lead on the case but it was purely supervisory. I sign off on the majority of cases. I had nothing to do with McClusky being set free. You're welcome to check my house. Judge Lloyd's not there. Your Chief Inspector's not there, either.'

'You disgust me, Wesley,' said Keane. 'How could you defend a man like that? He raped and murdered those two women.'

'We don't choose our clients, Sergeant Keane. Everyone has free access to the law and the right to be defended. Anyway, he was proven innocent. It would never have happened if his drink hadn't been spiked. Whoever did that, those are the people you should be searching for. I thought you said I was here for my protection. You said that McClusky had been kidnapped as well and I could be next. Now you're cross-examining me, for what reason I don't know. Why would I want to do anything to Judge Lloyd or Chessington?'

'No one has mentioned that you would,' said Swanson. 'But I know there's something you're not telling us, some other connection.'

She showed him a picture of Sarah Natal and Wesley winced. 'Christ, we've gone over this already. Yes, I slept with her. I wasn't the only one and I'm sure I won't be the last.'

Swanson showed him the picture of Nathaniel Jacobson and was surprised as he physically recoiled.

'You know Mr Jacobson?'

'Of course I know him. It was his wife and child who were murdered.' Wesley considered for a moment. 'I see, you think he's responsible. You think he's getting his revenge. Makes sense, I suppose, and I can see why you'd think maybe I would be next.'

Wesley paused, as if he was considering an internal dilemma. Eventually, he said, 'He won't be coming for me, don't worry.' His face contorted as the words left his mouth, as if he was experiencing some form of seizure, or as if he had said something he should not have.

'What makes you so sure?' said Swanson.

'This really is a farce,' said Wesley. 'You do understand

that I'm a senior public defender. I know my rights better than anyone in this building, possibly this whole city.'

'Yes, yes, we're aware of your credentials, Mr Wesley. What did you mean? Answer me that one question and you're free to go, at least under our surveillance.'

'What do you mean, "our surveillance?"'

'You'll be under our surveillance until this case is resolved. You're an obvious next target, unless you can prove otherwise to me.'

Wesley slumped. His skin was pale, almost translucent. His face was dotted with random spots of stubble and his eyes were heavy with fatigue. He sighed, a drawn-out noise signalling his compliance. 'Fine. He won't come after me because he's already taken his revenge on me.'

'How's that?' asked Swanson.

Colour returned to Wesley's cheeks. 'Because he destroyed my marriage.'

Chapter Fifty

It was one a.m. by the time they reached Jessica Wesley's house. She lived in a detached property in Sector Two. The palatial dwelling made Charles Wesley's townhouse look like a slum. The house was part of another exclusive gated community. Swanson pressed the intercom on the steel gates outside to be allowed access. Fortunately, Jessica Wesley was awake.

'You have to be kidding me,' she said, buzzing them through. By the time they'd parked, Jessica Wesley was outside her front door. She was dressed in a tight-fitting black dress with a silver-grey shawl over her shoulders.

'Inspector, I would start looking for a new career. I'll be calling the mayor first thing tomorrow morning,' she told Swanson.

'I understand your frustration, Mrs Wesley, but a number of things have come to light since we last spoke. Please may we come in?'

'No, you may not.'

'There can be a lot of negative kudos attributed to an arrest warrant,' said Swanson.

'Are you threatening me?'

Swanson shrugged.

Jessica Wesley opened the door for them both, and once they were in the hall she slammed it shut. Swanson had seen smaller hallways in the lobbies of five-star hotels. An ostentatious stairway filled the open plan area. The high ceiling of the hallway made the house feel even bigger than it looked from the outside.

A man dressed in a black tuxedo walked out from one of the side rooms. 'What the hell is going on, Jessica?' he said.

Swanson had seen the man before. He'd been loitering outside Jessica Wesley's office the first time they visited her law firm. Swanson thought he must be one of the senior partners.

'Nothing, James. I won't be long.'

Wesley ushered Swanson and Keane to the kitchen. The room was almost as large as Swanson's flat. Dark floorboards stretched towards glass-panelled doors which looked out onto a floodlit lawn. Swanson wondered if the money for the house had come from Charles Wesley's inheritance. Jessica Wesley poured some brandy into a thick crystal tumbler. She didn't offer any to the two officers. 'You've got two minutes. Make this quick.'

Swanson sat down on one of the high-backed chairs at the dining table. She told Jessica Wesley about the Jacobson case.

'What has this got to do with me?' Wesley asked.

'We didn't think it had anything to do with you until we spoke to your husband,' said Swanson.

Wesley gulped at her brandy. She gripped the slate-covered kitchen worktop and nodded her head.

'I'm sure you know of the case, Mrs Wesley. The brutal murder of Laura and Sally Jacobson.'

'I know only too well. And that bastard McClusky. The biggest travesty of justice I've ever seen in this city.'

'Quite,' said Swanson. 'You knew Laura Jacobson's husband, Sally Jacobson's father.'

This time Jessica Wesley sat down. 'What has Charles been saying?'

'Why don't you tell us?' said Swanson.

'You have to understand, Inspector. Charles lives in this fantasy world. I presume he's told you I had an affair or some such nonsense.'

Swanson didn't answer.

'I never had an affair with Nathaniel. I helped him, that was all. I originally attended the court case at Charles' request. He saw it as a great success.' She laughed, the noise cold and joyless. 'Some success, contributing to the acquittal of a man who'd admitted to murder and rape. That was what ended our marriage, Inspector Swanson, not any imaginary affair.'

'How exactly did you help Mr Jacobson?'

'I offered to pay for his counselling, and afterwards he worked for my firm for a while.'

'As what?' asked Keane.

'Security or something. I didn't organise it specifically, I just gave his details to HR and told them to give him a job.'

'When was the last time you saw him?' asked Swanson.

She studied the woman, looking for any giveaway sign.

Wesley looked away, towards the floodlit lawn. 'I haven't seen Nathaniel for at least two years.'

They sat in silence for some time. Swanson played over what Wesley had told her. 'Mrs Wesley, I'd like to search this house. I can either do it now or come back tomorrow with a warrant.'

'This is ridiculous. It's nearly two o'clock, Inspector. Do you really have nothing better to do with your time? What do you expect to find, anyway?' Her hesitancy had been replaced with an incredulous rage.

'One of our officers is missing and unless you want to become a suspect I suggest you help in any way you can.'

'Fine,' said Wesley, splaying her hands out. 'But my threat about the mayor is not an idle one. I will be speaking to him tomorrow.'

Swanson nodded to Keane, and together they began the search.

Chapter Fifty One

After knocking McClusky out, with more blows than was totally necessary, Old Blue handcuffed him and stuffed a gag into his mouth. He drove steadily back to the house and played out the final moments for the last time in his mind. He didn't know for sure how it would go. He could only guess as to McClusky's reaction.

Leaving McClusky in the car he walked into the house. He covered his face, first with a cycle mask and then with a green striped bandana he'd doused in aftershave. It made little difference. He pulled open the trapdoor for the last time and stopped to let the first wave of pungent air billow up from below. The four prisoners were asleep, each one having consumed their poisoned breakfast.

He tied up Chessington first. Having securely handcuffed him, he lassoed the rope around the man's thick gut and secured him to one of the four chairs. He did the same to the other three men, noticing how thin and insubstantial Judge Lloyd felt. Soon they sat side by side on the right-hand side of the prison, a mini jury facing out towards their executioner.

He set up the left side of the cell and returned to the car for McClusky. The man didn't struggle. Old Blue almost kicked him down the cellar stairs but remembered that he needed him unharmed for the last part of the act. He sat the man on the left side of the cell, secured his hands with a thin rope and pushed the back of his chair up against the front of the cell. He fed the rope through the food hatch so that he would be able to pull the rope free once he finished.

He arranged five knifes of various sizes onto the floor of McClusky's cell. On seeing the gleaming metal, McClusky struggled in his seat.

'These are not for you,' said Old Blue.

This didn't calm McClusky, so Old Blue punched his jaw and the man sat silent.

He grabbed McClusky by the throat and pushed the pills down his gullet. The man choked and spluttered. Old Blue grabbed the bottle of vodka and forced the man to drink it in large burning gulps.

'I hope you enjoy this,' he said.

The man tried to spit the drink back up but Old Blue pulled at the skin at the back of his skull and held his head back until over half the contents were swirling inside McClusky's swollen belly.

'What do you want from me?' the man slurred.

Old Blue left the prison, throwing water on the four other men and locking the glass doors securely. He waited ten minutes before pulling on the rope which held McClusky's hands in place from the outside. McClusky hesitated and slowly realised he'd been freed. The divider was down and he now shared a cell with the four men, all of whom were tied secure, unable to move. McClusky walked around the men and stopped at Thurrock and Wilson.

Old Blue could tell McClusky understood. He didn't try to free them. He returned to the other side of the cell, to the knives.

Old Blue shut the trapdoor and placed the battered rug over the hole in the ground. Taking off his mask, he vomited onto the living room floor.

Still carrying what remained of the bottle of vodka he walked upstairs to the bedroom. From one of the side drawers he pulled out a framed photograph. He smiled at the image.

A woman and a teenage girl smiled back at him.

Chapter Fifty Two

McClusky sensed the alcohol and drugs working through his body. He glanced at the knives, inches from his grasp, and savoured the memory of the last time he had been intoxicated, the time when he met Jacobson's wife and daughter.

The toxins entered his blood stream, his body surrendering immediately, his inhibitions fading. He had felt this way once before when the two men seated to his right poisoned his drinks with large quantities of what he later discovered was MDMA. The drugs had given him a wondrous freedom. They helped him fulfil his darkest passions. The desires had always been with him, for as long as he could remember. They had terrified him and filled him with wonder. He had always suspected that alcohol, or drugs of any kind, would lead to him acting on these instincts and as such he had stayed away from them. Thurrock and Wilson had proved the point. By drugging him, they had unwittingly awakened his dormant self and the two unfortunate women had suffered for it. But by some amazing quirk of law he had been freed despite the gruesome acts.

McClusky felt the ropes which held his hands in place loosen as Jacobson yanked the rope free through a two-way shutter cut into the prison door. The rope had rubbed away a thin layer of skin on his wrists, leaving two circular marks of swollen bloody flesh. He staggered to his feet, imagining how he would kill the four men in the room, with the added thrill of knowing that this time it wouldn't be a fantasy. He lifted the largest of the knives. It had a wooden handle and a smooth triangular blade. He turned to face Jacobson on the other side of the glass and waved the knife at him in an attempt to say thank you. He moved towards the shaking men and chose the first of his victims.

'Don't,' said Chessington.

The other three men trembled in their chairs, trying to break free. McClusky placed the largest knife under the policeman's neck. He looked for Jacobson but he had left the cell.

It didn't matter. He knew what he was supposed to do.

Chapter Fifty Three

They left the house three hours later, after searching every inch of Jessica Wesley's mansion. Keane asked Swanson what she had been looking for. 'Did you think Judge Lloyd would be hiding in one of the cupboards or something?'

Swanson was not too sure about her motivation. Regretfully, she thought it may have something to do with her dislike for Jessica Wesley. She wasn't sure where her animosity came from; certainly it wasn't the woman's wealth or elevated position which irked her. It was more her sense of superiority. The way she maintained the pretence of civility whilst secretly looking down on those she didn't believe were her equal.

It was nearly five a.m. by the time she reached her block of flats. It was light but the morning was cloudy and grey. She could taste particles of the river in the air. She was about to open the communal door to the flats when a flash of red caught her eye. In the distance, two to three hundred metres away, one of the prisoners had set off their suicide button. The pod was filled with red smoke which contrasted sharply with the greyness of its surrounding environment. The fallen body lay slumped on the floor of the glass prison. In her location, prisoners were normally only eight days into their sentence and it was rare for her to see the red smoke close to her building. She turned away and opened the door, feeling ashamed. She had become so desensitised to the pods that she hadn't even known that this particular one had been there.

She set her alarm for ten a.m. and fell immediately into an uneasy sleep. She woke every forty minutes, the stream of light through her curtains pulling her from sleep. Her phone rang at five to ten and tore her from an unpleasant dream where her father had been in one of the pods. He'd been about to press the suicide button when the shrill tone of her phone woke her.

It was Chief Superintendent Luce.

An hour later she was sitting in Luce's office. Tiredness overwhelmed her; it seeped deep within her bones. It was all she could do to keep her head from dropping to her lap as Luce read her the riot act.

'You could lose your job over this, Swanson,' he warned. 'You disobeyed direct orders and now the mayor's office is involved. These aren't the type of people you can just play around with. You better have something good for me.'

Swanson wondered how and why Jessica Wesley had such a close relationship with the mayor; if she was such a staunch supporter of Lenity then it made little sense. Even considering her relationship with Jacobson, whatever that was, it was unlikely that she was now a supporter of zero tolerance. Not with her son currently circling in the pods.

Swanson explained the situation regarding the Wesleys' connection to Sarah Natal and Nathaniel Jacobson. She explained the McClusky case, how Judge Lloyd had presided over it, how Chessington had been the prosecutor, and how she suspected that Thurrock and Wilson were the men responsible for drugging McClusky.

'I remember that case,' said Luce. 'Travesty. Though you have to hand it to his lawyers. It takes something special to win a case like that. But Swanson, this doesn't explain your harassment of Jessica Wesley. She said you were searching her house in the middle of the night. What possible justification could you have for that?'

Swanson considered for a moment. 'Charles Wesley claimed that the reason their marriage broke down was because of Nathaniel Jacobson. That Jessica Wesley had an affair with him.'

'Really?' said Luce, raising his eyebrows.

'I was looking for some link to Jacobson in the house. A letter, a photo, anything.'

'And you had to search for it at two a.m.?'

'I think you'll agree, sir, that time is of the essence.'

To his credit, Luce was giving her more time than she had expected. After being summoned to see him Swanson was sure she would be taken off the case, but despite the pressure he was under, he was listening to what she had to say.

'The fact is, Swanson, we've got bugger all else to go on at the moment and I can see why you would approach the case this way. But it's all circumstantial. I can give you twenty-four hours more; don't fuck this up or you'll be spending a lot longer than two weeks in your holiday home this year.'

'What about Garner, sir?'

'That's SI's business now, unless there is a link with these abductions.'

She met Keane in the canteen and gulped through three large cups of hot, black coffee. She told him what Luce had said.

'Do you have a holiday home?' asked Keane.

'I believe he was speaking metaphorically. Or maybe he believes everyone has a beachfront holiday apartment. Who knows?' By the time Flaherty arrived ten minutes later, the holiday home idea had been playing in her mind. She told the junior officer to check if Jacobson had ever rented anywhere previously, for a holiday or any reason whatsoever. As Flaherty was walking away she stopped him.

'Do the same for the Wesleys,' she ordered.

'It will show up as a recorded search,' said Flaherty.

'It's only a search,' growled Swanson. 'Get on with it.'

An hour later, Swanson was summoned to an interview room where Trent Hanson was waiting. No smiles were forthcoming from the man and Swanson wondered if he had been forced to report back to her by Superintendent Luce. Hanson placed a stack of papers on the desk before her. 'Again, thank you for your assistance the other day,' he said.

Without answering, Swanson began looking through the documents.

'Initial evaluation suggested Garner was interrogated for a number of days,' said Hanson. 'There were numerous puncture wounds over his body and enough drugs in his bloodstream to fell an ox.'

'Who did it?' asked Swanson.

'As you know, we've been investigating a group for a number of years now.'

'A splinter group from Lenity?'

'Most of those we are investigating began life in Lenity and became frustrated with their lack of action.'

'But why Garner?' asked Swanson.

'We initially thought they had released him because of his explosives expertise but after seeing the signs of torture we're not sure.'

'This group must have some serious resources to stage a breakout from the holding zone,' asked Swanson.

'Yes.'

'What about Dempsey?'

'Could have been suicide but more likely someone from their group inside. There's a chance Garner could have shared information with him so they just took out the variable.'

The explanation didn't sound very credible to Swanson. Garner could have shared information with anyone in the prison.

'We're close to a number of arrests linked to the bombings,' continued Hanson. 'Naturally, we'll keep you informed.'

'You think there's a link with Chessington's disappearance?' asked Swanson.

'I think we're looking at two separate cases here. I don't think the disappearance of Lloyd and Chessington are linked to Garner. They're not on our radar.'

'I will keep you informed then, sir.'

Hanson smiled and nodded. 'We've been impressed with your work, Swanson. After this is all finished, you should call me. We could do with an officer like you in our ranks. One thing though,' he added, getting to his feet.

'Sir?' Swanson remained seated.

'I would stay away from the Wesleys if I were you. It could seriously damage your standing here. They have friends in high places, if you understand what I mean.'

'I don't, sir, actually.'

'No?'

'They're supposedly big supporters of Lenity. Why would the mayor protect them?'

Hanson laughed. 'Inspector,' he said, turning and leaving the interview room.

Swanson tried to reconcile what she'd heard with what she knew but it didn't make sense. Why would this supposed splinter group free Garner only to torture him? Why would they take out someone as inconsequential as Garner's cell mate, Dempsey? Either Hanson was not giving her full disclosure or he was simply lying to her. It was no longer her concern, but the way Hanson had ended their conversation made her want to find out more.

At lunch, Keane presented her with a file on Jessica Wesley. He looked surprisingly fresh considering he'd had the same lack of sleep as she had. He sat next to her as they went through the file, his right arm in soft contact with her left. She struggled to concentrate with him in such close proximity and wondered why she had this troubling attraction.

Mrs Wesley had been a high achiever at University, finishing third in her undergraduate class and fifth in her graduating law school. Her politics made for the most interesting reading. She had been a member of a number of anti-zero-tolerance groups. They were all above board though some had controversial philosophies; although none had explicitly violent manifestos, neither were they as overtly peace-loving as Lenity. In the main they all promoted the idea of banning the policy of zero tolerance and the decommissioning of the pods.

Wesley had been a trainee at her current law firm for three years and gradually made her way to senior partner. From the files, it seemed she had relaxed her political views. She was clearly ambitious and a far-left approach in the city would not have been beneficial to her career. She had attended her last meeting, a Lenity conference, in the second year of her training contract and no records of any political affiliations existed since then. They reached a dead end.

Swanson tried not to dwell on her fear that Jacobson had somehow killed the five missing men and that their bodies would never be discovered. Unfortunately, it seemed not just conceivable but likely. There had been no further ransom note since Beck's suicide, which suggested that if Jacobson had abducted these men he had no motivation to keep them alive.

Flaherty called her from the office. 'This is probably another coincidence, ma'am,' he said. 'Jacobson never owned any second home or holiday flats so I started to check into his financial records. Something jumped out at me. It was the name really. About three years ago, there were a number of credit card receipts in Lake Rosslyn.' Lake Rosslyn was a man-made resort on the far outskirts of the city, in Sector Twenty-Nine. It was a large gated holiday complex and as far as Swanson was aware, it was very exclusive and beyond the means of a man like Nathaniel Jacobson. 'It wasn't just the resort that caught my interest,' Flaherty continued. 'It was what he spent. Just small amounts on groceries and a few bar tabs, but no large outlays, such as for accommodation.'

Swanson knew what Flaherty was going to say next. 'I cross-referenced with your other request, ma'am. Again, I'm sure it's coincidental, but the Wesleys have a permanent residence at Lake Rosslyn.'

Chapter Fifty Four

Swanson edged as fast as she could through the demonstrators until she hit the motorway.

'Do you mind telling me what the rush is?' said Keane.

Swanson told him what Flaherty discovered.

'Lake Rosslyn, think they had some sort of love nest there?'

'I think Jessica Wesley let Jacobson live there. The time he spent there coincided with the end of the court case.'

'You think he's still there now?'

'Let's find out.'

They reached Sector Twenty-Nine within forty minutes. It was the only gated sector in the city, open to residents and tourists with confirmed bookings. Swanson showed her warrant to one of the guards at the gate and was ushered through. She turned off the siren.

It was off-season at Lake Rosslyn but the area was alive with holiday-makers. It felt warmer in the resort than it had back at the office, as if the weather had been manipulated for the benefit of the tourists. The small man-made lake was less than a half-mile in diameter; it was not the reason people came to the area. They came to be seen in the exclusive bars and boutique shops that lined the central area of Rosslyn.

Jessica Wesley's holiday home was a ten-minute drive from the centre. It was a secluded building and although lake-facing, was covered by overgrown bushes and weeds. A padlocked wooden gate prevented the car's access.

'Shall we call it in?' said Keane.

Swanson hesitated. 'Okay,' she said.

The air was heavy with moisture. They clambered over the locked gate, Swanson landing in a puddle of mud. As they edged towards the house, a swarm of miniscule insects buzzed around their heads, small vibrations prickling Swanson's neck and ears.

The smell began as a faint odour of ammonia and excrement. By the time they stood at the end of the path, with the building directly in front of them, it had intensified into something much worse; something unidentifiable. The house was made of timber. From their position it looked like an overgrown garden shed, though Swanson knew it would have cost a small fortune to buy. A large people carrier sat in the driveway next to a small green hatchback. She drew her weapon and signalled for Keane to do the same.

Jacobson must be in the house.

They walked cautiously to the front door and Swanson counted to three in a growled whisper. Keane kicked the lock of the front door, almost taking it off its hinges.

A fierce blast of foul-smelling air rushed them. The house was dark: the windows boarded up with crude slabs of wood.

They edged from room to room, using flashlights. The house was dying. Litter was strewn across the wooden floorboards of the living room. Discarded cups and plates with rotting food were everywhere.

In the centre of the room, Swanson uncovered a trap door.

'Jesus Christ,' said Keane, lifting up the wooden handles to reveal a small staircase leading to the basement.

The smell was eye-watering. Swanson had been present at a number of autopsies in her years in the force. She'd become hardened to the sights and smells of decaying bodies but even she had to fight the gag reflex as the dead air drifted towards her.

They wrapped cloths around their faces. Swanson studied the staircase with her flashlight before descending. She ordered Keane to stay at the top of the stairs, as they still hadn't located Jacobson.

At the bottom of the stairs, she turned the corner and saw something she immediately wished she could forget. The underground prison was dimly lit. Four men were bound to chairs. She shone her flashlight on each one in turn, revealing Judge Lloyd, Chief Inspector Chessington, Glen Thurrock and Simon Wilson. At least, what was left of them.

The room was awash with blood. The men were covered head to foot in lacerations. Judge Lloyd seemed to be missing his lips, a knife still lodged into his neck. Chessington's lifeless eyes were open, staring into space, his face a crisscross network of cuts and puncture wounds. Thurrock and Wilson were coated in red as if they'd been skinned alive.

Amidst the chaos stood McClusky. Knife in hand, he was working on the corpse of Glen Thurrock. Swanson pulled out her gun and called up to Keane. 'Wait there. Jacobson isn't here but I've located McClusky and the others.'

'Drop the knife,' she told McClusky.

The man ignored her. He was a pitifully thin creature, covered in streaks of blood and matter. She shot at the glass panel. It shattered in a hail of crumbling glass. McClusky turned to face her. He was like some absurd creature from a zombie movie. Swanson had to check herself to believe this was all real, that the horribly mutilated corpses and the blood-soaked madman were not part of some elaborate invented dreamscape.

McClusky destroyed any such notion with a high-pitched wail. He launched himself towards her, his knife aloft.

Swanson held her gun steady in front of her and aimed for the man's heart. He was surprisingly quick and was almost upon her as the bullet entered his chest. He was thrown back from the blast, the gunshot instantly fatal.

She stood above his skeletal body which lay on the floor in an odd, unnatural angle. He looked as if he were smiling.

With her gun still poised, Swanson bent down towards him and felt for a pulse, which was non-existent. There was no need to check the other four men. She retraced her steps back up the stairs, forcing herself not to run. Keane was waiting for her. He looked at her blood-spattered face and checked her up and down with his flashlight torch.

'I think I heard something from upstairs,' said Keane. He

led the way this time. Swanson moved sideways so she could keep an eye on the trapdoor, as if somehow McClusky was still a threat. They reached a landing with three doors. The first was the bathroom and they made sure it was empty before moving on to what looked like the master bedroom.

'Oh no you don't,' said Swanson, as they entered.

Jacobson was lying on the bed, his round belly pointing to the ceiling, perfectly still. On the side table was an empty bottle of vodka and two empty tubs of pills. Swanson ran to the man, hoping there was still time to save him, but he had no pulse. She roared, a sound she'd repressed from what she had seen in the dungeon.

Jacobson had something clutched to his chest. Keane prised open the man's fingers, revealing the framed photograph of Jacobson's wife and child, Laura and Sally.

Swanson was about to call it in when a noise came from outside. Someone was in the back garden. With her gun still in her hand, she edged over to the bedroom window, hoping it was backup.

In the garden, a petite figure was opening the back door. The woman hovered by the entrance, as if transfixed. Swanson beckoned Keane over.

'Jesus Christ, what's she doing here?' he said, his face whitening as the figure of Sarah Natal disappeared within.

Chapter Fifty Five

'Why is she here now?' whispered Keane.

'My guess is Jacobson didn't let her in on all of the details of his plan,' replied Swanson.

Swanson's eyes had adjusted to the dark, but the gloom was such that she could only see a metre or two in front of her as they made their way downstairs. She didn't want to shine her torch in case it attracted Natal's attention. The overpowering stench of decay and death wafted up the stairs and Swanson put a hand over her mouth to stop herself from gagging. With Keane close behind her, she rounded the corner into the living room.

In the murkiness, the silhouetted figure of Sarah Natal stood by the hatch door. She was carrying a gun.

'Just hang back,' Swanson whispered to Keane, and retreated. She didn't want to startle the woman more than was necessary.

'Sarah, this is Inspector Swanson. I'm here with Sergeant Keane. We're both armed and have guns sighted on you. Drop your weapon.'

The silhouette remained motionless, arms by her side, still gawking down into the hole in the floor which led to the cellar.

'Don't go down there, Sarah,' said Swanson, her voice as steady and soft as she could make it.

The woman rounded and pointed her gun at them.

Swanson held out her left hand to hold Keane in place.

'Put it down, Sarah.'

'Where is he?' demanded the woman, taking slow steps towards them. Her figure blinked into focus as she reached the halfway point of the living room. 'What's happened, did he start without me?' Her questioning voice had a childlike innocence to it.

As the woman got closer, Swanson's voice became more urgent, the rasp in her throat more pronounced. 'Sarah, if you take a step nearer, I will have to shoot,' she said.

The woman lurched on one leg and came to a halt. 'Where is he?' she asked again.

'He's upstairs,' said Swanson. Keane's breath was hot behind her. He had made the right decision so far by staying quiet. Natal was in a fragile enough state as it was.

'And the others?' asked Natal.

'They're all dead.' Swanson hoped she was taking the right approach. 'Were you supposed to be there when it happened?'

Natal considered, her body swaying as though she was struggling to keep her balance. 'He told me to go and wait for him. He loves me, you see. He didn't want me to see what he was going to do.'

'Then why are you back?'

'Because I wanted to see,' said Natal.

'Why would you do this?' asked Keane.

Natal jolted her head, as if snapped out of a trance. 'Do you know what Lloyd did to me?' she said. The innocent quality had vanished from her voice. Its replacement was cold and distant.

'What did he do?' asked Swanson. She'd thought Natal's part in all this was to do with the rape allegation but maybe there was more.

'He killed him,' said Natal, her voice distant.

'Who did he kill, Sarah?'

'Daniel.'

Swanson looked at Keane, who shrugged his shoulders. 'Daniel?' asked Swanson, keeping her voice as soft as possible.

'Daniel Rye. They say he killed his wife, but he didn't. He loved me.' Natal took one more step towards them, her gun still poised. 'Is Nathan okay?' she said, a tremor of emotion in her voice.

'Do not move,' said Swanson. 'Nathan is fine. He's upstairs waiting for you. We'll take you to him as soon as you've dropped the weapon.' Swanson had been in similar situations a handful of times before. If Natal had any self-awareness left, she would realise that regardless of what happened next the pods would be waiting for her. This made her dangerous. 'Tell me more about Daniel.'

'Take me to Nathan, now,' demanded Natal, taking another step forward.

'Don't,' warned Swanson.

Natal hesitated. She was close enough now that Swanson could see her hand was shaking, her index finger poised on the trigger.

'We can talk about this,' said Swanson, as a thunderous explosion ripped through the living room. A flash of light briefly illuminated the woman in front of her, imprinting a snapshot of the woman's face onto Swanson's eyes. She had lost weight in the days since their last meeting. Her face was drained, white in the glare of the gun's flash, her eyes staring, hollow and cold. The impact of the bullet struck her to the ground.

With her firearm still raised, Swanson took out her flashlight with her spare hand. Natal was curled up, a pool of blood gathering close to her chest. Swanson shone her torch onto the woman's face. Her eyes were open, vacant and lifeless.

'She was going to shoot, I had no option,' said Keane.

Swanson stepped closer.

'I know,' she said.

Chapter Fifty Six

Swanson ran up the stairs of the newly refurbished central police station. It had been four weeks since they had found the bodies at the Wesley holiday home. Swanson was supposed to be on annual leave but there were too many cases for her attention at the moment. The streets were desolate. The mayoral committee had proposed a new bill to make demonstrations criminal unless prior consent had been granted. The bill was to be ratified at the end of the week but the would-be demonstrators were already less inclined to take the risk.

As always, Swanson felt the presence of the pods all around her. They reminded her of McClusky and the devastation he'd caused in the Wesleys' cellar, Natal's lifeless body, and her mother.

Jessica Wesley was with her lawyer Simon Wineman in one of the interview rooms. Both Jessica and Charles Wesley had been questioned intensively since that night but it was proving difficult to mount a case against either of them.

Swanson was less sure about Charles Wesley's involvement.

He had seemed genuinely surprised on discovering that Jacobson was using the holiday home and was sticking to the story that his wife had had an affair with Jacobson. Both of them denied knowing that Jacobson was using their holiday home and without further evidence it was likely they would escape punishment. Furthermore, the mayor's office was putting more and more pressure on them to stop their investigations, particularly against Jessica Wesley.

'Another interview, Inspector?' asked Jessica Wesley.

'There would be no need for any questioning if you could just tell us the truth. You previously admitted that you knew Nathaniel Jacobson. You were quite vociferous about the case involving his wife and daughter. Do you really expect me to believe that you had no knowledge of him staying at your holiday home?' asked Swanson.

Jessica Wesley didn't answer, only the slightest twitch of her mouth suggesting she had heard the question.

Swanson changed tack. 'I have asked you this question before, but to clarify, did you know Richard Beck?'

Wesley consulted her lawyer with a quick glance. 'No.'

'As you know, Mr Beck was a strident Lenity supporter. He sent us a hoax ransom note shortly after Judge Lloyd's disappearance.'

'And?' asked Wesley.

'He committed suicide a few days after his arrest.'

'A truly tragic story that we're getting a little tired of discussing. Could you tell me what this has to do with my client, Inspector Swanson?' asked Wesley's lawyer.

'We received a phone call today from Mr Beck's sister,

Sandra Thorn. It seems she will be receiving a very substantial check following probate on Mr Beck's will,' said Swanson.

'That doesn't answer my question,' said Wineman.

'The sum involved is extremely generous, particularly for a man who had never held down a job in his life. Would you happen to know how Mr Beck came to hold such a large sum of money, Mrs Wesley?'

Jessica Wesley sighed. 'I just told you I know nothing of a Mr Beck,' she said.

'I think you do. I think you paid Mr Beck to write the ransom note as a distraction. I think you knew Mr Jacobson was staying in your holiday home.

'I suppose I also orchestrated the recent bombings in the city?' said Wesley.

'This is preposterous,' agreed Wineman, getting to his feet. 'We have agreed to this questioning due to the unfortunate coincidences but I will not allow my client to be subjected to this ludicrous line of questioning again. Since you appear to have no actual evidence, we will not be attending any more meetings unless they are formal requirements.' The lawyer moved closer to Swanson. 'I would be very careful about making any formal arrest.'

'Once I prove where that money came from, I will do just that,' answered Swanson as Wesley and her lawyer left the office.

Yet she knew she would be unable to prove a link. Jessica Wesley was too meticulous to be caught out so easily and there was no evidence substantial enough to connect her with the Nathaniel Jacobson murders.

SI had made a number of arrests over Garner's escape and subsequent death. There was no apparent link to Jacobson or the Wesleys. The official line was that an unaffiliated subset of Lenity was responsible for Garner's kidnapping and the bombings. Due to the security implications, all interviews by SI had been conducted in secret. Trent Hanson had yet to divulge any information about why Garner was tortured and murdered.

Keane was still on paid leave following Sarah Natal's death. Swanson had played out the moment a thousand times in her mind and had convinced herself that Natal had provided a severe risk to them both. Since that day, they'd researched the podding of Daniel Rye who'd been convicted of the murder of his wife. No record of any Sarah Natal was found in the report of the case, though the prosecution at the time had suggested that Rye was having an affair with an unnamed woman.

Swanson had spoken in Keane's defence at the enquiry, and it was only a matter of time before he was back on the job.

As Swanson left the station, a woman called for her. Sighing, she looked for Jane Sutton. But it was another figure who was shouting, a petite lady with a shock of red hair falling from the hood of an oversized coat. 'Miss Hulbert?'

'Please, call me Natasha,' said the woman.

'What can I do for you, Natasha?' Swanson remembered the last time she had seen the woman, in her small flat where she had reluctantly given them a list of her clients.

Hulbert pulled the hood of her jacket tighter over her head, as if she could camouflage herself from the crowd. 'I'm not sure I should be here. But something happened a few weeks ago, on the day of the bombings. I wanted to speak to you sooner, but didn't know what to do.'

Swanson stepped closer to the woman and pulled her gently against the wall of the police station. 'Tell me in your own time,' she said.

'One of my clients called me on the evening of the bombings. Nothing unusual in that itself, though I normally only meet him once a month.'

Swanson nodded.

'I couldn't place it at first. But he looked different than normal, at least he acted differently. He was more sure of himself, more confident. It sounds a bit crazy but he was even a bit more *manly*. Anyway, I didn't think much more of it. I thought maybe he got excited about the bombings. Strange what gets some people off.'

Swanson hoped the woman was going somewhere with her story.

'Anyway, he started talking, you know, after we finished.'

'About the bombings?' asked Swanson.

'Yes, about what a good thing it was. How it had only been a matter of time. How glad he was that it had eventually come to fruition.'

'What had come to fruition?'

'Exactly. I played along with him; I always play along.' The woman smiled. 'I agreed with him, and told him how much I hated ZT and how I hoped this might be the end of it. But this just made him angry and then he said something which stuck in my mind which I didn't fully process at the time. It made me think about you and your investigation.'

'What?' asked Swanson.

'He said, "it's not the end of ZT, it's the start."' She handed Swanson a piece of paper. The man's name and address was scrawled on the paper in coarse, printed writing.

'Thank you, Natasha.'

'He won't find out that I told you, will he?' she asked.

'No need to worry about that,' said Swanson, touching the woman's shoulder.

Hulbert turned from her and disappeared into the crowd.

Swanson called Keane but his phone went straight to voicemail. Adrenaline sparked her back into life. The traffic was clear and she reached the man's house within ten minutes. The apartment was in Sector One, the building small but exclusive. A grey-haired concierge sat behind the apartment's reception desk. Swanson flashed him her warrant card and he directed her to the elevators. Inside the elevator, Swanson drew her firearm as the lift arrived on the fifth floor of the apartment building. She knocked on the man's door and stood to the side so she couldn't be seen through the peephole.

'Who is it?'

'Just reception, sir, we have a delivery for you,' said Swanson.

The man didn't reply. Swanson was about to knock again when the latch turned and the door opened.

Gun raised, Swanson turned to face Timothy Basle.

As Hulbert had described, Basle was a different character to the nasal-voiced spotty youth she had encountered first at the Lenity meeting, then at the bookshop. Even with a gun pointed at his face, he stood tall and stared back at Swanson. 'I presume you have a warrant?' he asked.

'I will be arresting you on suspicion of terrorism against the state but I need to ask you a few questions first,' said Swanson, her arms still outstretched, the gun an extension of her body.

'Come in,' said Basle, walking back inside.

'Wait,' growled Swanson.

The man turned to face her, a line of pink, scarred flesh creasing on his face as he did so.

'Walk back slowly and keep your hands where I can see them.'

The man smirked and edged backwards.

Swanson couldn't help but feel impressed by the man's previous deception. He edged back into his ultra-modern flat, which had white ceramic floors and clean pale walls. Swanson made him sit on a steel-backed dining chair. 'Place your hands behind your back and interlock them,' she said. She cuffed him, making sure the fine wire of the handcuffs dug deep into his skin.

His body tensed. 'You're making a huge mistake,' said Basle.

At that moment, Swanson felt so overwhelmed by the last few weeks that it was all she could do from hitting Basle with the blunt end of her firearm. She poked the gun underneath his chin. As he jerked his head back, he kept his eyes focused on her. He went to speak but she pushed the gun further into his scarred flesh.

'I can't prove anything against you but that doesn't have to matter,' she growled.

They stayed that way for some time, Swanson waiting for her body to decide what to do next. She was only half relieved when she felt her arms loosen.

Basle shook his head. 'You're not that sort of person, Inspector,' he said dismissively.

'You don't want to test that theory too much, Basle,' she said. 'Tell me who ordered you to set off those bombs,' she demanded.

'You must think I'm stupid.'

'Nothing is admissible,' said Swanson. 'You're handcuffed with a gun pointed at you. Nothing you say could take you to the pods.'

'I am not naïve, Inspector, whatever you may think of me.'

'How are the Wesleys involved?'

Basle looked genuinely surprised at the question. He laughed. 'My god, you are completely on the wrong track, aren't you?'

Swanson placed the gun on his temple and punched the man in his throat. Basle convulsed under the blow. His tried to bend forward but the handcuffs held him in place. His blotchy skin turned first maroon then purple, and Swanson thought he might pass out. Slowly he came to and Swanson placed the gun at his temple once more. 'Tell me who,' she demanded.

'You wouldn't believe me,' said Basle. He coughed and spat out a lump of bloody phlegm onto the white carpet.

Swanson unclicked the safety mechanism on her gun. 'No one knows I'm here. It's your last chance,' she said, ramming the gun farther into the man's skull until the red skin at the side of his head turned white from the pressure.

Something changed within the man. He shook, his arrogance crumbling, and started to speak.

After he had finished, Swanson cracked the butt of the gun against the back of his skull, knocking him unconscious. She uncuffed him and laid him on the ground in the recovery position. She took some pillows from his sofa and propped his back against them. From his sideboard she stole his wallet and mobile phone.

Chapter Fifty Seven

Swanson tried to control her breathing as she left Basle's apartment. What Basle had told her shouldn't have come as a surprise. It confirmed many long-held suspicions. Now she had a decision to make, one which could ultimately lead her to the pods.

She didn't want to rush but sooner or later Basle would wake and send word of what she'd done. She studied the nearest pod in her sightline which was mercifully empty and made her decision.

After making the necessary call she emailed Keane on her reader, programming it to be delivered in two hours. It explained where she was going, who she was going to meet, and why.

Trent Hanson, the head of SI, agreed to meet at St Christopher's church. It was nearly lightsout as Swanson made her way along the river bank. The city was at its most beautiful at this time of day, the lights from the buildings blinking out of existence one by one, the pods illuminating the city.

The streets were desolate. Swanson ignored the eyes she imagined were staring at her from the pods, fooled herself into believing she was the only one walking the empty streets of the city.

Light glared through the stained glass windows of the church. The illumination within clashing with the glow from the glass capsules of the pods which trailed above the church's steeple.

Swanson watched from the shadows as two SI guards paraded outside the church entrance. She knew if she walked into the church she might never walk out but she had to confront Hanson.

The guards let her through without checking her identification. Hanson sat halfway down the aisle on one of the wooden pews. Swanson considered how easy it would be to draw her firearm and shoot Hanson where he sat. She could get past the two guards at the door or escape through the vestry with ease.

Instead she walked up the aisle, the sound of her feet echoing in the cavernous space.

'Sit,' commanded Hanson.

Swanson sat down on the same pew two metres away from the man.

'Congratulations on the Lloyd case,' he said.

'It was hardly solved,' said Swanson, unable to hide the deep resonance in her voice. 'Everyone was dead.'

'One less perpetrator on the streets,' said Hanson.

'Are you for real?' asked Swanson.

Hanson held his hands up. 'What is it that you want?' he asked.

'I've spoken to Timothy Basle.'

'Is that supposed to mean something to me?'

'He seems to think the mayor's office had something to do with the bombings and the breakout from the holding zone.'

Hanson laughed, the humourless sound echoing in the hollow room. 'You forced me out of a meeting on the say-so of some political youth?'

'A youth who works in a bookshop, yet lives in a top-rent apartment, beyond my meagre salary.'

'Jesus, Swanson. People have other income sources, you know. I'm sure Basle comes from a rich family or something, probably inherited that flat. What's it got to do with me?'

'I'll tell you what Basle said to me, and what I worked out for myself,' said Swanson.

'Are you wearing a wire?'

'We can do this at the police station,' said Swanson.

Hanson shook his head.

'There was never any splinter group. It was all a fabrication, created by SI. You are responsible for the bombings. You are also responsible for the escape from the holding zone of Oscar Garner and his subsequent torture and murder.'

Hanson shook his head. 'You have a very active imagination.'

Swanson continued, undeterred. 'With the elections less than a year away, what better way to drum up support for the mayor? The escape from the holding zone and then the bombings. You knew the fear it would all cause, that everyone would be searching for a strong, militant government as a response.'

'For the sake of argument, let's accept this theory of yours. Surely such unrest, such negligent security, would result in citizens voting against the mayor.'

'You made it very public that you had located Garner after his escape, that SI had found the dangerous fugitive with the mayor providing all the necessary resources; and I'm sure these arrests you have made in secret will be worked to your advantage. A few special days of celebration as those responsible are podded. I guess you'll even use the Lloyd case to help drum up support for the mayor.'

'Wonderful piece of investigative police work, Inspector Swanson. Although I am guessing you have no actual evidence?'

Swanson stared at the man.

'So what next?' asked Hanson. 'You realise if you go public with these crazy accusations your career will be over. No one will entertain them. Basle is not credible and wouldn't testify anyway.'

Swanson stood. 'For now, it's enough that I know,' she said.

'Sit back down, Inspector.'

Swanson felt the weight of the gun in her inside jacket and walked away.

'Suit yourself, but before you do anything stupid, just remember we've had our eye on you for a long time.'

'Meaning?'

'People don't get positions of authority without being vetted first. You've been watched closely for a number of years. More so recently.'

Swanson's hand moved towards the gun.

'Let's just say, there may or may not be certain visuals of you. We all have vices, Inspector, but there is nothing that would stop Superintendent Luce making you next Chief Inspector as long as you don't cause a commotion; a commotion you would never be able to control.'

From the altar, Swanson heard footsteps. She turned to see Father Annerley. Her arm went limp and she left the gun in its holster. She turned without a word and left the church.

Keane was outside. 'These fools wouldn't let me in,' he said, pointing to the SI guards.

'Don't worry, thanks for coming. It's good to see you.'

'Is Hanson still in there? We're not going to let him get away with it, are we?'

'There's nothing we can do at the moment. We know he's responsible. He'll slip up one day,' she said.

'I've been cleared,' said Keane. 'Drink?'

'Not tonight,' she whispered.

'So there'll be another night?'

'You never know your luck.'

She had yet to tell her father about the incident with McClusky. He knew the basic details but she had not told him about what she'd seen in the cellar. He was waiting for her at home. As usual, he held a large glass of blood-coloured wine in his hand. 'Another wonderful day,' he said, toasting her as she walked through the door.

'What's for dinner?' she asked.

'Fish,' he said, 'I'll have to open the white wine soon.'

Swanson went to her room and changed. She heard her father singing away in the kitchen, the aroma of fish and fried onions drifting towards her. She locked her door and took the treasure box out from beneath her bed. She added Basle's wallet and phone and flicked through some of her recent acquisitions: Chessington's watch and diary, which she now treasured, and the pen she had stolen from the solicitor, Dave Legg. A small ornament she had taken from the Wesley summer house in Lake Rosslyn, and her fondest treasure, the books she had taken from Abigail Thompson's apartment.

She flicked through the second volume again, to the page she'd looked at every night since confronting McClusky in the cellar of the Wesleys' summer house. The picture had been taken in the daytime. The light had shone across the pod, creating a perfect silhouette of the figure within. A beautiful woman in her thirties gazed towards her. She had fierce green eyes with a symmetrical angular face. Her high cheekbones seemed to have been carved from marble, such was their perfection. Swanson thought the woman was smiling. As if perhaps she knew that Abigail Thompson was taking a picture of her, and that one day her daughter would gaze upon it.

Acknowledgements

Zero has been a long term project for me and I would like to thank the following for their contribution to the book:

Michael Bhaskar, Iain Millar, and the whole team at Canelo.

Beth Eardley, Warren Eardley, and Samantha Saboviec for comments and advice on earlier versions.

All the amazing bloggers and reviewers for promoting *Dead Eyed* and *Dead Lucky*. Too many to name, but sincere thanks for each and every review. So many great blogs out there!

All my friends and family, with special thanks to Matt Wulff and Alexia Capsomidis for their support.

My agent, Joanna Swainson, for her advice and help finding a home for the book.

Freya and Hamish for their inspiration and love.

Dr Alison Brolly for all the editing and suggestions, and her unwavering belief in Kate Swanson and the world of Zero.

DEAD EYED
BY MATT BROLLY

DCI Lambert Book 1

Gritty, complex and effortlessly chilling, Brolly's *Dead Eyed* is a grisly crime thriller that will keep you on the edge of your seat.

DCI Michael Lambert thought he'd closed his last case…

Yet when he's passed a file detailing a particularly gruesome murder, Michael knows that this is no ordinary killer at work.

The removal of the victim's eyes and the Latin inscription carved into the chest is the chilling calling-card of the 'soul jacker': a cold-blooded murderer who struck close to Michael once before, twenty-five years ago.

Now the long-buried case is being re-opened, and Michael is determined to use his inside knowledge to finally bring the killer to justice. But as the body count rises, Michael realises that his own links to the victims could mean that he is next on the killer's list…

The gripping first novel in a thrilling new crime series -by Matt Brolly. Perfect for fans of Tony Parsons, Lee Child and Angela Marsons.

DEAD LUCKY
BY MATT BROLLY

DCI Lambert Book 2

A fast-paced crime-thriller, full of chilling twists, turns and grisly surprises, Matt Brolly's *Dead Lucky* will have you gripped from beginning to end!

DCI Michael Lambert is back…

When a woman is murdered, the twisted killer forcing her husband to watch her slow and painful death, DCI Michael Lambert knows that his next case might be his toughest yet.

And when a second set of killings are discovered, with exactly the same MO, the race is on the find the lethal sociopath before he strikes again.

But Lambert never expected to receive an anonymous call from the killer. This time, it's personal: if Lambert doesn't find the murderer soon, his own loved ones will be next…

The gripping second novel in a thrilling new crime series by Matt Brolly. Perfect for fans of Tony Parsons, Lee Child and Angela Marsons.

DEAD EMBERS
BY MATT BROLLY

DCI Lambert Book 3

An explosive fire. A double murder. And that's just the start

When **DCI Michael Lambert** is called out to an apparent house fire, he knows it can't be routine. Instead he finds the remains of a burnt house, a traumatised child and two corpses - one of whom is a senior police officer.

Lambert's got other problems. Anti-corruption are onto his boss. His relationships is on the rocks. He can't get over his ex-wife and he keeps blacking out.

But when a detective has been murdered the stakes are too high to get distracted. All is not as it seems. As the investigation continues Lambert realises he is getting drawn into something altogether bigger and more terrifying than he could ever have imagined...

Trust no one.

Gripping, chilling to its core and full of twists, the powerful new DCI Michael Lambert from Matt Brolly is perfect for fans of Angela Marsons, Helen H. Durrant and Michael Hambling.

Printed in Great Britain
by Amazon

50137197R00231